"Thoughtful as well as suspenseful . . . rich in characterization."

—*San Francisco Chronicle*

"[Kat is] funny, sexy, and admirably determined."

—*Chicago Tribune*

"[Kijewski] has a gift for writing characters . . . The terse, breezy dialogue . . . is downright hilarious . . . perfectly etched."

—*Washington Post*

"Kat Colorado is a winner."

—*Detroit News*

"Crisp styling and spunky supporting characters . . . verve and charm."

—*Library Journal*

"Funny, thoughtful and ingenious . . . everything works . . . right up there with the best stuff being published by anyone, anywhere."

—*Drood Review of Mystery*

"Definitely a writer to watch."

—*Kansas City Star*

continued on next page ...

"A smart, funny, sharp private eye."
—*Mostly Murder*

"Hard-boiled . . . carefully plotted and briskly paced."
—*New York Times Book Review*

"Kat Colorado is sure to win the hearts of mystery fans."
—*Publishers Weekly*

"[Kat] is sassy, savvy, tender and tough—more than a match for any of her macho male counterparts."
—*Worcester County* (MA) *Newspapers*

"Exceptional . . . Kijewski is a master at combining psychological suspense with traditional P.I. stories."
—*Romantic Times*

"Karen Kijewski is . . . one of the best."
—*Mystery News*

"A great read . . . This author, whose first Kat Colorado book, *Katwalk*, won the Shamus, Anthony, and Best First Private Eye awards, is just getting better and better."
—*Cape Cod Times*

HONKY TONK KAT

Karen Kijewski

BERKLEY BOOKS, NEW YORK

This is a work of fiction. The events described are imaginary and the characters are fictitious and not intended to represent specific living persons. When persons or entities are referred to by their true names, they are portrayed in entirely fictitious circumstances; the reader should not infer that these events ever actually happened.

HONKY TONK KAT

A Berkley Book / published by arrangement with
the author

PRINTING HISTORY
G. P. Putnam's Sons edition / June 1996
Berkley edition / July 1997

The Putnam Berkley World Wide Web site address is
http://www.berkley.com

ISBN: 0-425-15860-8

BERKLEY®
Berkley Books are published by The Berkley Publishing Group,
200 Madison Avenue, New York, New York 10016.
BERKLEY and the "B" design
are trademarks belonging to Berkley Publishing Corporation.

PRINTED IN THE UNITED STATES OF AMERICA

10 9 8 7 6 5 4 3 2 1

ACKNOWLEDGMENTS

A S LONG AS I CAN REMEMBER, I HAVE LOVED COUNTRY music. But loving something is not the same as knowing it from the inside out or understanding how the business works. For help and insight I am indebted to many: Bones Howe, Pat Higdon, Bill Carter, Jerri Carter, Michael Webb, Lari White's band (Jim Christensen, Kevin Crampton, Frank Fogerty, Bryan Grassmeyer, Matt McClure, Dean Rose, Bruce Wallace), and Lieutenant Tommy Jacobs, Homicide, Nashville Metropolitan Police Department.

My particular thanks and deep appreciation to Lari White, who welcomed me on tour, was generous in sharing information, time, insight and inspiration, and who is a delight to know!

Thanks to Steven Womack, my Nashville colleague, for the inside view, the historical overview, and the gracious hospitality. And to Detective Russ Martin, Sacramento County Sheriff's Department, who, as always, patiently straightened me out on legal technicalities and criminal possibilities.

It goes without saying: All the above expert help was theirs; the mistakes, if any, are mine.

We are five in the Sacramento Writer Gang (aka Karen and the Boys): myself, John Lescroart, Richard Herman, William P. Wood and Dale Brown. Thanks, guys, for everything. I want to say a particular thank-you to John Lescroart, whose friendship, support, common sense, humor and inspiration have made a huge difference. Thanks is too small a word, but here it is anyway.

My love and appreciation to my daughter, Sonia, for always being there, for always being supportive. Once again, thanks is too small a word. Once again, here it is.

For Deborah Schneider,
my agent and my friend

HONKY TONK KAT

one

PLATINUM AND BALONEY

THE SOUND OF HEELS ON CONCRETE WAS LOUD. ECHOES reverberated in the long windowless cement corridor. The quick click of the woman's shoes was lost in the noise made by the boots of the four men, two in front, two in back. Nobody spoke. Occasionally we passed other corridors. At first I looked down each, then I stopped. No one. Nothing. The man in front of me rolled his shoulders under the smooth shiny-blue fabric, flexed them like a prize-fighter.

We could hear the roar now, distant, undefined. Then, as we turned the final corner, the sound smashed into us. Twenty thousand people hollering, stomping, clapping. It was like standing in the path of a locomotive, feeling the physical force and power of the energy coming toward you, the sound filling your ears, then your brain, then leaning on your soul. I stumbled. Maybe everybody does the first time. The man behind me caught my elbow, held it firmly for a moment. No one else missed a beat. No one spoke. The roar was everywhere, then it died into the music, then we were backstage.

It was dark, almost black, after the harsh light of the corridor. I saw people in the background and scattered here and there. Occasionally a hand was raised in salute as we threaded our way around equipment and over heavy cables.

The music ended, drowned in applause. Briefer this time. Then the thunder of voices.

Dakota . . . Dakota . . . Dakota . . .

The stage lights cut and the crowd fell silent. Dakota gripped my hand briefly, then walked on stage. She stood there, lost in the darkness, then the spotlight hit her. Lights sparkled in the thousands of black sequins on her tight black sheath, in the gold ones on her slim gold jacket. She tossed her long blond hair back and held her arms out wide. The crowd roared with approval.

"Y'all having a good time? I hope so. I sure plan to. Here's the song that started it for me."

The pedal steel guitar whined and sobbed. The crowd recognized the opening chords of "Leftover Love," and went wild.

> "You found a new darlin',
> you found a new life.
> Well, honey . . ."

Standing with her hands balled into fists and tucked into her slim waist, her head at a cocky angle, Dakota drew out the *honey* so we could hear the sweetness and the acid both. The crowd roared.

> "I ain't no leftover love.
> I ain't no leftover life."

Someone pushed by me in the dark, equipment loaded high on a hand truck. Sound rolled over me in waves. I looked past the spotlight that showcased and framed Dakota into the blackness that was the audience, twenty thousand fans who adored her.

And one who wanted to kill her.

The concert was a blur of lights, noise, costume changes and choreography. And the roar of the audience. The music itself was often lost, sometimes secondary. My attention was not on the music, or on Dakota, but on the stage, on the possibility of danger. With the first encore I started to breathe more easily. Almost over. Almost safe.

The second encore was an old favorite, "Honky Tonk Angel." Slowly the houselights started coming up. I saw him right away, a lanky cowboy with pressed jeans, starched shirt, buffed-out boots and a hat shielding his face, holding a huge bouquet of long-stemmed red roses. He slipped past a guard, vaulted over the lights, hit the stage running.

What was in the bouquet besides roses?

It seemed like an eternity but it was seconds. He never reached the spotlight, never even came close to her. One of our boys, in a blue satin shirt and black hat—you can't tell the good guys from the bad guys by their hats anymore—took him down halfway, dragged him to the edge of the stage, tossed him over like you'd toss garbage over a fence. In a final futile gesture the cowboy flung the bouquet on stage.

Dakota drew out the last note, threw the audience kisses and thank-yous, tried to leave. They hollered for one more song. Finally the last encore, the last kiss thrown into waiting hearts and Dakota turned, walked out of the spotlight and across the black expanse of the back stage. Waiting hands caught her, guided her—blind from the stage lights—past obstacles and back to the unforgiving bare-bulb glare of the corridor.

We moved fast trying to beat the press and fans. I had forbidden meet-and-greet time with fans after the show, forbidden interviews with media. Twenty thousand people. Nobody can control a situation with twenty thousand people.

As we walked back, our words and laughter ricocheted off the concrete walls, almost drowned out the sound of the men's boots. There were five of them now, all dressed in jeans, blue satin western shirts and black hats. They were built to push through a crowd. Smiling now, the look would change to mean the minute the last door flew open and they had to get Dakota across the parking lot and into her bus.

"Hey guys, how'd I sound?"

"Honey, you were great."

"Knocked 'em sideways, Dakota. But you always do."

Dakota laughed, the pre-performance silence and jitters long gone. She would be excited, high for an hour or two—the music, the applause, the adrenaline hot and wild in her veins.

"You were something, Dakota. You always are, sweetheart." Admiration hung heavy and thick in his voice, like maple syrup in winter. I didn't know him by name but I turned slightly so that, now, I would know him by face.

"Ready?"

The point man was five seven by five seven with a low voice, a gap-toothed grin and a hand that completely covered the doorknob on the steel door. He opened the door and the guys rushed us out. I blinked and stumbled in the sudden glare of flashbulbs. A hand caught my elbow, stayed there. Dakota and I moved swiftly in blue-satin-black-hat momentum.

People screamed for Dakota, reached out to touch her, to present her with flowers and food and gifts. A woman held up a child who solemnly waved a little plastic American flag. Faces appeared and disappeared, smiling and mouthing endearments we couldn't hear. One woman stood silently, tears streaming down her face. Someone waited by the bus, opened the door as we neared. We ran up the steps. Momentum. The door slammed behind us and Dakota sank into a chair, kicking her shoes onto the floor and peeling off her jacket. A gold sequin tumbled to the carpet.

"Well, Katy?"

I shook my head, still stunned. "It's like nothing I ever imagined."

She laughed and stretched her arms above her head, then opened the small refrigerator, grabbed a bottle of water and chugged thirstily. "Have a glass of wine with me, Katy?"

"Okay."

She grinned at me, looking suddenly like the kid I'd grown up with. "Sandwich?"

"Sure." I stared blankly at a tightly curtained window as she made sandwiches and spoke in rapid-fire sentences, spilling her thoughts like gumdrop jewels.

"It's all I ever wanted, all that I worked for my whole life, Katy. I feel real lucky. And I sure don't want it to end." She put a plate of sandwiches on the table, pulled paper napkins out of a dispenser and sat.

I looked at the sandwiches, then at Dakota.

"You remember." Her voice was soft. "Plain white bread, one skinny little ol' slice of baloney and a hunka mayonnaise. You remember how often we ate that when we were kids, Katy. Hey, that was on the *good* days. Bad days it was just white bread and mayonnaise." Her smile twisted until it was something besides a smile.

"I don't want to lose those days completely. I don't want to forget where I came from and how much I have to be thankful for. I don't want to forget how many of my fans have white bread and baloney days, and how maybe my music makes things a little better, a little brighter."

I thought of the child waving the American flag, the woman with tears running down her cheeks, the kisses and notes and flowers.

And the threats.

Dakota grabbed a sandwich and handed it to me. There was a lot I didn't want to lose either. Dakota was part of that.

"Mmmmmm." She savored the first bite. "Tastes better than steak, I swear."

I smiled and shook my head. I didn't agree but I ate.

"Where did it start, Katy? I look back and I can't tell. I know it was wrong for a long time but I don't know where, or when it started." She wiped mayonnaise off her chin.

"Somewhere back in the string of yesterdays, I guess."

two

STRING OF YESTERDAYS

*T*HE VOICE ON THE PHONE WAS A CAPPELLA, THE BALLAD *sad and wistful.*

> " 'Ain't no today or tomorrow, ain't
> nuthin' but a string of yesterdays.' "

"Dakota?"

"Katy, thank God you're there." *She laughed with some of the same sad notes of the song heavy in her voice.*

There were tears behind the laughter and something else behind the tears. I knew—I've known Dakota for twenty-odd years. I knew her when she was Cody Jones, though now I, too, call her Dakota. Three albums had gone platinum or double platinum, two gold. Dakota Jones, country singer and recording artist. Country Star.

"Katy, I need help."

"What, Cody?" *Without meaning to, I slipped into the past. The past always has a hold on you.*

"Someone keeps sending me letters. Anonymous letters."

"Threatening? Obscene?"

"Yes. No. Katy, I don't know. It's things you wouldn't think a person could know."

"What kind of things?" *Blackmail was on my mind.*

"It's creepy, Katy. It's like someone wants to have power over me or . . ." *The hesitation hung heavy in her voice.* "Or like they already do and I just don't know it yet. Who *would know all this stuff? Who would care? I hate this."*

"Is it blackmail, Cody?"

"No."

I waited.

"No. And what would it be, anyway?" she asked.

I didn't answer; I wasn't sure. Much of Cody's life sounds like a country song—a childhood without enough money or love, an early marriage she jumped into to get away from home, not realizing that she was running to something just as bad.

Cody sucked in a breath. In the background I could hear music. *"Katy, when you're young, you don't understand. You think you can start over with anything, with the first dream that catches your eye and fancy. And you think if you marry him even the leftovers will be great. Growing up is learning that what you see is what you get and, nine times out of ten, the leftovers are worse. Much worse. I got so sick of leftovers—leftover love, leftover life, leftover dreams . . ."*

"Leftover Love." It was Dakota Jones's first hit song and it took her to the top, made the poverty of the past a memory.

"Since then I've tried to make myself up as I go along. Make up something good. Can you, Katy? Or are you always made up of leftovers and of your past?"

I know Cody better than I know Dakota but I tried to come up with an answer. Dakota spoke before I could.

"Do I want all that old stuff to come out? No, of course not. But it's not something someone would blackmail me about."

"Some of it has come out in the interviews."

"Yes." Her voice was dead, flat. There was no high note or promise in it. No song. *"Some of it has."*

"Cody, is there something in your life that is blackmail material?"

"No!"

She said it fast—way too fast—so I knew there was.

"Oh God, Katy, you know how life goes?"

I know. "Yes?" I asked, knowing the answer.

"Katy," she whispered, *"please come. Please stop it. I need you. I need help real bad or I wouldn't ask—you know that."*

I WAS ON A PLANE TO NASHVILLE IN LESS THAN TWENTY-four hours, had arrived last night. The past has a hold on us all.

"You want the last sandwich, Katy?"

I slipped out of that yesterday, that memory. "You eat it." White bread, baloney and mayonnaise have no hold on me.

There was a thump on the door and the bus started filling up with guys: Ted, Dakota's road manager; Steve, who played keyboard; James on guitar and Tommy on acoustic; Nat on bass; Rolli on drums. Security, in black hats and blue satin, was introduced as a group. People talking, laughing, goofing off. Tension before the show, energy and adrenaline during—we were all coming down now. Tabs on beer cans and sodas popped. Sandwiches and potato chips appeared. Something that smelled like chili, that smelled good, was on the stove.

"Guys, you were terrific. It was a great night. Thanks. Jimmy—"

A blue satin shirt turned. Now that he'd taken his hat off, I could see I'd guessed wrong. Not five seven by five seven, maybe five five by five seven. He tipped a Bud at Dakota in acknowledgment.

"Good work. The guy on stage—had you ever seen him before?"

Jimmy shook his head and reached for a fresh beer. "No. I'll recognize him now, though."

"Chili's hot. Kat, Dakota didn't make you eat baloney, did she?" Everyone laughed at Steve's question.

Dakota winked at me. "She *loved* it." Laughter again.

It was a big bus, but even a big bus gets crowded. We were in the kitchen/living area. Behind that was a three-bunk tier, a small bathroom and Dakota's spacious state-room with a bed, sofa and makeup table, a large closet and bathroom.

I'd flown into Nashville last night just in time for the
midnight departure of the bus. Sleeping, eating, sound
checks, rehearsing—there'd been no chance to talk to Dakota.

"Chili?" Dakota asked with a smile, handing me a bowl.

"Dakota, we—"

"Tomorrow, Katy. I promise."

The chili was a lot better than the baloney.

"KATY."

In the quiet of the bus Dakota's voice sounded strained.
She stood outside her stateroom, eyes wide, face otherwise
expressionless. "Could you come here for a minute,
please?"

Dakota shut the door behind me as soon as I entered. I
glanced at her dark stricken eyes, then around the room. A
huge bouquet of long-stemmed red, almost black, roses had
been tossed on the bed. A few leaves had crumpled and
broken and lay in fragments on the spread. They looked
like the flowers Dakota's admirer at the concert had tossed
at her.

Only these were dead.

And tied with a black ribbon.

"Dead roses," Dakota said, her voice dull and heavy.
She picked them up, held them to her chest, hands modestly
folded over them, closed her eyes. "How do I look?" she
whispered. "Black on black. They're meant for me. Dead
roses for—"

I shook her slightly—reality check—and took the roses
out of her hands. "Look around, Dakota. Tell me if anything else looks wrong or out of place."

"I don't know. Kat, why—?"

I made her look. Closets, drawers, makeup table, desk.
It didn't take long. And we didn't find anything.

"Who has access to the bus?"

"Now? Well, theoretically only me, you, Ted and the
driver."

"Ted is your manager?"

"My road manager, yes. But this is the first time we've

had new rules about the buses. Everyone still comes and goes pretty much as they please. Like tonight. No one really thinks of this bus as mine, as private, yet.''

''It could have been anybody?''

''Yes.''

''A fan? Someone from the outside?''

She hesitated. ''Ted says no, that it's either locked or he's here, or Hoss, the driver, is. Still, there have been times when he wasn't. He gets mad when I say something, says he was right by the bus the whole time and nobody could have gotten by him. But I have, so someone else could too.'' Dakota sank down on her bed.

''I thought that with you here it would be over, that they would stop. There was no letter tonight before the show. I hoped . . .'' Her voice trailed off.

''Why would someone blackmail you, Dakota?'' I was thinking about our earlier conversation.

''This isn't really blackmail, Kat.''

I revised the question. ''What could someone threaten you with?''

''I don't know.'' Her wide blue eyes met mine. No fear. Total control. Being on stage had taught Dakota something; I'd never seen her lie like this.

''I'm leaving tomorrow,'' I said. I could hear the fatigue in my voice.

''Why? No, *please*.'' Panic in hers.

''You've already decided how to handle this. You don't need me. And I won't play by your rules.''

''Katy, I don't understand.'' Wide blue, guileless eyes. Her left eyebrow arched. As a child I'd spent hours in front of a mirror trying to lift a single eyebrow like that. There was something so innocent, quizzical, quixotic about it, I thought, wishing even now that I could do it with her style.

''You're in trouble, Dakota. It's not going to go away. Letters. Dead flowers. And it could get worse.'' *Probably will.* ''I think your best choice is to face it, not run away, not hide. But that, of course, is your decision.''

I heard voices, the slam of a door. I'd gotten used to the sound of the bus engine idling. Now it changed. There was the sound of gears grinding, changing. The bus wheezed and then jerked into motion.

"What time do we get to Memphis?" I asked.

"Tomorrow morning around ten." Dakota knuckled her eyes like a tired child. "God, I'm tired. Let's go to bed now, okay? One more day, one more show tomorrow night, then home to Nashville and we'll talk. I promise." She stood and stretched, then slumped slightly. "Someone's trying to scare me, Kat."

"Yes." I looked at Dakota's serene and beautiful face. There was fear in her eyes now.

three

LOST AND FOUND

IT WAS THE LACK OF MOTION THAT WOKE ME. MY WIN-
dowless bunk, the privacy curtain opening onto the corridor closed, was absolutely dark. I yawned, pulled the
comforter up under my chin. Had it been seven hours? It
couldn't have; I was exhausted still. Outside I heard voices,
muted and distant. Gas, I thought, not Memphis. I drifted
back to sleep once we were on the freeway. No stops, starts
or turns, just forward motion, the occasional bump or pothole, and the singing of the tires. *On the road.* Motion in
time and unknown space. I loved sleeping on the bus, the
sounds and the motion, the waking up to a new place and
a new day.

When I woke up next, it was nine. I unsnapped the curtain, pushed it back, stumbled into the main cabin and the
sunlight. I brushed my teeth and pulled a comb through my
hair, then started coffee. I poured two cups, walked up front
to ride shotgun.

"Coffee, Hoss?"

"That's a thought." He took the mug and thanked me
with a nod. I sank into the seat next to him, sipped coffee
and stared out a clean windshield into blue skies, sunshine
and white-lined asphalt unwinding in front of us.

"A boss driver named Hoss. Does that make sense?"

" 'Bout as much as anything, I guess."

"Do you know why I'm here?"

"I heard somethin' about it. That don't make sense, neither."

"You got any ideas?"

"About Dakota's troubles?"

"Yes."

"The world's full of people who are filled up with hate and lookin' fer someone to lay it on."

"Like?"

"Like maybe she's got what someone else don't and ain't never gonna have. Don't matter they didn't work for it so of course they ain't got it. They don't think that way. They just want what they don't got. Or maybe it's the other way around—they don't want another to have what they ain't got."

"You think that's it?"

"How the hell I know? I'm outta coffee, that's what I know."

I got up to get him some more. "Have you seen anything odd or unusual, Hoss?"

"No, but I got an eye open. Dakota's one hell of a nice lady." He stuck his jaw out and looked mean, looked like a Hoss should.

I drifted back for a second cup of coffee and flipped through today's schedule. Full. I frowned. The bus swayed and the coffee and I almost parted company. Traffic was thicker now. We had left the freeway and were headed for downtown.

Still in the sweatsuit I'd slept in, I pulled on socks and sneakers. I tapped on Dakota's door, opened it, stuck my head in. "Want coffee?"

"Please." A small and muffled voice from a mound of covers.

By the time I got back Dakota was propped up, her hair fanned out on the pillow. I sat at the chair at her makeup table.

"Hey, Katy."

"Hey. I'm going to be your shadow all day."

"Good. Ted will have an update of my schedule when we get to the hotel."

The bus slowed, then stopped. Memphis. Ted showed up on our bus twenty minutes later. By then Dakota was in a sweatsuit too and we were both on another cup of coffee.

"Room keys. I got you a suite like you wanted." Ted handed us keys and a printed list with the names and room numbers of the band and crew. "Update of your schedule." Another couple of sheets. "You going up to your room? I'll get your bags up there in the next ten minutes."

"Thanks. Is there an exercise room, Ted?"

"Yeah." He blanked. "Forgot where, though."

Dakota winked at me. "Let's go pump iron, girl."

The exercise room was all ours. I pulled off my sweatshirt, peeling down to a T-shirt, and tugged my sweatpants up to my knees. We started off with a fifteen-minute warm-up on bicycles.

"Enough with the problems. Tell me what else is happening, Katy. Tell me the news from home, from Sacramento."

"Everything's fine." I smiled. "Alma's as wild as ever, Lindy's doing great—just graduated from high school. Charity's writing a book." That list was my grandmother; a kid, very dear to me, that I pulled off the streets several years ago and whom Alma later adopted; and my best friend, a syndicated advice columnist.

"And Hank?"

Hank. "Almost everything's fine," I amended. I reached down, turned up the resistance on the bike. "We're—" I stopped. After more than two years I wasn't sure what we were. "Katy?" Dakota's voice was encouraging. I looked over into her warm and gentle smile, her eyes wide, questioning, caring. It's no wonder people love her so. It's not just the music.

"Maybe it's a song." *A sad song*, I thought. *A song of betrayal, of broken hearts and forgotten promises.*

"Tell me."

"There was a case and another woman. Hank got too involved in both."

Dakota sucked in her breath. Hank's a detective with the Las Vegas Police Department and as good and kind, as loving and steady as they come. Usually.

"It tied into a case I was working on—a bad combination. He got into trouble, I pulled him out. He was grateful but—"

"Yes," Dakota said. "I see. And now?"

"We're still picking up the pieces. Trying to," I modified. "It's a lot easier to break something than to put it back together." In my mind delicate hand-painted plates, beautiful vases and exquisite crystal goblets smashed to the ground. Impossible to restore. Maybe relationships were like that. Or maybe you could put them back together but the cracks would always be there. Or maybe you couldn't. *All the king's horses and all the king's men* . . .

"But the love's still there—for both of you?"

"The love's still there; the trust is gone."

The timer on Dakota's bike dinged. Obediently we climbed off, Dakota headed for the stair-stepper, me for the Nordic Track.

"That's a song," Dakota said.

I nodded. "Do you ever cry when you write sad songs?"

"Do I ever write sad songs and not cry?"

And that made us laugh, which was good.

"I'm glad you called, Dakota. I'm glad I can help and mostly—"

"Mostly, it's been way too long," she finished.

"Way too long," I agreed. "That was another thing we didn't see as kids."

"What?"

"How complicated life would be. And how the minute we figured out one set of complications we'd walk right smack into another set."

"Or how much it would hurt." Dakota made no attempt to hide the pain in her voice. "Whichever way you turn, there's a world of hurt waiting for you."

"Speaking of hurt," I said, sweating and breathing hard, "is our twenty minutes up? No wonder skiers are in such great shape."

"That's *it*." Dakota was definite. "We ought to go for jocks. People in the music business and in law enforcement are too—"

"Fucked up," I finished. We were quiet then, since we also fall into those categories and that was a can of worms we didn't feel like opening. "That's *not* a song," I said finally, and we cracked up again.

"Oh God, Katy, I've missed you. Okay, let's pump a little iron and we're out of here." We moved over to the weight machines.

"You know what I hate?" I asked.

"Shush up," Dakota said sternly, "you can't breathe right if you talk."

"*Do* you?" I asked, screwing up my breathing.

"What?"

"People who pump so much iron that they become huge mounds of muscle-bound mass. It's not only ugly, they can't even walk right."

"Yeah. Well, you know what they say: Everything in moderation."

That one silenced us for a bit. Dakota and I know what moderation is but only theoretically. We have almost no hands-on experience with it. *Go for broke. Hell-bent for leather. All or nothing.* That's us.

"Eight . . . nine . . . ten." I panted, then stopped and unwound myself from stainless steel without a heart. "Almost done?"

In the elevator we stretched a little and laughed the carefree laugh of people who exercise hard and are thus, by definition, virtuous. Not that virtue is logical. An overweight couple—tourists, I'd put money on it—looked away from us. Ha. Virtue may not be logical but it is intimidating.

I stopped at the pop machine on our floor. So much for virtue. "Want one?" I fed in dollar bills and punched down two diet Dr Peppers.

Our suite was attractive in the bland way that most hotel rooms are, with a central living area and a bedroom and bathroom to each side. Our bags were stacked neatly in the middle of the floor. Besides that, the only personal touch was a basket of fruit, cheeses and crackers. No threatening letters, bombs or vials of poison. I checked.

Bags in hand, we headed for clean clothes and a shower. Ooops. I stuck my head back into the living room. "Do you want to order room service or shall I?"

"You. The usual for me, unless they have apple pancakes."

"CHRIS IS COMING AT ONE." DAKOTA WAVED A SHEET OF paper at me and spoke through a bite of apple. The debris from breakfast was on the table in front of us. Dakota's legs were carelessly stretched out in front of her. Wearing jeans, boots, a scoop-neck T-shirt and a short, soft-gold suede jacket, she looked simple, unabashed, unadorned. And beautiful.

"Who's Chris?" the suspicious investigator in me asked.

"Our escort. No problem, Katy. My manager in Nashville arranged it all."

"And?"

"And I do a radio interview and one-liners, and a TV interview. Over to the venue for a general meet-the-press interview at four. Sound check at five. At six-fifteen a quick meet-and-greet autograph party at the hotel. Then back to the room to eat and get ready." She took another bite of apple.

I stared at her. "Is every day like this?"

"On the road, yeah. Pretty much."

"And you're on the road how many days?"

"I've cut back. Probably only two hundred a year now."

"Jeez, Dakota. It's a good thing you pump iron. I hope you take vitamins, too."

She wrinkled her nose at me. "It's hard work but it's what I *love*, Katy. It's more than work. It's my life, it's . . ." Her voice trailed off. "You ready?"

"Almost. Do something with my hair, will you?" I shook back my tousled mop of slightly below-shoulder-length curly brown hair.

"Why? It looks great."

"I want a different look. This makes me too easily iden-tifiable. I want to notice rather than be noticed."

"Oh."

The laughter was gone from her voice now. I felt the sadness touch me, too. Sadness? More like danger.

"What shall I do?"

"A French braid?" Three minutes later I stared into the mirror. "Wow! Talk about different."

"You look lovely, Katy. You should wear it like this more often. It shows off the shape of your face, your cheek-bones, your beautiful eyes."

"*Wow,*" I said again. "This is *much* better than just stuffing my hair up in a baseball cap." Which is what I usually do.

Dakota laughed at me.

The phone rang.

"Yes." My voice was businesslike, even harsh. I left *wow* behind just like that. "Five minutes. In the lobby. Thank you."

Dakota looked at me sideways as we walked to the el-evator bank. "Maybe we could do something about your clothes, too?"

"People have tried before." We both laughed. "I'm okay," I said, looking at black boots, worn jeans, a white blouse and a black blazer.

"You look *great*, Kat. It's a good look and it's *you*. But there's no reason we couldn't go for drop-dead gorgeous once in a while."

I looked at her suspiciously.

"Is there? Drop-dead gorgeous is good. Change is good. You know you like your hair like that."

I touched my hair gently. "Like it? I *love* it."

"So we'll try it, okay?"

"Okay."

"Where do you carry your gun, Kat?"

She asked this as we rounded the corner to the elevator bank. Good timing, huh? Two middle-aged ladies, one with a matching middle-aged man and a lively ten-year-old in pigtails gaped at us. Did I mention that Dakota's voice was loud, her words well enunciated and emphatic?

"You've got a *gun*?" the ten-year-old asked. "How come? Can I see?"

"Shush up, Mary Ellen Jeanette Rose Louise," one of the women hissed. The man stepped forward slightly. I smiled—benignly, I thought. He stepped back.

The elevator bell dinged at us. Down. The child of many names lunged for it but was yanked back. We rode down alone.

"Dakota!"

"Oh, Katy, you should have *seen* your face!" She giggled. "So, where do you?"

"I don't always carry a gun," I said stiffly. "Hardly ever, actually."

"Are you now?"

The elevator slid to a stop and the door opened. I didn't answer.

"Hey!" someone said, a voice in the background moving into the foreground. "Hey, aren't you Dakota Jones?"

We moved quickly toward the lobby, the revolving front door and the car that awaited us outside.

"Hey!" A cowboy hat and an attitude. Right in our face. He moved quickly too.

Dakota smiled and dodged. The cowboy hat lunged for her. I signaled to the doormen. Why use muscle when you can use brainpower? We slid past the three of them, cowboy hat struggling with a doorman locked onto each arm, slid into the back seat of the waiting car.

four

SEE YA!

I SEE NOW WHY CELEBRITIES BECOME JERKS. *SOME* CE-
lebrities. I see why they start to believe that they can
walk on water, turn lead to gold, and that their dirt don't
stink. This is not an exaggeration.

People fawned on us. Me, too, because I was with Dakota. They reached out to touch her, crowded in to look at
her, begged to meet her. Sometimes the expressions that
flickered across their faces reminded me of figures in Eu-
ropean paintings, their faces frozen in centuries-old ecstasy.
It was almost worshipful. I found it a little frightening,
definitely unnerving. Here we have no saints, no royalty.
We make celebrities our royalty. We make them more than
they are, or want to be.

Dakota was instantly surrounded at the radio station.
Chris stood to one side chatting with someone. People who
had at first shyly hung back now pressed forward, closing
in on us. Dakota smiled, shook hands, chatted. After a few
minutes of this she leaned back and whispered to me.
Someone jostled us, hard. All I heard was "out of here."

"Chris!" I had to call her name twice to get her attention. "We're on a tight schedule here. We need to do the
interview."

"Oh." She looked at the man next to her, who pointed
down the hall, then waved at us to follow.

I grabbed Dakota's elbow and pushed my way through the crowd, pulling her along with me. We were ushered into a small soundproofed studio. An advertising jingle played in the background and the DJ stood to welcome us.

"Are you ready?" He was polite and businesslike, a welcome change. Dakota nodded and he placed her in front of a mike and adjusted it. "Right after the weather." He returned to his seat and we listened to the weather. Dakota stood at the mike, feet slightly apart, one hand gently tapping her leg, her face blank. She came to attention as the DJ introduced her.

"A warm welcome to Dakota Jones who's in Memphis for a concert tonight . . .

"Dakota, I know there's a special story behind your latest hit song . . .

"Is there any truth to the rumor that . . .

"What's in the future for . . .

"Where else are you going on this tour . . ."

Dakota answered in a warm, friendly voice, making it sound as though it were the very first time she had been asked those questions. After the third commercial break, the DJ turned to us.

"Okay, that's a wrap. You were great. Thanks, Dakota. Any chance for a few one-liners?"

"Of course." Dakota smiled and we were ushered to another studio.

"Hey, y'all, this is Dakota Jones and when I'm in Memphis I listen to station . . .

"Hi, y'all, when you're looking for country, you're looking for station . . .

"Hey, y'all, this is Dakota Jones and I'll see y'all at the concert tonight."

She stepped away from the mike. "Katy, get Chris to bring the car around to the back and someone to walk us out of the station without any fuss, okay?"

Later, in the car, there was silence for a moment. Chris broke it. "That went pretty well, don't you think?"

"Are you new in this business, Chris?" There was a *very*

polite note in Dakota's voice which meant, I knew, that she was furious.

"A l-little." She stuttered on the *l.* "Is something wrong?"

"The mob scene in the lobby."

"Y-yes."

"It's your job to see that that never happens. We walk in, say hello, smile, shake a few hands. Keep moving. Always. Don't let me get surrounded and trapped like that. There's no way we can keep to our schedule that way. And it's way too much for me." She grimaced, that to me alone.

"All right. Sure. Sorry."

The television stop was quick, a short promotional piece for tonight's concert. They walked Dakota in, made her up, walked her in front of the camera and next to an interviewer who was moussed and hair-sprayed as well as made up. He had good teeth and a great smile, although the smile only came into play when he was on camera. He was polite to Dakota, whose name he couldn't remember without looking at the TelePrompTer, and viciously rude to the camera crew. Eight minutes and we were out of there, listening to the retreating sounds of Mr. Big Shot hollering for water, for the makeup person, and about something the grip had done wrong.

"Katy, if I ever get like that, shoot me."

I nodded. "No problem."

We paused at the door of the studio looking for Chris and the way out. Radio and TV stations are a maze of endless corridors and identical closed doors with no clues as to where you are. If that's the maze, were we the rats? Performing rats? "Remember Randy Newman's song 'Lonely at the Top'?" she asked, a little sadness in her voice.

"Hey you guys. *There* you are." Chris bounced over and led us out of the maze.

ON TO THE VENUE AND ANOTHER PRESS CONFERENCE. Again I watched Dakota graciously answer questions about her life, her tour, her plans, her music, her future. There

was a pattern, a sameness about the questions that I was
beginning to recognize. Not simplistic exactly, but the kind
of query interested people who know nothing about your
work would ask.

We finished a little ahead of schedule. "For a change,"
Dakota said as we followed Chris to the arena, the site of
that night's concert, for sound check. A sellout crowd was
twelve thousand. We were sold out. Except for the stage
the arena was almost dark, only a few lights scattered here
and there.

"C'mon, Katy." Dakota took off. Past the chairs on the
ground floor of the arena, up the stairs in the gradually
sloping lower sections, then up into the steeply climbing
upper sections. Last row. Cheap seats. Nosebleed seats. We
sat.

"I want to *know* what it's like sitting up here, only being
able to afford the cheapest seat in the house. Some fans
will scrimp and save all year just to go to one concert.
When I'm on stage, Katy, I can't even see up here—the
distance and the lights. But I know they're there and I look
up at where they are. The folks in these seats are just as
important to me as the fan who comes to every concert and
buys every CD the minute it hits the store."

From here the stage was far away and small, the people
scurrying around like little two-legged bugs.

"Do you mind all the—" I gestured with both hands, at
a loss for words but thinking of the press and the people
at the radio station, of the double-edged sword that is fame
and stardom.

"All of it? Today?"

"Yes."

A guitar twanged. Someone played the same riff on a
drum over and over.

"No. Remember when we were in high school? I was
always in my head, wrapped up in music and ideas. I wasn't
academic, though, so I didn't fit in that way. I never really
fit in anywhere. I had friends but I wasn't one of the 'popular' kids. I felt like I was always on the outside looking
in, like looking at the stage from here. Everything was far

away, a different world, and definitely not my world.

"I always envied the girls who were cheerleaders. Or I envied what I *thought* their life was. I didn't know what it really was. They were popular—everyone wanted to hang out with them, to be part of their group, their crowd. They could go anywhere and always be welcome.

"Being an artist, being known, is kind of like being a cheerleader, making it, being one of the popular kids. People accept you. No one criticizes me for having my head in the clouds now. No one tells me to forget music, to get a job and get a life. People accept what I do.

"It's not who I am, it's what I do, I know that. People don't want to meet Cody, the dreamer kid who made good. They want to see Dakota, the star. I understand that and I don't mind, just as long as—" Dakota poked me in the ribs with her elbow. "As long as I have a few friends who know and like me as a person, who don't care about the star part and do care about me."

Below us the band finished an instrumental and someone took the mike. "Dakota, you out there?"

"C'mon. Race you!"

Going down was a lot faster than coming up.

It always is.

I SAT IN A CHAIR ABOUT FIFTEEN ROWS BACK AND watched. It was a round stage placed at one end of the arena. The band was set up in the center, leaving pathways so that Dakota could cross the stage at two points. After three false starts they ran through "See Ya!," a sassy song Dakota wrote about a woman who tells off her no-good boyfriend and walks.

"Take it from 'You said I wasn't good enough,' and Nat, not quite so much bass."

"One more time."

"You got it."

"How about this on vocals?"

"Okay. Good."

It was, Dakota told me later, the last song they had added and she was still playing with it.

Overhead hung a huge skeletal structure. Two men
scrambled around moving lights—adjusting, trying, adjusting. A spot hit Dakota, then moved across stage and back.
In quick succession spots hit each of the musicians. I
watched one of the light men clamber, crawl and climb
around. Goose bumps. Up in the last row it hadn't seemed
high at all. From here? It was a good fall. Perspective. The
light man climbed down the free-swinging wire-and-pipe
ladder. More goose bumps. Guess who never dove off the
high board even on a double dare?

Someone was fussing with Dakota's mike, a wireless
hand mike, and she was talking with James, the guitar
player. One more walk-through with the mike, a quick
wave to the band, and Dakota headed for the back of the
stage. I joined her there. Chris was waiting at the exit to
take us back to the hotel and the autograph party. Dakota
looked fresh. I felt wilted.

A small convention room had been reserved at the hotel.
Banners advertising a local radio station had been slung
around and the room was filled to capacity, three hundred
people. Ted waited to escort us. A small hush started as we
entered the room and walked across to a table that had been
set up for Dakota. A long line stretched away from the
table.

Almost everybody was in western clothes, fancy dress-
up western clothes, not just jeans and a jacket. Mostly
boots—men and women—and a bunch of hats—men.

Dakota had a stack of eight-by-ten photographs in front
of her. She was smiling and signing.

Hey y'all.

Three young couples giggling and shoving. Parents with
a little guy, five maybe, dressed like Garth Brooks.

How ya doing?

Two shy overweight girls dressed in brand-new western
duds with dreams in their eyes. A couple in their sixties
holding hands. Four guys, early twenties, strutting and
chewing tobacco.

Thanks for stopping by.

An old man in a wheelchair, hat on his knees, pushed
by a smiling young woman. Two couples, the guys shrug-

ging and grunting, the girls talking to each other.

See you at the concert.

A young woman in a navy business suit with red accessories. A gaggle of teenage girls. A cowboy with a chip on his shoulder and a toothpick in his mouth. Two women—mother and daughter?—the younger one pushing a double stroller with cranky twins.

Y'all take care.

They were all looking for something, wanting Dakota to answer a question they hadn't spoken, feel a need they couldn't articulate or understand. Everyone was polite. No threats. No deranged fans.

Ted got us out. Hotel security escorted us through a locked door, down a long corridor, through the kitchen and up a service elevator to the suite. Dakota sank onto the couch, closed her eyes. Seven o'clock. She was on at nine.

Later I watched as Dakota deftly, quickly did her makeup. Tonight she wore a silver dress and the gold jacket of the night before.

Ted drove us to the venue. Traffic was snarled and police had cordoned off several access streets. We used them. Dakota's two buses were inside a cavernous garage at the arena, as were two others I didn't recognize and a number of cars. We parked and followed Ted to the dressing room, walking in silence. Pre-performance silence. And jitters.

The dressing room was ugly but lively. Cream concrete walls, institutional-gray carpeting and a long table with refreshments and chairs. Hyped-up musicians and a couple of blue satin shirts. Everybody was joking around, goofing off. Dakota poured herself a glass of mineral water and sat to one side. No one disturbed her.

"Okay, guys. Time. Let's *move!*" Ted hollered.

After the band left, there was only Dakota and me and silence. Her band would play for fifteen or twenty minutes and then she was on. Dakota stood, walked back to the bathroom area. Scales climbed and fell and climbed again, notes bouncing off the tile bathroom walls and flying around. I shivered.

"Dakota." Ted's voice.

She walked out. "Hey."

"You ready?"

A nod.

We followed blue satin shirts again to the arena. There were no seats at that end of the stage/arena area—just equipment and cables—and no one was allowed there without a backstage pass. We waited in a corridor lined with security people, guys who didn't smile. I watched a muscle jump in the cheek of a young, clean-shaven, well-biceped guard.

When Dakota's cue came, she ran down the corridor. A spotlight picked her up twenty feet from the stage and followed her on.

"Hey, y'all! How you doing? It's great to be in Memphis!" Dakota walked the stage greeting everyone. The crowds were on their feet cheering, hollering, ready to have a good time. They went wild with the opening bars of "Leftover Love."

I walked through security onto the main floor. People move around a lot at concerts. They go for a beer, or for the stage and a better look at the star. They toss flowers and gifts, try to take a picture. The *FULL ACCESS* backstage pass was tucked into my jacket; I didn't want to stick out.

On stage Dakota moved around a lot, playing the audience, playing with them and to them. It wasn't choreographed, wasn't predictable.

Neither was the bomb.

five

RIPTIDE ROAR

I SAW IT. I JUST COULDN'T STOP IT.
A man stood up, pulled his arm back as though to throw a baseball.

High and on the inside? Curve ball? Slider?

It doesn't matter with a bomb. You don't need the same accuracy with a bomb as you do with a baseball.

I started to drop to the floor, to shield my head and body as much as possible. I wasn't fast enough. An oversize supersize firecracker and flashbulb went off. Blinding light. Deafening noise.

The pandemonium was instant. I looked for the bomber but there were spots in front of my eyes, flashes and stars, and I couldn't see much. I didn't see him. Thousands of people on the floor of the arena were in a state of total panic, shoving, screaming, every man for himself and to hell with women and children. Like a riptide. Only the strong survive a riptide. Sometimes not even the strong.

Out of the corner of my eye I saw a lost child of five or six, her face a frozen tableau of stark terror. Two men knocked her over, almost trampled her. I lunged for the child, grabbing roughly for the clothing on her chest, jerking, hauling her up to my height. I didn't dare bend over. You could be lost then, snapped in two or trampled. The child wrapped her legs around my waist, her arms around my neck. I could feel her hot breath on my cheek. The noise around us was deafening, people screaming and crying out, chairs smashing.

There were several riptides. With the child clinging to me, I fought my way through a thin crust of people into the smaller tide that washed us toward the stage, the bomb target, and the back exit of the arena. I could hardly breathe, staggered with the weight of the child. I could keep myself afloat; I wasn't sure about the two of us.

So I didn't let myself think about that. I didn't let myself think about Dakota, either. The tide roared onto some unknown beach, pulling us along though we were on the edge of it. Someone slammed us into a metal barricade and the child cried out in my ear, her leg taking the force of the blow. We were carried through the corridor and then, suddenly, it opened up and we were spun along, spit out into a clear area behind the stage and into a pool of quiet. People eddied around us but not on top of us. The riptide ripped on toward the exit.

"Are we safe?" A small voice breathed words into my ear.

"Yes. We'll stay here until things quiet down." We were, I thought, at much less risk here than if I were to try to take the child out. I chose not to consider the possibility of more bombs.

"Where's my mommy?"

"I don't know. We'll find her as soon as we can."

There were figures moving on stage. I could see them but not make out details. I tried to count. Three figures merged into one, then divided again. I blinked, started my count over.

"I want my mommy."

I hugged her. I wanted her mommy too.

"My leg hurts."

The light on the stage picked out a slim figure in silver and gold that stepped over something, then stepped into the shadows. Dakota. Relief washed through me, another kind of tide.

"Can we go now? I want my mommy."

The arena floor had almost cleared out but there would be crowds outside, I knew. A few lone fans clung to their seats, waiting. For what? The finale of the show had come and gone.

"Pretty soon," I said to the child. She whimpered at me. I thought about the stuff in my pockets. Maybe a package of Life Savers? *Yes*. I fished the candy out and handed it over.

"Thank you," she said formally. "My name is Julie."

I started for the stage still holding Julie. God, she was heavy. Was it safe to put her down? Someone jostled us, nearly knocked us over. No. I clutched Julie a little tighter and kept on moving.

The stage. Dakota. And sooner or later, police. A shadowy figure on stage turned into Steve and I hollered at him.

He peered down at me, then grinned. "All right! One more accounted for."

"This is Julie," I said, holding her up. He reached down and took the child without question. A thousand pounds lighter, I clambered up on stage hollering for Dakota.

"Katy!"

"Dakota." We hugged, clutched each other like drowning people. Riptides, eddies, pools, drowning people—I needed to get away from water.

"Is everyone all right? The bomb—" I let the words go. Coward.

"Everyone's okay." She wrinkled her nose, "I don't think it was a bomb."

"Not a bomb?" I looked at the destruction that surrounded us. Instruments were knocked over, busted up and abandoned but the stage wasn't blown up. No ripped boards, no holes.

Flash bombs? Flash grenades? Is that what they were called? Intense light and noise with minimal destruction of property and people. Temporary blindness and deafness if you were too close.

"Whatever it was didn't do this." Dakota swung an arm at the wrecked instruments. "This was people trying to get away and not caring what was in front of them. Or under their feet.''

"Miss? Dakota Jones? Are you all right?" A polite and soft-spoken police officer touched Dakota on the shoulder.

Dakota turned, smiled and nodded, opened her mouth to answer.

"Hi," said Julie, still holding Steve's hand and dragging him into our circle. "I've never seen a lady policeman before. Will you take me to my mommy? *Please*. Do you want a Lifesaver?" she asked no one in particular.

WE WATCHED TV THAT NIGHT—NEWS UPDATE AT ELEVEN— and we made every channel. The opening shots were wonderful. Long shots of Dakota and then the gold and silver of her clothing, slightly out of focus, pulling back to a clear head-and-shoulders shot of her belting out "See Ya!"

That was the end of the wonderful part.

The camera caught the light but the explosion was muffled. The lens zoomed in, then shots became a tumbled kaleidoscopic jumble of the stage, the crowd, the arcing dome of the arena—as though the camera had lost control. Then it went black. Riptide.

Aftermath: Shots of Dakota and the band, of the police officer holding Julie's hand, of other officers—plainclothes and uniform—prowling around the devastation and outlining it with crime scene tape. And then there was blood. How had the camera resisted it so long? Broken arms and stomped feet and cuts and bruises. Several people had been hospitalized. One, a child, was in critical condition. The camera panned the trashed arena and the injured with no voice-over—just Dakota singing "Solid Gone." The final image was a shot of a woman with beautiful hair crying uncontrollably, blood smeared across her face from cuts under her eye and on her cheek. "Coming tonight was my dream," she said, "my *dream*, and it's nothing but a horrible horrible nightmare!" The last notes of "Solid Gone" faded out.

A Barbie anchorgirl—I'm not being snippy here, she wasn't old enough to be an anchorwoman, *barely* looked old enough to drive—smiled (smiled?) at us and said the police were on the trail (*on the trail?*) of the culprit (*culprit?*) and to stay tuned for more news, sports and weather. Someone punched the remote.

"What the hell is going on?" Rolli. The drummer.

That was the question, all right.

We were all jammed into the suite. The guys had come back with a case of beer. I looked again—okay, two cases. Then we ordered half a dozen pizzas. Room service said they would be happy to send up a bottle of Chardonnay but sounded a little puzzled at my request for two wineglasses and twenty napkins.

"Dakota, is this tied in with her?" Rolli pointed a Miller Lite at me. Then: "Sorry. With Kat and you being as jumpy as a goddamn water bug all the time now, with the extra security and god*damn*, who knows what goddamn else?"

"I don't know." Dakota spoke quietly. She held her wineglass as though it were a mug of coffee that could warm her. "I should have spoken to you before but I hoped I could make it blow over, be nothing. Obviously, that's out of the question now." She looked at her wine, took a sip, put the glass down.

"Somebody's been writing me letters. Anonymous letters. Somehow they get on the bus or someone, not one of us, is asked to be sure to get it to me. They're not physically threatening—just, just kind of awful. Kat's here to help. Ted knew. I had no idea anything like this could happen. I don't even know if it's connected. I . . . I'm sorry if I didn't handle it well. I don't know what will happen now. We're working with the police, of course. I hope . . . I don't know, guys." She sounded lost.

"Hey, Dakota, no problem, girl. We're behind you all the way."

A chorus: "Yeah." "Damn right." "No shit."

"Thanks, all of you. Y'all take the bus back home tonight. I'll come home tomorrow. Or as soon as the police . . . as soon as I can," she corrected. She took a deep breath. "We lost a lot, equipment, instruments—" A lot more that no one wanted to talk about yet. "I hope the insurance will cover it all, but you have my promise that no one's going to be out of pocket on this. What the insurance doesn't cover, I will.''

''You're the best, Dakota.'' Rolli again.

No one asked what we were all thinking: What next? Would the scheduled concerts go on as planned? Could we pick up the pieces and walk away from this concert to the next one and the one after? Would people come? Would there be more terrorist actions?

The guys left. With the pizza. With the beer. Ted wanted to stay but Dakota wouldn't let him, begged off until tomorrow. The suite seemed suddenly very big and very quiet, very empty. Dakota picked a bunch of grapes out of the fruit bowl, pulled one off, looked at it, ate it, put the rest of the fruit back.

''I'm ordering another bottle of wine, Katy.''

I nodded. Good idea.

THE COPS WOKE US UP EARLY. THEY HAD QUESTIONS, NOT news. Big deal. We had the same thing. After we pooled our information, here's what we had:

• An unknown assailant threw a flash grenade for an unknown reason.
• Dakota was the presumed target, but the band—or something (someone?) else—couldn't be ruled out.
• No descriptions, no leads, no nothing.
• Julie's family thought I was the best thing ever.

It was a relief to leave Memphis.

six

BUG UNDER A MICROSCOPE

"KAT, LOOK AT THIS." THERE WAS A NOTE OF WONDER, or nostalgia—something I couldn't quite pin down—in Dakota's voice. She sat at the pine table in the kitchen nook, the midmorning early-spring Nashville sun climbing over the trees and splashing through the leaves and window and onto us, the dappled patterns of the leaves dancing merrily around the room.

I looked at Dakota, not the photographs. Her hair was pushed back behind her ears, her face scrubbed and clean and without makeup. An oversize T-shirt was tucked into her blue jeans. No star quality, no glitz and glitter. No insanity, no bombs. We were supposed to be talking about that.

"Are you listening, Katy?" She looked up and smiled at me, her eyes a startling, dazzling shade of blue.

"What?" I answered back. I was not listening. I was thinking. I was trying to get the background clear. The background which, right now, was letters and bombs.

"This picture. Look."

Two little girls smiled out at us. They were nine or ten with trusting eyes and lopsided ponytails. One had blond ponytails and blue eyes, the other brown ponytails and green eyes. A large scruffy panting dog sat between them.

"It seems like a long time ago, doesn't it?"

I nodded.

The ponytails are gone now. Dakota's hair, long and straight and silky, tumbles down her back. Mine, brown and curly, is just to my shoulders. We are the same age, thirty-three. For different reasons, our eyes are no longer trusting.

"The letters, Dakota," I reminded her gently, refusing to be distracted for long. Ignoring letters was one thing; ignoring bombs was another.

"Look at this one." Dakota laughed at the photograph of the child holding a large metal kitchen spoon and singing into it as though it were a mike, mugging for the camera. "Remember how I pretended to be a singer? What did you want to be, Kat? Back then, I mean. Funny." She frowned slightly. "Why can't I remember?"

"I didn't want to be anything, I wanted to escape. You would make up stories about being a singer, a star, and I would make up stories about living in a place where people were nice and laughed and smiled and didn't say mean things." *Everything my early childhood wasn't.*

The leaves danced in the sun around us. Outside I heard the screech of wheels and then tires squealing. Everyday sounds, reassuring sounds.

"We did it, Katy. We rewrote our lives."

We stared at each other, not smiling because we remembered how hard it was and how we almost didn't make it.

"You're still doing the same thing, you know. Only now it's for other people."

Hmmmm? I wrinkled my nose. There is no one in the world who has known me as long and well as Dakota, but I didn't understand. "What do you mean?"

"When you became a private investigator you said you'd be doing background checks for corporations, fraud investigations, that kind of thing. When's the last time that cases like that were most of your caseload?"

I shook my head. I couldn't remember.

"When they went after the whistle-blower, you helped her. And the guy everyone believed had killed his wife even though the police had nothing on him? You helped him. And Lindy.''

Lindy, yes. Lindy had been a street-smart but very frightened fourteen-year-old hooker when I pulled her off the stroll. My grandmother, Alma, adopted her, as she had me years before. Lindy graduated from high school this year with honors and is now trying to decide whether to be a forest ranger, a vet or a novelist.

''You help people rewrite their lives, Katy. And you help people escape bad things. That's what you really do. Investigator is just kind of a convenient label.''

I was silent, trying to work my way through what Dakota said. ''I don't think of it like that.''

''No.'' Dakota shrugged. ''We live our lives without looking at the pattern that's there, without recognizing it. I see it because I know you so well, that's all. Maybe we can't figure it out for ourselves, see the pattern on our own. That's why I need you now.''

''To figure it out?''

She nodded. ''And to help me fix it. Obviously something's gone really wrong. And I can't even begin to fix it until I know what it is. I sure don't want it messing up my life right now. I'm scared, Katy. Not just because of the letters, though they're bad enough, but because—'' She looked at me helplessly.

''Because of the hate,'' I finished.

She shivered. ''Do you think the flash grenade was meant for me?''

''I think we have to assume that.''

Outside a dog barked nearby. I heard footsteps on the porch. Dakota jumped slightly.

''The mail.'' She sighed. ''I used to look forward to it and now I dread it. Sometimes I let it sit around all day before I can make myself look at it.''

I walked through the house to the front door. It was a small house in Hillwood that Dakota had recently bought, still sparsely furnished and without a lot of personal touches. Except for the handmade quilts. There was one on the couch, on Dakota's bed, on the spare bed where I was sleeping. All from her grandmother.

There was a bundle of mail. I flipped through it. "Do you subscribe to *Seventeen, Road and Track, Prison Life, Playboy* and *Retirement Living*?" I asked, knowing the answer.

"Aw shoot," Dakota said wearily.

I put the mail on the table. She started to pick it up, then swept the pile onto the floor in disgust. A letter slid out. Typed name. Cheap envelope. No return address. No stamp. It had been hand-delivered. I hadn't seen it. Did it slip out of a magazine? I reached for it.

"*No!*" Dakota's hand hovered on my arm. "Let's just burn it, let's burn them all and forget them. Let's—" Dakota sucked in her breath on a note of panic.

"It won't work," I said gently.

"No." Her voice was defeated now.

I opened the envelope, removed a sheet of folded paper. There was nothing on it. Or in it.

"Oh God," Dakota said, and put her head in her hands.

"The other letters. May I see them?"

Dakota left the room, returned with a pack of letters banded together. She held them away from her body—as if to keep filth at arm's length.

Some of the envelopes were blank. Some had her name, Dakota, printed in block letters. None had arrived in the mail. Dates and places were penciled in on the back of the envelope.

"Is this your writing?" I asked, referring to the penciled notations.

"Yes."

I sorted through the letters. There were five of them, six now, and all were written in block letters, just as they were addressed.

"These didn't come to the house." I was looking at the place names.

"No. Today's was the first one. The others I got on the road, usually just before a performance. Somebody hand-delivered them to me or to one of the guys. Or they just showed up on the bus.'' She shivered. ''It's spooky, Kat. It's as though someone's trying to make me jumpy.''

I nodded, skimmed the letters, then went back and reread them slowly. They were short, a line or two at most.

YOU'RE FULL OF BALONEY.

YOU CAN'T BUILD ON LIES. AND STEALING. YOU WON'T GET AWAY WITH IT. YOU'LL SEE.

ASK YOUR GRANDMOTHER ABOUT THE QUILT. ABOUT THE DEBT.

YOU'RE NOT THROUGH WITH LEFTOVERS. NO WAY. AND LEFTOVERS GET ROTTEN.

YOU'RE JUST ANOTHER PRETTY FACE. PRETTY DOESN'T LAST.

They weren't overtly threatening. Just menacing. Unnerving. *Just?* Impossible to dismiss. I glanced at Dakota. She was neither dismissing them nor taking them lightly. It was telling on her.

''The blank one is the worst, Kat.''

''No it's not. The writer is counting on you to fill in something horrible, to imagine what he or she doesn't know but would be frightening to you. It's reasonable to be annoyed by the letters, but don't help the writer scare you. Don't scare yourself.''

She looked at me mutely, then nodded.

I stacked the letters. ''What do they mean?''

Dakota looked at the top one, the baloney letter. ''I guess that's in reference to my sandwiches but it also sounds like a variation of 'You're full of shit.' ''

It did, yes.

''And the next one, about lies and stealing. I don't get it, Kat. Really I don't.''

No. Dakota was the kind of kid who turned in lunch money she found on the playground. She wouldn't lie; she

wouldn't tell on someone. I'd seen her take another kid's
licking more than once because of that. And nothing had
changed over the years I'd known her. I'd bet my life on
it.

"The next one? The quilt?"

She frowned. "You remember Granny Mae"—it wasn't
a question. I did, of course—"and how old-fashioned, in a
funny sweet way, she could be. Like her hope chest. In the
attic, remember?"

*Whenever I hear Dakota's song "String of Yesterdays"
I think of things like this—not just about a lost love and
living in yesterday but about how everything is built on that
string of yesterdays. I remember how Granny Mae would
let us play in the attic, the sun filtering in through dirt- and
rain-streaked windows and dancing off the dust motes we
sent flying in our abandon.*

*There was a trunk with old clothes that we were allowed
to try on, dresses of shimmering silky fabrics, accessories
with feathers and sequins. A birdcage whose occupant had
long flown sat with its door open, occupied then by a di-
minutive teddy bear and a lop-eared rabbit. We dressed up,
acted out stories and danced with an old sewing form, pins
stuck in its ample waist still.*

*Often we heard the skittering of mice and once we found
a dried-out bat. We made stories of everything, Dakota's
imagination running wild and free like the mustangs I was
to see many years later in South Dakota. We got her stage
name from the horses I'd seen and, that time, the stories I
told. The rest of the time Dakota's part was the imagination
and the stories, mine was the happy endings. Then and now
I could not bear stories with unhappy endings.*

"I remember the day I was home sick. It was raining, I
remember that too, and you were in school, Katy. I was so
bored I dug deep into the corners and found the chest. Inside the chest was a coat of black velvet, creased where it
had been folded for so long, and a quilt. They were
wrapped up carefully in heavy linen sheets with crocheted
edges that looked like long-ago wedding gifts saved for a
special tomorrow that never came.

"I knew that the things were beautiful but not the words to describe them. Later I learned that it was velvet and linen, satin and silk. Later I learned the term 'crazy quilt.' Do you know it, Kat?"

I shook my head.

"Bits of fabric, often velvet and silk, of any odd size and shape stitched together, sometimes with fancy and intricate top stitching. Quilt patterns are called by names, Wedding Ring, Log Cabin, Drunkard's Path, Wild-Goose Chase. But a crazy quilt has no pattern. Each is unique in colors and piecing and stitching."

"The pillow Alma has—?"

"Yes," Dakota said, "like that. I put on the coat, holding it up so the hem wouldn't drag in the dust, and wrapped the quilt around me like a cape. Then I went to show Granny Mae.

"Katy, I don't remember ever seeing her so upset. She took the things from me and sat me down. Then she told me the story of Pandora's box—a kind of garbled version, I think—and of how some things had evil in them and must be locked up. She kissed me and said she would not let the evil come to me and I must not go to it. I didn't understand.

"Later I saw the chest in her room at the foot of her bed. It was hand-hewn cedar with metal fittings. In the old hasp hung a brand new padlock. Since that day I have never seen the chest opened, nor has Granny Mae ever referred to it. I asked about the coat and quilt just once."

Dakota looked at me. I had no sense of what was coming.

"She didn't get angry or reprimand me, just said matter-of-factly that it must not be spoken of and that we must try to keep some things safely locked up, to keep the evil away. There were tears in her eyes as she spoke, love in her voice. I never had the courage to bring it up again. Nobody in the family knows anything about it. Nobody. I asked. So how could someone else know? It seems impossible. If that's the quilt they're talking about. I don't know anything about a debt, do you?"

I didn't answer. The possibilities that occurred to me were not ones that I wanted to share. I turned back to the letters. "The one about leftovers seems an obvious reference to 'Leftover Love.' "

"And the rotten part?"

I shrugged. Another thing I didn't want to get into yet.

"The 'just another pretty face'?" She didn't say what we were both thinking. The rest of it: "Pretty doesn't last."

I didn't say it either. "Who knows about the baloney sandwiches?"

Dakota shook her head. "It's no big secret but probably only the band, Ted, the roadies, close friends. You know."

"Have you mentioned it in an interview?"

She frowned. "No, I'm sure not. It's something I like to remember but not talk about. God, this makes me feel, I don't know, dirtied. Or like a bug under a microscope. The bug doesn't know, doesn't have a clue that someone's watching, planning . . . Ugh." She shook herself.

"Dakota, do you have *any* idea who's sending these letters?"

"No."

"Forget idea, then. How about wild guess, shot in the dark?"

"No. Nothing. That's what's so scary. Katy, I don't think of myself as someone with enemies, but I guess that's wrong."

Enemy? That might not be the word. I thought about other words that would qualify.

"Want to go for a run, Katy?"

"What are my other choices?"

She laughed. "C'mon, it'll be good for us. It'll blow the cobwebs out."

The cobwebs and the fear.

I didn't like it that the last letter had come to Dakota's house. He, or she, knew where Dakota was. And knew her schedule, her world.

Like looking at a bug under a microscope.

seven

DREAMS IN HER EYES

I WANT TO TALK ABOUT CAL."

Dakota twirled spaghetti around her fork. The kitchen was redolent with the smell of spaghetti sauce, hot spicy sausages, meatballs and garlic. Our plates were piled with that, with green salad and garlic bread.

"Remember the spaghetti we had in college, Kat?"

It was an old joke. When we were always-broke students at Sacramento City College we used to dump ketchup on spaghetti and call it a meal. Or eat the stale pizza and greasy chicken wings that passed as happy hour hors d'oeuvres at the restaurant where I worked as a bartender.

Dakota speared a huge meatball and held it on her fork as though it were a microphone. " 'Hey, good-lookin', whatcha got cookin' . . .' "

"Dakota."

She nibbled a piece of her meatball mike. "Katy, you know how I hate even thinking about him. Talking— yuck." She ate the rest of her meatball and sampled her bread. "Do you think we used enough garlic?"

"Gilroy would be proud."

She giggled. Gilroy is a town in California that is reputed to be the garlic capital of the world. People who don't know California as we do think of our state as LA and SF, as big city, not small towns and ranches. They don't know about the garlic in Gilroy, the artichokes in Castroville, the cray-fish in Isleton. They don't know our California, the Golden State where dreams are born and die hard, the state Dakota had left for Nashville.

It makes me angry when people think of California in stupid generalizations but I realize I do the same thing with Nashville. I don't think of it as the Athens of the South, a Bible-publishing center, or an insurance hub, and it is all of those things. To me, Nashville is country music. A little knowledge is a dangerous thing.

Dakota clicked her knife absently against her plate.

"Cal?" I asked again.

She sighed.

"Tell me the story as if I didn't know anything, as if I were a total stranger and you didn't want to leave anything out."

She sighed. More heavily this time. "Why, Kat? It's over. A done deal. History. Leftovers. A song written and best forgotten."

"And he would never try to hurt you in any way, or threaten you, or scare you, or get back at you, or—"

"Katy," Dakota said helplessly, *"please."* Her voice ac-knowledged the truth of what I said, surrendered.

We finished our dinner first, licked our fingers after the last piece of garlicky, buttery bread. With the table cleared, the coffee made, there was nothing left. Just Cal.

"You remember the song he did, 'Honky Tonk Hero'?"

It was a rhetorical question. Everybody remembered.

"That's what he was to me, a honky tonk hero. I put him on a pedestal. I saw a man he wasn't and would never be, never even pretended to be. At least not after he got the patsy, the sucker, the girl. Katy, I was all three." Her voice was bitter, condemning. Not of him, I thought—she accepted what he was—but of herself.

"You were young, Dakota, with stars in your eyes. It's difficult to see clearly then, for any of us."

"There are a million girls who dream of Hollywood or Nashville." Her voice was faraway and dreamy. "Girls in Flatbush, Kansas City, Austin and Fayetteville. In Sacramento, in Bumfork, Anywhere. Most of these dreams die, most of these girls give up. But some actually come here, try to make their dreams come true. Sooner or later almost all go home, whipped, busted, broken, disillusioned, the dreams in their eyes betrayed or dead.''

That was another of Dakota's songs, ''Dreams in Your Eyes.''

''When they come here, they don't know how hard it is, how many fail. I was one of them and I didn't know either. I didn't have a clue. Katy, I didn't know anything. It was luck and timing and I don't know what.''

I remembered. The day she left marked the worst fight we'd ever had. I thought she was leaving something for nothing. I stopped, my mind in instant replay—Dakota hurling things into her beat-up-running-on-a-prayer Toyota. Everything was chucked in haphazardly, even her guitar and the notebooks with her songs.

''You were so mad at me for quitting school.''

''I was wrong, Dakota. You can't put fear in front of a dream and that's what I did. I'm glad you didn't listen.''

''I didn't listen to anyone, Katy, not then. Not you, not Granny Mae. God, I made it to Nashville on a wing and a prayer and not much else. Flat broke. Busted.'' She laughed.

''With dreams in your eyes.''

''Yeah. They stayed for a long time, too, before the clouds moved in. Things happened so fast my head was spinning. I never did have a chance to think it through. When it looks like your dream is coming true, you don't ask questions, do you?''

''No. Not at twenty-four.''

''I got a job in a mini-mart and I made the rounds. I had a letter from a musician/songwriter in Reno whose sister was a good friend of mine—we were in a band together once. It was an introduction to a guy at MCA. I thought it was a big deal but it turned out he was nothing and nobody. Anyway, there I was asking for him and some guy blows in having a fit because the singer he'd hired to do demos hadn't shown. I took a deep breath and said I could do it.''

Dakota has guts, I thought. It wasn't the first time it had occurred to me.

" 'Sing,' he said to me."

"There? In the office?"

"Yes."

"And?"

"And I did. And he hired me. And I thought I left all the bad times behind me."

In her eyes, then, there were only memories, no dreams. Memories that I shared of the times we left behind.

WE PARKED IN THE BACK AT THE EDGE OF THE CRACKED asphalt lot. I thought Cody would throw up in the bushes, though she'd done that twice already on the way over—she was that scared. It was light still, summer, and the late dusk and heat played with us. The building was long, low, squatting somewhere on the edge of Rio Linda in Sacramento County. Crummy bars always look better at night, when the dark hides the ugliness and dirt and the neon in the windows tarts them up. Now, in the dusk, the bar looked like just what it was. A dive with no hope, no pretension, no promise.

I followed Cody inside, hung back a little as she walked over to the slightly elevated stage where the band was setting up.

"Hey," she said. "I'm Cody Jones. I'm trying out tonight."

"Yeah?" One of the guys turned. "Well, hey yourself, Cody Jones. I'm Hawk, the bass player." He leaned over, plugged in his amp, fiddled with dials and switches, hit a chord. It sounded lousy to me. He grimaced. Sounded lousy to him, too, I guess.

"You're expecting me, right?"

Hawk shrugged. "Dunno. We've been looking for a girl singer for a while. Lenny's always telling some chick to come over." He hit another chord. That one sounded a lot better. "Lenny talk to you?"

Cody nodded.

"Most of the chicks he finds can't sing worth a good goddamn. You sing?"

Cody nodded again.

Hawk peered at her. "Don't talk much, do you?"

"I sing better." Cody croaked it out.

"Hope so"—Hawk grinned—"'cause you can't talk worth a damn. Lenny tell you what we're doing now?"

Cody shook her head. "He told me to get two songs ready."

"Yeah, okay. Get a drink, kick back, we'll call you." He turned his back on her.

She stood there staring for a moment, then walked over to me. We got Cokes from the bar and sat at a table on the edge of the crowd. Cody's eyes were haunted and scared. She gripped her Coke—white-knuckled—and watched the ice melt.

I watched the place fill up. Couples who sat at tables— old married folks who had been drinking and dancing together for twenty-five years, young courting couples who leaned into each other's words and hearts. Single guys leaned on the bar and looked cool, looked at the women who came in pairs. The women, girls really, sat at tables mostly but moved around a lot, visiting people, going to the ladies' room, fluffing their hair, strutting their stuff.

It got louder and warmer and smokier. The jukebox played nonstop.

The last guy in the band to arrive was Lenny. Cody stiffened when he came in, nudged me. It only took me half a look to recognize it, it was that easy: macho guitar player with asshole attitude. Hawk spoke to him, pointed. Lenny turned around, stared at us, turned back to Hawk and shrugged. A minute later he went to the bar. Cody was almost in tears.

"Maybe we should leave, Katy?"

"Not yet. Stick it out a little longer." I squeezed her hand quickly. She had, I knew, already made up some horrible story in her mind. A story that was nothing like the dream she had come in with.

"I hear you gonna sing for us tonight." Lenny lounged

at Cody's elbow, crowding her. He wore cowboy boots, a pair of jeans that had been clean three weeks ago and a black tank top. His arms and chest were tan and muscled and he leered at Cody. I despised him immediately.

"That right?"

"Yes," Cody said bravely.

"Well, what's your name again, darlin'?"

"Cody. Cody Jones."

He nodded. "Second or third set." And walked—no, swaggered—away. I despised him some more.

Cody's face was white and pinched. "Katy, he didn't even remember."

"It doesn't matter. You got what you wanted. You get to sing. He doesn't matter."

She would have left, I knew, if I had let her. But I didn't. I didn't like the gig, the bar or Lenny but if Cody left I didn't think she'd ever come back. Dreams are fragile and easily broken.

I was glad when the lights dimmed, when they no longer picked out Cody's white face and big scared eyes. The bar was too warm now, way too smoky and loud. I could smell sweat and perfume and feel the lust and expectation crackling in the air like electricity before a storm.

The music sounded good to me, hot up-tempo tunes mixed in with slower ballads that pulled all the couples out on the floor.

"Are they any good?" I asked Cody.

"The band? Yeah. Good, not great."

Hawk took the mike at the end of the second set. "We're going to take a short break and when we get back we've got a surprise for you. Cody Jones, a great little gal with a big voice, is going to do a couple of songs."

Guys starting stomping and whistling. First liquor talks, then it hollers, then it fucks up. We were getting closer to fuckup now.

I have forgotten how we got through the endless minutes and hours that evening. Cody stared at her ice a lot and made herself respond when I said something. When that got too hard, I gave up. Guys asked us to dance at first, then they gave up too. It was her eyes, frightened eyes with a big stake in something they couldn't understand and didn't want to hear about.

"You ready?" Hawk was at our table. Break was over. She nodded.

"Let's go." He winked at her. "You'll be fine." He put his hand on her elbow ready to steady her and they walked to the bandstand. Cody swayed a little as though she'd been drinking something besides Cokes. They got to the stage and Hawk planted her in front of the mike. She clung to it like it was her last chance, last hope. The band hit the opening notes and something almost imperceptibly shifted in her.

Cody sang "Crazy Blue Eyes," her voice climbing, soaring over the band, then falling into the low notes with a catch in her voice and a sob deep in her throat.

She wasn't fine, she was fantastic.

When she finished, there was a stunned silence and then the place exploded. Cody stood there in the spotlight like a deer caught in the headlights. Finally, grinning, Hawk nudged her and she managed to smile back at the audience and teeter slightly at her mike.

She sang half a dozen songs that night. The crowd went wild. The cowboys were beside themselves. They let her go, but reluctantly. We sat out the last set, Cody turning down dances, drinks, drugs, phone numbers and other offers. I was happy for her and afraid both.

It was one-thirty before the band stopped playing, before Lenny called out to Cody, beckoned her over. By then she was practically in a trance state. I went too.

"Well, Cody Jones, you did real good." He nodded. "Real good. I reckon we could use a cute little gal like you." He smiled at her and reached out to fiddle with the top button on her blouse, his hand brushing across her breast. "No reason you can't show your stuff as well as sing it." He gave her a long slow wink.

Cody didn't move, didn't budge. His hand rested lightly on her breast. She didn't exactly speak, kind of hissed and spat like a sexy, well-dressed snake. "Take your hand off *me. I'm a singer, nothing more. You don't like it, you can lump it. I can get another job."*

Lenny snatched his hand away, like he'd hit a hot stove. Hawk started laughing. "Well, Lenny, looks like you're going to have to mind your manners for a change. How's that for different?" Lenny stalked off, everything about him screaming angry male.

"Do I still have the job?" Cody's voice was soft, hesitant.

"You've got the job—he'll get over it. You've got the right idea, too. There's plenty in this business will use you and walk on you you give them a chance. Especially a girl. Don't ever let 'em. Friday and Saturday nights. Thirty-five sound okay to you?"

"Yes."

It was way too low. We didn't know that then. Cody didn't know a lot then and neither did I.

SHE KNEW IT BY THE TIME SHE LEFT SACRAMENTO FOR Nashville. And she knew what she wanted to leave behind. I looked at her across the table. She had left it, no question.

It was memory now.

Except for the letters.

And maybe the grenade.

eight

EVERY WHICH WAY BUT RIGHT

I DON'T EVEN HAVE PICTURES OF HIM ANYMORE.''

"Cal?"

"Cal," she agreed.

"Not even wedding pictures?"

"Yes and no." Her grin was impish. "I have the wedding pictures but I cut him out of them. Every single one of them."

I didn't laugh. It reminded me just how bad it had gotten. "But it didn't start out that way." I remind myself of that, too.

"Oh no, it didn't start out that way. It didn't even start out with Cal. My first break was filling in for the demo singer who didn't show that day for her recording session. It was my first demo tape."

I lifted an eyebrow in silent question.

"Demo tapes are made so producers and performers can hear a song. You need to know what it sounds like, not just how it looks on paper. The tapes are pretty much slammed together. You go to the studio, listen to the tape from the songwriter, rehearse for a few minutes and record. If you don't get it right the first time, you don't work much. The songwriter or the publisher is the one paying the demo singer and musicians and they're not paying to listen to your mistakes. Basically you're nothing and there are a

whole lot of other talented singers who would give anything
to be in your place, who would cut you out if they could.''

Dakota said that quietly and without expression. I wondered how difficult it had been for her—a small-town kind
of kid, loyal and honest as an Eagle Scout—wanting to get
to the top but not cutthroat competitive. And I wondered
how much Dakota had changed over the last few years, a
time when we had seen very little of each other.

''They liked it?''

''They loved it. It took me a couple of tries the first time
but I was new at it. Word got around. Pretty soon I was
getting calls and working two or three times a week, up to
three sessions a day cutting demos. The manager at the
mini-mart where I was working got pretty mad.'' Dakota
smiled wryly. ''I was calling in sick, late, out of town, or
working all the time. They put me on notice. I quit just
before I got fired. It was tough for a while—ketchup spaghetti again.

''It helped that I could do my own harmonies; that way
I was two singers for the price of one. Even so I was afraid
I wasn't going to make it. I was about down to my last
bounced check. Remember how we'd talk about getting so
broke we'd have to live in our cars? I wasn't joking about
that anymore.''

''When did you write 'Solid Gone'?''

''Right about then.'' And she grinned. ''And Doug Stone
almost did it. It's the kind of down-and-out song he does
really well. He didn't pick it up but things turned. I started
getting called a lot more for demos. And occasionally I got
called when someone was looking for a harmony singer.
One-shot deals, but worth it. I cut my own demos and sent
them out. I did everything I could to be seen and get noticed.

''Katy, when it comes right down to it, there are only
two ways you get signed to a record deal. You produce a
demo tape, send it to an A and R—artists and repertoire—
executive at a record company and hope to God it somehow
stands out from the two hundred already on his desk and
the two dozen he got that day. Or you do a showcase—

rent a club, invite people who count, hope to God they
come, hope to God they love you, hope to God they sign
you. It's a lot of hoping.''

''Did they?''

''I couldn't afford to do a showcase and Cal found me
before an A and R exec did.'' She stood and walked to the
windows, hands clenched at her side. ''At the time I
thought it was a lucky break.'' She idly traced patterns in
the dust on the windowsill.

''Then it was just a break, then it was unlucky. And then
. . . then it was a disaster.''

''I wish I'd known back then, Cody.'' I slipped into yesterday.

''Do you know how many times I picked up the phone
to call you?'' She shrugged. ''I don't. I lost count. Most of
the time it was in the middle of the night, after the gig,
after Cal's drinking, after he had passed out.''

''Was he hitting you then?'' I'd known for a while but
she'd never said the words, never let me help. Her eyes,
fierce and protective, met mine but she didn't answer.

''I wish you'd called,'' I said, at a loss for something to
say.

''I wish I had too,'' she said wearily. ''Maybe it would
have been over sooner. Maybe the damage would have
been less.''

''What was the damage, Dakota?''

She sat down again. ''He stole, he cheated me, he
cheated on me, he used me every which way but right. Ask
me what he didn't do. That's the short list.''

''Did he love you then?''

She shrugged. ''Did he ever love me? I thought so.
Maybe even he thought so. Now I honestly think that he
doesn't know the difference between loving and using.
Probably he figured it was a fair trade, him giving me a
start, me . . .'' Her voice trailed off, lost, bitter.

''I should have been smarter, Katy. I was so hungry to
make it, to have someone hear my songs, hear me and think
I was something. It ate away at me. I guess it ate away a
bunch of my good sense.''

"What did you give him?"

She held out her hands helplessly. "Not just what did I give but what did he take. Everything. My love, my trust, my songs, my talent. What *didn't* he take? But that was later—at first everything seemed fine. He made it sound so good. I didn't know then that he wouldn't keep his promises to me."

"Promises?"

"He said that he'd feature me, that he could get me a recording deal. For a while there—after 'Honky Tonk Hero'—the world was his. He promised to make it mine and I believed him. I let him take charge of my life, my career. It was one of my biggest mistakes."

"Dakota, we have to trust and believe in the people we love." I said it gently.

"I should have paid more attention, Katy."

"Did he feature you?"

"Sort of. I sang with him but it was almost always harmony. Backup, Katy, not headline. When we toured I opened for him in a thirty-minute set. When he couldn't get someone else. *He* took 'Solid Gone' to the top, not me, and it was my song."

Sorrow and fury were mixed in her voice. And something else I couldn't quite pinpoint but didn't like.

"On his next album we did 'Solid Gone' as a duet but only because I made such a big deal out of it. He would still give in to me then. Sometimes."

I wondered if to be a songwriter, you had to live what you wrote. I hoped not.

"A lot happened because of that duet. I just never knew it." Her voice was soft and dangerous. "By then Cal was acting as my manager and there was a lot I never knew. Turns out there was a bunch of excitement. Two recording offers came in. The buzz was that I was hot, really hot, and going places. Cal turned both offers down. I wasn't going anyplace. Not without him. I figured it out later."

"Were they good offers?"

"MCA and Arista? Yeah, they were good. No, they were great."

"Why didn't—"

"Katy, I didn't find out until it was too late. Even then I tried. They'd signed someone else. When things happen, they happen, and you have to jump on it. You know how that works."

Yes. I know.

"That was our first big fight."

"You stayed."

"Yeah. I guess I couldn't believe it. Not then. He said he turned them down because they weren't right for me, because he was waiting for something better. I can believe he said it, I just can't believe I bought it." She sighed.

I could though. I had known them when they were in love. He had loved her—I had seen it, though it was his way, not hers. Always it was his way, even in the beginning.

I WAS AT THE AIRPORT IN SACRAMENTO TO PICK THEM UP— first trip home after the wedding. Dakota ran to me, dragging Cal behind her. "Kat, I want you to meet Cal, my husband." She stammered the word out in tongue-tied pride.

He wasn't tongue-tied. He was smooth and slick—an operator, but very attractive—and he held my hand maybe a little too long. Because of Cody I smiled. And because he was so charming.

He was still good-looking then, tall with dark hair combed back and just graying at the temples. His face was deeply lined, the first signs of the ravages of drugs, alcohol, loose living and loose women—we just didn't know what it was then.

He wore cowboy boots, tight jeans and a shirt that looked custom-tailored. He had big shoulders, a tight ass and legs two miles long. The women figured they were missing something when he walked by. He figured they were too. We didn't figure out that part of it until later either.

They were only in town two days and Cody had a long list of things to do, people to see, places to go. They had dinner the first night at Granny Mae's and she listened to

Cal without speaking, with eyes like shiny black pebbles in a white and serious face.

Afterwards Dakota, Cal and I went dancing.

The band was Gold Rush; Cody had played with them once. I think she wanted them to know that she had made something of herself, that she was singing in Nashville and married to Cal Jenkins, America's honky tonk hero.

He played the part, played it well.

The bar should have had swinging doors, like the movie doors in old Westerns, I thought. The buzz started the moment we walked in.

"Hey, doesn't he look like Cal Jenkins?"

And Cody was mobbed.

"How you doing?"

"You made it yet, girl?"

"You a star?"

Cody laughed. "I'd like you all to meet my husband, Cal Jenkins."

There was a collective gasp, as if they'd rehearsed it. Cal smiled in acknowledgment and casually saluted the crowd. It went on like that for three hours. We couldn't buy a drink all night.

They begged him to sing and he said no, thanks, that he'd come to hear the band, not— They ignored that, drowned him out, cheered him on. And so he agreed. Everyone went crazy, especially the band—now they could go to their graves saying they'd played with Cal Jenkins.

Cal picked up the proffered guitar and the place fell silent. "I'd like to dedicate this song to my wife, Dakota Jones, who talked the hero into me and the honky tonk out." There was love in his eyes that night, I swear it. I saw it and I believed it. He's a con man but not that good. The crowd cheered. Cody looked like she'd died and gone to heaven.

It wasn't heaven.

Eighteen months later I got a call. Middle of the night. Those are always the bad ones.

"Katy, please come as soon as you can. Please!"

Cody was crying.

nine
HONKY TONK HERO

I'D NEVER FLOWN INTO MEMPHIS. I PICKED UP THE RENTAL car and thumbed through the maps I'd brought and the directions Cody had given me before starting out. Nine-thirty p.m. I was on a job. On the road.

A pickup hit the horn and ran a red light through the intersection I was entering, just missing me. Beer bottles flew out the windows. One of them landed in the bed of the truck; the rest hit the road, exploding on impact. Local color and excitement. Memphis.

I could see the Wagon Wheel quite a ways off, the neon, the signs. "It's a dance club outside of town," Dakota had said. "Cal used to play there a lot when he was just getting started. They think he's the best thing since bottled beer."

I pulled into the dirt-and-gravel parking lot where at least a hundred and fifty trucks and cars were parked, most of them pretty beat up, a hundred thousand miles on the odometer easy, and found a space under a light. The new rental stuck out badly, a debutante at a beer hall but I was grateful for the light and the added security.

I shook my hair back, bunched it in a loose knot on the top of my head and pulled on a baseball cap. I was wearing worn jeans, scuffed boots and a lightweight jacket, and I wouldn't stand out at all. I got out of the car and slung my bag over my shoulder. There were rolls of quarters in the bottom and it was heavy enough to use as a weapon. Flirting with danger was one thing, courting it unprepared another.

It was a squeeze but by holding my breath and turning sideways I almost managed to scoot past a bunch of rowdy guys and into the Wagon Wheel. Almost. I eyed the hairy lower arm, then the rolled-up T-shirt bulging with a bicep that blocked my way. The smell of deodorant was almost overpowering. I followed the arm up as muscles rippled and tensed. Nice eyes, blond beard stubble and front teeth that overlapped slightly in his smile.

"Cover's three bucks, miss."

I paid up and he gave me the smile again. Better than neon, I swear. I glanced again at the biceps—I'm kind of a sucker for muscle definition—then followed the noise and music in. I stood there on the edge of things for a while letting my eyes adjust to the dimness, making a mental note of the layout and the exits. All this is information that you hope you don't need. Far better to have it and not need it than to need it and not have it. Guess how I know this?

It was a big place with an oval dance floor the size of a basketball court, the band at one end, the bar at the other and rows of tables along each side. It was hot and smoky. The crowd was mixed, maybe half couples of all ages, the rest singles, mostly young. A lot of people had on Saturday night clothes but there were plenty of jeans and T-shirts, plenty of hats and boots. The dancers circled smoothly around the dance floor, the men occasionally twirling their partners, dipping their heads so as not to lose their hats. The crowd was noisy and happy. The music sounded good.

The spotlight bounced off the band but held the lead singer, played with him as he sang how he was so lonesome he could cry, an old Hank Williams tune. On stage a singer is somehow larger than life. You begin to believe the myth then, you feel the power of it pulling on you. I looked at Cal and realized that even then I couldn't separate the myth from the man. Even now. I threaded my way through the tables on the left, found an empty two-top all the way up

*front. I could see the band easily; I wasn't worried about
being seen.*

The minute I sat down the band took a break. This is
some kind of immutable law of nature that I neither understand nor like. It includes waiters who ask you how you
like your meal when your mouth is full, and the fact that
the line you pick at the bank is always the slowest.

Cal stepped off the stage and ambled in my direction. I
rested my chin in my hand and pulled the bill of my cap
down. Another guy in the band was with him.

"Cal, oh-ma-god Cal," a woman's voice called out.

"Hey sweetheart, how ya doin'?" Cal turned and waved
at the middle-aged woman who was moaning his name in
orgasmic tones. The smile fell off his face the second his
eyes left her. He was her idol; to him she was nothing.

"You got some in the van?" Cal asked the guy with him
as he brushed past me, close enough so I could have stuck
a foot out and tripped him. Close enough so it was tempting. I held myself back.

"Hold your horses, I got some," the man replied.

"You want something?" I slanted my eyes away from
the retreating forms of Cal and his buddy and up to a
skinny, fortyish bottled blonde wearing a size 10 knit top
on size 14 breasts. Very dramatic. There was a pencil behind her ear and fatigue in her eyes. I ordered a Dr Pepper
and she nodded, pushed her way back through the crowd.

At the beginning of the next set Cal took the mike, his
voice heavy with emotion. "I'd like to dedicate this song
to a real special little lady here tonight, someone who
talked the hero into me and the honky tonk out." The band
swung into "Honky Tonk Hero," the dance floor filled and
Cal sang and gazed into the eyes of a long-haired brunette
in tight jeans who sat at a table beside the dance floor and
gazed back at him, enraptured, oblivious of the world and
the dancers that swirled around her.

It was the kind of real-life stuff that country songs are
written about. Cheatin' eyes, cheatin' hearts. It's the kind
of thing you love, or hate, but rarely are neutral about. I
tried to be neutral. This was an investigation. I am an in-

vestigator. I looked at Cal looking at the brunette. I wasn't neutral, I loathed him.

Another two sets and two Dr Peppers later the band wrapped it up. The lights on the stage dimmed as the guys in the band turned off amps, packed away instruments and closed up shop for the night. Cal walked across the dance floor and pushed up to the bar.

The long-haired brunette was waiting for him. She leaned forward as Cal pulled up a barstool, her breast against his arm, her hand on his thigh. No need to read between the lines there.

It was simple: a cheating heart, a man thinking with his pants, and a woman willing to buy into it for a night. Oh yeah, she would say to her friends the next day, tossing her hair, I was with Cal Jenkins, you bet I was. It was great. She would say that even if it wasn't, even if he was drunk and drugged and couldn't get anything, even her name right. She would say that even if he popped off like a firecracker. He was something, she would say, caught up in and creating the myth both.

I moved to a table not far from the bar, nursing the dregs of my soda and watching them sort of make out. At last call they stood. She had stars in her eyes and he had a bulge in his pants. It wasn't a match made in heaven.

"Let's go to your place, sweet thing." Had he forgotten her name already? She nodded.

"Hey, Cal." I stepped in front of him.

"Hiya darlin', how ya doin'?" His eyes didn't focus on me but slid past, his attention on smooth slick bodies slipping between the sheets.

I pulled off my cap and shook out my hair.

He focused, his eyes narrowed. "Well, goddamn."

Okay, he had something right, maybe for the first time that evening. Too bad he wasn't pleased about it.

"Hey, sweetheart." Without looking he reached out and took his companion's elbow. "Wait for me outside."

Sweetheart stared at me with eyes like huge smoldering coals. I know that sounds like something out of a romance novel but it was true. Sweetheart stared at me a little

*longer, then tossed her hair and pouted. "Don't be long,"
she admonished Cal coquettishly. I stifled a yawn.*

*Cal waved her off, again without looking. She didn't
count anymore, not in that moment in time.*

*"Well, Kat. How ya doin'?" He rubbed his chin. Hard.
"What are you doin' around here anyway?" Then he
frowned, realizing, I guess, that he might not want to hear
the answer.*

"Hi, Cal. Fine, thanks. How are you?"

*He tipped his hat back and rubbed his forehead this time.
"Doing fine. Look, I'd like to talk with you but I got to
walk that young lady—the uh, uh, daughter of a friend—
to her car."*

*I laughed. I couldn't help it. "I've been watching you
for the last two and a half hours, Cal."*

*He frowned at that one. No, maybe it was closer to a
snarl than a frown. Big surprise. "Dakota sent you, didn't
she?" The pupils in his eyes were large and dark.*

*"No." I shook my head solemnly. "Of all the beer joints
in all the world, I just happened to walk into this one."*

"Huh?"

Oh God, *I thought wearily,* how could Cody have married him?

*"I hate to be fucking spied on," he shouted, spraying
spittle on me, and then stomped off. I leaned against the
wall and watched him go. Righteousness—what a nice
touch, though his timing was poor. Still, it's always worth
a try.*

*On my way out I passed the cute doorman and smiled.
He smiled back and flexed a bicep. I think he did. Maybe
the dim lights and fantasy had gotten to me, too. Outside
two guys were arguing in the parking lot. Another was
throwing up. I saw several couples, the guys leaning back
against their cars, their feet apart, holding their girls
tightly against them. My-place-or-yours time.*

I walked quickly to the rental.

*The night air was cool but once on the road I opened
the car windows for as long as I could stand it. My hair*

and clothing reeked of cigarette smoke. Eau de Ashtray—that was me.

It was five-thirty in the morning when I pulled up to the house in Nashville that Dakota and Cal shared. The curtains were drawn but thin streaks of light leaked out around the living room windows. Dakota was up still, waiting for me.

She answered the door in sweats, her hair disheveled, her eyes sleepy. Behind the sleep I could see the questions. Behind the questions I could see the hope.

"Kat, you look so tired." She took my overnight bag from me, gave me a quick hug. "I'm so glad you're here. Did you—?" She caught herself in midsentence as I half stumbled in fatigue. "Do you want something to eat or drink?"

"Sleep." That was it. Everything else would have to wait. I followed her down the hall to what I assumed was the guest room. The bed was turned down, the light on the night table glowed softly.

"Good night, Katy. We'll have breakfast when you get up."

I barely remember pulling my clothes off or turning out the light. Strains of "Honky Tonk Hero" played in my mind as sleep dragged me down and knocked me out.

ten

HEARTBREAK IN PANTS

WE SAT AT THE BREAKFAST TABLE IN A HOUSE THAT felt more like Cal's than Dakota's. It was expensive and tasteful but heavy and impersonal somehow.

Dakota and I were on our second pot of coffee.

"Now, Katy. Please."

"Do you care a lot still, Dakota?"

She heard the gentleness in my voice and turned away, troubled. I picked up the plates and flatware and stacked them in the sink. I was going to tell her the truth, I just wanted to know if I needed to sugarcoat it.

"I don't know. That sounds funny, doesn't it? Sometimes I think the love is gone, that now I'm just grateful for the help he gave me. Other times he can still hurt me so bad that I think that it must not be all gone."

I searched for a good way to tell bad news, though I know from experience there isn't one.

"Just tell me, Katy."

"There's a good chance he's doing drugs." The trip to the van, the size of his pupils. "He was drinking a lot."

"That's it?" The relief—relief? at drugs and alcohol?— in her voice begged me to say yes, to tell her that her other suspicions were all wrong.

"No."

"A woman." Not a question, a statement.

"Yes. I don't think they had known each other that long. Maybe they only met last night—I couldn't tell." Maybe she was just one of many. I thought that was the most likely.

"Did they—" She looked the rest of the question at me.

"They left together, yes." I took a deep breath. "That's not the worst thing, Dakota."

Does the truth set you free? I operate on that principle, but sometimes I can't believe it. So often it rips you apart. Free but destroyed? Free to put the pieces back together? Dakota had made her face a blank. I couldn't read anything there as she waited for the pain I was about to dish up. No, not me, I thought angrily. Cal.

"He dedicated 'Honky Tonk Hero' to 'the special lady who found the hero in me and took the honky tonk out,' to the woman waiting for him."

Dakota crumpled.

That was his dedication to her.

That was the beginning of the end.

I wanted to stay in Nashville for a while then but Cody said no, she needed to think things out and she needed to do it alone. Before I left, I saw the bruises. Numerous dark marks on her arms as though someone had grabbed her, fingers biting into flesh. It was news to me then. After that I changed my mind. I didn't want to stay, I wanted Cody to come with me.

She refused. We fought over it. We've always argued a lot. Cody is as stubborn and hardheaded as I am. But the stakes were different now—they were high. Too high. In the end she stayed, I left.

The next phone call wasn't really a surprise. I know the calls weren't all in the middle of the night but, in my recollection, it seems that way. I think it's because from then on almost all of them had the midnight urgency. That one wasn't midnight, it was three a.m. and it was a year or so later.

"Katy, did I wake you?"

"Dakota?"

"Did I wake you?"

*"At three in the morning?" I asked sleepily. "No way.
I was playing Parcheesi."*

*She laughed the kind of laughter that has no amusement
in it. It woke me up pretty fast.*

"Are you all right, Dakota?"

"No. Katy, you won't believe what I found out."

*I thought that she was wrong, that most of it wouldn't
even be a big surprise. I climbed back into bed with the
phone, mashing the pillows behind me and pulling the
comforter up under my chin. "Bad?"*

*She laughed that same awful laugh. "Real bad. It's bad
when you have to hire a private detective to find out what's
in your husband's bank accounts. When you have to hire
an accountant to try and figure out how much of that money
should have been yours. When one of the roadies really
isn't a roadie, he's a bodyguard.*

*"I searched, Katy, and hard, but there was a whole lot
of stuff I couldn't even trace. He did everything he could
in cash—clothes, furniture, cars, you name it. He bought a
lot of things for me, too. Remember how then I thought I
was lucky—" Her tone was ugly. "I was a wife whose
husband gave her presents. That was a long time ago, before I found out how much of it should have been my
money. I didn't want a diamond ring or a sequined dress,
not like I wanted credit for my songs and work, and money
of my own."*

*There were tears in her eyes. I couldn't see them, but I
could hear them in her voice.*

*"He always came first. Always. Granny used to say that
he was always talking him him him and he surely wasn't
singing in church. I don't just blame him. I blame myself,
too." She sighed. "In the beginning I thought he hung the
moon. I was blind. I was young and naive.*

*"Katy, I never told you how bad it got, how he would
call—drunker than a skunk—every night I was on the road
away from him and accuse me of sleeping around. Slut slut
slut, he'd yell at me, loud enough so everyone on the bus
could hear. And it wasn't me that was doing the running
around, it was him. He was seeing an old girlfriend. God,*

I was dumb. He gave her a ring he bought with my money.''

I had never heard Dakota so wild and bitter. I pulled the comforter tightly around me, reaching for solace that wasn't there.

''No shit but my life sounded like an Oprah show: 'Women Who Stay with Men Who Treat Them Like Dirt.' It took me too long to wise up. And if you act like a rug everyone will walk on you and that is that.

''And then, when I did wise up, it was hard. He was cheating on me every which way but he didn't want to let go. He had me under contract—no one wants to turn a moneymaker loose—and he fought it all the way. That was a real hurting time. Real ugly. When I finally did it, cut him loose, he said to me, 'You'll never make it without me but if you do, I won't let you enjoy it.' He ran his finger across his throat and grinned.''

I was wrong and Dakota was right: It was much worse than I had imagined. ''Did he threaten you any other time?''

''Oh yes, it's been going on since I filed for divorce. He hit me too.''

I sucked in a breath.

''On the face. I was glad. There were witnesses. That was even better. I got a restraining order.''

I loosened my grip on the phone. It was so tight my fingers were cramping up. Restraining orders are good but still—it's only a piece of paper. It tells us where to look when we find the body, a cop told me once.

''Did it help?'' I asked.

''It got better. I moved and didn't tell anyone where. I got an unlisted phone number and registered my car through my manager. You know.''

''Yes.'' I knew.

''I think maybe his manager told him to put a lid on it. He was starting to lose bookings. He even lost a recording contract. Not just because of what he was doing to me. It was all the drinking, the drugs, the crazy stuff.'' She laughed and this time the laugh was real. ''And all the time things were going downhill for him they were picking up for me."

"Is the divorce final?"

"Pretty soon."

"Did you get—"

"Nothing. He stole it, spent it, snorted it, did anything but give it up to me."

"Bastard."

She ignored me. "No, that's wrong. I shouldn't say I got nothing. I got everything. I got my songs back, my name, my self-respect." Her voice was high and lilting. "I got my freedom."

I smiled. This was the Cody I'd known and grown up with.

"And Katy, I'm writing again. I didn't tell you, I didn't tell anyone, but when it got really bad I quit writing. I don't know if it was because I couldn't, or because things were so bad I didn't want to, or if it was to keep Cal from getting his hands on any more of my songs. You know what's funny, Katy?"

I started to answer but she rushed on.

"He never thought he was stealing. Cal is a very honest person. And generous. Really, he has a lot of good qualities. I think he just kind of rewrote reality the way I would rewrite a song. I think that he figured that whatever I became, he had found me, and that a part of everything I had or did should be his. Of course that's not right but—"

"You are being way too nice." I was furious—Dakota heard it and was silent—and I saw things very differently. Cal had taken credit for everything. Always. "It must have been a struggle for him sometimes," I said when I could control my anger. "On the one hand he wanted you to do well so he could take credit for it and make money on you. On the other hand he couldn't let you do so well that you would leave and go out on your own. He was jealous and possessive."

"I know." Dakota's voice was subdued. "And I never gave him reason, though I had plenty of chances if I'd wanted them." Her voice turned wistful. "Once I really *was tempted. He was a nice guy and Cal was being so awful to me then.''*

"But you didn't.''

"No. I didn't. Never.''

"It wasn't just men. He was jealous of your success. He sabotaged your career more than once—the recording contracts he turned down, for instance. He wanted the big time but he didn't want to be in your shadow and he didn't want you to get bigger than he was.''

"For a long time he wanted what was best for me.''

Her voice was defensive. Defending him, I wondered, or a younger Dakota? I made my voice gentle. "You decide what's best for you, Dakota. Don't ever give anyone that power again.''

"He can't stop me now, Katy.''

"No." I hoped she'd heard what I said.

"What you said—about the fear of being in someone's shadow?" I nodded to the phone. "I'm going to write a song about that. I can almost hear it, it's in the back of my mind now." Her voice was excited.

"Nobody can stop you, Dakota.''

"No," she agreed.

And after that, nobody did.

"YOU DIDN'T ANSWER MY QUESTION." WELL, IMPLIED question.

"About Cal?"

I nodded.

"Do I think he's a threat to me now?" She shook her head. "I think he's a threat to himself. He's drinking more than ever before and he was drinking a lot back then. Drugs again, too, from what I hear.''

"What else do you hear?"

Her face darkened. "He talks bad about me, Katy. Nobody listens but he still does it. If it weren't for a few big songs he wrote, songs he's still making money on, he'd have a hard time getting by. He's talk, Katy, that's all.''

She smiled at me and I smiled back.

Just talk? Or letters? Or a flash grenade? Maybe. Maybe not. I needed to find out.

It wasn't all I needed to find out.

eleven

HURT ME SO BAD

TWO OUT OF THREE. I'D GOTTEN DAKOTA TO TALK about Cal and about the letters. It was a start.

"Dakota, what could someone blackmail or threaten you with?" How many times had I asked this question? How many times hadn't she answered it?

"I don't know who I am, Katy."

I waited to see if this would turn into an answer. Dakota answers questions like this. Answers that sound like songs and stories, not like answers. Answers that are like life, but make you long for simplicity, for black and white and yes and no.

"Remember times in your life when you thought you knew who you were, when it was clear and simple?"

I wrinkled my nose and tried to think of times like that.

"When you were a kid maybe, or a student in college. You know," Dakota prompted. "Life just was. You went to school and did homework and looked forward to Christmas and summer vacations and you didn't think a lot about anything else."

I nodded, though I didn't remember it quite like that.

"Now practically the whole world knows who Dakota Jones is."

The phone rang.

"And I don't."

Dakota answered the phone in a harsh businesslike voice, then squealed. "Granny! Granny Mae, how are you? Oh *God*, is everything all right? You're calling on day rates." The squeal died and I could hear the tension in Dakota's voice. Granny Mae distrusted the telephone and rarely called, *never* called at "expensive time," as she termed it.

"It is? Good! Look, you hang up the phone this *instant*. I'm calling you right back. *Right* back." There was a smile in her voice now. She winked at me, disconnected and punched the number out.

I drifted off to the kitchen to get a diet Dr Pepper, drifted back.

"Aunt Louella's *first* husband. You mean Uncle Elmer *wasn't* her first? . . . No, Granny, of course I don't remember. A *scandal*? What kind of a scandal?"

I leafed through Dakota's unsolicited magazines. *Seventeen* was packed with beautiful young women with gleaming, glossy hair and flawless complexions. The teenagers who wrote in were a different story. They had zits and split ends and self-doubts and the "wrong" parents and boyfriends. Wrong values, too. Nobody in *Seventeen* worried about hungry children, recycling or world peace.

Prison Life was another world, an ugly one. It had articles by two different groups of writers: guys in the slammer and guys out of the slammer. There was a "Convict of the Month" feature, an "Ask Bubba" advice column and a "Tattoo of the Month"—a fire-breathing dragon covering half a guy's back, which was, the convict said, "an expression of his sensitive and creative side." I wondered what side the murder of his wife expressed, but he didn't go into that. Nobody in *Prison Life* worried about world peace either.

"Who is she? . . . A second or third cousin? . . . What does once removed mean? It sounds like spots on a party dress. . . . Why? . . . Now? . . . How important? . . . Well, sure. Yes, of course. . . . I love you too, Granny." Dakota cradled the receiver, then stared at it. "Well, I'll be damned." She wandered into the living room where I was sitting, plopped down onto the arm of the sofa and shook her head slightly. "Making sense out of that is a challenge."

"What?" Bored with *Seventeen*, disgusted with *Prison Life*, I was ready to hear Granny Mae's story.

"I guess it starts with Aunt Louella, who is really my great-aunt. She and Granny are sisters. I don't really know how close they were—they were always bickering but they were always together. Louella was a good one for bickering, she could be a real sourpuss. We used to call her Aunt Vinegar behind her back when we were kids. Everybody loved Uncle Elmer though. It turns out that he was her second husband. She married her first when she was seventeen. Shoot, I wonder if it was even legal? Now that I think of it, Granny never said the word 'marry.' Maybe they ran off together."

Dakota's eyes had the faraway look they sometimes get when she's singing or telling a story. She stood and walked to the window, tapped the glass softly.

"It seems there was bad blood between Grandpa Billy and Louella's Homer—that was the one she married at seventeen."

No one ever called William Parneter anything but Billy. A hard-working man who loved to sing and fiddle, he and Granny were married for over fifty years.

"Granny Mae wouldn't tell me what it was, just that Homer and Billy didn't get along and that Grandpa lit out after Homer more'n once. The law caught up with Homer before Grandpa did, though." Dakota shook her head.

"Homer died in prison in a fight with another man. He was nineteen. By all accounts he was a no good, sweet-talking ladies' man." She glanced sideways at me. "Hmmm, add music and we could be talking Cal."

Prison? I hoped Cal wasn't that bad.

"Granny called long-distance to tell you all this *now*?" I asked, not even bothering to hide the incredulity in my voice. It is a family joke that Granny's dislike of the telephone is so strong that she will only call for a birth or death.

Dakota smiled an odd, twisted smile that puzzled me.

"Louella was pregnant. She found out when Homer was in prison."

I stared at Dakota. It had been talk in the family for as long as I could remember how much Louella and Elmer had yearned for a child of their own. Maybe it was that loss that had turned the sweetness in her life to vinegar.

"She had a backdoor abortion—botched and incomplete. She didn't abort the baby and she didn't carry it full-term. It was a month or so early, but healthy enough. Louella wouldn't even look at it, never mind hold it or nurse it. She refused to name the child and cursed the day it was born. Then she gave it up to Homer's family. Granny said she just about broke her heart over that, said she and Billy begged to raise that child as their own. Louella would have none of it.

"So she gave up the baby, never saw it again. Homer's people moved a few years later, after Homer died in prison, and nobody ever heard of them again."

"Until now," I said, feeling the goose bumps.

"Yes." Dakota tossed her hair back, her eyes here now, not far away. "It haunted her, Katy, for all those years, Granny said, wondering and worrying and praying over that motherless unnamed child that she felt our family had so wronged."

It *would* haunt Granny. Had it, I wondered, haunted Louella too? She gave up the only child she would ever bear.

"They named the child Pity."

"No," I said. I could hear the sadness in my voice. I didn't ask how someone could do that to a child. I don't ask those things anymore.

"Pity had a child and named her Hope. Hope came to Granny Mae. She's twenty-five, a singer and a musician. Granny wants me to help her."

"How does Granny know she's who she says she is?" Always the skeptic. Ever the investigator.

"She had pictures and letters, old family records. Granny said one photo of her mother, Pity, was the spitting image of Louella when she was young and beautiful still. And she had a quilt. Half a quilt."

I saw it coming. "A crazy quilt?"

Dakota nodded. "Louella made it when she was pregnant, then cut it in half. Granny Mae has one half. She saved it when Louella threw it out. Hope has the other."

It wasn't evidence, but it was compelling.

"What is she like? Hope," I clarified.

"Granny liked her."

We shrugged in unconscious unison. Here is what we both know about Granny: One. Granny Mae is a rock-solid, sensible, no-nonsense person. Two. She would bend over backwards, do cartwheels and handstands, to right a wrong she, or the family, had done to someone.

"She said Hope was shy and quiet and not very talkative at first. Sweet and unassuming."

I frowned. "Asking a major artist for help is not unassuming." Not by a long shot.

Dakota nodded. "I agree. Granny kind of skated around on that one. She implied that Hope had just mentioned it and that she, Granny, suggested that I might be able to help. Granny said she didn't make her any promises on my part, just said she'd see."

"Is she any good?" I asked without thinking.

Dakota busted up. In a family of musicians, Granny has a tin ear. I didn't ask if Dakota would meet Hope. We both knew the answer to that one. She would. Dakota would do anything she could for Granny Mae.

"Hope is in Nashville. She's coming over."

"Now?"

"She'll call first, I'm sure."

"Here?"

"Oh, for *goodness'* sakes, Katy," Dakota said crossly. "She's family, not an unknown-stranger-possible-serial-killer-maniac-off-the-streets. I know it's your job to think like this, but if Granny says she's okay, she's okay."

Yes. That almost made it all right. Granny Mae is as eccentric as they come but full of common sense. *And family guilt*, I reminded myself.

"I said I would, so I will. You can meet her too. Then we'll decide. Granny said she would call soon."

I took a deep breath. "Dakota, we're in the middle of three conversations here—blackmail, how you don't know who you are, and Hope's story. I don't mind but . . ." I bit my lip slightly, which is what I do when I'm trying not to frown and look disapproving.

Dakota stuck her tongue out at me. She knows exactly what that gesture means.

"Okay," I amended. "I do mind." Dakota nodded. "And you do this when you don't want to talk about something. Every time we might be getting somewhere you slide into a new story. And the more you do this, the more important the first thing—the one you're trying to avoid—was. Is."

"I know." She said it contritely, but there was laughter in her blue eyes. "It's just that Hope—"

I sighed like a person flat out at the end of her rope and still drowning.

"I'll just finish up Hope, Katy." She started out humble but ended up laughing.

"Okay." I'm big on graceful capitulation when surrender is inevitable.

"Hope first contacted Granny three months ago. Of course Granny put off doing anything."

Of course.

We sighed in unison. Aunt Louella had been Aunt Vinegar. Granny was the World's Greatest Procrastinator. *Good news can't git here too fast and bad news can dang well wait till hell freezes over.* Naturally the bad, or maybe bad, news category was a lot bigger than the good news one.

I did some quick figuring. "So Granny put off Hope—who is now upset or hurt or confused—and Granny is in a lather and you're supposed to do something right away." That was Granny's MO in a nutshell.

"You got it. But of course it doesn't have to be right this minute, Kat." She used her placating voice.

"Good. Back to blackmail, or why you don't know who

you are. Your choice," I said, gracious again.

"Remember how we used to talk about roots, Katy?"

"Dakota, *no*!" I wailed.

"It's all connected, I promise."

I sat, silent and grumpy. We had talked plenty about roots as children, both of us neglected by our parents and raised by grandparents, but I didn't see how it figured into this.

"Your roots are in Sacramento, Katy. You love Sacramento and the Valley, the rivers and ranches, old mining towns and wineries just a jump away. And the history, like the stories Alma used to tell us about her daddy, how he would walk for hours on the levees and swim and play in the irrigation ditches. How they made little paddle wheel boats and one summer a kid drowned. How her brother bought their mama a washing machine on time with the money he made on his paper route.

"Remember when she told us that in the winter you couldn't go to San Francisco, except by boat or rail, because the rivers would flood and there would be miles of water everywhere you looked. And how if the levees failed, parts of Sacramento would be under water and the Delta islands would disappear.

"It's roots. A tree can't grow without roots and maybe people can't either. Even though I grew up in Sacramento it's not my roots like it is yours, Katy. My roots are country and I feel like I belong in Nashville. I grew up on stories of how Grandpa Billy played once at the old Ryman Auditorium, how he met Kitty Wells—well, he always said *Miss* Kitty Wells—and Patsy Cline and Roy Acuff. By the time I was six years old I could sing most of 'Wings of a Dove,' 'I Fall to Pieces,' and 'Honky Tonk Angel.' I'm country. I'm music through and through, Katy."

"Yes." I wondered if we were getting any closer to an answer.

"I tried to talk to Grandpa Billy about Nashville and the Grand Ole Opry. You know, I'm not even sure he was there. Maybe he made it up, but it's real for me. I'm country. Sometimes it's the only thing I'm sure about, Katy."

"What did you mean by saying you don't know who you are?" I asked gently.

"When I was young I thought that as you got older you left behind each person you'd been. Of course looking back you could remember it, or trace it, just as you would mark out where you had been on a road map. You could see the roads you'd taken and the ones you hadn't. But it would be a record of the past, only that. Now I know that's not true. You can't leave the past behind, you carry it with you all the time."

Yes. That was what blackmail was about—the past that couldn't be forgotten or hidden.

"I changed my name from Cody to Dakota but Cody is still a big part of me. Granny Mae hardly ever calls me Dakota."

It wasn't a non sequitur and we weren't at blackmail yet.

"And there's not just one Cody either. There's the little girl who was afraid of noises in the night, the college student who dropped out, the young woman who came to Nashville."

This wasn't it. Instinctively I knew it. Dakota's eyes were clear and blue. Though her expression was a little puzzled, the words came easily. I waited.

"Katy, sometimes I think I've spent my whole life running from myself. My mama made a career out of looking for a heartbreak in pants. My daddy was a back door man. Who am I?"

Questions, not answers.

twelve

MILLION-DOLLAR BABY

BEFORE YOU GET FAMOUS, BEFORE YOU EVEN THINK IT'S a possibility, you say things you wouldn't say later when you know enough to keep the door to your life closed. It's innocence at first, the thought that the truth can't hurt you. Then you were nobody and you knew it and everybody else did too. You didn't see that things would change, that people would be interested in every little fact or rumor they could drag up about you."

Overhead a jet roared, a sound full of promise and possibilities, full of the unknown.

"Facts? Rumors?"

"Or dirt," Dakota said bitterly. "Sometimes the truth becomes your enemy and the past, even if it's not yours, comes to haunt you."

Truth is rarely easy, I think. And almost always a double-edged sword.

"Now I try to be more understanding of my mother, of Jo."

We always speak of her as Jo. She pounded that into us when we were younger.

"I know now she didn't have it easy," Dakota continued.

"She was the first to make it difficult for herself." *And everyone else.* Sometimes I am not very tolerant or understanding. "And whenever it was"—I searched for the right word—"inconvenient for her to be a parent, she let your grandparents take over."

"Katy, I was so lucky to have them. Without them . . ." We both let that go. "The word 'inconvenient' doesn't quite cover it." I raised an eyebrow in question. "Hormone surges." We giggled like schoolgirls. "The car salesman, what was his name?"

I searched my memory bank. "Herbie?"

"Yes. Remember she started wearing those horrible navy polyester pantsuits accessorized with plastic globs of red-and-white jewelry?"

"And the stockbroker, Alec," I added.

"That was trim little suits with silk shells and matching purse and pumps."

"Robert?"

We laughed out loud at Robert, a minister who had permanently pursed lips in disapproval of the world and its ways and who, we later learned, screamed obscenities while having sex.

"What did she wear then?" I couldn't remember anything but disapproval and obscenities.

Dakota thought about it. "Dowdy housewife dresses that looked like they had been ordered from a Sears Roebuck catalogue in the fifties. Oh God, Katy."

Dakota dragged a hand wearily across her eyes.

"It was all she knew. It was all I ever remember back then—how she tried so hard to become the dream of the man she was with. She stepped into a new identity like we would a party dress, only to toss it aside after the party, after the guy. She was always moving out of the house we shared with Granny Mae and Grandpa Billy and in with some man. A fight or a divorce and she was back again. For a while. I loved her and hated her both. She could turn her interest in me on and off in a heartbeat, like turning off a faucet.

"I still hold it against her. I didn't want her to die but, in an odd way, it was a relief when she did. No more hopes and spoiled dreams. I wouldn't get all excited, then disappointed, then bitter. I'm still bitter," she said. "I'm still hungry for family. I don't mind about Hope even. Katy, you see, don't you?"

"Yes."

"And you know how I feel about you?"

"Sisters."

"Sisters," she agreed. We had decided that at eight years old. "I've had to find my family as I go along. I wish that I could reinvent mine. Everyone in country music seems to have had this wonderful family and childhood. 'Poor but happy.' 'Hardworking but content.' 'Life was tough but there was always enough love.' " Her voice was plaintive.

"Not everyone. The rest just aren't talking."

"Oh." She thought that one over, shifted in her seat. "Daddy was no better but at least he was consistent. He left when I was two and he stayed gone. Solid gone. It was only later I heard the stories."

"What's a back door man, Dakota?"

"Those stories, yes," she said wryly. "Company comes to the front door. A back door man might be expected but he's not company you want the neighbors to see. So he would come and go by the back door—sometimes, rumor has it, just slippin' out the back door before the husband walked in the front. From what I hear, my daddy's reputation as a ladies' man was well earned and well deserved." She grimaced. "Not exactly what you want to hear about your father, is it?"

"No. But you have Granny. You had Billy."

"Full of love and kindness."

"Solid as brick houses."

"Granny let something slip once."

Only once? I thought. *Good for her.*

"I was still pretty young, ten or eleven maybe. And, like every kid, I wanted a daddy who loved me and thought I was something. I wanted Granny to make up a story and tell me, or let *me* make up one and just agree with me, but she wouldn't. She said it was better to know the truth, however hard."

The truth again.

"I wanted to think that he loved me and thought about me, that he wrote and sent money for Granny to buy me presents. That he asked how I was and would she please send my school picture and report card."

Sometimes I think that, in the long run, the stories we make up to get by hurt more than help. Maybe we wouldn't survive, though, if we didn't make them up. Survival is expediency, is short-run. And why do you think it is that I wonder about things like this?

"It turns out he *had* written."

I looked at Dakota's face, closed over, impassive.

"He wrote to Granny. Billy would have told him to go to hell and helped him on his way with a kick in the pants. He didn't write about me, he wrote for money and he threatened to come back and raise hell if he didn't get it. Granny said it was only a couple of times but I think it may have happened more than she wanted to let on to me. The truth was he wanted nothing to do with me."

"Or with responsibility. A child is a big responsibility, Dakota, and he doesn't sound like someone cut out for responsibility of any size or kind."

"At least I got a song out of it, a *good* song."

"Yes. I guess a lot of us have run into a back door man. Especially the irresponsible, fun-loving ladies' man kind."

"Ain't that the truth!"

"A-*men*," we said, just the way Granny would have said it, which made us laugh again. Dakota dusted her hands off as if to dust off the past. *And move on to blackmail*, I hoped.

"It's not pretty but it's not blackmail," I prompted.

"Does anyone have a perfect childhood, Katy?" she asked wistfully.

"Not perfect, no, but good. Better than ours." Not that that was saying much.

"Cal and Daddy."

It wasn't an out-of-the-blue comment, Dakota was back to telling her story. I'd about decided to give up on asking direct questions for a while.

"Remember what you used to say to me, Katy? About Cal."

"Yell at you, you mean. You wouldn't listen when I just said it."

"I didn't pay it any mind when you yelled either but I still remember it word for word."

Yes. I did too. I spoke softly. "Don't try to find your daddy in a husband."

"Cal was twenty years older."

"And twenty years more experienced. Twenty going on a hundred and twenty," I corrected darkly.

"Katy, did I ever tell you you were absolutely right? Did I ever thank you?"

I crossed the room and hugged her. She put her forehead against mine. "Know what I'm thinking?" We used to do that when we were kids, pretend we could read each other's mind with our foreheads smacked together.

"Uh-huh. No more back door men."

She giggled. "Yeah, and I'm thinking I got a couple of good songs out of Cal, too."

"Spinning straw into gold. You've always done that, Dakota. I admire that about you."

She tossed a couch pillow at me, then started pacing restlessly around the room. "Did I ever tell you how Cal sued me for a million dollars?"

"*Sued* you? A *million* dollars." I shook my head admiringly. "That son of a bitch has nerve."

"It was all written up in legalese but basically he said that without him I'd be nothing, so therefore he was entitled to a percentage of my earnings forever and ever but, since he was such a sweet generous guy, he'd settle for a token million. It wasn't the money, he said, it was the principle."

So, of course, we busted up right there, flat out lost it on that one.

"Principle! *Shoot*, Cal wouldn't recognize a principle if he tripped over one."

"If it landed in his lap with a label on it."

"If it came boxed up and with directions."

"A-*men*!"

"What happened?" I asked.

"The court dismissed the case as frivolous and made him pay my legal costs."

"Good."

"It's going to be a long time before I'm done with that man, Katy, and he's about as friendly as a black widow spider."

I didn't disagree.

But I wished it weren't true.

thirteen
BUSINESS AS USUAL

WE HOLED UP IN DAKOTA'S PLACE IN NASHVILLE UN-
til we could tell which way things were going to go.
The papers played it down. The cops did too.

Okay, that statement is a little misleading: There was a
massive amount of coverage—newspaper, TV and radio.
What was played down was any indication that Dakota was
the target of the flash bomb. We told the media nothing.
We leveled with the cops.

Correction: I made Dakota level with the cops.

"*Absolutely* not!"

That was her opening statement. I didn't argue at first. I
wanted to hear her reasoning.

"Why?" I queried.

"We don't know that this . . . this . . ."

"Attack," I supplied helpfully.

"Incident." She glared at me and continued. "Is in *any*
way connected with me and the other incidents."

"Just a coincidence?" I asked, still being helpful. "The
anonymous letters, the magazine subscriptions you didn't
order, the dead flowers on your bed, and now a flash grenade at one of your concerts, apparently aimed at you. It
doesn't sound like a coincidence to me."

"Okay, not all of it maybe. But we don't know that the
flash grenade is connected. Anyway, I don't see any point

in making a big deal of it. And I certainly don't see any point in making my private life public."

It wasn't reasoning. *Surprise*. It was fear. Fear is a hard one, tough to reason with. I tried anyway.

"Throwing a flash grenade in a public place and causing a riot is a criminal act, not an invasion of your privacy. As citizens we will naturally go to the police with any information that could help them catch this person." Not to mention stop additional, probably worse assaults. I was still trying to reason, not scare, so I didn't say that.

"No."

Okay. Reasoning was over. "A number of people were injured seriously enough to be taken to the hospital, one child is still in critical condition. You may choose to jeopardize your safety in order to protect your privacy; you may not choose that for others. Especially children." I said it mean and hard—my take-no-prisoners attitude.

Dakota's mouth dropped open. "Oh God, Kat, of course I can't. What was I thinking? I wasn't, I was just being selfish." She looked ready to burst into tears. "We'll do it right now. But—"

I waited in silence for the rest of the sentence.

"I can ask the police to respect my privacy?"

"Of course. And they will as much as they can. They're interested in both your safety and the safety of the public, not tabloid headlines."

She nodded, still miserable. But she told them, spit it right out like a good Girl Scout. The consensus of both the Nashville and Memphis cops was that this guy might be after Dakota to get attention, particularly media attention, and that the most effective strategy would be to downplay it and to limit that attention. "Would Miss Jones be willing to go along with that?" Gravely Dakota agreed to it.

"Oh thank God, Katy," she had said as we walked away from cops and into Nashville sunshine and headed back to whatever came next. "Thank God," she said again, as though everything was resolved, as though the worst was over.

We didn't have any control over the next part. Nobody

knows better than an entertainer how fickle the public can be. So we waited. A lot was at stake: the rest of the tour, a major financial investment, maybe Dakota's career. We held our breath as we waited for the media's reaction.

"Police search for concert bomber."

"Singer visits injured child in hospital." There was a picture of Dakota holding a teddy bear and flowers and the child smiling up at her.

"Police think bomber acted alone."

"Police following 'several promising leads.' "

"Dakota tells band: 'Don't worry, I'll cover the loss.' "

"Singer starts charity drive for those injured at concert."

Flowers, cards and letters poured in. The rest of the scheduled concerts on the tour sold out in a heartbeat. CDs were flying off the shelves. It was a million dollars' worth of publicity. It was more than publicity, it was sympathy and support.

"I don't get it, Katy." Dakota was frankly dumbfounded. "Just because of the attack?"

"No. Because of you. Because of your courage and compassion. Because of your dedication to your music and concert commitments. Maybe even because we all have sympathy for the victim, not the criminal."

"Back to business as usual, then."

"Back to business as usual with increased security. What's on your schedule today?"

"Kick back a little, work on a song if there's time. I'm still playing catch-up. I'd like to go to the health club and work out. Want to?"

"Sure."

"Tonight Garrett wants me to go into the studio, redo one song, cut a new one. We're trying to come to a decision on the last two tracks for my new album."

"What time is the recording session?"

"Eight."

"Where?"

"A studio just out of town."

"Who's Garrett?"

"Garrett Hunter, my manager."

Okay, I thought. *Time to straighten this out.* "Please take it from the top, Dakota—all the people you work with and exactly what they do."

She shrugged, bored but agreeable. "Garrett is my general manager. He knows where I want to go; it's his job to figure out how we get there—a combination of career planning and vision. He's involved in my choice of music, the feel and direction of an album; in marketing decisions; even in publicity photos, clothing and style if I need his advice on it. He decides what kind of venues I should do, arranges media interviews, contacts, press releases, and works with me on production.

"Ted, as you know, is my road manager. He makes it all come together on the road, organizes trip schedules, daily schedules, books us into hotels, accompanies me to on-the-road media events and generally stands between me and the demands of the public.

"I have a booking agent to schedule particular concerts and appearances in a doable, efficient way. A lawyer who oversees my contracts and other legal stuff." *Like Cal*, I thought. "And an accountant who keeps track of the financial end of things. She figures out income and expenses, does payroll and taxes, decides if we can afford a new bus and so on."

I whistled. Dakota grinned.

"This is a business and it's in everyone's best interest to run things as smoothly and efficiently as possible. I expect to add on more people at some point. This is a pretty standard setup, Katy. What I do isn't much different from any other singer at my level." She looked at me and smiled wryly. "I have a personal reason for it as well, of course."

"A six-foot-two honky tonk heel reason?"

"Yes. Or rather, Cal taught me a lesson I don't need to repeat. Country music's full of stories about stars who made millions, millions that vanished because they either didn't pay close enough attention to the money or to the people managing it. A corporation like mine is structured so that everything is accounted for, is checked and double-checked and triple-checked."

"And everyone's accountable."

"Exactly. C'mon, let's work out, eat, then head on over to the studio."

THE STUDIO WAS LIT, CARS PARKED IN MOST OF THE nearby spaces. Eight o'clock is not late by Nashville recording standards, where a working day is just as easily two to nine as eight to five. And sometimes much later than nine. We walked into a waiting room furnished with sofas and chairs, a coffee table with magazines, a TV in the corner and a Coke machine. Behind the waiting room I could see a corridor and what looked like recording areas and glass-walled control rooms. Guys who appeared to be musicians wandered around.

Dakota looked puzzled.

I got wary. Just like that.

"Hey, Dakota," a man in faded jeans and a baseball cap called out. "You doing harmony? What song?"

"No," Dakota said. "I thought we had the studio tonight."

"Not unless your name's Joni Ames."

Dakota looked at me, shrugged, then headed on back to one of the control rooms. I stuck to her like glue.

"Jamie, what's up?"

The sound engineer looked up from his control panel. "Hey, Dakota. They didn't get ahold of you in time, did they? Someone in the band couldn't make it at the last minute, so Garrett called, canceled and rescheduled, and we booked these guys in."

"You spoke to Garrett personally?" I asked.

Jamie looked at me, then at Dakota.

"This is Kat," Dakota offered in a voice that said I was okay.

"Yeah, I spoke to him personally."

"Thanks, Jamie."

"Sure, Dakota. Oh, one other thing. Some guy called for you earlier, before Garrett canceled, wanted to be sure you'd be here, sounded real eager to catch up to you. He didn't leave a message."

"Anybody you knew?" I asked.

"Nah. Probably a songwriter with a tape and a hard-luck story." Jamie shook his head and went back to work.

We walked. "That's how writers submit songs?" I asked.

"That's not the way it's supposed to be done but jeez, Katy, I've had songs dropped in my pocket at a salad bar, shoved under the door in the stall of a ladies' room and thrown at me on the stage. It's not like everyone plays by the rules."

I put my hand on Dakota's arm as we reached the front door. "Wait here. I'll bring the car up."

She shook my hand off and started to walk out with me.

"Dakota—" The tone in my voice stopped her. "We're dealing with someone who doesn't play by the rules, remember?"

We got home just fine. No problems. No incidents. There were two messages on the machine. One was from Garrett saying the session had been canceled and why the hell wouldn't Dakota get a cell phone? The other was from Link, who said he'd missed her, he hoped she was back in town, and he wanted to see her. He didn't leave his name. Dakota filled me in on that. And blushed.

Blushed? I wondered.

"Tell me about Link."

"Let's go out, Katy. Let's go over to the Bluebird Cafe. Maybe Link can meet us there. I'd like you to meet him." She smiled, blushed again, picked up the phone.

He was a guy who defied description, I guess. I am wary of that kind of guy.

"We're going to meet Link at the Bluebird in an hour. Come talk to me while I get dressed, okay?" Dakota hadn't bothered much with her clothes or with makeup to go to the studio. Link and the Bluebird had changed all that. I got so swept up in the beauty and fashion excitement I put on lipstick, then sat on Dakota's bed as she looked through her closet.

"What's the Bluebird?" I asked conversationally.

"A club. Always good music, a lot of new music. Everyone goes there—it's a fun place.'' She disappeared into the walk-in closet.

"Big club?" Yeah, I was thinking security.

"No. Maybe a hundred."

Her voice was muffled. She tossed a boot out. I heard scuffling and muttering, then another boot emerged. Dakota reappeared, her face flushed.

"Dakota, please finish what you were telling me the other day about—"

"Katy, have you seen my brown leather belt, the one with the big buckle?"

"No. Dakota—"

"How about my silver and turquoise bracelet? I thought they were—" She pushed a pile of stuff off her dresser. "Nope."

"Cody."

She looked up into the mirror. Our eyes met and held.

"I'm sorry, Katy. It's just so damn hard for me.'' She reached under the dresser, pulled a belt out and walked over to the bed where I sat, the silver buckle of the belt dragging on the carpet as she walked. "I don't know where to start, what matters or doesn't. Mostly I don't want to face the pain."

I didn't say that facing the pain was good, was the way to leave it behind. She knew that. I didn't say she had no choice now either because someone had forced the issue. She knew that, too. We knew these things and more, just like we knew how hard, how awful, pain could be.

Dakota sank down on one end of the bed. The belt slipped from her hands, landing next to the boots on the floor.

"When I met Cal I was young and had a lot to learn but I felt like a whole person. I knew I was talented—as a singer and writer both—and pretty. And very determined and hardworking. The world was mine for the asking. I believed that. I believed all of it and more the first years I was married to Cal. I don't even know when it started to change.

"It wasn't so much that I lost that sense of myself but

that it always seemed to be slipping away. I thought, then, about my mother, about how she tried to become whatever her man of the moment wanted. How she lost herself. And me. When I was younger I couldn't define it but I hated it. I hate it now. I was afraid I was starting to lose myself like that. And Cal? All the things he loved about me before we were married he hated afterwards.

"Before, I was independent and gutsy. Afterwards that became selfish and contrary. My determination became hardheaded stubbornness. Anytime I didn't agree with him, I was wrong. So after a while I didn't feel whole anymore."

She picked up the belt, dropped it again. I said nothing. I couldn't think of anything to say.

"By then I was getting known. I was making a name for myself as a singer and writer. Things were happening, though not as fast as I had hoped. Cal had something to do with that of course. I thought about it a lot, even spoke of it. He denied holding me back. He told me I was crazy."

I bit my lip. I didn't trust myself to speak.

"By then he was picking on me all the time. Hitting me too." She spoke softly. "So I left, and slowly started to rebuild my sense of myself. I threw myself into my work and my career. I got a divorce lawyer and met Garrett. And that changed everything. I had the talent but I didn't know how to get where I wanted to go. Garrett did. And he and the lawyer knew how to get me out of where I was, my marriage."

She picked up the belt. She was looking at me as she spoke, but her fingers traced the patterns on the silver buckle. "That was the first time in my life I realized I didn't know who I was. When I looked, I couldn't find me.

"Now I'm a major artist, a star. That's not who I am as a person, though. Maybe it shouldn't be that way, or needn't be that way, but it is. People treat you . . ." Her voice trailed off.

I nodded. I knew; I'd seen it.

"The bigger and more well known you become, the more difficult it is to keep a part—even a small part—of your life private. Difficult? Oh God, Katy," she said despairingly. "Sometimes it seems impossible."

"Difficult, not impossible," I said gently. "And you have a lot of people around you who care, who will do their best to protect you."

The smile she smiled at me was a wan one, one that said: *You don't know. You can't know.*

"It's not just that, either, the struggle to be yourself and to keep something private. You have to keep reminding yourself to keep your feet on the ground, to be sensible, to remember you're you and not the myth, the 'star' that the fans and the media create.

"Things happen so fast, Katy. Too fast to keep up with. By the time I've adjusted to something, it's outdated and something else has happened. It's like being in a speeding car. Everything outside the car is blurred.

"It's not just me, either. Friends and associates change. You lose a lot of people, Katy. Maybe they're jealous. Maybe they can't or don't want to come along with you. Maybe you'll never know—but you lose them. And that hurts too."

Dakota looked up at the clock, then leaned over to pick up a boot and pull it on.

"A lot of people you never even heard of suddenly want to be your friend, your associate, your lover, anything at all that you'll allow. I had never thought about any of this and I certainly hadn't expected it. When I finally did think it through, I guess it wasn't much of a surprise. It wasn't much fun, either. *That* was a surprise." Dakota made a face at me and pulled on her other boot.

"I think that often happens."

"What?"

"The dream that comes true is not quite what you expect, is not what you dreamt."

Dakota stared at me openmouthed.

"That's a song, huh?" I sounded pleased, even smug.

"Yes." And we laughed. Dakota glanced at the clock. "We're late, Katy, and you know how I hate to be late. We'll finish talking about this. Or keep on, I guess; I don't know if you ever finish with stuff like this. There's something else, something important I haven't told you about Cal, something it's hard for me to admit.''

"What?"

She glanced over at me sideways as she threaded her belt through the loops on her jeans. "Shame," she said. "And blackmail. His was the blackmail, mine was the shame. I don't know if he feels shame."

The phone rang.

"It's probably Link wondering where we are."

Not Link. The police.

And they wanted us back at the recording studio. Immediately.

I wasn't wary, I was certain.

It was bad.

fourteen
DEATH AND BROKEN CHINA

REVOLVING LIGHTS.
  Police cars.
Yellow crime scene tape.
And the body of Joni Ames.
As we approached the cordoned-off area a uniform glanced at us, then impatiently waved us away. We ignored that. He looked at us, at our approach, and started to get mad. I spoke before he could, but I had to rush the words out to do it.
"Sergeant Deeter, please. This is Dakota Jones and I'm—"
"Wow!" the uniform said. *"Dakota Jones."* His voice was awed, his mad look gone. "This sure is an honor." He stared at Dakota; I could have been a mailbox. Dakota stared back—not at him but at life—white-faced, wide-eyed, silent and stunned-looking. The revolving lights hit her face, then left it in shadows. Close by a siren started up. The lights hit us again as the officer lifted up the crime scene tape for us to scramble under. I had to nudge Dakota to get her moving. The officer hollered for Deeter. Dakota froze.
In front of us, in a pool of lights set up for the cameras a young woman lay sprawled on the concrete. Her head was flung back, her mouth slightly open, her expression

almost surprised. One arm was tossed out palm up with fingers slightly curled and supplicating; the other was twisted and hidden beneath the body. There was a lot of blood everywhere, centering on her chest like a bull's-eye, spinning out from there onto clothing and concrete. Her face was untouched, unmarked. Except for the surprise.

"Oh my God, oh my God, oh my God," Dakota cried.

She was mid to late twenties, I thought. Slim but full-breasted; wearing jeans, boots, a denim jacket. Her complexion was fair; her hair long, straight and blond. She had been very pretty. Even now, so soon, whatever it is that makes us human and alive was fading, ebbing away. Soon there would be nothing but a body. The beauty was already gone.

A live and perky young woman with a no-nonsense business attitude and a camera moved about purposefully taking pictures of the victim and the crime scene. Next to the coroner's van a uniform was conversing in quiet tones with a man in khakis and a sweater. Someone stepped in a pool of blood and swore loudly but briefly.

"Oh my God, Katy. Oh my God."

It would have been difficult—without an audition—to find someone who looked more like Dakota. Same general build and height, skin coloring, hair color and style. Even the style of dress.

Dakota started crying. I put my arms around her, turning her away from the scene. Behind us the camera flashed frantically, then stopped. The man in khakis started toward the corpse that had been a young woman who looked like Dakota.

"Ma'am."

I turned and looked up into kind brown eyes. Dakota sobbed into my shoulder.

"Sergeant Deeter, ma'am. Could you and Miss Jones step over here please?"

I stepped, hauling a stumbling and dazed Dakota along with me. The sergeant headed for the studio at a brisk pace. We followed at a slower one. He held the door and then escorted us into a small soundproofed room furnished with a wooden table and four metal folding chairs. Deeter waited until we were seated, then followed suit.

"Did you know the dead woman, Miss Jones?" he asked politely.

"Joni!" Dakota said fiercely. "Joni Ames. Not the dead woman. Can't you call her by name?"

"Forgive me," he said gently. "You knew her then?"

"Yes. Not well but we had met. At award ceremonies, at the Bluebird, at parties. We all know each other."

"What did you know of her?"

"Her music and her talent." The fierceness was gone. Dakota was subdued, her voice just above a whisper. "And she seemed very nice."

"Had you spoken to her recently? Today?"

"No. Was she leaving the studio when—when it happened?"

"Yes." Deeter's voice was easy and noncommittal and didn't match his eyes, which were hard and alert.

"A recording session?"

"Yes."

Dakota swallowed hard. "Did you know that—my manager—we were supposed to—" She burst into tears, put her arms on the wooden table, her head on them, and wept.

Deeter's eyes didn't change as he waited for the emotional tumult to subside. When I opened my mouth to pick up the story he silenced me with a gesture. As the sobs became snuffles he spoke again. Same gentle voice, same hard eyes.

"Miss Jones, if you could explain that again, please. It was difficult to understand you."

Dakota wiped her eyes and snuffed up a last lost sob. "We, Kat and I, were here at eight this evening. My manager had booked the studio for a recording session. When we got here Jamie, the sound engineer, said Garrett, my manager, had called to cancel because someone in the band couldn't make it. Apparently the studio booked someone else—Joni—at the last minute. So we left."

"Was there anything unusual about that?"

"About the cancellation and rebooking?"

"Yes."

"That's not what was unusual." Dakota's eyes met Deeter's, then dropped.

"No? What was, Miss Jones?"

"Jamie said a man called earlier to make sure I would be here tonight. At a distance"—Dakota broke off and gulped in a breath—"Joni and I look somewhat alike. Who was that person trying to kill?"

That was the question, all right.

Dakota's wide-eyed, white-faced stunned look was back.

"I was hoping you could tell me that."

She shook her head. "I have to go now," she whispered. "I feel sick. And sad. And scared." She added each on as an afterthought postscript. There were tears in her eyes again.

"Perhaps you could go to the ladies' room while I talk to your friend?"

She nodded. Deeter held the door for her, loomed over me for a moment, then sat again. He was still polite but he didn't bother with gentle.

"You were with Miss Jones all evening?"

"Yes."

"In what capacity?"

I hesitated. "I don't understand." And stalled for time.

"I gathered from Garrett Hunter that you are a private investigator in California, Miss Colorado."

I nodded. I hadn't given him my name.

"Why are you here?"

"Dakota Jones and I have been friends since we were eight years old. You are aware, I'm sure, of the flash grenade thrown at her concert in Memphis last weekend?"

His turn to nod.

"That was not the first incident. Miss Jones had received half a dozen anonymous letters—unpleasant but not explicitly threatening. There were other incidents: a bouquet of dead flowers, a number of unordered magazine subscriptions. Dakota asked me for help." I shrugged. "I have both a personal and a professional interest in this, sergeant."

He nodded again. "What have you found out?"

"Nothing that makes sense of this. It seems reasonable to assume that whoever threw the flash grenade had chosen Dakota as a target. But that's all it is, an assumption. We don't know. Perhaps the victim—" I stopped, thinking of Dakota's impassioned protest. "Maybe Joni Ames was mistaken for Dakota. Maybe someone knew that Dakota was scheduled to record tonight and didn't know of the last-minute changes. Maybe Dakota was the intended victim."

Three maybes in a row. Deeter wasn't any more impressed with this than I was.

"And there's no way of knowing if the flash grenade, the harassment and the homicide are connected."

Not with what I had, anyway. I didn't think Deeter had any more. Hard to tell, though. Hard to fool cops too. I wasn't trying exactly but I wasn't offering anything either. What I said wasn't news to Deeter but it gave, I hoped, the illusion of sharing and cooperation. "Illusion" is the wrong word. I'm happy to cooperate with cops. It's their job to find the bad guys and they get paid a lot more than I do. But first I like to know that we're on the same side. And I don't speculate and dish dirt with cops I don't know. Right now speculation and dirt was all I had. And it was the last thing that Dakota needed more of.

Deeter looked at me appraisingly for two or three beats. Translation: *You're not telling me everything. You're not fooling me either.*

I looked right back at him, a friendly, guileless out-of-state-P!-eager-to-cooperate look on my face. Translation: *Hey sarge, you can count on me.*

"She was shot?" I asked.

"Yes."

"A mugging?" Not that that was likely in this neighborhood. "A drive-by?"

"We have very little information at this point." Translation: *And you're not going to hear any of it.*

Dakota pushed open the door looking worse, not better. "Katy, let's go home." She turned on her heel. I followed.

"You're both staying at Miss Jones's?"

"Yes."

He didn't ask for details. He'd known my name; he knew, or would know, Dakota's address. Unlisted doesn't faze cops.

"You'll be in town for the next few days?"

I agreed to that, too. The police officer stationed at the entrance of the studio escorted us to our car. Dakota walked holding her hands up at her temples like blinders, blocking out the lights and the activity. Blocking out the body and the blood. Trying to block out death and fear. We can't do that, but we still try.

"Okay, let's load 'er."

Two men hoisted a body bag onto a stretcher.

"Sam, you got a cigarette?"

"Nah. You don't slow up, you'll be in a body bag too."

Harsh laughter. Voices and laughter carried well in the night stillness. Dakota shivered. The officer watched us get into the car, tapped solicitously on the passenger window to remind Dakota to fasten her seat belt. She did. It's the kind of thing you can do on instinct and without looking, which was just as well because Dakota was crying again.

"Maybe that was supposed to be me, Katy. All the time I was looking at that poor dead girl I was thinking that. Over and over. Here she is dead and all I can think of is me. All I can see is me lying there on cold concrete in a pool of blood feeling nothing. How could you hate someone enough to do that? Was it supposed to be me, Katy?"

"I don't know." I had to fight the impulse to lie. Sticking our heads in sand wouldn't help, wouldn't stop another attempt, wouldn't keep Dakota safe.

"But it could have been?"

"Yes, it could have been. It could be another senseless urban crime statistic. It could be that Joni Ames had an angry boyfriend or an enemy. It could be a lot of things."

"What do the police think?"

"I don't know. I asked but got nowhere." It was like talking to a wall. Deeter, the Polite Police Wall. "We'll try tomorrow. Maybe we'll have better luck inquiring through Garrett."

"Katy, what am I going to do?"

She didn't wait for an answer, which was just as well. I didn't have one.

"I said I'd keep on with my concert schedule if the fans supported me but now I don't know." Her voice was tight with fear. "I don't know. I'm scared."

"Dakota, stop. It's too soon. We'll decide when we know more." I tried sensible.

The radio was on. Dakota reached over and turned the volume up. A slow, sad voice dipped into a low register singing "It's too late now" and faded out. An announcer with a frantic, excited tone said: "Folks, that was Joni Ames's last song. She died tonight, shot outside Studio Sixty-Two after a recording session. Police declined comment on why she was attacked or who her attacker could have been. The music world is stunned and saddened at this sudden and tragic loss of one of its most promising artists."

Dakota snapped the radio off.

"We take things so much for granted but we shouldn't."

I reached out to touch her hand but I couldn't think of anything to say.

THE SMASHING WOKE ME UP. I HAD NO IDEA WHAT TIME it was but it was dark still. I rolled out of bed, grabbed for the .380, was out the bedroom door in a heartbeat. I was wide awake. Hope—no, pray—that you never learn to do this.

I headed for the kitchen. Top speed. Every light in there was high-volt, the rest of the house dark. I didn't bother sneaking up. A stumble-footed elephant could have moved with impunity in the ruckus. One person in the kitchen, one noise: Dakota. I leaned against the doorframe, my gun hand hanging at my side, swinging loosely. There was smashed stuff everywhere and Dakota was in the middle of it.

"Hey!" Dakota looked up between smashes. "So *that's* where you keep your gun." She grinned at me. "Is that a bulletproof vest?"

Smash went a bowl—soup tureen, I think.

Bulletproof? I was wearing underpants and an oversize

T-shirt that said *SACRAMENTO* and was illustrated with a huge lush tomato. You've heard of the Big Apple and the Big Easy—well, guess what?

SMASH! A couple of salad plates bit the dust. Dakota reached into the cupboard behind her, grabbed, then handed me a stack of saucers, sailed a dinner plate into the floor and off to the Great Cupboard in the Sky. I put the saucers down. She picked them up. Smash. There was quite a pile on the floor by now. I glanced into the cupboard. Not much left. Not much longer now. A couple more teacups and it was over. Smashsmashsmash. We said goodbye to the teacups.

The silence was loud.

I broke it. "In California, earthquakes take out more dishes than people do."

"What about guns?" She was grinning like a demented Cheshire cat on Happy Pills.

"Nah. With guns you shoot cans and bottles, not dishes." I left to put the gun away. Dakota was clearly not a person who should be anywhere near a loaded firearm. I put my boots on too. Barefoot was not the way to go in that kitchen.

"A tomato T-shirt and boots. Ride 'em, cowgirl!" Dakota giggled at me.

"How about I make us a nice cup of tea," I said carefully as I waded through the smashed-up stuff.

"Oh for godssakes, Kat." Dakota sounded cross. "Get a grip. Tequila or wine?"

It was three a.m. "Wine." I picked the lesser of two evils.

Dakota hauled a bottle of white wine out of the fridge, holding it by the bottom. She was about to open it by smashing the neck of the bottle against the counter. I knew that. I know her. I lunged for the bottle. Slid on dishes. Saved the wine, saved me. Barely. By the time it was uncorked I had changed my mind; I was ready to drink.

I searched through the almost barren cupboard and found a couple of plastic tumblers. Dakota giggled—what was *with* the giggling?—and handed me two wineglasses. I poured.

"Bad dream?" I asked. Okay, I was being sarcastic. It was hard not to be at three a.m. standing ankle-deep in broken china, wearing a T-shirt and cowboy boots. "Great idea, smashing things up."

"Yeah." Dakota drained half her glass in a gulp and nodded in satisfaction. "*Exactly.* I learned it from you."

"What?" I stared at her, stunned into temporary silence.

"Sometimes after a night of studying or working I'd be all keyed up and I'd come by River City at the end of your shift, remember?"

I nodded. River City was a restaurant where I had been a bartender for a good part of my college years. *So? So what did this have to do with smashed-up nights?*

"You'd give last call and we'd have a drink while you counted out your tips and your drawer. Some nights you were still cleaning or doing your liquor count."

She downed the rest of her wine, filled up her glass and topped off mine. In my mind I could see the rows of empty bottles on the wiped-down bar. In my mind I filled out the printed form: "Vodka—5; Gin—2; Bourbon—3; Scotch—1; Daniel's—1," and so on. Twenty-seven bottles, or thirty-six; fifty-four on a real busy night. Fifty-four bottles to haul out with the rest of the trash. Liquor bottles are heavy.

"One night I caught you, remember?"

Caught me? No, I didn't remember. "What?" I asked. I was beginning to sound like a parrot with a limited vocabulary.

"You were out back standing on the loading dock by the Dumpsters. I watched you grab those empty bottles by the neck and sling them into the Dumpster. It was maybe two-thirds full and you aimed so you'd hit the side, the metal. The bottles would explode. I watched you do that, bottle after bottle, until finally you noticed me standing there. Remember?"

I nodded. I remembered that night and many like it.

"I'd never seen you like that, Katy. Like—" She

stopped, maybe not wanting to define it further.

River City was a busy restaurant and bar. Bartending is a hard job. On a busy night at a busy bar a lot of shit goes down. Some of it—too much mostly—catches the bartender. I didn't want to take it home with me: the anger and hatred and disgust and other things that alcohol releases that it is better not to name. So I smashed it up, left it in the Dumpster. I went home lighter, freer. You cannot carry the burdens of strangers. If you do, one day you will stumble under the weight and be crushed. You cannot even carry the burdens of those you love for very long.

Enough. I looked at the mess on the floor. Not the liquor bottles of my past. Not crockery. "This is your wedding china. Didn't it cost a million dollars a place setting?"

"*Was* my wedding china. Watch your verb tenses, Katy. And it did but who cares?" She sipped at her wine complacently.

Was. Yes. "Why?" I asked. The adrenaline and anger were gone now, I was just puzzled. Wedding china is a little different from empty liquor bottles.

"I woke up suddenly in a state of total panic. My heart was pounding. I was sweaty and shaking and every brain cell I had was screaming fearful messages: *Someone hates you and wants to kill you. Soon you will be cold and dead just like Joni and it will be over. They will get you. There's nothing you can do.* There were pictures, too. One that repeated over and over like a stuck record was the broken bloody body of a blond singer. The echoes of that image were chalk lines—like the kind police draw around bodies—chalk line figures filled with blood. The dead girl wasn't Joni. It was me."

She picked up her wineglass, looked at it, set it down. "Katy, I couldn't let the fear fill me up like blood inside the chalk lines. Fill me up and take me over."

"Some people pound pillows," I said, sounding like a middle-of-the-night grump, which I was.

"You didn't. I didn't either. Some things you have to smash."

No grin, no giggles. You can live with fear but not if it

rules you. I swept up. Dakota decided we needed breakfast, scrambled eggs, grits and toast.

"What was it, Dakota, that was blackmail on Cal's part and shame on yours?"

Dakota was whisking the eggs with a fork. She stopped whisking but didn't look at me. "He threatened to tell the past—the past I want so much to leave behind—if I didn't record some of his songs. *'I treated you like shit, babe, and you took it. You don't think the world will be interested in that? I think they'll fucking eat it up.'* That's what he said to me."

She whipped the eggs hard, as if she wished it were Cal. "It's not that I don't want to tell you, Katy. It's me. I don't want to tell *me*. I want to keep it from *me*. I don't want to see it, or say it, or relive it again. *I don't.*"

"Dakota—"

"I can talk about how Cal stole my songs, my money, but—my pride, my sense of myself? God, that's hard. Because he didn't just steal it, I let him take it. I know." She waved away my objection. "I was young. Still—"

"When did he threaten this? Recently?"

She nodded.

"What did you do?"

"I put him off and took it to my lawyer. He said that I should try to get Cal to put it all in writing."

"And?"

"Nothing." She shook her head. "It's not that Cal's too smart to fall for that, it's just that angry verbal threats are what he does."

"Co-opt him."

"Huh?"

"Write a song about it, about a woman who starts off in love and then begins to lose herself. Call it 'Lost and Found.'" Mmmm. I liked that. Was I getting good at this or what? Maybe I'm in the wrong job.

Dakota stared at me with a little frown, the eggs forgotten.

"That's the name of the song," I explained. "You don't have to tell your life unless you choose to, you don't owe anyone that. Just tell stories in songs. And tell Cal to go to hell.

"Or—" I was warming to my subject now. "Do a 'Tell All' or a 'Tell Some of It' piece for *Redbook* or *People* or Barbara Walters. Say you're telling your story in the hope that it will help others, that it will keep other women from getting caught in the same trap. You'll look like a brave and loving person with the guts to do the difficult, but right thing. Which is absolutely true," I added simply.

"And he'll look like a jerk. Which is also true. Tell about his blackmail threats. Then he'll look like a jerk with criminal intent. True and even better."

"Katy, I couldn't. I *can't*."

"Okay, it's just a thought. We'll play it however you want. I'll help you deal with Cal on your terms." That was hard for me to say. I wanted to do it my way, to kick ass and take no prisoners. *Really* wanted to. I tried to be content with planting the idea.

Dakota went back to eggs and grits.

"Blackmail has no power in the light, Dakota. If you take things out of the closet and into the sunshine there is nothing left for blackmail. You are free of it."

Dakota stirred the eggs in the pan.

"I'm going back on tour, Katy. I'm a singer, I'm going to sing. I'm not letting someone run my life ever again."

The toast was burned but the eggs were perfect. We finished the wine and went to bed.

I dreamed of a bull in a china shop.

A bloody bull.

fifteen

REFRIED DREAMS

I WOKE UP AT FIVE AND AGAIN AT SEVEN-THIRTY. HEAR-ing noises outside and being jumpy inside is a bad combination. I got up both times and walked the house, looked out, looked around. Nothing.

That I could see.

I slept fitfully after that, got up tired at eight-thirty. Dakota was still asleep. It had been after four when we went to bed. In the shower I imagined that the shampoo and hot soapy water washed the death, ugliness and fear of yesterday off me. Wouldn't it be something to have the patent on a soap like that?

I made coffee, swept the kitchen again, wiped down the counters, finding more bits of broken china. The phone rang. After two rings the answering machine picked it up in silence. Then I hauled the trash (coffee grounds and smashed china) out and prowled around the house. Nothing suspicious. No footprints in the flower beds, pipe bombs or threatening communications.

Nothing but murder.

Back inside I poured a fresh cup of coffee—well, mug; the cups were all casualties—and sat at the kitchen table. Joni Ames was dead. Homicide. I could come up with three possibilities: One. Random killing—that seemed unlikely. Two. Someone gunning for Joni. Three. Someone gunning for Dakota. *Hope for the best, plan for the worst.* I was going with number three, that someone was gunning for Dakota.

Okay. Who?

She didn't have any enemies, or if she did, we hadn't been able to come up with them. From anonymous letters and dead flowers to murder? It was a stretch—big stretch. More than that; it didn't make sense. I played with it and I still couldn't make it make sense. The thing is that in order to understand an apparently senseless action, you have to get into the mind of the one who conceived it. And that's impossible. The twisted imaginings of the criminal and the insane are inconceivable to the sane.

I sighed. What it added up to was nothing. So I figured I'd go out and beat the bushes, see what I could scare up. And I figured to start with Cal. He was handy; he was a no-good jerk with a record to prove it; he was a black-mailer. It was not only a start, it was a good start.

I turned on the TV looking for news and found morning talk shows, hit the mute button and tried the radio. The dial was already set to a country station. I listened to the end of a song I didn't recognize and then to two DJs talking in shocked tones about Joni Ames's death.

They couldn't believe a country artist had been gunned down. Maybe a gun-toting, drug-sniffing, woman-raping, trouble-hungry rap star, but a *country* artist?

They couldn't believe it had happened in Nashville. New York, LA, Chicago or Miami, sure, but *Nashville*?

And they especially couldn't believe it had happened to someone as nice and sweet and kind and talented as Joni.

The phone rang. The answering machine got it.

On the surface I agreed with them. Unfortunately we were using our sense, common sense and good sense, not the warped and distorted sense of a killer. I wanted to know what the police were thinking. *Yeah. Right.* For that I needed an in. I wasn't guessing. I knew.

He picked up on the first ring. "Henley. Homicide."

"Hey, Bill, it's Kat."

"Jesus, Kat, you're an early bird today."

I looked at the clock; ten-fifteen, eight-fifteen at home in Sacramento. "I'm in Nashville."

"Yeah? What for?"

"Long story. Short version is it turned into murder. I think the intended victim was a woman I'm working with here."

"Kat." I heard him slurp at the coffee that's never far from his hand. "You're young, smart and pretty. You need to work a job with a lot less corpses. Trust me on this." Another slurp.

"I know. You're right. Meanwhile, I need help." Chewing sounds on his end. A frosted cruller, I'd put money on it. "Hey, what happened to your diet?"

He grunted, a little grumpy maybe. "Whaddya need, Kat?"

"Would you call Sergeant Deeter, Nashville PD—homicide, I assume—and put in a good word for me? Right now he wouldn't give me the time of day if he were wearing two watches and standing under a clock."

"You got it." He spoke through a mouthful of doughnut. "When you getting back?"

"I don't know. Murder really screws up your schedule."

"Yeah. Tell me about it. Keep me posted."

"Thanks, Bill."

"Yeah."

"You want cowboy boots?"

He laughed.

I crossed my fingers for the next call. Hank was hard to catch. Cops often are. An all too familiar voice answered. *Shit!* Where was Voicemail when you needed it?

"Homicide. May I help you?"

The voice trilled musically in my ear. I gritted my teeth.

"Sergeant Parker, please."

"I'll see if he's available. Who's calling?" Jewel inquired sweetly, smoothly.

She knows my name, just as I know hers, but she won't admit it.

It's her way of getting back at me because I have Hank and she doesn't, though God knows she's tried.

"Amelia Earhart."

"Huh?"

"Amelia Earhart."

Silence. It was a problem, all right. I was lying and she knew it—that part was easy. Unfortunately she couldn't call me on it without admitting she knew who I was. After all, there *could* be two Amelia Earharts, or I could be Amelia Earhart's illegitimate granddaughter. Actually I was amazed she knew the name—history never struck me as her strong point. Maybe she picked it up on *Jeopardy*? Score so far: 1–0. My favor.

"One moment, please." Her tone was frosty and she thunked the phone down. Apparently I didn't rate the hold button. "I'm sorry, he seems to have stepped away from his desk. May I take a message?"

Ha! It would never get to him, not in a million years. Guess how I know this? "Is Davis there? I'll talk to him." Davis is Hank's partner. Davis and his wife, Maggie, are good friends of ours.

"One moment, I'll check." From frosty to glacial. "Your name again, please?"

"Emily Brontë."

"Emmmm . . ." More lies, but once again, she couldn't say that without admitting she remembered the first name and was just being a jerk by asking. "Emmmm . . ." She gave it up. 2–0. Still my favor.

"I'm sorry," Jewel said after a *very* brief pause—too brief to have checked. "He doesn't seem to be here either."

Notice there was no helpful offer to take a message or direct my call elsewhere. 2–1. I thought it over quickly as I listened to the sounds of a roomful of detectives talking, occasionally laughing.

"Give me a cop, *any* cop." She *couldn't* say there wasn't a cop there. She didn't. 3–1. Without a word she clicked me on hold. The phone rang once, was picked up.

"Sanders."

"Hi, this is Kat Colorado. I'm Hank Parker's girlfriend and—"

"Hey, Kat, sure. Hank's spoken of you." He said it like

I was someone he would like to know, which was nice.

"Detective—"

"Joe."

"Joe, I need to talk to Hank and I'm out of town and hard to reach. May I leave a message with you?"

"You bet, but hold on a minute, I just saw him. Let me try 'n' track him down."

"You're a peach."

He chuckled and put me on hold. I listened to Tim McGraw singing about how he was messed up in Mexico living off refried dreams. I sang along with the radio. Refried dreams are not news to me. Unfortunately.

"Katy?"

"Hey Hank."

"Where are you, sweetheart? Joe said you were out of town."

"Nashville."

He took that one in. "Dakota?"

"Bingo. And murder."

Silence. I know this silence well, have heard it often in our two years together. I explained, being as low-key as possible without actually lying. Not that it fooled him. He knows me too well.

"I need your help," I finished up. "Would you call a Sergeant Deeter here in Nashville and put in a good word for me? Please," I added.

"Against my better judgment," he said, but he was smiling, I could tell.

"You're okay, I don't care what they say about you."

He laughed.

"Now?" I asked.

"Now," he said. "I'm looking forward to Yosemite, Katy." Translation: *I love you and I miss you. Can't wait to see you.*

"Me, too." Translation: *Ditto.* "Here's Dakota's number." I raced through it. "Talk to you soon." We both hung up on a smile. I gave Deeter twenty minutes and then I called. Having Bill and Hank call might not help, but it couldn't hurt. He was in. *Hot damn*. This was my lucky day with Ma Bell and cops.

"Hey, Kat. You got any more out-of-state cops gonna call me?"

"You need 'em, sergeant, I got 'em."

"Hell, you might as well call me Jimmy. Everyone else does. And no, I don't need 'em. Two's enough. What can I do for you, Kat?"

Wow, he was almost cordial. I love being on the inside loop. *Start off with a polite disclaimer*, I thought. "I don't want to get in your way, Jimmy. I'm just worried about Dakota."

"You got the right to be."

"And the reason?"

"I think so. Can't prove a thing yet, but I think so. She should take it easy and careful. *Real* easy. *Real* careful."

He had something; I was sure of it. I wasn't sure how to get it though. "You know something even if you can't prove it?"

He hesitated. So I was right.

"I know something," he agreed finally. "No reason you shouldn't know it. Miss Jones as well. In fact I was going to call you with it later anyway. For now I don't want it going any farther than you two."

"All right."

"We found a note on the body."

"A note?" It was the last thing I expected.

"It said: 'Now we're even, Dakota.' "

"Typed?"

"Handwritten. Block letters, all capitals. No punctuation."

"Unsigned?"

"Yes."

"And you think Dakota was the target?"

"Not necessarily, although it does make it a much stronger possibility. I'll say it again. Miss Jones should be *real* careful."

We were in perfect agreement on that one.

"Thanks for the information, Jimmy."

"You're welcome."

Dakota walked in as I was hanging up the phone. "Katy." She looked awful. "I didn't sleep very well, did you?" She looked at me closely. "No. Dumb question, huh? I wish I knew more about Joni. I've got to find out, talk to her family. I don't even know if she was married, if she had children, if—"

"Dakota."

She looked at me wordlessly.

"You can't change it. She's dead."

"Because of me."

"No, you don't know that. We can't know that. And even if we were certain she was mistaken for you it wouldn't make you responsible. You didn't harm her or wish her harm. You didn't, couldn't have known about this and you couldn't have prevented it. Don't assume responsibility or feel guilty. Don't play God." I poured her a mug of coffee. "Milk? Sugar?"

She shook her head and cupped her hands around the mug. "It's so hard," she whispered. "So sad."

"Yes."

"She was young and talented and—"

"Dakota—" I stopped, trying to think of a way of saying this without sounding harsh and unfeeling. There really wasn't one. "Joni Ames is dead and we can't change that. Let's focus on something else, on who killed her."

"No one knows."

"Not yet," I agreed.

"But how—?" She stopped, stared at me with huge, hurt eyes. "Oh. That's what you do, isn't it?"

"That's what I do." *If I have to,* I amended silently.

She sipped at her coffee, made a face, then got up and poured it into the sink. "You're not a coffee drinker, are you, Katy?"

"Not really. I drink it when it's around but I prefer tea or diet Dr Pepper."

"I can tell." She made a fresh pot. "So," she said as she waited for caffeine input, "so, let's nail this sucker." Her voice was soft and dangerous.

Good. Her spunk was back. The fear was there still, I knew, but it was controlled.

"What do we do?"

"Start where we are. Let's listen to your messages."

"Okay, but—never mind," she added quickly as she caught the expression on my face. "C'mon then, let's."

We walked into her office. The red light blinked at us and the machine told us there were eight messages. Dakota punched the message retrieval button.

"Dakota, call me at once. It's important." Garrett sounded serious. Joni was dead, I bet, and the cops had just called him.

"Dakota, I'm at the Bluebird. Where are you? Call if you've been delayed."

It was a male voice, deep and sexy and pissed. I looked the question at Dakota.

"Link," she answered.

"Dakota, call me whenever you get in. Anytime, it doesn't matter. Call!" Garrett. Very serious, very worried.

"Dakota, what the hell is going on? I thought we had a date."

Link. He wasn't pissed anymore—it was way beyond that. He sounded like generic ugly male to me and it didn't make me want to like him. *Pissed?* Why not concerned or worried?

sixteen

MURDER: CAREER OPPORTUNITY

DAKOTA CALLED GARRETT FIRST. LINK HAD STOPPED calling last night after the second message but Garrett called four more times, last night and this morning both.

"Garrett, I'm fine. I'm pretty upset, of course. You must see if we can do anything, help in any way. . . . No, I just got your messages this morning. Last night I talked to the police and—Garrett, *for godssake*, a woman we know is *dead*. Not just anyone, someone we knew and liked. . . . I know, I *know*. Of course we have to consider the fallout and what to do about it, but not yet. Joni's dead and we have to deal with that first. . . . All right. Yes. . . . Yes. One-thirty. . . . *No.* We'll do it my way." She hung up, walked over to the stove and poured coffee.

"Is it so hard to understand, Katy, that right now I just want to mourn Joni, see if I can help, things like that—not use this in some way to further or enhance or publicize my career? Garrett didn't come right out and say it but he was talking about how to use Joni's death to my advantage. He wants to make a career opportunity out of *murder*!" She slammed the coffeepot down.

I was less shocked than Dakota, more aware perhaps of how much it happened. More cynical, too.

"I'm sorry, Dakota. Tell him to go to hell. You're the boss."

"He wants me to hold a press conference this afternoon." She spoke as though she hadn't heard me.

"Are you going to?"

"Yes. I want to make a public statement, to apologize."

Uh-oh. I was on Dakota's side, not Garrett's, but I didn't like the sound of this. "Apologize for what?"

"For her death."

That's what I was afraid of. "People make public apologies when they've done something wrong, when they're culpable. What did you do wrong? How are you guilty?"

"Well, I'm not but—"

"But you think it should have been you instead of her? That you should be lying on a slab in the morgue, not Joni?" I was deliberately harsh.

"That's not what I think. God knows it's not what I want, it's just—just that life isn't fair," she said bleakly. "And it sure wasn't fair to Joni."

"No."

"What should I do then, Katy?"

"Express your sympathy. I wouldn't say anything about the possible connection between you and Joni and the last-minute scheduling change without running it by the cops first. Play it the way they tell you."

"Okay."

"What time is the press conference?"

"This afternoon. Garrett's sending a car for me at one-thirty. He said it would be easier and safer that way."

"Good." I nodded in agreement.

"He said not to talk to the press or anyone else. I have to call Link, though. What shall I tell him?"

"That we were late leaving for the club last night, that we heard it on the news and you were too upset to go out to a club. That's not only understandable, that's pretty much what happened. Abbreviated version, anyway."

She looked up the number and picked up the phone. He answered quickly.

"Link, it's—"

"What the hell is going on?"

I could hear his angry response easily. I poured myself

another cup of coffee. *Whoa!* Dakota was right, her coffee was a lot better than mine. And I listened, assuming that if Dakota had wanted to be private she would have gone into her bedroom.

"Link—" Dakota tried again and didn't get anywhere.

I couldn't hear the words this time, just his voice, a loud, irate, unpleasant voice.

"Shut up and listen!" Dakota was angry, though I thought from the sound of her voice that there were tears behind the anger. "Joni Ames was killed last night. *Shot* at a recording studio. I heard about it and was too upset to remember to call you and cancel. It wasn't rude and impolite, it was *murder*. I don't owe you an apology, *you* owe *me* one. Don't bother to call again without one. In fact, don't bother to call at all for a while!" She slammed the phone down.

I applauded her—silently on the outside, loudly on the inside. I was afraid that Link might be a younger, prettier, only slightly nicer version of Cal. I didn't want that for Dakota. Whatever it was, Dakota was playing it very differently this time.

"Are you hungry, Katy? I'm starving. Let's have breakfast again." We left the office for the kitchen. "I think I have onions and peppers. Want an omelet?" She foraged around in the refrigerator. "Oh good, mushrooms too. And cheese. Will you make some juice?"

The phone rang and Dakota ignored it, letting the machine pick it up. We ate huge omelets and mountains of toast with homemade Granny Mae preserves. Death, especially sudden death, makes you very appreciative of the sweet taste of life.

"Do you want me to go with you?"

"To the press conference? No, I'll be fine. Garrett's a good manager, he really is. And I'm grateful that he puts me and my best interests first. Most of the time I am. When he gets it wrong, like today, I only have to tell him once. Why don't you take the time off, relax, grab a nap?"

"Okay."

"Good." She smiled at me.

"Do you have Cal's address, Dakota?"

The smile disappeared. "That doesn't sound like a nap to me."

"I need to talk to him." More than that: I was looking forward to it. A lot.

"I know the address. He has an unlisted phone number, although I'm sure I could get it if you want?" She tipped the last phrase up in a question.

"I reckon I'll just pop on by for a friendly little visit."

She gave me a serious look. "Don't underestimate Cal, Katy."

"No." I started stacking dirty dishes into the dishwasher.

seventeen

SILVER-TONGUED DEVIL

THE HOUSE LOOKED LIKE CAL. OLDER AND KIND OF run-down, but with a hint of devil-may-care charm. It needed paint, the shrubs needed pruning and the windows hadn't been washed since sometime in the Nixon administration. The car had, though; a sleek and spotless vintage Cadillac sat in the driveway. I wrote down the tag before I got out of Dakota's Pathfinder and headed up an unswept walkway to the house.

The sun was out but the place looked dark and silent, almost forbidding. The curtains were drab and frayed. Someone had tried to pull them closed but here and there they gapped and the sunshine struggled inside through dusty windows. I leaned on the doorbell, heard it clamor somewhere in the house. No answer. Leaned again. No answer. And again.

"Son of a bitch!"

I smiled. *Off to a good start.* Cal is a charmer all right, a silver-tongued, sweet-talking devil. The door opened. A man wearing jeans, a two-day growth and a scowl lounged against the doorframe. His feet and chest were bare. There was gray in the abundant dark hair on his head and chest. He held the door open about two feet, bracing it with an arm held at a perfect angle for a clear bulging bicep-and-armpit shot. Lucky me.

"Well, I'll be damned," he drawled. "Just about the last person in the whole fuckin' world I wanted to see. Even a Jehovah's Witness would be better than you, Kat."

See what I mean about the charm? Practically irresistible. "Hey, Cal."

"You're a long ways from home, aren't you, Kat? Not a long enough ways from my home, though." He slid his hand down the door, re-forming the bicep and losing the armpit view—a refreshing change. "Notice there's no welcome mat? It ain't no accident." He slammed the door shut.

At two feet it wasn't much of a slam. It was nothing at all with my boot stuck in the door.

He opened the door again, looked at me for a long time, face expressionless. Lines were carved deep into his face now. Not laugh lines, I thought, but anger and greed, fear and revenge and hard living.

"Never one to take a hint, were you, Kat?"

"Yes and no. In this case, no."

"Always turning up, just like a fuckin' bad penny."

"Yup," I agreed cheerfully.

He stepped back, pulling the door with him. It was the closest thing to an invitation I was going to get. I followed him in, blinking in the dim light.

The decorating scheme was an interesting combination of white trash and guy mode: bulky furniture that I could barely discern in the dimness in shades of what seemed to be brown and gloom; full ashtrays and empty beer cans; a tipped-over bottle of Jack Daniel's; an empty pizza carton open on the coffee table. A guitar leaned comfortably against a La-Z-Boy, a beer can kicked over beside it. The place smelled worse than it looked, which was saying something.

"Nice place. Who's your decorator?"

He grunted. I followed him back to the kitchen. Same style but fewer beer cans and a whole lot of dirty dishes. A cast-iron frying pan with at least an inch of congealed gray fat sat on the filthy stove. It had a lived-in look although the homey touch was missing. Maybe he thought adding garbage to a place was homey?

"How you doing, Cal?"

Cal kicked open the back door, letting sunshine and fresh air in—what a concept—then hauled a carton of orange juice out of the refrigerator. He drank thirstily from the carton, spilling a little, then dragged the back of his hand across his mouth. He didn't offer me anything, which was neither a surprise nor a disappointment. Manners were never his strong suit.

"You can't stand me. I can't stand you. So what the fuck you want, Kat? What are you doing here?"

"Dakota," I said softly.

"We don't have nuthin' to do with each other anymore. Nuthin'. And I don't want nuthin' to do with you, either."

"Half right, Cal. She doesn't have anything to do with you. You prove you don't have anything to do with her and I'm gone."

"What the hell you talking about?" He shrugged with (studied?) nonchalance and hauled on the refrigerator door, treating me to the sight of another housekeeping nightmare. I stared in fascination—I couldn't help myself.

Okay, I didn't try that hard.

I identified ketchup, barbecue sauce, pickles, a bucket of take-out fried chicken, individually wrapped cheese singles tossed gaily around. A carton of ice cream, fudge ripple maybe, that someone had mistakenly put in the refrigerator instead of the freezer dripped onto plastic-wrapped chops of suspicious color and character, and a shriveled head of iceberg lettuce. Plenty of Pabst Blue Ribbon.

Cal pulled out a Blue Ribbon, twisted off the top, tipped his head back and sucked it down like a starving baby. He drained it, belched—there was that charm again—reached into the still-open refrigerator for another.

"Wanna beer?"

"No, thanks." It was eleven-thirty in the morning.

"So what are you talking about, Kat?"

"You. History."

"Huh?"

He kicked a kitchen chair away from the table and sat, waving at me to do the same. I did. I checked the chair before I sat down, though. Seemed like a good idea in this house.

"I remember the bruises on Dakota's arms and legs, the swelling and the black eyes."

His face darkened and he slugged down his beer. "Like you said—history."

"I remember how you stood in the way of Dakota's career, how when that didn't work and she left you, you sued her for a million bucks. And lost."

"What's your point, Kat?" He tried with the nonchalance again. Failed.

"Even now you don't miss a chance to bad-mouth Dakota, to run her down and try to tear her up."

"You got me confused with someone who gives a shit." His voice was light but his face was still dark. And wary, I thought.

"Oh, you care, Cal, you care a lot that Dakota's doing so well. Especially now that your singing career is history, a sad memory. A memory getting sadder every year."

He got up to get another beer. *A sad drowning memory,* I amended. *A sodden, drunken, drowning memory.*

"Recently you asked Dakota for help, you asked her to record one of your songs. She turned her back on you, laughed at the thought."

He was getting riled. Good. I laughed too, as Dakota had, thought I'd see if I could work him up some more—not usually a tough task with Cal. His hands clenched the beer bottle, knuckles whitening. Good.

"Who could blame her?" I spoke so softly that without thinking he leaned forward to hear. "You used her, lied, stole money and songs and recording opportunities, cheated on her, sued her, and then you were surprised when she didn't record your song?" I laughed again. "But you hadn't run out of ideas yet, had you, Cal? So you tried extortion. Now that's a nice little felony. Everyone loves a blackmailer." The sarcasm was heavy in my voice.

"Fuck you, Kat." His teeth were clenched.

"You're angry and bitter and still trying to get Dakota. Someone's harassing her, threatening her. Someone threw a grenade at a concert. Who do you think looks like number one on the suspect sheet? Where do you think the smart money's going, Cal?''

''Hell with you.'' He slammed his beer bottle on the table. It foamed but didn't spill over. He had that one down all right; Cal was a man who hated to waste beer. ''You can't prove a thing. I wasn't even in Memphis that Saturday, the night the guy threw the flash bomb.''

I smiled. *Did I say Memphis? Or flash bomb? Or Saturday?* Sheesh. Oldest trick in the book. Only the bad guys on *Murder, She Wrote* are still dumb enough to walk into that one.

''Memphis? Saturday? Flash bomb? I didn't say that. How did you know?''

''I read it in the fucking papers, just like the rest of the country. Get a grip, Kat. And get the hell out of here.''

''How come you're so defensive?'' I didn't bother to wait for the answer he wasn't going to give me. ''I'm not the only one asking, Cal. The police are too.''

''What do I give a fuck?'' The bravado was forced, the beer courage faltering. He smiled, a smile so fake it made the bravado look natural. ''Look, I'm not a monster, Kat. Sure, Dakota and I have had our differences. That's no secret. But I wouldn't hurt her. Hell, I wouldn't want to see her hurt by anyone.'' He smiled again. Insincere again. He got up for another beer. ''Hey, sure you won't have one? Old times' sake, all that?''

''Maybe it started out as a game, Cal—the harassment, the threats. Maybe. But the stakes are a lot higher now.''

He turned, his body silhouetted in the light of the refrigerator, an unopened beer in his hand.

''What do you mean?'' The corner of his left eye twisted in a nervous tic. ''What the hell you talking about?''

''Murder.''

''Huh?'' He kicked the refrigerator door shut and sat, the unopened Blue Ribbon still in his hand. ''Someone *killed* Dakota?'' He sounded surprised but not shocked or saddened. *Interesting.*

"A woman similar in appearance to Dakota. Who was the killer after, Cal?"

"How the hell should I know?" He shook his head as if to clear it, as if things were coming too fast now.

"I suppose you have an alibi for then, too?" I winced. *Alibi.* Sheesh. I think they only say that on *Murder, She Wrote* too.

"I don't need a fucking alibi, I didn't do it." He brandished the beer bottle like a weapon. "I didn't fucking do it, get it?" He hurled the bottle at me. It missed, but not by much, not by enough, and smashed an out-of-date girlie calendar on the wall, splashing glass and beer everywhere.

Cal was breathing hard, as though he'd been running, pumping iron or fighting. The sweat stood out on his forehead in beads. The volatile temper, the violent streak in him hadn't mellowed, hadn't changed much at all.

"You didn't do what?" a plaintive voice asked.

She was slim and dark and wore black leggings and cowboy boots and an XL man's denim shirt with pearl buttons. Cal's size. Her hair was tousled and her young face had the vague unformed look of one who had just woken up. Her features were simple and regular with no hint of prettiness, only youth. Serious youth. Old enough to drive but maybe not to vote, was my guess.

"Didn't do what?" Her voice was petulant and she rubbed her eyes with both fists. "Didn't do what, Callie?"

He growled. *Callie?* I bit back a smirk and a smart-ass comment.

"Hi." I smiled at her. "What's your name?"

"Trudy. Trudy Montell." She spoke like a third-grader answering a teacher.

"Did you—"

"Get the fuck outta here, Kat." Cal started toward me. I knew by his face and voice that he meant it. So I moved fast, stayed ahead of him.

"Didn't do *what?*" Trudy whined. "Cal? Didn't do—"

The door slammed shut on her whine.

eighteen

GOOD AND GODDAMN SORRY

IT WAS A TOSS-UP.

I tossed it around as I climbed into the Pathfinder and drove off. Worth a shot, I decided, and pulled on the sunglasses and baseball cap I'd stashed on the seat next to me, slid around a corner and parked. Cal could leave his house in either direction but I was betting on this one. It fed directly into the main road in this part of East Nashville, from there into downtown or the freeways; the other way out meandered off into a residential part of town.

I smacked a perplexed-and-lost-driver look onto my face as I opened a map and spread it out on the steering wheel. I didn't have a lot of time, maybe half an hour. People tend to notice you in residential districts. And right after they notice you, they tend to call the cops. That was something I could do without right now.

It wasn't thirty minutes, it was seventeen. And it wasn't the cops, it was the Cadillac. I heard it first—it was way overdue for a trip to the muffler shop—watched as it growled through the intersection. Cal didn't bother to check the side streets for traffic. Or for me. So far so good. I folded up my map, tossed the hat on the seat, started the car and headed back the way I had come. I only had to ring once this time.

"Hey Trudy."

"Oh . . . hi." Her eyes were red and puffy and her voice had gone from whiny to wan. The voice was an improvement but not much of one. The eyes were definitely worse. I started to feel sorry for her.

"I forgot to tell Cal something. Could you let him know I'm here, please?" I lied like a rug.

"He's left."

"Oh!" I hit just the right note of surprise and annoyance. "Well, *shoot*, now what am I going to do?"

She stared at me blankly, moving fast from wan to pathetic. Cal sure knew how to pick the helpless and vulnerable ones. With a stab I realized I did too.

"Maybe you could help?"

"Oh . . . I dunno, I don't think so." Her eyes teared up. "I—" She broke off and flapped a hand helplessly.

"Are you okay? You don't look like it. Can I help?" I switched gears fast, opportunistic as well as concerned.

"Look, I'm in a hurry. I've got to go. I don't want to be here when—I don't have a car and—"

"May I give you a ride somewhere?"

"Okay." There was relief in her voice. "Lemme get my purse and stuff." When she returned I noted that she had traded Cal's shirt for an oversize sweater that reeked of cigarette smoke. She was carrying a jacket and a huge purse. Almost running, she beat me to the car and jumped in the minute I opened the door. She locked her door immediately and slumped down as if to make herself less visible.

"Where are we going, Trudy?"

"Oh, ummmm, just drive, okay. Just get *out* of here. Please. I sorta should make a phone call before . . . Just drive, *okay*?"

"How about getting some breakfast? You can make your phone call and figure out what you want to do then."

"Oh, yeah, great. Just—just I don't want to go anywhere where I'm known or where . . . ummmm . . ."

Where Cal might be, I silently finished for her.

"Not near Music Row or anything, you know, nothing popular, nothing like that."

"Okay."

We drove for a while in silence, then Trudy turned on the radio and fiddled with the dial until she found a country station she liked.

"Why are you afraid?"

"Who? *Me? I'm* not afraid." Her voice was startled and afraid. She was lying like a rug too, but she wasn't very good at it.

"Who are you afraid of?" I asked the obvious again.

"*No* one. Why should I be? Why are you asking these dumb questions?" On the radio Travis Tritt was singing "Here's a Quarter (Call Someone Who Cares)." Trudy burst into tears and started rummaging through her bag.

I glanced at her, then looked back at the road. Green light, gas station, strip mall, McDonald's. Glanced back at Trudy again.

She looked at me and said, "He's never hit me before. I don't like it." She blew her nose, wadded up the tissue and stuffed it back in her bag.

I turned into the asphalt parking lot of the Country Diner. "Does this look okay?"

She nodded, fished around in her purse, pulled out a lipstick and made her lips a vampire-red slash on her pale face. She looked around the restaurant carefully as we entered, then picked a seat in a corner booth with a good view of the action. There was a huge crash in the kitchen. Trudy jumped and gasped, grabbed at my arm before she could catch herself. Someone in the kitchen yelled "*Shit!*" Trudy sank into her seat and disappeared behind the menu. Her hands were shaking.

I *despise* men who prey on women and children.

Trudy carefully placed the menu on the table, pushed her silverware around, then piled it on her napkin. "You've been awful nice to me 'n' all and I don't even know your name."

"Kat Colorado."

"Oh. Are you a singer?"

"No. Cal and I used to be friends," I said, stretching the truth out to a thin black line, then watching it disappear.

"Really?"

"You ready to order?"

The waitress snapped her gum and acted like someone who didn't care one way or the other. I glimpsed a shabby, stained bra between the buttons of a gaping uniform that had fit her two sizes ago.

I ordered iced tea. Trudy ordered eggs, sausage, grits, hash browns, biscuits and gravy and hesitated over the apricot Danish. The waitress—Ruby, her name tag informed us—listened in silence without writing anything down, smacked her gum and left.

"How often does Cal hit you?" I asked as Ruby swung her ample rear and walked away. Trudy had said that it was the first time that Cal had hit her. Not that that was necessarily the truth. Women frequently lie to protect their abusers. Or what's left of their pride and self-esteem.

"That was the first time, I swear." She held a hand up like a child. *I pledge allegiance to the flag of the . . .*

Ruby brought our iced tea and Trudy dumped a pound or so of sugar in the large glass without tasting it.

"What didn't Cal do? What did you mean by asking that? Is he seeing some other woman, is that it? He's fooling around with someone, isn't he? Oh God, is that it? Is it?" There was pain in her voice. "Is it?"

"No, that's not it."

"He's not fooling around with anyone?" Relief flooded her voice.

"I don't know that." But I did, of course. Cal was probably fooling around. If he wasn't now, he would be soon. I left that issue behind. "Does he ever mention Dakota?"

"No. Well, not to me. I overheard him talking to someone on the phone one time. It's not her, though, he wouldn't fool around with her. I think he hates her. He called her a two-timing, scheming little bitch." I could hear the satisfaction in her voice. Her eyes were wide, happy that Dakota wasn't in Cal's life.

I was saddened. For Dakota in the past and Trudy now, Trudy who was afraid she was going to lose the man who hit her. The food arrived. Trudy slashed open her fried eggs and mixed them in with the grits. Carefully she cut up her sausage into bite-size chunks. Then she sighed and looked at it contentedly for a moment before eating.

"He said that she was gonna get hers, that she was gonna be good and goddamn sorry. 'One sorry bitch,' he said."

Good and goddamn sorry. I'd forgotten that expression of Cal's. "She?" I asked, just to be sure.

"Dakota." Trudy ate without pausing, speaking through grits and eggs. "And that he was gonna be good and goddamned glad."

"Did he say how she was going to get hers? What she would be sorry about?"

Trudy shrugged, chasing a bite of sausage around her plate with her fork. "I dunno. I didn't bother to listen real close. He was mad about some songs, I think. And money. He was real mad about money. Cal says that anyone who does him wrong—well, he says 'fucks with me'—is a dead man." She shivered. "He can be real mean. *Real* mean, I've seen it. I think he'd do just about anything to hurt someone he didn't like."

She looked at me solemnly. "He doesn't like you, you know. You said you were friends once. Well, those are the people he hates most, the ones who were his friends and aren't now." She mopped up the last of her gravy with a biscuit—a little gal with a big appetite for food and bad judgment in men.

"Who does Cal hang out with?"

"I dunno. The guys in his band, I guess. Other musicians, songwriters, you know."

"Anyone in particular?"

"I dunno. Sonny, I guess. Sonny Graves."

"Where would I find Sonny?"

"At Sal's. It's a crummy bar in East Nashville around Five Points. Seems like Sonny's 'bout always there. Cal goes there too." She looked at me sideways.

The waitress ambled over and filled up our iced teas. "That it?" The southern hospitality and graciousness I was getting used to was conspicuously absent. I nodded. Too soon. Trudy ordered a sweet roll.

"Are you and Cal together a lot, Trudy?"

"How do you mean?"

"Do you do things together—dinner, movies, going away for the weekend, that kind of thing?"

"Not really. I work nights. If I get off early enough, we'll go out for a drink or a bite to eat or to a club, but mostly we just go home."

"Your home?"

"Cal's. He doesn't like to sleep alone. He likes to have somebody—well, me—there."

"And then you leave in the morning?"

"Yeah. Hey, don't be making it sound like something cheap. It's not that at all. Cal likes me a *lot*. He does. He *does*. One night I got off work so I could go hear him play and he saw me come in and dedicated a song to me. It was real sweet. I won't never forget it. The song was 'Honky Tonk Hero' and he said he was singing it to the gal who took the honky tonk out of him and put the hero in." She smiled and fluttered her eyelids at me. "Isn't that *something*?"

"Yes." It was a one-syllable word but I had a tough time getting it out. Slimeballs don't improve with age, they get worse. I put down a twenty to cover the check.

"Oh, you don't have to do that," Trudy said halfheartedly, without even pretending to reach for her wallet. "Look, you won't tell on me to Cal, will you. Man, he'd *kill* me if he knew I'd been talking to you like this." The words came out in a rush.

"Kill you?"

"Hey, it's just an expression. *Jeez*. He hit me *once*. It's no big deal. It was an accident. He said he was sorry and it would never happen again."

"Accident?"

Her face darkened. "It's over, okay? Leave it be."

I nodded. I would try. That kind of thing is real tough for me, though.

"Did you and Cal go out last Saturday?"

"No. I was working."

"What did he do?

"That night?"

I nodded.

"I dunno. He gets mad when I ask stuff like that. He says his life is none of my business. Like the Saturday night you're asking about? Well, he was supposed to pick me up and he didn't. He didn't answer his phone all that night. I know 'cause I called him and called him. You think it was another woman?" Trudy's voice rose on an anxious note.

Maybe, I thought. *Or maybe a flash grenade bombing in Memphis.*

"Do you?"

"I don't know. Where do you work, Trudy?"

"The Horseshoe Lounge."

"Cocktail waitress?"

"Yeah." She picked up her iced tea, then put it down untouched. "He *said* he was just playing music with some guys and lost track of the time." Her voice was plaintive and her eyes didn't meet mine. "Look, I gotta make my phone call." She stood and walked off stiffly.

The waitress sullenly slapped my change down on the table, snapped her gum and yanked Trudy's plate away. I left her a five-dollar tip. Maybe it would change her day? She looked like she needed a break.

Trudy came back to the table but didn't sit. "I'm all set, going over to my girlfriend's until—well, for now. You ready?"

I was ready. We walked.

"If you need help or want to reach me, call me at this number. Leave a message. I'll call you back."

She shrugged. *Yeah. Right.* That kind of a shrug. I dropped a slip of paper with my name and Dakota's manager's phone number on it into her bag.

"Cal hit Dakota. And cheated on her. She wasn't the first." *Or the last.* "The cheating, the hitting—it doesn't just stop."

"You got it all wrong," Trudy said sullenly, climbing into the Pathfinder and slamming the door.

I used to think that nothing could make me despise Cal Jenkins more than I already did.

I was wrong.

nineteen

COUNTRY COUSIN, CITY MURDER

AFTER I DROPPED TRUDY OFF, I HEADED BACK TO DAkota's. I told myself it was to check on messages and be available for Dakota, but really it was in hope of peace and quiet. I had had enough of distraught females for a while. On the road "Your Cheatin' Heart" played over and over in the airways of my mind. I turned the radio on to delete the stuck record in my head. Dakota was singing "See Ya!" which made me smile.

Dakota's house was quiet, serene. No messages, no notes, no threatening mail, no nothing. I could hear the quiet tick-tock of the old-fashioned clock on the mantel. A huge basket of flowers sat on the dining room table. Not fancy flowers but simple traditional blooms, sweet-smelling and fragrant.

I made a cup of tea and sat at the table to scan the paper for news updates. Political squabbles, a spring flood, a hit-and-run. I saw nothing about Joni's death or the flash grenade or Dakota.

No news is good news?

Not in a murder investigation.

Or a bombing investigation.

I pushed the paper away, cupped the tea in my hands and tried to recapture the measured tick-tock of the clock, the beauty of the flowers, the peace of mind.

Then the police called.

And Hope stopped by.

And I gave up.

Sergeant Deeter wasn't a bundle of joy or optimism, even considering that joy and optimism are a reach when you're a cop.

"Kat. Jimmy Deeter."

It wasn't just so-so news, it was bad news. I could tell from his voice. "Hey, Jimmy."

"We didn't come up with anything. Nobody saw the shooting, nobody saw anything or anybody suspicious. Nobody saw a vehicle. Nobody heard the gunshots. We can't even pin the time down more closely than the coroner's estimate."

Days like this no one goes to Vegas.

"Now what? Where does that leave you?" I couldn't think of much but they were the professionals.

"We watch, we wait."

Not great. That sounded like the kind of stuff I did. "Is that anything like up shit creek without a paddle?"

"Yeah," he sighed. "It is. My gut instinct on this is that it's one person at work. I'm talking about Miss Jones here, not the murder. So far the intention has been to scare. Dead flowers, anonymous letters, a flash grenade—all the time the pace picking up. No reason not to expect that to continue. Just the opposite."

"And the murder? The note? Was Dakota the intended victim?"

"I don't know. We haven't found a connection other than the fact that she was originally scheduled to be at the recording studio and that she and the victim are similar in appearance. And the note. But it's a connection, no doubt about it, and it don't set that easy with me. We haven't found anything in the victim's life to indicate a reason for murder."

"No jealous husband or boyfriend; nobody who inherits

a million if she dies; no record deal that she cheated someone out of?''

''If it's there, we haven't found it. Look, this is all off
the record.''

''I understand.''

''I'm telling you because it's my strong recommendation
that Miss Jones maintain a real low profile, preferably stay
completely out of public view, even leave town for a month
or two. *Strong* recommendation.''

He emphasized strong. *Really* emphasized it. If he'd been
Dakota's mom, he would have grounded her indefinitely.
TV dinners, blackout curtains, bulletproof vests, the works.

''What's Plan B?''

He was silent for a three count. ''You're not taking this
seriously.''

''Yeah, I am, Jimmy. I'm not the problem, though. Dakota is. She held a press conference earlier today.''

His turn to be silent.

''She's in the middle of a concert schedule and the many
other commitments that go along with that. And it's not
just the schedule, of course; it's her career.''

''I understand. Course, kinda hard to sing when you're
dead.'' His voice was laconic in the extreme.

I shivered, Joni's bloody image in my mind. ''There's
nothing to directly link Joni's death with Dakota?'' I asked
again. Just in case we'd missed something. Just because I
was nervous and jumpy and couldn't let it drop.

''No. Helluva coincidence though, don't you think?''

I did, yes. And I knew enough cops to know how they
felt about coincidence. In the background I heard someone
hollering for Deeter.

''Hey, gotta go, Kat. I'll get back to you I get anything
new.''

He hung up and the doorbell rang. Today was starting
to feel like a soap opera. Same back-to-back pacing, same
building suspense and sense of foreboding. Only thing
missing was the commercial breaks so you could go to the
bathroom or grab a cold drink. Which was too bad. I looked
out the front window and saw a mud-spattered, beat-up,

rusted-out blue pickup. There was a wheelbarrow, dirty
tools and what—to my uneducated eye—looked like trash
in the bed of the truck. It was parked haphazardly and I
could see a Confederate flag decal in the back window.

Company time.

The peephole in the front door framed a cherubic face
almost dwarfed by a mass of golden-red curls in a halo
around the young, frowning face.

I opened the door.

"You don't look like Dakota," her voice chastised me.
"Not one bit."

"I'm not."

She smiled. "Oh, okay then. I'm Dakota's cousin, Hope.
Hope Delaney." Her smile got bigger. Expectation and excitement blazed out of her eyes (soap opera again, I know)
like headlights stuck on high-beam.

"We expected you to call first."

The excitement flickered and started to die. I felt like a
party pooper.

"Oh. Yeah. Well, I shoulda, I know, but I was just so
charged. I was coming into town anyway—I borrowed my
cousin Tommy's truck and boy, can he change his mind
fast, he always was an Indian giver, that stinker, so I just
wanted to scoot out of there real quick before he could get
to it. Anyway"—she paused and gulped in a breath—"I
didn't even think about it until I was already on the road
and then I didn't see a pay phone that was real handy and
I just kept telling myself that it would be okay, me being
family and all. But . . ." Her voice wavered and skidded to
a stop. "I guess it wasn't." The excitement and expectation
were gone now.

"It's not that." I spoke gently. "Dakota's not here."

"Oh." She brightened a little, the excitement surging
back. "When will she be back? Who are you? Where is
she? In town? *Not* on the road?" The excitement died
again, the anxiety back.

How did she handle such constant and widely fluctuating
emotions? I was already exhausted by them. I took a deep
breath.

"Well?" Her eyes were almost yellow with little flecks of brown in them. Feral eyes. Not hostile, just untamed. The sunlight caught in her hair and fired it up in reds and oranges. Her face was round and plain, unadorned by makeup. Still, plainness wasn't the overall impression. She was dramatic, striking and arresting and, at the same time, seemed oddly vulnerable and innocent. I considered discreetly grilling her. No. Better to talk to her when Dakota was there.

"She's in town. I know she expects you and will certainly be in touch. Why don't you leave me your phone number?"

"Yes. Of course. I don't suppose I could come in and— Well, no, I suppose not."

I nodded, my expression encouraging the latter rather than the former.

Hope dug into her tight jeans and extracted a torn slip of paper with a phone number scrawled on it. No name. "Here." She thrust it at me. "It's the number where I'm staying. Tommy isn't very good about remembering messages and stuff so I might call Dakota too, just to check in and all. Don't let her think that I don't want to see her or anything. Okay? *Please*," she added quickly.

"Okay," I answered.

She ducked her head in a quick thank-you, turned and walked down the path to her truck. She was short—five two or three, I thought—a little bit chubby, although not unattractively so at all. Faded jeans, boots and a sweatshirt one stop away from the rag pile fit her like old news. I wondered if this was the way she always dressed or whether this was the poor-country-cousin look. If so, she had it down, no question. I leaned on the doorframe and watched as she drove away. She made a careful U-turn, tooted on her horn and waved to me. The Confederate flag gleamed in the sunshine and a beer can fell off the back of the truck as she accelerated.

I waved back, the dirty blue truck almost lost now in the black exhaust, watched her turn the corner, then walked to the street and picked up the beer can.

I realized for the millionth time how easy it is to be cynical in my job. I really have to watch it. Maybe it's death—well, murder. Either you become frightened, which makes you want to stay in bed until it's over, or you detach. That's a protection, as is cynicism. It's tempting to stay there, but the price is high. Hope and optimism are among the first casualties. I tossed the beer can in the trash and walked into the house.

What would it be like to be named Hope?

A car pulled up to the curb and honked at me before I had the answer. See what I mean about soap opera and pacing? The back door of the sedan flew open and Dakota blasted up the walk, practically smacking into me. "News, Katy." She grabbed my arms tightly, her face contorted by an emotion I couldn't read.

"Good or bad?" I asked, reading the answer then in her tense posture, hard eyes and strained voice.

"We're going to Garrett's office. A meeting." She spat the words out rapid-fire. "C'mon."

"What is it, Dakota?"

"Clyde."

I looked at her blankly, uncomprehendingly. The name meant nothing to me.

"Clyde T. Jones. *My father.* He's here."

Talk about surprise and shock. Talk about getting smacked from *way* out in left field.

The soap opera continued.

twenty

BACK DOOR MAN

W E SAT IN THE BACK SEAT, THE GLASS PRIVACY PAR-
tition between us and the driver closed.

And Dakota laughed. It was a laugh that I recognized
immediately though it had been years since I had heard it.
Years since I had hoped, heart and soul, that I would never
hear it again. It was the laugh of the little girl who had
been hurt and abandoned once more and was trying to pretend that it didn't matter. Granny Mae would have known
what to do; I didn't. I reached out for her hand.

Cold fingers gripped mine tightly. "I always wondered
what the *T* stood for in Clyde T. Jones. Clyde The Jerk
Jones? Clyde The-World's-Biggest-Asshole-Dad Jones?
Clyde Tightheart Jones?"

"Why is he here?" I cut past the bitterness and to the
chase.

"Not out of fatherly love, bet on it. No, *bank* on it."

I squeezed her hand.

She tried to smile. "I called Granny Mae. She told me
the story almost in tears. It seems he's been calling and
bothering her for the last ten months or so. He wanted my
address. She refused to give it to him. Then he threatened
to hire a private investigator. Granny didn't think he'd do
it—after all, private investigators cost money—but it worried her. She didn't want him just showing up on my door-

step one morning. She gave him Garrett's number and then she *called* Garrett—"

Our eyes met, knowing Granny and how much she hates long-distance telephone calls.

"She explained it to Garrett, said not to tell me because Clyde is more bluff than anything else and she still hoped that nothing would come of it. But it did. He called."

She pressed her hands to her temples. "Garrett side-tracked him, put him off. It worked for a while. Then it didn't. Clyde threatened to go to the press with the news that Dakota Jones refused to see her own father. Isn't that something?"

I whistled. "Yeah. Almost as good as Cal threatening to sue you for a million dollars."

Dakota laughed, a real laugh with an edge of sunshine in it. "Garrett asked me how I wanted to handle it. I said that we would meet at his office, a short meeting, and that was it." Her voice drifted off.

We were close to Garrett's office now, a new building on Music Row.

"I guess the hope never quite dies, Katy."

I looked at her quickly. *Her hope? His? Both?*

"It's just that this isn't my hope," she explained.

Hers. I thought about it and thought that it was good that hope didn't die. Mostly. Though probably not in this case. "Don't let hope be stronger than reason."

"Oh no." She flashed me a quick reassuring smile. "I'm glad you're with me."

The driver pulled up in front of the office building.

I stated the obvious. Just for the record. "You're a star, Dakota, not a lost and lonely little girl."

Another quick smile. We walked up the steps, Dakota calm, poised, almost regal. I'd seen this kind of calm descend on her right before a performance.

The receptionist whisked us into Garrett's office. He was on the phone but got off immediately, standing to welcome us.

"Dakota, you sure you want to handle it this way? It's not the only option."

She nodded. "Garrett, this is Kat."

He shook my hand warmly. "Delighted to meet you. I've heard a lot of nice things about you."

"Is he here?" Dakota was focused.

"In the meeting room."

"Then let's do it."

We followed Dakota down the hall to the meeting room. I realized I had no idea what to expect. There was a round table that would seat six in the center of the room. Clyde sat in a side chair and stood as we entered.

"Hi, Cody." He smiled.

I was stunned by his good looks, his easy self-assurance, his resemblance to Dakota.

"May I call you that?" His voice was low and warm as he approached her.

"My name is Dakota." Her tone wasn't icy but it was formal. "You've met Garrett, of course, and this is Kat Colorado."

I nodded, not caring to shake his hand. *To fraternize with the enemy.*

Dakota continued with a calm assumption of authority. "Let's sit, shall we."

Like Dakota's, his hair was thick, not blond but almost white, and beautiful. I thought about the women who had run their fingers through it, whispered endearments in his ears, women he had preferred for years to his wife and daughter. *It's hard not to be bitter.* His features were regular and pleasing, his eyes large and dark, deep with promises of things unrevealed. The kind of eyes that draw women in. His mouth was strong, his lips full. It was the kind of mouth that was built for kissing and lying. *Bitter and cynical both.*

He was almost six foot, with wide shoulders and narrow hips. His clothes were Nashville—a western shirt, jeans that were worn just enough, boots. His smile brushed over all of us like a moth's wing, landed on Dakota. Smooth. *He was good.*

She didn't smile back. "You asked for this meeting, Clyde."

I was surprised at the easy, indifferent way she spoke his name.

"I was against it, as you know," she continued. "After all these years I do not have a great deal to say to you. I cannot comprehend what you might have to say to me, particularly when you forced this meeting by threatening me."

Clyde leaned forward, his elbows on the table, a slight frown creasing his handsome forehead. I did the math quickly: Dakota was thirty-three; Clyde, who had been in his early twenties when she was born, was now in his mid-fifties. Didn't look it. The white hair didn't age him.

"I regret that very much, Cody. *Dakota*," he corrected smoothly. "I apologize. I'm sorry it's come to that between us."

"*It?* It hasn't come to that. Our relationship, or rather, lack of relationship, is what you made it years ago."

He opened his hands, almost supplicating. Pleading. "I'm sorry. I hope we can do better now."

"We?"

"I, then. Dakota, it was years ago when I left. I was young and irresponsible. I make no excuse for my behavior. It was wrong. I offer you my deep and heartfelt apologies. It's not possible to make up the past, I know. I'm hoping that we can try again, that we can start over. No, please—" He held up a hand at Dakota like a school crossing guard. "Let me finish. I read in the paper about the bomb attack, about the threat of other attacks." His voice was low and troubled, concerned, almost loving.

God, he's good, I thought. *Convincing*. It would be easy to believe everything he said. You wanted to believe everything he said. No wonder the ladies fell for him. He reminded me of someone but I couldn't pin it down. At first I thought it was Cal, that same ladies'-man charm and arrogance. But it was more than just a style; it was a physical resemblance. Had I seen him before? No. I couldn't imagine where or when. That wasn't it, but it was something.

"Dakota, you need people around you you know and trust. You need help. I'm your father. I want to help."

There was a long heavy silence in the room. Dakota stared expressionlessly at Clyde. He almost looked away, but didn't. He sat, waiting, his face composed and concerned.

Dakota began laughing, merrily at first and then with a hysterical edge, and then she put her arms on the table in front of her, her head down, and was silent. Clyde was frozen in his seat. Garrett started to get up and I shook my head. I thought Dakota should play this however she wanted. I stared at Clyde, who stared at the wall until Dakota sat up straight and spoke.

"I needed your help, Clyde, you're right. I needed you to help me learn to walk and to listen to my first words. I needed you to take me to Sunday school and come to my school plays. To tell me stories, kiss me good night, and take care of me when I was sick. I needed you for words of encouragement. And I needed a father especially because I had a mother who was always gone.

"I needed that but I never got it. I had Granny Mae and Grandpa Billy and you, a father who threatened Granny with trouble if she didn't send you money."

His face darkened.

"I don't need you anymore. I'm not a lonely defenseless child. I have friends to help me—you're looking at two of them. I don't want you in my life. Now get out."

Silence.

Garrett stood and opened the door.

Clyde stood slowly, as though each movement was painful, and looked sorrowfully at Dakota.

"What's the *T* stand for, Clyde?" Dakota's voice was light.

"What?"

"In Clyde T. Jones."

"Thomas."

She nodded as if there was nothing more she needed to know about this man who claimed to be her father.

"I hope you'll change your mind. If you do, please let me know. Your manager"—he nodded in Garrett's direction—"knows how to reach me."

"Jo always said you were a back door man, a scam artist. What's the scam this time, Clyde?"

"Your mother was a bitter woman, Dakota."

"Yes. Understandably so."

He shook his head sadly. He had sad and sorrowful down real well. I didn't think I was being cynical here at all. Garrett escorted Clyde out.

"What's his scam, Katy?"

"I don't know." Translation: *I'm not sure. Yet.*

"It *is* a scam?"

"Yes. I think so. Not concern anyway, something else."

"Money?"

"Probably." My voice was sad. Not about the scam—scams are a dime a dozen—but about the old stuff. About the sadness of not having a father. Or having a father who was at best a ladies' man and an opportunist. At worst . . .

"That son of a bitch!"

"Yes."

Anger was better than sadness.

Who the hell did Clyde remind me of?

twenty-one

PROFESSIONAL DETACHMENT

W E TALKED ABOUT IT, FIRST IN GARRETT'S OFFICE,
then in the car. Dakota wasn't paying much attention. While that was understandable, it was a luxury we
couldn't afford.

"Are you listening to me, Dakota? Shall I repeat what
Sergeant Deeter said, what his recommendation, *strong* recommendation is?" I asked patiently, though I wasn't feeling very patient. I was determined not to be someone who
tried to push Dakota around, like Cal and Garrett. Maybe
Clyde and Link, too?

"No, Kat, I heard you. I appreciate all you're saying.
The sergeant, too, but I've made up my mind. I announced
at the press conference that I would be organizing a benefit
concert to set up a trust fund for Joni's child. She had a
two-year-old son." There were tears in her eyes. "We,
well, I—and you're welcome, of course—am going to the
Bluebird tonight. It's going to be an informal tribute to
Joni. A number of other artists have called volunteering for
the benefit so we'll start putting that together tonight too."

"I understand how you feel but—"

"In a sense we're all one big family, Katy. We bicker
and squabble, sure. There's rivalry and jealousy, too, but
when trouble hits we pull together, we stick together. And

we take care of each other. I need to go, Katy—not just
for Joni, for me as well.''

''All right.'' There's more than one kind of family, one
kind of survival. I know that as well as Dakota. ''The Bluebird's not so bad''—*so dangerous* is what I meant—''especially when it's an informal, unpublicized function.''
*Unless the threat is from someone very close to Dakota.
No. Even then it's unlikely that he'll show his hand in public. Or she.* ''It's the large, well-publicized venues I'm worried about.''

''I know, Katy. Me, too. A lot. I can't get the image of
Joni out of my mind. I can see myself like that, bloody and
lifeless. There are a lot of songs I want to write and sing.
I want to get married. I want to have a family. I want a lot
of things, Katy, before I want to be dead. I'll be careful, I
promise. We'll work it out as we go.''

''What about this weekend's venues?'' *Big venues. Well-
publicized venues.*

''I don't know. I think Garrett's going to cancel. He's
still trying to see if the venues can be secured.''

''How? Extra security, police, metal detectors?''

''I don't know. I didn't ask.'' She shrugged helplessly.
''There's too much happening. I can't keep on top of it all.
Will you come to the Bluebird tonight?''

I nodded. Control is first choice; damage control is second.

Dakota was humming, playing with a melody.

''How much family can you take in one day?''

''Hmmm?'' she asked absently, singing and playing with
a musical phrase over and over, changing it, repeating it,
changing it again.

''Hope came by.''

''*Did* she? What is she like? What did you think?''

I considered all the cynical things I could say and decided not to. Not yet. ''I liked her.''

''Really?'' Dakota's voice was pleased and happy.
''What's she like?''

''Young and unsure but eager, enthusiastic.''

''Pretty?''

"Attractive. Red hair in curls around her head, nice eyes, a short not quite plump figure, crummy clothes."

"What did she say?"

"Not much. She wants to see you."

"Hmmm. And she left her number?"

"Yes."

"I'll have Garrett call her. She can show up at the Bluebird tonight, maybe play with us."

"Is that the same thing as an audition?"

"Pretty much. First step, anyway."

"That's a lot of pressure on a kid who's just hit town."

Dakota shrugged. "It is, sure, but this is the same kid who wants me to hire her, who wants to go on stage in front of ten thousand people. The Bluebird is nothing compared to that." Her voice was businesslike. "Not everyone can perform, Katy. Some of the best players or singers in the world never get on stage, never sing 'Happy Birthday' in a crowd or join their church choir. Their only audience is the walls of their bedroom. 'Hello walls . . .'" She sang the mournful opening words to a Willie Nelson song.

"I'm sure there are wonderful manuscripts saved in computers or stashed on dusty shelves, paintings stuck in the back of closets. It's not enough to have talent. You have to have the courage it takes to show that talent to the world."

Yes. So much of it is courage.

"It's tough out there, Katy. They might love you but they'll also stomp on you, bruise your heart and soul, kick you until you are bloody and broken. Sooner or later it will happen." She sighed. "It's another thing you can bank on."

The driver took the corner slowly and a shrunken frail-looking woman of at least ninety, standing on the corner with a huge black dog that practically came to her shoulder, smiled and waved at us. We waved back.

"Do you think she is sweet and kind, Katy? Do you think she walks her dog and pets him and loves him, makes cookies for her great-grandkids—their *favorite* kind of cookies, not whole wheat bars with prune filling—and takes them to *The Nutcracker* and baseball games, sings at her church, always votes and says her prayers, and has a kind word and smile for everyone?''

Is what seems to be really what is?

"I think that's the longest run-on sentence I've heard in a while." And I wondered what the real question was.

"Wouldn't it be so much easier if people's insides and outsides matched?"

"Clyde," I said, understanding.

"Yes. He's such a handsome man, Katy, the kind you'd like to have for a father. He has a nice voice and manner and when you hear him you want to believe every word he says."

Her voice was detached, without emotion, as though she spoke of a local politician, not the man who was her father—who *said* he was her father, I corrected quickly, thinking of the roll of film in my purse. I'd asked Dakota to call Garrett from the car, to have him take pictures. I'd wanted Jones's prints, too, just fingertips on a stamp pad, then on paper, but Hunter had balked at that. "Forget it. I'm a manager, not a cop," were his exact words.

"Do you remember him, Dakota?"

"Clyde? No. Two is too young, I think. All that I 'know' or 'remember' about him is from stories that someone told me. Jo or Granny Mae or Grandpa. Some of them were told so often, so vividly that they seem real to me. I see pictures in my mind now to go with the stories but I know they didn't really happen that way. It's just my imagination, or the pictures the words of others painted in my mind. It's funny that something can seem so real and yet not be."

"It happens a lot."

Dakota ignored me, attentive still to the memory, not to me. "I seem to remember him coming home once. I would have been about eight, I guess. I didn't see him to talk to, just caught a glimpse of a strange man in the house. Later, from something I heard Granny say, I thought it was him. No one would tell me or talk to me about it. They meant it for the best, I'm sure, meant to protect me. But how can you protect a child from the lack of love? How can you hide that from a child? I think it would have been better for me to have seen him, to have faced it and him.''

Yes. I did too.

"Maybe it would have spared me all those silly dreams and hopes.''

"Not silly. Dreams and hopes are important.'' I searched for the word I wanted. "Futile. And that was his fault.''

"Futile. What a hopeless-sounding word.''

"Not something a child would understand. Children do understand about hopes and dreams, how necessary they are.''

"Yes. I had hopes, though I didn't pin them on people. I pinned them on songs, on singing and performing.''

I understood that, too, not pinning your hopes on people.

"I guess I'm not surprised that this happened. I guess I expected that it would, that he would show up, that I would have to deal with it. Now it's over. I'm glad. I feel lighter, freer.'' She stretched languidly, like a cat, and smiled at me.

I smiled back.

I wasn't sure it was over.

Dakota hummed a now familiar refrain. "A song,'' she explained. "A song I'm writing for Joni.''

THE BLUEBIRD WAS HALF FULL WHEN WE ARRIVED. THERE was a hum, a buzz I couldn't quite define. Anticipation? Or something else? Garrett, who had picked us up, pulled several small tables together. Dakota and I sat at the center table.

"Dakota.''

"Yes.'' She turned and smiled at me, a kind of dreamy look on her face. Was it the way the lights hit us? There was a soft glow about her and she looked extraordinarily beautiful. Tonight she was a star, not just the kid I had grown up with. "Look, is that Patty Loveless?''

She looked and nodded.

"And Amy Grant? See, over there?''

She nodded again.

"Wow!''

Dakota grinned. "You sound like a little kid."

"I am. A kid in hog heaven. Hey! Over there. Is that—"

"Hi."

A whispery, breathless voice addressed us. "You're Dakota."

And stated the obvious.

"I'm Hope. Hope Delaney."

Dakota held out a hand. Her voice was warm. "I'm glad to meet you. Please join us. You've met Kat, I know, and this is Garrett, my manager, with whom you spoke on the phone." Dakota was welcoming but formal, a little reserved.

Hope nodded, opened her mouth to speak, shut it again. *Cat got her tongue?* Her clothes were the same as earlier, looked—even in this subdued lighting—as shabby and no-account as before. Not that we were dressed up. Dakota seemed not to notice. Hope held a battered violin case in her arms, clutched it to her chest as though it were something incredibly precious that someone might try to tear from her. She gazed at Dakota, her eyes sliding away shyly, then back again.

"Won't you sit down?" Dakota asked, still formally. Hope slipped into a seat, perched on the edge like a terrified wobbly little bird, and clutched her fiddle case even tighter.

"Did you just arrive in Nashville?" Dakota asked.

Hope nodded.

"And you had a good trip?"

Hope nodded again.

"Have you had a chance to look around much?"

Hope shook her head. This conversation, if you could call it that, was making me feel sad. I looked around the club instead. Everybody at the table looked at me when I gasped.

"Dakota!" I whispered loudly.

She arched an eyebrow in inquiry.

"Is that Mary-Chapin Carpenter?"

"Ka-a-aty." She giggled at me.

"Quick! Look! Is it?"

She looked and shook her head. "What are we going to

do about you? We can dress you up but not take you out?''

"I *whispered*," I said, in an aggrieved tone of voice, and we both started laughing. Hope stared at us, round-eyed and puzzled, and as though she didn't get it, or us, or a lot of things. And who could blame her?

"Dakota, do you think I could meet—"

"Yes, of course, if it comes up. Now, shush."

Dakota went back to vainly trying to engage Hope in conversation and I went back to gazing (okay, stargazing) with what I hoped was an air of casual nonchalance.

"Pssst, Dakota, that guy who just came in, is it—"

"I thought you had shushed."

"Just *look*."

She turned, following my gaze. "Never saw him before in my life."

"Oh. Doesn't he look like George Jones?"

Dakota shrugged. "Maybe twenty years and a vat of bourbon ago." She looked at me, amused and exasperated both. "I mean it. If you don't hush up, I'm going to stick you over there next to Garrett and tonight he's about as chatty as a clam. We're working, remember?"

I blushed. It had slipped my mind for just a bit there. So much for professional detachment and investigator alertness.

Dakota winked at me. "We'll play, I promise. And I'll introduce you to everyone in town. After all, my friends want to meet you too, Katy."

"Meet me?" I was genuinely puzzled.

"Sure. They've heard about our growing up together, about college and my getting started in the music business with you as my 'manager.' ''

She smiled a crooked happy/sad and something-else-I-couldn't-tell smile over those days when she was too timid to stand up for herself, so I did it for her. Well, *with* her. Those days that we never refer to as the good old days. There were good times and fun, but not enough to qualify them as good old days.

"Okay?" she asked.

I nodded. Then gasped. I didn't mean to, honest. I

couldn't help it. A tall good-looking guy was threading his
way through tables across the room. *Alan Jackson?*

"Dakota?"

She gasped too.

We weren't gasping at the same thing.

We weren't even looking in the same direction.

twenty-two
CADILLAC COWBOY

L INK." DAKOTA'S VOICE WAS COLD. NO, FORGET COLD.
Try glacial.

He smiled. It was, I thought, a smile that could melt ice,
a smile that started with his mouth, hit his eyes, then
reached out to Dakota, splashing down on her like the first
warm summer rain, washing over her with promises, some
of them sexual. He was either very sincere or very good. I
couldn't tell. You can't when they're that good, not without
more information.

"Another time, Link." Dakota turned away, turned back
to Hope. I was seated on one side of her, Hope on the other.

"Link." Garrett's voice was a hearty echo of Dakota's,
only his was welcoming. "Join us, won't you?" Garrett
couldn't have heard Dakota and he hadn't bothered to read
her expression, gestures or eyes. Sensitivity didn't seem to
be his strong suit. Garrett pushed back and Link pulled up
a chair, parked between Hope and Garrett. He leaned forward and smiled at Dakota—I gave him ten points for
balls—then turned to Garrett.

Me? I wasn't used to a night out being so complicated.

But of course it wasn't a night out. It was work. And
this wasn't a friendly get-together; it was a group of people
who all wanted something from Dakota.

Across the room I could see Cal. The Bluebird was a hot

spot, all right. He started over to a table, then saw us and changed his course. Nothing Cal likes better than a little barroom brawling.

''Evening.'' He drawled it out, looking around the table, including everyone in his greeting. He passed over Hope, then looked back and winked.

Hope's hands flew around in her lap until she caught herself, blushed and ordered them down, started to reach for the violin on the floor, caught herself again. Link and Garrett nodded at Cal—Garrett throwing in a frown—both of them going for the strong, silent, macho-type response, a response pretty much wasted on everyone but Hope, who slid an interested sideways glance first at Cal, then at Link. Link stiffened, folded his arms across his chest and stared stolidly at Cal.

''Evening, Dakota. Kat.'' Cal dipped his head slightly and touched the rim of his black hat. He could play the lout, he could play the gentleman—whatever the situation called for.

''Hello, Cal.''

A faint smile played around Dakota's face, darting from her mouth to her eyes and then back again. She was enjoying this. So was Cal. Cat and mouse? It was a game they had played often, I thought, and played well. Or maybe Dakota was playing this out for Link's benefit? Garrett stared at the floor. Uncomfortable. Why? Link was still in tough-guy mode, annoyed maybe that no one paid him any mind. He tipped his light gray hat back, then refolded his arms across his chest and added a small sneer to complement the hard eyes which blinked a little too often in the smoke slipstream of Cal's cigarette.

''Heard you were putting together a benefit for Joni.'' Cal dragged on the cigarette, then held it loosely at his side so the smoke curled up and wreathed Link in a gray cloud. Link blinked again.

Dakota nodded, the same smile playing around her mouth.

''I'd be honored to be involved. Anything I can do, you give me a holler. *Anything* at all.'' The way he said ''anything'' made it as big and wide open as Texas, as dangerous and unpredictable as a rattlesnake. He said it with a straight face. That Cal, what a guy.

"I sure will, Cal. Thanks for offering.'' She said it with a straight face too.

I could see Cal in the movies easy. A Western. Not a John Wayne kind of Western but a Clint Eastwood one, with guys dressed in shades of brown and gray and despair and a four-day stubble on their faces. I could see Clyde in that movie too. They would all ride spiritless but sturdy horses and carry guns. Lots of guns. And knives on their belts. Their boots and pantlegs would be caked with dried mud, their cuffs and collars frayed and filthy.

The eyes of this kind of man are hooded and dark and don't ever give anything away. Not drunk. Not in sex. Not in storytelling and lies. Not even dead.

Clyde. Clint. Cal. The *C* made their names sound harsh and hard. Which was okay. These are men who are harsh and hard, who like harsh and hard. Good guys don't have names like that. But that's the movies.

Real life doesn't work that way. Look at my name.

While I was thinking in fast-forward Cal was still playing a movie role. He was the star, waving and calling to people at other tables, making sure he was seen by everyone. Seen with Dakota. He was all in black, wearing the eight-hundred-dollar kind of cowboy boots. These days you can't tell by color anymore either. The good guys wear black; the bad guys wear whatever they want to.

"Well darlin'.'' He leaned down over Dakota. B-grade movie dialogue. "You take care of yourself now, you hear.'' And he kissed her on the cheek, straightened up, pushed his hat back, waved his cigarette one last time in Link's face. "Kat, y'all remember you ain't got nine lives.'' He laughed, turned on his heel and sauntered off.

"Coming or going, he's still a good-looking man,'' Dakota whispered softly to me. "I'd rather see him going, though. Anytime. Any day.''

Cal stopped at a table to talk to someone, shoving a hand in his back pocket, his handsome face in profile. From here you couldn't see the lines, the dissipation. He was just good-looking, sexy trouble. Maybe TROUBLE. A Cadillac cowboy.

"I've got a name for a song," I said. We were both staring at Cal still.

"What?"

"Cadillac Cowboy."

"Katy, that's *good*!"

"Yeah. It is, huh?"

I was pretty pleased with myself, I admit. She was too. We sat there grinning and giggling like a couple of kids at Christmas.

"Did you know that Cal drives a Cadillac?"

I nodded. I'd seen the current one and he'd been driving them as long as I could remember. "Hey, I think Hope is flirting with Link." I whispered that, too.

An eyebrow darted up in surprise. "Really? Well, good, they can amuse each other."

"Hey, Dakota, ma'am, could y'all sign my hat, please. I'm a big fan."

Dakota flashed him a big-fan smile and signed his hat.

"Thank you. You got lots of friends where I come from. I could tell you stories till the cows come home." He shifted his weight from foot to foot, dallying around for the invitation no one trotted out. "Well, hey there. Look, someone gave this to me to give you." He thrust an envelope into Dakota's hand, was gone before she could thank him.

I got a bad feeling about it—immediately—and started to reach for it.

"Dakota!"

Artists I sort of recognized but whose names I wasn't sure of stopped by the table, eager to be a part of the benefit concert. Kind words and tears both, as well as a sense of pulling together and working together. I thought it was really something. God knows PIs would never do that. A couple joined our party at Garrett's end, leaving a single vacant chair next to me.

Someone slid into it. "Hey Dakota!"

Dakota looked up and smiled her real smile, her big smile, the one that friends get. "Lari!"

It was Lari White! I was speechless with excitement.

The music started.

twenty-three

TWISTED NOTES

IT IS DIFFERENT IN A SMALL CLUB. YOU'D THINK THAT IF the music is the same the experience would be the same, but it's not. In a large venue, the kind Dakota played, the music slams into you. Decibels, not subtly. The artist is far away, remote in distance and experience. Ten to twenty thousand people come and go, sing, holler, stand up, spill their beer and their emotions into the aisles, onto you if you will allow it.

In the Bluebird music washed over you. Notes twisted into your soul and words lodged in your heart. The music filled you up, spilled out electrically and emotionally charged, captured you and set you free both.

"Are you singing?" I asked, puzzled at the setup. There seemed to be more than one performer. "How does Hope fit in?"

"I've been asked to join in on a couple of songs, that's all. Hope?" Dakota shrugged. "She could too, or we can wait until later."

I glanced at Hope, rigid and intense at Dakota's side. She looked like one of the condemned waiting for her turn in front of the firing squad. The drink on the table before her was almost untouched. She felt my look, turned and gazed at me, her odd yellow eyes unblinking, then she turned back. Maybe I was wrong about the firing squad.

That look had been almost feral, as though she were watching, stalking her prey.

Dakota stood.

"Where are you going?" Investigator on alert.

"Bathroom."

I stood too.

Her eyes flickered in amusement. "I'll be all right."

But I followed her, threading around tables and past occasional knots of people. There was no one else in the ladies' room, a small room with tulip wallpaper.

"They look a lot alike," I said.

"Who? What are you talking about? That's nonsense. They do *not*. Not at all!" She slammed the bathroom door and snapped the latch into place. "Honest to God, Katy, your imagination's on overtime now."

I washed my hands, ran my fingers through my hair, fluffing it out, made a face at myself in the mirror. Okay, I was about out of things to do. I started humming.

"You're off-key," Dakota pointed out crossly, and flushed the toilet. She washed her hands without looking at me, then put on a fresh layer of lipstick.

"Where do you get this stuff, Katy? Honestly, I don't know how you come up with such junky ideas. They don't look *anything* alike. Anyway, Clyde's a much better-looking man than Cal."

"If they don't look anything alike, how did you know who I was talking about?" I asked, trying—but not quite succeeding—to sound reasonable and not smart-alecky.

"Oh for *Pete's* sake, Katy, I know how your mind works, that's all." Still cross. Crosser, actually. "Ready?"

"No."

I took the envelope out of my purse. A look of dread flashed across Dakota's face, like a storm cloud at warp speed.

"Who knew you were going to be here tonight?"

She frowned. "A lot of people were calling all afternoon about the benefit concert and Garrett passed the word on."

Her eyes weren't on me, but on the envelope, on the single sheet of paper I slid out. Glossy and in full color, it looked like a page ripped out of a brochure. It was a picture of a coffin, white with brass fittings and lined with white velvet. There was even a spray of white flowers. On the velvet, red ink on white, was written:

THE PAST WILL GET YOU.

The well-formed block letters were tucked perfectly into the velvet of the coffin. It was a neat, well-executed effort. Someone knocked on the door of the ladies' room.

"Katy, who would do that? Why?"

"I don't know who—someone who wants to scare you."

"It's getting closer. It seems more threatening."

I nodded and opened the door. A slim woman in blue jeans and a smile came in on a blast of music as we exited. I refolded the paper and put it back in the envelope. Dakota's face was too pale now for the bright lipstick. Mentally I sketched out a picture of the fan who had wanted his hat signed, who had hand-delivered the envelope. *Somebody told me to give you this.* He would be gone by now, though I would look. Dakota put her hand on my arm, her face all scared eyes and red lipstick.

"Go back to the table." I kept my voice low. "I want to look around."

"Is he still here?" She matched her voice to mine.

"The man who delivered it? I doubt it. We don't know who wrote it, of course."

Fear flickered in Dakota's eyes, then settled right in, like a drop-in visitor choosing the comfiest easy chair. "He might be here?"

I nodded. "Or she."

Fear stretched out, comfortable, languid, right at home.

"Try to act as though nothing's bothering you. In case someone's watching."

"All right."

She pinched her cheeks until there was color in them, straightened her shoulders, kicked fear out of the easy chair and showed him the door, then stepped back into the noise and music and life of the club. I watched Dakota walk with a light and carefree step, seat herself, then lean over to say something lively and vivacious to Hope.

I looked around, covering the place thoroughly. The "fan" was gone. I stationed myself by the bar, looking for I wasn't sure what. There was a break in the music and I heard Dakota's name and an invitation to come up on stage. Dakota sang harmony on two songs, then introduced a new song of hers, "Broken Angel." I had never heard it before. "Broken angel . . . broken wings . . . stumbling over yesterday's hopes, yesterday's dreams . . . reaching for the rainbow still." It was haunting, despair and hope lyrically intertwined and climbing a cappella into uncharted heights.

The audience exploded in applause. I slipped back into my seat.

Garrett was grinning, dollar signs in his eyes. Link acted proud and pleased. Hope had a look of dumb horror on her face. *Horror?* Was she way out of her league here, was that it? She glanced over sideways, caught my look and smiled slightly, ditching the horror like a bad habit. I smiled back, not meaning it any more than she did.

Dakota spoke about Joni, about the benefit.

I thought about broken angels. Some got fixed; some died; some changed. And sometimes you can fix what is broken but it is never the same again. Broken angels are—

"Pssst."

I looked over at Hope.

"When do I get to play, do you know?"

I shook my head.

A pained expression flitted across her face. Watching Hope was like reading a large-print book. Dakota came back to the table as the music started again. Hope's face was blank now, a tabula rasa for the next feeling.

"I'm sorry, Hope." Dakota spoke lightly. "I didn't get a chance to include you this evening. We'll work it out. Soon."

Before Hope could answer, Garrett spoke and Dakota turned away. I waited for the next expression to pop up on Hope's face. It wasn't pissed off, it was much stronger than that. Rage. Rage that was barely controlled. *Murderous* slammed into my mind before I could figure it.

Hope caught me looking again, ditched that glance like another bad habit and smiled and shrugged. *Oh well,* her shrug said. *Too bad, but that's life. No big deal.*

An expression is just that, an expression. No big deal. But murderous is something else, murderous is a big deal. I learned this the hard way.

Hope slid over toward Link and favored him with a 2000-watt smolder, leaning well back so Dakota could enjoy it too. Jeez. Subtle just wasn't in her repertoire. Link turned away and Hope's face fell to pieces, crumpled up in emotions that distorted her features. She took a deep breath and gazed, fixed and abstracted, at the stage.

Broken angel? I wondered. Broken and murderous? Who had broken her? Why was there horror and rage in her face when she looked surreptitiously at Dakota?

Too bad I get paid for answering questions, not asking them.

We left early. Before the music stopped and without saying goodbye. It was a security move, not a lack of manners. And it was my idea.

Garrett's driver got us home, walked us to the door. From the outside everything looked okay.

We almost stepped on it coming inside. Dakota cried out, shied and skittered away like a startled pony. She came to rest with her back slammed to the wall, hands down, palms pushing back against it.

It was another page torn from the funeral brochure. The coffin in this picture was black, black and sleek and glossy, and it was pasted on another magazine ad. The rough collage showed the coffin balanced on a Mercedes, also black and sleek and shiny. Little cutouts of black bats had been pasted on the background of both pictures.

It had been shoved under the door. Probably. I looked at the driver, a barrel-chested burly guy with bulging biceps and hands like hams and nodded. He nodded back and stepped in. I locked the door.

"Stay here," I said to Dakota, who was still doing her shadow-glued-to-the-wall routine. The driver, whose name turned out to be Howie, and I walked the place. He did muscle, I covered the fine points. We found nothing else until we got to the kitchen and the back door. A picture had been slid under that door too, this one a coffin in golden-blond wood with brass appointments and a gold velvet lining. I honestly had no idea coffins came in such a dazzling variety. I guess I rarely see death from that angle.

"Hunnh," Howie grunted.

I found a plastic sandwich bag and tucked my hand in it to pick up the paper. I probably should have done it with the one at the front door too, but better late than never. "No sign of entry."

"Naw," Howie said, agreeing.

I placed the latest epistle on the table and headed back to the front door. There I peeled a still-speechless Dakota off the wall, plopped her on the couch and retrieved the black coffin.

"Ma'am."

"Kat," I corrected.

"Yes, ma'am," Howie agreed. "I got to go to the car, make a phone call."

"Garrett?" I asked.

"Mr. Hunter, yes, ma'am." He exited. I did a visual check on Dakota, now a shadow glued to the couch, and called the cops, although I didn't call it in as an emergency. Briefly I explained the situation, mentioned Deeter and his concern, requested that—if possible—they alert the patrol cars in the area and ask them to keep an eye out. They were very polite.

As I hung up there was a loud knock on the door. Dakota leapt up and pasted herself against an interior wall.

"It's Howie, ma'am," a loud voice announced. I let him in, closed and locked the door behind him. "Mr. Hunter has requested that I stay here until he arrives. I can wait here or outside, whatever you say."

"You're welcome to stay inside. Warmer." I peeled Dakota off the wall again and headed for the kitchen, coaxing her along. Howie lumbered after us, large and comforting.

I put water on to boil and then bagged the coffins and

stashed them away on the off chance that I could interest Deeter in checking them for prints.

I made herbal tea for Dakota, who would have gone into orbit on caffeine, and a pot of coffee for everyone else. I figured there would be a crowd here soon. Dakota looked pale and frightened and sat without speaking. Joni had died last night; Clyde and Hope had shown up this afternoon; the anonymous letters and threats had been continuous. It was too much.

Too much, too fast, too ugly.

Broken angel.

Dakota wobbled to her feet and left the kitchen. Food, I thought. Maybe that would help. I fried up a package of bacon, then made grilled cheese sandwiches with bacon, slices of tomato and mayo. Dakota drifted back in.

"That smells good, Katy. Thanks." She cut her sandwich up into triangles and nibbled at it. Howie's hands were bigger than the sandwich I offered him. He ate like a backhoe, snapping pieces off. It took him four bites. A car pulled up in front as I started grilling more sandwiches. We all heard it; we were all fine-tuned. Howie looked at me and I nodded for him to check it out. A loud knock beat him to the door. "Police," the voice announced.

I walked into the front room, opened the curtains, saw the squad car. "Let them in."

Him. One came in. The other was outside. I could see the light of a flashlight moving around the house and yard.

"Evening, ma'am."

"Kat Colorado," I said.

"Yes, ma'am." He nodded. "Everything okay now?"

"Yes and no."

"Miss Jones?"

"Shocked and upset."

He nodded. "Could you tell me what happened?"

I could, but not here. I smelled toasting cheese from the kitchen. Or burning cheese. He smelled it too. "Would you come back to the kitchen?" We left Howie stationed at the door.

I flipped the grilled cheese over. Just in time. Toasty but

not burned. Dakota was white and still but at least she'd eaten half her sandwich. I started to explain, stopped when I heard the commotion at the door, then heard Garrett's voice. The kitchen filled right up: Dakota, me, Howie, Garrett, and two cops. After checking his name tag I asked Officer Smitte if he would mind getting mugs out of the cupboard behind him and passing coffee around.

"No, ma'am. Wouldn't mind at all."

I winced. Bad enough I was a fry cook without being ma'amed continuously. I talked, finished grilling a bunch more sandwiches (the most domestic I'd been in years), cut them in half, filled up a plate and passed them around.

Everyone acted like they weren't hungry and were just having some to be polite. Ha. I stared at the empty plate and started another sandwich for me. The radio on one of the officers' belts crackled, then hummed and buzzed with words too low to make out. I finished the story and the sandwich at the same time and sat down to eat. Smitte asked a few last questions, gazed enraptured at Dakota, then politely put his and his partner's coffee mugs in the sink and departed with assurances of increased surveillance.

And one last "ma'am."

"Dakota, honey." Garrett spoke directly to her for the first time. "Are you all right?"

She shook her head.

"Dakota can't do this weekend's concerts." I stated the obvious.

Dakota shook her head again. Agreeing? Disagreeing? And drank the last of her tea, toyed with her sandwich.

"No." Garrett spoke immediately. "We'll cancel, reschedule for a later date." He helped himself to the last portion of Dakota's sandwich.

"Dakota." I made my voice gentle. "What do you think about flying home?"

She stared at me.

"Stay with Granny Mae for a week or so. You need to rest. You need to get away from all this. You need to feel safe."

"All right." There was relief in her voice. "You're coming too, aren't you?"

"Soon. There are a few things I want to do here first."

"What? Oh, God, Katy, I'm so tired."

"Have a bath and go to bed."

"All right." She smiled. First time in a while.

"Howie will stay here tonight," Garrett announced. "Don't worry. Sleep well." He stood and patted Dakota on the shoulder as she left the room with a little wan smile that frightened me.

"Why are you staying?" His face was creased with a frown, his voice something else on top of curious.

"We need to address the security issue." I answered his question with a comment of my own. "An alarm system should be installed before Dakota returns. We need a tracer on her phone line, maybe a security patrol."

He nodded. "I'll take care of it. The benefit concert is scheduled three weeks from Sunday."

"Tight security?"

"Yes."

"Where is it?"

"At the Ryman Auditorium."

"If Dakota's ready."

"She will be."

Commanding. I didn't like his attitude. We both spoke in clipped sentences now.

"I'll have my secretary get Dakota's tickets. Howie will take her to the airport."

"Never mind. I'll do it."

He started to answer, then shrugged.

"Don't tell anyone where Dakota is. Or how to reach her. Don't give out the phone number."

He bristled, not a man who took directions well.

"The stakes are high now," I reminded him.

"Yes." Clipped. Short. He walked out.

Dakota trusted him.

I didn't. Not yet.

twenty-four

DEAD COWS AND COUNTRY
BUMPKINS

"WHY, KATY?"
Dakota asked it again the next morning as she
was pulling things out of the closet and I was folding and
packing them. Plain things, dark things: sweaters and T-
shirts and jeans. Nothing that would stand out or draw attention to her, nothing that made her look like a star.

"It would be more fun to travel together," she added.

Fun. Right now fun was future tense, not present.

"I came out to keep you safe, to try to stop the letters."
Damage control. "We're way past that now." *Murder.*
Way past that. "It's getting worse. We don't have much to
work on. The cops don't have time to follow up on a bunch
of maybe—no, probably—unimportant leads. I do. But
only if you're safe somewhere. Staying with Granny Mae
is perfect." *And Rafe*, I added mentally. Rafe is one of my
best friends. A good guy to have on your side, a bad guy
to be up against. Very bad.

"*What* leads?"

*Cal. Garrett. Link. Maybe Hope and Clyde? Well, that
was stretching it. I wanted to talk to Sonny, Cal's buddy;*

again to Trudy, Cal's girlfriend; to Garrett's secretary.
That was the beginning of a long list.

"Let's finish packing. I'll tell you later." I was in a
stick-with-the-big-vague-picture-and-skip-the-details mood.

Dakota picked up the bedroom phone. "You finish while
I call Garrett."

"Tell him you're leaving tomorrow."

She looked at the clock. Her plane left in three hours.
"Why?"

"The fewer people who know anything, the better. Remind him not to tell anyone where you are."

"At a fat farm?" She giggled.

I looked at her slim figure. "Make it a health spa for rest
and recuperation. Somewhere in—" I broke off, clueless.

"Florida."

"Perfect."

She punched buttons, spoke in a quiet voice. I folded up
socks and leggings during the short conversation.

"I feel bad about all of this, Katy."

"What?"

"Canceling this weekend's concerts. Hope. It's not like
me. I can't bear it when I don't live up to the commitments
I've made. It happened so often to me and I hate—"

I hugged her. "This isn't your choice. Your safety has
to come first, you know that."

She acknowledged it, but with a downcast look.

"Is Garrett going to talk to Hope?"

"Yes. And have her play, try out a few songs with the
band. If she's good we'll take her on for a three-month
trial. Will you talk to her too? Garrett can be kind of abrupt
and I don't want her to think—"

"I'll talk to her." I closed the suitcase. "Be careful,
Cody." The "Cody" slipped out. "Don't visit old friends.
Don't let Granny tell anyone. Don't go *any*where without
Rafe."

"Alma?"

"Of course." We were all close, Alma and Granny particularly. "Just act like—" I broke off, not wanting to say
it.

"Like my life depends on it," Dakota finished soberly for me.

"Yes."

And maybe it did.

"The tickets are under the name Cindy Alexander. Rafe will pick you up at the airport. He's six foot three and will be carrying a rolled-up magazine under his arm. He will greet you by name, 'Cindy,' and will have a recent photo of me and Granny."

"You're making it sound like a spy novel." Her voice was edgy and anxious.

I hugged her. "Don't call *any*one but me and Garrett. It's too easy to let something slip. Can you do that?"

"Not call Link? Is that what you were thinking?"

"Yes. Or people about the concert. *Anyone.*"

"I won't call." She looked forlorn.

I hugged her again. Does it take the threat of death to make us realize how precious a friend is? "Better safe than sorry." Dakota nodded, looking utterly woebegone.

I put "Cindy" on the 2:15 plane, watched it leave, called Rafe from the airport to confirm and went back to Dakota's.

Back to work.

To murder and coffins.

To Cadillac cowboys and broken angels.

DAKOTA HAD LEFT ME WITH HER ADDRESS BOOK. I skimmed through it. Link Davidson immediately caught my fancy. There were two numbers: one for work, one for home. It was three-thirty. I called the work number. The secretary was pleasant and helpful. Link was reserved and cool. Good thing I see situations like this as a challenge.

"Yes, of course I remember you," he said impatiently as I finished my intro.

"I didn't have a chance to speak with you last night," I continued, unruffled. "I was hoping I could do so today."

"Why?"

Okay, let's face it: Link was not in the running for Mr. Polite, Mr. Accommodating or Mr. How May I Help? Not even considered for a nomination.

"What's all this about?" he queried, impatient again.

"Dakota."

Silence. "I don't see what this has to do with me."

More silence, this time mine. I hoped he was thinking how bad that sounded.

"I mean . . . uh . . ."

He was. Good. I moved in on it. "What time would be convenient for you?"

He cleared his throat, dropped his voice into a low register. Manly and decisive? "Now is fine. How can I help?"

"Great. I'll be right over."

"I *meant*—" his voice not quite as low now. "I meant on the phone."

Oh *sure*. Like I was going to miss his expressions, his body language. "In person would be better."

"Why?"

"You don't care to help?" I asked, making my voice surprised. "Oh." I went for disappointed and saddened. Sometimes I wonder how Hollywood gets along without me.

"Fine." He sounded resigned. "How soon can you be here?"

I looked at the clock. "By four."

"I have an appointment at five," he said firmly. "Sharp."

"All right. I appreciate your time." I threw that in in an attempt to be gracious.

I was singing "See Ya!" as I flew out the front door and jumped into Dakota's Pathfinder. The address jotted in Dakota's book was a downtown one and it turned out to be a huge modern glass-and-concrete edifice solely inhabited by Charitable Insurance. Now there's an oxymoron. It's stuff like this that makes me cynical. I parked in a multi-level parking garage across the street and zipped over to Charitable. Three fifty-nine. Right on time.

The revolving doors tossed me out into a vast expanse dotted with oases of palm trees and smaller more welcoming plants that hovered over sterile and peopleless couch and chair groupings. Modern paintings of the pastel line-and-blob variety dotted the walls the way the greenery dotted the floor. Expensive and soulless, it was a perfect metaphor for the insurance industry.

Two uniformed security guards who looked as though they were paid not to smile glanced at me as I walked toward the elevator bank. The open doors of the waiting elevator hissed as they closed behind me. Another metaphor?

Davidson's office was on the third floor. Just a number on the door, no clue as to job or title. The office was done in tones of soft gray and green with more vague pastels on the wall and slightly dusty silk plants on the floor. The secretary sat behind a remarkably clean desk and spoke in hushed tones on the phone. I dropped into one of the three upholstered green chairs and waited my turn.

The woman behind the desk glanced up at me and smiled a perky be-right-with-you! smile. Her hair was short and dark and moussed into a dazzling curly display. Red earrings matched a red jacket, red lipstick and nail polish. She was in her early twenties and cute as a button.

"Miss Colorado?" she asked, hanging up the phone. "Mr. Davidson is expecting you. This way, please." She stood, revealing a short red skirt and long, slim, shapely legs, and opened the door to Davidson's office. "Miss Colorado is here, Mr. Davidson." I heard the door click shut softly behind me.

Link didn't look real pleased to see me but he made an effort, half standing behind his desk as he greeted me. His smile was forced, his eyes calculating. "Hi, Kat." His tone falsely jovial. Hollywood wasn't missing a thing. "Won't you sit?" He remained standing until I was seated.

"I'll get right to the point. Dakota's life is in danger."

"What?" He was startled. At the news? Or at my announcement of it?

"She's been receiving threatening anonymous communications. You know about the flash grenade incident, of course. There was also an attempt made on her life." Okay, I exaggerated. Okay, I lied. "I am not at liberty to talk about that," I added quickly, anticipating the question as he opened his mouth. Why stop at one lie? "There is very little to go on, though the police are doing their best. I am here for two reasons. The first is that Dakota asked me to let you know that she would be out of town and unreachable for an indefinite period of time." Lie number three. He swallowed hard. "The second is that although I am one of Dakota's oldest friends I am here as an investigator. I am talking to all of her friends and associates in an attempt to get to the bottom of this.

"I know you will want to help," I finished firmly. Okay, I didn't *know* that, but why stop at three lies?

"Whatever I can do. I had no idea." He leaned forward, elbows on the table, and looked genuinely concerned.

"Allow me to backtrack a little, to fill in the gaps in my knowledge. How did you and Dakota meet?"

"We met at a party through friends. Dakota is an extraordinary artist. I love music but have very little talent for it. I pick a little, sing a little, like to hang out with people in the business. I knew of Dakota, had for several years. It was a pleasure to meet her." He shrugged.

"We met. We hit it off. That's it."

"How long have you known each other?"

"About three months."

"And you do a lot of things together?"

He frowned.

"I don't mean to be personal," I explained quickly, though of course I did. "I'm wondering if you know most of Dakota's friends and associates, if you would be in a position to assess a person or situation that might be, or become, threatening to her?"

Perfect. A personal question that sounded professional. His face cleared. He rolled his shoulders and cracked his knuckles. Concentrating, I guess. I waited patiently.

"We did a fair amount together. I knew her manager, the guys in the band, most of her friends. Yeah, I was in a position."

That was important to him, I thought. He liked knowing that he was on the inside loop, and he liked knowing that other people knew that too.

"In a position?" I asked.

"To see, to pick things up."

"And what did you see, pick up?"

He frowned again. "Everyone loves Dakota. She's not just a great singer, she's a great person. Still, people get jealous. There's a lot of that in this business."

"Jealous enough to threaten her? To hurt her?"

"Hard to believe. Usually it's just gossip, backbiting, more or less hidden meanness."

"But someone's gone further." His face darkened.

"Who do you think?"

The words exploded out of him. "Cal Jenkins, that son of a bitch."

Cal. Everyone's favorite for bad guy.

"Why?"

"He can't let the past go. He thinks that Dakota owes him, that he's the reason she's a success and that she should pay for that. One way or another," he added, his face ugly with emotion.

"Meaning?"

"Dakota owes him nothing. But all the threats, the danger—she's paying, isn't she?"

"Anyone else?"

He shrugged. "There's a million people who want something from you when you're hot. They're hangers-on. They don't threaten you."

Or try to murder you.

"Those kind of people, they want you around as long as possible. You're no good to them a loser. Can't milk a dead cow." He looked at his watch, then back to me. "No one wants a dead cow."

Cadillac cowboys, broken angels and now dead cows.

"Her manager, the guys in the band?"

He rolled his shoulders, shrugging it off. "Seem like straight-up guys to me."

"Other artists?"

"I wouldn't know."

"Last night at the Bluebird, you sat next to Hope."

He flushed slightly. Flushed? I pretended not to notice.

"What was your impression of her?"

"Seems like a nice enough kid." Casual in the extreme. "Any ulterior motives?"

"She's family, right? Just a kid who needs a break. Anything else—I don't know. I take things pretty much at face value."

An insurance man who takes things at face value? Give me a break.

"How did you get into the insurance business, Link?" He was wearing a three-hundred-dollar suit and a Rolex. This business, or something, had been good to him.

"Started young, worked my way up." He gave the Rolex a long, careful scrutiny. "Hope this has been a help, Kat. You be sure and call me now if I can help you out again." He started up from his chair. I followed his lead.

"How do I get in touch with Dakota? I'd like to send flowers or something."

"She's not taking any calls. I'm sure she'll appreciate the thought, though."

"Yeah," he said, but he looked pissed.

I preceded him out the door he opened for me and into the reception area. The woman in red looked up from her computer.

"Mr. Johnston called. He asked if you could meet him this afternoon to go over the—"

"Put him off. You through with the Bradley report?" He spoke to her as though she were a performing bug. And not a very talented one, either.

"I'm working on it, sir." Her voice was soft. I thought she sounded as though she was close to tears.

"Get it done. Today."

"It's after four-thirty, Mr. Davidson. It'll take me at least another hour and a half, and this evening I—"

"Is your social life more important than your job?"

"It's not that. It's—"

"Whatever." He snapped it out, turned to me and smiled. "Kat," he said politely, and nodded goodbye.

"Thanks for your help, Link."

"Anytime." His office door clicked shut behind him.

I looked at the woman in red. "What's your name?" I

spoke gently, softly.

"Barbie." There was a frightened flicker in her eyes. "It isn't my social life, honest. My cousin is real sick and in the hospital. I've been helping take care of the kids. It's not right, him wanting me to work late on such short notice." There were tears in her eyes now.

"Barbie, my name is Kat Colorado. I'm an out-of-state investigator. I've been talking to Mr. Davidson. I'd like to talk to you." Badly treated employees don't have much loyalty.

"About?" she asked cautiously, her emotional outburst over now. I tipped my head toward Link's closed door. "There's reason to believe—" I broke off and left it there, left it wide open for assumption.

"About Mr. Davidson?" She spoke in a low voice, almost a whisper.

I nodded. "It would all be confidential of course."

The residue of tears disappeared. Her cheeks flushed, her eyes brightened. Treat people like performing bugs and they're real happy to drop a dime on you.

"Oh. Okay. Sure. I'd be glad to help."

"May I buy you dinner tonight after you're through at your cousin's?"

"It's eight, eight-thirty 'fore I get the kids to bed. Is that too late?" she asked doubtfully.

"Not for me." Not at all. I love to hear dimes drop. It's something I'd stay up late for any day.

"Okay. Great." She brightened even more. "Where?"

"Since I don't know my way around, will you pick a restaurant? A *nice* one. Expense doesn't matter."

"Mario's, then." She smiled.

I smiled back. "I'll be at Mario's at eight. See you when you get there." She was still smiling as I walked out.

I didn't go right back to the car.

Temptation was too strong for me.

I cruised the street slowly on foot, enjoying the spring weather and keeping Charitable Insurance in view. I didn't have long to wait. Link Davidson exited Charitable at four-fifty. I was right behind him as we headed down Fourth, half a block and a bunch of people between us. We walked past the Ryman Auditorium, the first home of the Grand Ole Opry, with flowers out front and a statue of Tom Ryman standing next to a huge paddle wheel, past an old brick building in the process of being restored. The faded paint of advertisements from another era graced the buildings. *The Alamo of Nashville*. I wondered what that was. We crossed the street at Broadway. He made it on the light, I didn't. I watched as he entered the Merchant Restaurant & Grill.

It looked like an elegant, upscale restaurant that catered to the professional crowd. Brick, stone and iron grillwork graced by canopies. Business lunches and cocktails and all on the corporate tab. Link's kind of place. The light finally turned green and I followed him. I was cutting it close, closer than I like to. Life in the snoop lane. If I got caught I'd have to tell lies. If I didn't, I'd be ahead. Not a tough call.

I pulled open the heavy old doors and entered a lovely foyer with intricate parquet flooring and a hostess stand with a sweetly simpering hostess. The downstairs bar was to my left. I walked in with my chin tucked to my chest (my face—I hoped—difficult to see) and a tissue held to my nose, making delicate, ladylike sneeze sounds—*pftooi, pftooi*—and trying to disappear into the dark wood, marble-topped, copper-detailed, people-packed background.

Davidson was standing at the bar with his back to me, drinking what looked like a double bourbon on the rocks. Drinking fast. What a lush. The place, fortunately, was crowded. I scooted past him and around to the far side of the horseshoe-shaped bar where I snagged a stool at the end of the bar. I could see Davidson by stretching, but was out of his direct line of vision.

"What can I get y'all?"

"Chardonnay, please."

Speaking of lushes. I could have had an iced tea. Oh well, when in Rome . . . Davidson was talking in an animated fashion to a three-piece suit but his eyes frequently checked his watch and the entryway.

I was focused on him, so I missed the entrance. He didn't. I could tell by the way his jaw dropped. Somewhere in his conversation with the suit he had claimed a barstool. He stood now, in greeting, and spoke. I wished I could see his eyes. Not to mention hear the conversation.

The woman wore black leggings and boots, her legs shapely and muscled rather than slim. The jacket was long and of some kind of silky, shiny material I didn't recognize. Under the jacket she wore a low-cut lacy red top. The black of her bra peeked through the lace, showcasing her full breasts. A tiny black bag covered with jet beads dangled on a long strap from her left hand. Jet earrings hung from her earlobes. The red of the top set off her beautiful hair. Her right hand reached out to Davidson and they embraced affectionately.

Hope had left country bumpkin way behind her.

twenty-five
HEY SAILOR!

THEY STAYED LONG ENOUGH FOR A QUICK DRINK—
real quick, I'd finished less than half of my wine—
then left, Hope clinging vinelike to Link's arm. Smiling at
each other, not talking. It was clear that they had places to
go, things to do.

I waited just long enough to give them a head start. No
point in trying to follow—my chances of getting out of the
parking lot and on Link's tail were slim and none. Anyway,
I had other fish to fry. Back to Dakota's where I looked up
the number I'd gotten from Trudy and placed the call. A
familiar man's voice answered. If you can call snarling answering.

I pitched my voice high, added a nasal twang and twisted
the receiver about six inches from my mouth.

"Overseas operator for...uh...Can Jenkins." I
couldn't resist, honest, and it could have been worse. Crud
was my first choice. Cad wasn't bad either.

"*Cal* Jenkins. You mean Cal Jenkins?"

"Is Can Jenkins there, sir?" I waved the sentence up and
down in loud and soft tones. "I have a call for—" I clicked
the button on the receiver a few times. "Are you there,
sir?" My voice faded at the end of the question. "Trying
a new line. Please hold on." I drifted off, clicked the button
some more and broke the connection.

Looking good so far. Cal was home, hopefully would stay parked for a while. Not me, I was ready to speed. First stop, Dakota's closet. We're about the same size and we've always traded clothes. Dakota's got great taste and I have the fashion sense of a stray dog so basically it's a much better deal for me than for her. Although I do have a bunch of exceptionally fine swimsuits. California, you know. Oh, and baseball caps, too.

Fashion and style weren't uppermost in my mind today. Snooping was. I looked through the closet quickly. Nothing jumped out. Hmmm. Hope's look was something. Maybe I'd take a page out of her book.

Ten minutes later I smiled in satisfaction as I gazed into the full-length mirror. Black leggings; black boots that were a little too small—hope I didn't have to do any running; hot-pink bustier—also a little small so we are talking *fan-*tastic cleavage; a loose black jacket with the sleeves rolled up. I was all gobbed up with makeup, too.

A little slutty and tarty with a dash of hey sailor!

Perfect! Maybe I had more fashion sense than I thought? I whistled and posed briefly. If this didn't charm Sonny's socks off, what would? Shoot, where was a camera when you needed it? I headed for the Pathfinder and hit the road.

Okay, there were a few possible flaws in this line of reasoning. The only thing I knew about Sonny was what Trudy had told me. That he and Cal hung out and drank a lot together, that one of their favorite spots was Sal's. So, I reasoned, if he was Cal's buddy how likely was he to be a class act with a taste for elegant women? Not. Tarty, slutty and hey sailor! were a pretty good call. Not just for him, for Sal's too. I might strike out but it was worth a shot.

I'd never been there but, from location alone, I could tell you what Sal's looked like. Exactly. Every town has a Sal's. Long bar, wooden stools with no cushions; tables with scummy surfaces and metal ashtrays stamped out sometime in the Eisenhower administration; cigarettes, booze, disinfectant and half-rotten/half-drowned dreams.

By and large the people are okay but they are mostly losers with nowhere else to go.

I rolled down the window and sucked in fresh air. Just thinking about it made me feel queasy. I was back in East Nashville, on Main near Five Points. And Sal's wasn't the only thing that made me queasy.

What Jimmy Deeter had said did too. "Five Points is okay, but there are parts of East Nashville that aren't. It's salt 'n' pepper there. There are projects and guns and drug deals on the corners. It's a bad place at night, Kat. Hell, it's a bad place anytime. Don't get lost in East Nashville."

I drove past Sal's and parked half a block away, leaving some distance between me and the sprinkling of cars parked in front of the bar. Two pickups, a beat-up El Camino, an even more beat-up van and a couple of compacts.

No Cadillac. No Cal.

Good so far.

I took a deep breath before I walked in, my last fresh air for a while. The smell of urine and disinfectant from the rest rooms to my right blasted me briefly. I blinked, waiting for my eyes to adjust. My description? Right on the money. I'd forgotten about the pool tables, though. There were two here. Five guys at the bar, two at a pool table. No bartender.

My hot-pink bustier was a big hit. Well, that and my pushed-up breasts and ample cleavage. The guys didn't fall off their barstools but in one case it was a close call. The bartender walked in from the back carrying a case of beer and looked at me without interest. Dead eyes. Seen-it-all-and-don't-give-a-shit eyes.

I walked up to the bar. "I'm looking for a guy named Sonny. Know where I could find him?" I inhaled. (Go with your strengths.) My breasts bulged out of the bustier.

He looked at me briefly, eye level not breast level, then ripped open the box and started stocking beer in the cooler in front of him. Not rotating it either. Good bartenders stock the fresh to the back.

"Sonny," he said in a leaden voice that wasn't quite a question.

So I knew Sonny was there. Dead Eyes wasn't going

to help me either; it was Sonny's call. I inhaled again, breasts bulging again, and looked around.

The guy in the middle of the bar was the best bet. Hard to tell sitting down but he looked to be medium height. Stocky build, with dark hair pulled into a short ponytail. His face was pockmarked but pleasant with even, regular features. I guessed that he was mid-forties but he could have been younger. Drugs, sex, and rock 'n' roll take their toll. He wore a T-shirt with a picture of "cool" Joe Camel playing a guitar, cigarette dangling from his fingers, and blue jeans.

I smiled at him. "Would you know Sonny?"

He stood politely. "At your service, ma'am." He kept his eyes on my face. Very gentlemanly.

"You're Sonny?" I waited for his confirming nod. "Could I, uh, talk to you? Please," I added quickly, shyly. Hey sailor! and shy—nice combination, don't you think?

"Sure." He pulled out a barstool.

"Maybe over there?" I pointed at one of the tables.

He nodded, reached for his Pabst Blue Ribbon and followed me to a table by the window facing onto the street. No sunshine, just kind of a hazy blur. The windows had probably last been cleaned about the same time the *Hindenburg* went down. The chair scraped across the floor as I pulled it out, leaving marks in the ingrained floor slime.

"Get you a drink, miss?" Sonny pulled out a chair and put his drink on the table.

"Thank you." I smiled beatifically, really into the angel/slut role now. "Maybe a light beer?" I almost ordered a Pepsi but caught myself in time. *Never* order anything in a glass in a bar like this, where they change the cold, scummy water in the washtubs twice a day. Maybe.

Sonny brought me a Bud Light, a glass and a napkin, and smiled at my thank-you. I arranged my beer on the napkin and then gazed into his eyes. "I don't know how to start."

Sonny smiled again, encouraging me. His eyes traveled to my hot-pink display when I took a sip of beer and he thought I wouldn't notice.

"I had this friend Susie who had a friend—" I wrinkled my brow in apparent concentration, then gave up. "Oh, I can't remember now. Anyway, that girl said she knew you and that you were nice. *Really* nice." I fluttered my eyes just a tad.

He didn't look like he had a clue. Sonny was a man who had put his boots under a lot of beds. More than he could remember—the beds or the women. It didn't bother either of us.

"Well, now," he said, accepting the reference point and arching an eyebrow in question.

"She said maybe you could help me. Being as you're such a nice guy and all." I stressed the "all" slightly so that it covered a lot of territory.

"*Well,* now," Sonny said.

Okay, I had him hook, line and sinker. All I had to do was reel him in.

"You see, I've always *always* wanted to be a singer. Country music, it's my life. So I came to Nashville."

Sonny kept the expression on his face alert and interested but his eyes were bored. He'd heard this a million times and, like the bartender, didn't give a shit. Maybe he'd wanted to be a star once. Maybe music had been his life. It wasn't now. He might still pick but the passion was gone. He was up for a trade, though, no problem. A cute little gal with big knockers wanted to talk and looked like she was offering? He was ready. He'd have a hard-on in a minute and who cared what kind of bullshit got him there.

"You came to the right place." Sonny eased a cigarette—a Camel, to match his shirt—out of the pack and offered it to me. When I shook my head he lit up.

Bait and switch. "I heard tell you know some really *big* stars. I heard tell you know Cal Jenkins."

"Yeah." He nodded. "I do." *So what?* his tone said.

"The honky tonk hero," I breathed out in feigned ecstasy.

He caught the bored look before it settled in. Barely.

I kept on talking. "Do you know Dakota Jones, too?"

"Yeah. I do." A look of a different kind flickered across his face.

"What's she like? Is she as nice and sweet as she seems?"

"Nothing's what it seems. What's your name again?"

"Rita." Though I hadn't said before.

"Know what I mean, Rita?"

"Cal's a friend of yours, right? That's what I heard tell."

"Right." He was humoring me, talking me around to the clothes-dropping part which—he hoped—was coming soon.

"What's he think about Dakota? I mean they were married and all."

"Well, he ain't fooled by the surface. I guess you could say that he's met the real Dakota, the one underneath the smiling surface."

"Yeah? What's she like?"

"Really?"

"Really." I coaxed him along with a little smile.

"A bitch."

"No!" I said it in the kind of voice that means *Oh God, I love this kind of dirt—give me more*. "Like what? What do you mean?"

"Once she made it, she forgot who her friends were. She was too damn good for—them." He almost said *us*. "Just plain old greedy. Uppity from there on out. A bitch." Sonny was caught up in his topic now. Passionate.

"But didn't Cal steal songs from her or something? That's what I heard. And money, too, or—I don't know. Something."

"Lies." His face darkened. "Them are the lies she told. Nobody believes them."

The courts had. I didn't bring that up though.

"Jeez, I never would have thought. I guessed they were friends and all still."

"Naw, he hates her guts." Sonny slugged down his beer.

"I feel sorry for her though, don't you? I mean after that bombing and everything at the concert. No one deserves *that*."

Sonny glanced at me, chugged his beer. He was sick of

this subject. I didn't have much longer. He set his bottle on the table a little too hard.

"What goes around comes around. She'll get hers, she'll get it good. She'll be good and goddamn sorry."

"Was it Cal who did that? To get even? Wow! I'm impressed, *really* impressed," I said, switching sides again.

"Naw." Sonny smiled at me. "Don't be thinking that now." Only his words were a denial.

"I sure would like to meet Cal." Sonny frowned slightly. "I bet he can't hold a candle to *you*, but it'd be fun, a story to tell back home." I leaned forward, elbows on the table, and batted my eyes at Sonny and hoped to hell I wasn't about to tumble out of my bustier.

He fell for it. The frown disappeared.

We're all so gullible, I thought sadly, so desperate to be appreciated, to be loved in some way, any way, that we bought into almost anything.

"I reckon that could be arranged," Sonny said, buying in. "In fact, speaking of the devil." He grinned at me. Cal had just walked in and was standing at the bar, his back to us, the dark hair unmistakable even in the gloom.

"Oh God, don't say anything!" Panic in my voice. I wasn't acting anymore either. "First I've got to—to go fix my hair," I said, improvising wildly. "And my makeup."

"You look great, Rita. Purty as a flower."

"I'll be *right* back. Y'all wait for me!" I made a dash toward the rest room—around the corner and right by the entrance, thank God—and was out of the bar and halfway down the block before Sonny could say "I'll have another Blue Ribbon."

I didn't breathe easily until I was in the car and standing on the gas pedal. Didn't breathe easily then either.

The damn bustier was too tight.

twenty-six

PHILANTHROPISTS, PHILANDERERS AND LOVERS

TIME FOR A COSTUME CHANGE. WHAT PLAYED AT SAL'S wouldn't fly at Mario's. Not to mention that slutty and hey sailor! wasn't really me. I headed back for Dakota's, braking sharply as a little old person in a big old Lincoln pulled into my lane without looking or signaling.

It's not just cars and driving, it's people. We live the way we drive, taking off for we're not sure where, changing lanes and directions without thinking it through or checking things out, making sudden impetuous moves without counting the cost or assessing possible damage. Driving blind, living blind.

I thought about Link and Hope. Was that connection sudden and impetuous? Was the evening at the Bluebird the first time they had met? Their demeanor at the bar this afternoon didn't suggest that, although they could be people who got to know each other real fast. I thought over the implications of see-through lacy tops. And were going to

get to know each other even better in the very near future?
I didn't like it.

What was Link doing fooling around with Hope while
he was dating Dakota? What was Hope doing going after
Link? (Uh-oh, soap opera again.) And she was. Pursuing
his acquaintance in jeans and a sweatshirt—the only thing
I'd seen her in until now—was one thing. Slinky black, red
lace and a quarter acre of smooth pink flesh was another,
one with highly questionable implications.

And Sonny?

I sighed. There sure were a lot of good ol' boys around
Dakota. Although Sonny didn't count much except as a
reflection of Cal. *She'll get hers, she'll get it good. She'll
be good and goddamn sorry.* I didn't like that either, I
admit it. Still, there was a big difference between bitterness,
hatred, a desire for revenge, and murder. Not that murder
didn't often start with hatred and revenge. And Cal was a
volatile man with a hot temper whose relationships with
women were marked by violence. I pulled into the driveway at Dakota's, then walked around checking things out
before going in.

Once inside I just about ripped the bustier off. Big time
relief. How does Madonna do it? I jumped into slacks and
a blouse, flats and a blazer. And washed the makeup off
my face. Goodbye Rita, hello Kat.

I was a little late getting to Mario's but I still beat Barbie.
I sat at the bar, ordered a mineral water and looked around.
More elegance. The foyer had marble flooring with a white
iron grill overhead. Lush green plants spilled down from
there into the room. The floor was black and white marble
squares; small marble-topped tables were scattered invit-
ingly about. A magnificent old wooden bar presided at one
end and all around were walls of wine cabinets stocked with
wine I'd probably never heard of and undoubtedly couldn't
afford.

I had a ten-minute wait. Barbie was hard to miss—perky
and bright in red—but she scooted in and looked around
with a tentative air, an I'm-not-sure-I belong-here look. I
walked over to the foyer to join her.

"Oh! There you are," she gushed. "Gosh, what a nice place. I've never been here before, just heard about it."

The maître d' materialized next to us holding menus. We followed him to a corner table, cozy and private. The mood was muted and expensive, starched white linen, flowers and delicate antiques. I reined in my impatience until we'd ordered and Barbie was settled in and wrapped around a drink.

"Tell me about Davidson." *Investigator rule #4: Give them plenty of room to fill in the big picture, to bring up things you don't know about or wouldn't have heard of. Then go for specifics.*

"What kind of an investigation did you say this is?"

I hadn't. *Details.* "There have been some complaints and questions about policy decisions. I'm here to try to answer all those points. Some of them involve Davidson. I cannot be more specific at this point, of course, because it could impact on privacy and personnel issues." *Whew, talk about verbal gobbledygook.*

"Of course," Barbie agreed, looking understandably dazed.

"Mr. Davidson?" I prompted.

Barbie took a fortifying sip of her cocktail. "What exactly are you looking for?"

"How long have you worked for him? How well do you know him?" I answered her questions with ones of my own.

"I've worked for Charitable for six years, two of those years as Mr. Davidson's assistant." I noted the bitterness in her voice. ' "Secretary," he says, or 'girl.' 'I'll have my girl set up a time for you.' I just *hate* that. I worked hard to get where I am and I want to be called by my correct title. Is that too much to ask?"

"No." *Reasonable.* "Actually, I would think it's the *absolute* minimum you should expect." *Fanning the flames.*

"Well, exactly! I've lasted longer than anyone, you know. Before me he went through assistants faster than Murphy Brown. The company has given me good raises and benefits but, even so, sometimes I wonder if it's worth

it. And I do a lot of his work. I mean, if he didn't have me
to organize and keep him on top of things, he'd be sunk.
He'd be a fish out of water,'' she announced in an interesting twist of metaphor.

"What does he do?"

"He's a manager. He runs a division." She snorted.
"Everyone else worked his or her way up the ladder. Not
Mr. Big Shot Davidson." She was on a roll now, eating
her salad in angry little bites and waving her fork to punc-
tuate her comments.

"Oh?"

She broke off a piece of bread, slapped butter on it,
popped it into her mouth and chewed furiously.

"His grandfather was one of the founders of the company. He, the grandfather, has been out of the picture for
some time. The company is run by CEOs now but obviously the family still has enough influence—stock holdings,
probably—to pull this one off."

"Is Davidson incompetent?"

"No. That's the funny thing about it. He's really very
smart. Every once in a while he'll give his whole attention
to the business and it's amazing what he gets done. Everyone likes him at first, too, before he acts like a jerk one too
many times. He has a real head for the insurance business
and could really do something with it but he doesn't seem
to want to. He's just in it for the ride. If it weren't for his
family connection he'd be out tomorrow. Yesterday,'' she
amended and buttered another piece of bread before con-
tinuing.

"You want to know what the gossip is?"

I nodded. That was exactly what I wanted to know.

"That management is getting really fed up. If he doesn't
shape up even his family might not be able to stop him
from getting canned."

There was a gleeful note in her voice. I thought of Cal
and Sonny. *She'll get hers.* Everyone wants to see other
people get theirs, especially if it's bad.

"He's been on his toes a lot more lately. Still, I just
don't see how it can last. He was born with a silver spoon

in his mouth and thinks the world owes him a living. He didn't start off in insurance. Oh no. He wanted to be a musician. I guess his family tried to buy him a record deal but it didn't work. He's got some talent but that isn't doodly squat in this town. This town is full of *real* talent."

She paused to take a breath and watched as the waiter removed our salad plates and served our entrees.

"Mmmm." Barbie licked her lips at a steak the size of a small briefcase, picked up her steak knife and attacked it. It was rare and juicy and she made happy little sounds as she chewed. "So, where was I?" she asked as she blotted her lips.

"He thinks the world owes him a living." I picked a point of considerable interest to me.

"Oh, yeah. And not an everyday scratch-along living either. He's got expensive tastes—drives a Porsche, wears expensive suits and fancy made-to-order boots, eats at all the best places, lives in a good neighborhood." She shrugged. "The phrases 'self-denial' and 'economize' mean nothing to him. Even if he tried, he couldn't do it. I mean if he can't keep this job he's going to have to get himself a rich wife." She grinned.

"Is he dating anyone like that?"

"I don't know." Genuine regret in her voice. "He's really close about that part of his life. Once a woman complained because I asked for her name so then he told me never to ask lady callers to identify themselves, just to put them through. So I do." She sighed and popped a large bite of steak into her mouth, chewed it thoughtfully for a moment. "You know what I think?"

I shook my head.

"I bet you're looking into insurance sales to the elderly, misrepresentation and maybe fraud, aren't you?"

I wasn't, but I could, at least in a peripheral kind of way. "Boy, you're sharp," I said and shook my head in admiration. "Tell me what you know about it."

"It's so sad." She sniffed. "He's preying on old people, on all their fears and worries. He talks about how inflation's going up and how no one can really count on Social Security and how they could be sick and penniless in the streets. Of course, that's not going to happen, not with the folks he's talking to. They've got money, investments and property, or he wouldn't waste a minute on them. Not a minute. But by then he's got them shaking in their seats and just beside themselves with worry.''

She pushed the remains of her steak around on her plate with her fork. ''And then he says, 'But don't worry, I can take care of you,' and they start to breathe again. They're ready to sign whatever he puts in front of them, just to keep the fear away.

''He's good at this, Kat, really good. He could sell electric blankets to people in hell. He's soft-spoken and polite. Very respectful. And he has a way of acting like the person is his grandma or grandpa and it's *terribly* important to him that they be taken care of. They totally believe him. It'd be hard not to, he's that good.''

''What exactly does he do?'' Detail time.

''He gets them to buy insurance for the future—these people are in their seventies or eighties, I mean how much future do they have?—using their investments or their houses, which they almost always own free and clear. So basically, they're throwing away real assets—real estate, savings and investments—for an insurance policy they may never use that liquidates their assets.''

''You mentioned fraud. Is this illegal?''

''It's kind of a gray area. It certainly is if he lies or misrepresents the policy in any way. I haven't heard him do that, which is not to say that he wouldn't when there weren't any witnesses,'' she added darkly.

''But it's immoral, playing on people's fears and getting them to turn their real assets into paper they won't use and certainly can't leave to their heirs. And old people scare easily, get confused easily. He doesn't help them see through that, he plays on it. For Mr. Davidson, it's simple: no insurance, no commission. And he wants that commission.

''I *hate* it. I just think it's lower than dirt on a snake's belly. If someone sold that bunch of lies to my grandparents I'd be ready to skin them alive.''

"Coffee? Dessert?" the waiter inquired, not raising an eyebrow over such bloodthirsty talk. Barbie had both. Fuming over injustice really works up an appetite. I know this from experience.

Barbie dug into a piece of mocha cheesecake with enthusiasm.

"What was his name, the grandfather who was one of Charitable's founders?"

"Harter Hodges Davidson. He had three sons and named them all for presidents he admired. Washington Harter Davidson, Jefferson Harter Davidson and Lincoln Harter Davidson. He was a real fine old man from what I hear. I mean, for one thing he was a Southerner and he named a son after Abraham Lincoln. That's guts for you.''

"Or conviction."

"Yeah." She nodded. "Whatever. And he believed in the vote for women—his wife was on a lot of boards and things—and they contributed to charities and the arts and worked for the preservation of historical sites. The family is very respected hereabouts.''

"You know a lot about them." I was a little surprised.

She shrugged. "I got it from a brochure the company puts out. The human-interest angle and all that.''

"And Link is Lincoln Harter Davidson's son?"

"Yes."

"Are there other children in the family?"

She nodded. "A brother, Jeff, and a sister. Isabelle, I think.''

"Are they in the insurance business?"

"No." She chased the last crumb of cheesecake around her plate. "She's married to a well-known attorney and does a lot of charitable work. Her husband works for the company though; he's one of the head lawyers.''

"And the brother?"

"I don't know. I only know about Isabelle because her husband works for Charitable. *Really* works,'' she added in a snotty tone.

"Do Link and his brother-in-law get along?"

"The talk is no. The talk is that Link doesn't really get along with anyone in the family. Except for his mother. She favors him and always sticks up for him. Apparently they're real close and he's always sweet as pie to her."

"Does the brother live in Nashville?"

"I think so, I don't really know." She wrinkled her nose. "What does this have to do with Mr. Davidson?"

"Background. Very important."

"Oh." She didn't look entirely convinced but said nothing. Well, except for: "That cheesecake was *really* good. Do you think I could have another piece?"

"Sure." I signaled a waiter and she ordered.

"This is such a treat, Kat. Mario's! I wish I could come to places like this all the time."

I had a one-track mind and food wasn't the track. "Charitable is an unusual name for an insurance company."

The waiter placed the cheesecake in front of Barbie and she sighed happily, contemplated it blissfully but briefly before she dug in.

"It is, huh? That was the grandfather. He was a great, ummm, phil—ummmm, philanderer I think the word is. You know, he did good works and things."

"Philanthropist," I corrected. "A philanderer is someone who runs around with women."

She giggled and popped a hand over her mouth. *Like Link*, is what we were both thinking.

"Anyway, Harter Hodges Davidson said that a certain percentage of the profits *had* to be put back into the community. Into charity. After he married, it was the arts, too, because of his wife."

"Is that still the policy?"

"I don't think so. I don't think it has been for some time. Does this have to do with your investigation?"

"It could." I nodded and glanced at a grandfather clock. "You don't always know at the beginning."

Barbie dumped cream and sugar into her coffee and stirred. "Oh. Well, I hope you nail him," Barbie said and sipped her coffee delicately. She seemed eager to linger, reluctant to end our conversation. "Call me *any*time." She scribbled her phone number down on a cocktail napkin. "I'd love to help."

"I'll do that. Keep your eyes and ears open."

She grinned. "I always do."

I gave her my office number in Sacramento and told her to call collect, I'd get back to her.

As we parted in the parking lot she said, "I wish I had a job like yours. Investigating. Getting the bad guys." Her voice was wistful.

"Why don't you then? You're not stuck in an office. Or perhaps you should consider being an investment counselor or advocate for the elderly? You got real fired up over that. The world needs more fired-up people."

"Oh, I wish. Nobody takes me seriously, though. Not like you." Wistful again.

I smiled. "They will if you have the training. You've already got the fight and the nerve. May I make a suggestion?"

"Sure." Her face was turned up, young, eager and excited in a circle of lamplight.

"Instead of Barbie, go by Barb or Barbara."

"Oh? Why?"

Barbie is a doll. "It's more powerful."

"Barbara Ann? That's my full name."

"That's good too."

"Thank you. Good night, Kat."

"Good night, Barbara Ann."

I watched her walk to her car, her high heels clicking on the pavement in the staccato certainty of youth.

IT WAS QUIET AT DAKOTA'S. GOOD. I WAS READY FOR A hot bath and bed. Three phone messages. One from Garrett to say that the alarm company was coming tomorrow and he was sending someone over to let them in and supervise. One from Dakota and Rafe. One from Hank. First I poured a glass of wine, then I made calls.

It sounded like a party—music, voices and laughter. I wished, in a sudden rush of emotion, that I was there too.

"Granny? It's Kat."

"Katy, dear, how are you? Is everything all right? Bless you for sending Cody home. We miss you." Her voice faded out.

"Katy? Is everything okay? Has anything happened? What are you doing?"

I laughed at Dakota. She sounded young and carefree. Happy. "Everything's fine. Me, too. How was your flight?"

"Uneventful. We're playing charades. Would you believe it? Just like years ago. Alma's here too. And Rafe. They both want to talk to you."

I talked to everyone. And then I called Hank. The phone rang six times. I was ready to hang up when he answered. He spoke in his hard voice, the one I think of as his cop voice. My heart sank a little.

"Hank."

"Katy, sweetheart, how are you?"

The hardness was gone—it was love and warmth. I felt like I was sinking into a down comforter. We talked about everyday things, the known and familiar, in the way that is so comforting. A stray thought was nagging at me but I couldn't quite catch it.

And then I did. "Hank, does anyone ever kill out of love?"

"No. In passion, but not for love. People kill when they have lost love, or are angry with one they love, or won't let go of a love that has left them. But that's not love. It's control, or hatred, anger or greed. Love builds. Killing, like hatred and anger, destroys."

And we are silent because it is not only killing that destroys. Broken or betrayed trust does too and we are too close to that one. We say our goodbyes with love. We are very careful with our love now. We do not take it for granted.

Later I thought about killing for love. About the young father, tears in his eyes, who unplugged the machines that were keeping his severely disabled, painfully and terminally ill infant alive, holding hospital personnel at bay with a gun until his son died quietly in his arms.

Or the eighty-three-year-old woman who shot and killed her husband just before they came to take him away. She sat holding her dead husband's hand, and surrendered the gun quietly. He, too, was eighty-three but crippled by arthritis and in the last stages of Alzheimer's. "We have been married sixty-two years and, except for the Great War, we have never spent a night apart," she said to the police.

"He made me promise that I would never let this happen. I would have killed myself, too, but that would be a sin, for I am still strong enough to bear what God has given to me. He was not. It wasn't a crime," she explained to the police officer, who listened quietly. And she kissed her husband's cheek, tenderly smoothed his thin white hair back from his forehead. "God understands. I pray that I am with him soon."

When the police arrested her there was such an outcry in the small rural community where she lived—and they recognized love—that the authorities let her go again. She died a month later, her face serene and composed, a slight smile on her lips. "She was going to him. They would be together again," a neighbor said. "And she was happy."

They had killed out of love, those two.

But that was rare.

And not what worried me.

twenty-seven

SEX, LIES AND CROSSES

I LOOKED UP DAVIDSON IN THE PHONE BOOK. BINGO. A Forest Hills address not far from Dakota. My concern wasn't that Link was a faithless philandering boyfriend. After all, Dakota was a big girl, and not only could she take care of herself, it was none of my business. Not that that had ever stopped me.

My concern in this was the Hope/Link connection. If it wasn't a case of simple lust (best bet so far), then it got interesting. If they knew each other, then it got really interesting. If they were in cahoots—ooops, I was starting to sound like a bad Western—then it was off the charts. But motive was still a luxury. Right now facts would be nice.

I set the alarm for six.

I am not at my best in the early morning. Not even second or third or— But you get the picture. I hit the alarm and jumped out of bed and into the shower without giving myself time to think. I was dressed and in the Pathfinder, rolling through a fast-food drive-in lane for coffee still half asleep. Two large coffees. Black. Go-for-jolt time. Then over to Link's neighborhood. I stayed on Hillwood to West End, where I headed south, then east on Harding and on into Forest Hills.

It was a quiet residential area with a number of cars parked on the street. I tucked the Pathfinder into a space between two resident cars just down from Link's place and hoped we'd fit right in. It's always iffy parking and snooping in nice neighborhoods like this. The fact that it was so early was in my favor but this is the kind of area where people notice and care about what is going on. And—more to the point—report suspicious stuff to the cops. Like strangers lurking in parked cars. Like me.

I slumped down into the seat so I could just see over the wheel. I had a clear view of the house and the street in front of me and a limited one through the side mirrors. I saw no familiar vehicles. Hope's beat-up truck would have stood out here like a panhandler at a prom.

It was seven forty-five and I was on my second cup of coffee when I saw a downstairs light flick on. *All right*. Lights. Camera. Action. The boring part was over.

The metallic rap on my window caught me completely off guard. *Rats*. I sat up suddenly, barking my shin and spilling my coffee. A large face pretty much filled up the driver's-side window. It was red, freshly shaven—one nick on the chin—and scowling. Maybe swearing, I couldn't tell. My shin hurt like hell. I powered the window down.

"Who are you and what are you doing? I been watching you the last hour. This is a nice neighborhood. We don't take to strangers hanging out." He jabbed his keys in the air at me in some kind of unclear but threatening rhythm.

I coaxed out the tears in the back of my eyes—the ones from the shin barking and the coffee spill—and encouraged them to spill down my cheeks. I stuttered as I spoke, snuffled too. This was a clear case of give-it-all-you've-got and head-'em-off-at-the-pass.

"Oh *God!* I am *so* sorry. I don't mean any harm, it's just that—" I thought about the possibility of being questioned by cops and the tears spilled right out. "It's just that my boyfriend lives over there." I tipped my head toward Link's house. "I think he's been seeing *sniff sniff sniff* someone else. I just *had* to know. Oh God, I can't believe I'm doing this. I'm *so* ashamed." I hung my head and forced out a sob. It was a little feeble but better than nothing.

When he patted my arm, I looked up. The scowl had disappeared, the red face had taken on a kindly look. I sniffed again.

"Over there?" he asked. We both looked at Link's. I saw a shadowy figure move behind the curtain.

"Yes." I nodded sadly.

"Lot of traffic. Lot of girls coming and going."

I almost sat bolt upright in interest, just remembered in time to clutch the steering wheel and moan.

"Look, you're a pretty girl. You deserve better'n that. Why don't you run along home now?"

"I will. Soon," I amended, in case he planned to stand around and watch me drive off. "I just have to know," I explained, squeezing a few more crocodile tears out, my last ones for sure. "I just have to catch that son of a bitch and then I'm leaving him, you bet," I said with considerably more spirit.

He laughed and patted my arm. "That's more like it."

"Don't tell on me, though. Please?" I let my lower lip tremble. Or tried to. I made a mental note to stand in front of a mirror and practice that.

"Naw, your secret's safe with me. Hell, I weren't a family man, I'd take you out myself. You're a cute thing. Don't let anyone tell you different or treat you like dirt. He ain't worth a gal like you."

"Thank you." I stuttered and peeked up at him through half-lowered lashes. Simpering is really an art form and not as easy as it sounds, trust me.

He winked, thumped the car door lightly and walked off. I slumped back into the seat exhausted. The morning air was cool and I shivered as I put up the window. I glanced at the clock on the dash. Seven forty-nine. Only three or four minutes had passed. It had seemed like a week. There was more action at Link's now, a light on upstairs as well. Not much longer. I assumed he would get to work around nine. If Hope was with him he'd have to allow time to drop her off.

The front door opened at eight-twenty. I slumped way down in the seat although I needn't have bothered; they were totally engrossed in each other. Hope had the happy, almost smug look of a woman who's been recently laid. I looked at the satisfied smile on her face again.

Make that recently and repeatedly laid.

Her hand caressed the Porsche before she got in. She liked Link, hot sex and hot cars. That was established now. How did she feel about Dakota, about music and her career? That was unclear still.

I didn't know if they had known each other before. It was clear they did now.

Link backed out of the driveway at about thirty miles per hour, slammed into first and blasted off rocket-style. I followed at a much more sedate pace, and at a distance. If I could pull this off without him noticing me—I was, after all, driving Dakota's familiar vehicle—fine; if not, I'd do it another way.

There were enough stop signs to keep his speed down and keep the Porsche in sight, though I trailed him by about a block or so. After twisting around on a couple of local streets we ended up on Hillsboro which turned into 21st at the overpass of 440. Later it turns into Broadway. Nashville streets frequently change names and always without warning or helpful clues of any kind. Half the streets don't even have street signs. Getting somewhere in Nashville is a challenge. We ended up at the Wild Boar near 21st and Broadway in the same area as Mario's. Link pulled into the now deserted parking area. Not for breakfast, for Hope's truck.

I zipped on by, made a U-turn and headed back. Half a block from the restaurant I pulled into a metered spot on the street, put the engine in neutral and slumped down behind the wheel again. Snooping is *very* bad for your posture.

They were enjoying a prolonged goodbye that involved a lot of hand and (I squinted. Where are your bird-watching binoculars when you need them?) lip action. After a few minutes of this Hope hopped out, leaned down to say something to Link, then closed the car door. He revved the engine a few times, waved and sped off. Not only didn't he walk her to her car—well, shit-heap truck—he didn't even wait until she got in. What a clod.

Hope smoothed her hands down her arms and thighs, smiling dreamily—or dopily, it was hard to tell from this distance—then walked to her truck and climbed in. She wasn't, I noticed, wearing red lace anymore, but a simple white top that looked like a man's undershirt.

Hope drove off. I followed. She drove rather erratically, changing lanes at the last minute, slowing down to look at signs, then speeding up again. Maybe she was wobbly from love; more likely she didn't know her way around Nashville very well. After about fifteen minutes of this her driving smoothed out and improved so I assumed she now knew where she was going.

I had only the vaguest notion of where we were. Okay, that's an exaggeration: I had no idea. We were getting more rural, though. Rural as in white trash, not country estate. Shacky houses with a number of vehicles parked on the property; laundry on lines; dogs and chickens—that kind of thing. I was grateful for the steady stream of early-morning traffic and kept two or three cars between me and Hope. She didn't know the vehicle of course, and certainly wasn't on the lookout for me, so I felt pretty safe. The countryside was beautiful, green and lush. I was just starting to get into it when Hope made a quick—unsignaled— left turn onto a dirt driveway. I zipped on by.

I didn't want to be right on her heels. Even a largely unsuspecting person might wonder about the timing. I did want to catch her in last night's clothes, though. That's enough to throw most of us. Fifteen minutes is what I figured. I made a U-turn and doubled back. The truck was the only vehicle at the place, a small, neat-looking house with an overgrown weedy yard. I saw no signs of anyone else. Good. I wanted Hope all to myself, without backup.

I pulled onto the dirt driveway, fifteen minutes on the dot, and climbed out, slamming the car door. No people. No dogs. I knocked on the door. Nothing. I knocked again. Louder.

Hope yanked the door open. "Yes?"

"Hi!" I said cheerily.

He face crumpled in surprise, consternation and something else I couldn't identify. She fell back a little. I took it as an invitation, though of course it wasn't, and stepped in.

"Just going out?" I scanned her clothes, her face—still smeared slightly with last night's makeup. "No," I corrected. "Just coming in. I guess you're settling into Nashville pretty well."

"Why are you here?" We stood by the open door, cold air following me in. She was upset and trying not to show it. I didn't blame her.

"I'm going to skip the formalities." Yeah, I know. I already had. "It's about your working for Dakota. Shall we close the door? Maybe sit down?"

She closed the door. Grudgingly. I looked around. The decorating scheme was back-to-basic. Or maybe barebones. Also dark colors, minimal light, and religion. Somber faces of Jesus gazed mournfully at me everywhere I looked. I sat on an old wooden rocker keeping my eyes pitched low so the large three-dimensional bleeding Jesus on the cross wouldn't get to me. Hope sat across from me on a clean but threadbare and sad-looking sofa.

"This is very early." She toned down her disapproval—not, I was sure, out of politeness but because apparently I had a great deal of influence on Dakota.

"So?" I spoke almost rudely, a perfect example of how power goes to your head. Or manipulation. Here's how the manipulation works: Nervous people lose control. Out-of-control people say indiscreet things. And indiscreet was *exactly* what I was in the mood for. Hope's eyes dropped, flickered around the room, then settled on her hands. Her demure look was back. "Where were you last night?"

"That's none of your business." Her eyes flashed.

I shrugged, stared her down.

She capitulated. "I was out. With friends."

"Hope, this is not impertinence." *Wrong*. "And I am not just a friend of Dakota's, I am an investigator. Someone is trying to kill her."

She gasped, eyes wide. I would have believed the emotional display without question if I hadn't already seen the easy and skillful transformation from country mouse to city tart and back again. I was impressed though. It was nicely done.

"We can't afford to take things at face value," I explained soberly. The dripping blood—also three-dimensional—on Jesus˙ looked almost real. "She has received a number of threatening communications; a bomb was thrown at one of her concerts; an attempt was made on her life."

I was thinking of Joni. It wasn't random; it wasn't a coincidence; it just wasn't Dakota—not that time. The agony in Jesus' face seemed even more intense now, the blood redder and drippier. I shifted the rocker so He was out of my sight. Mostly. Hope's eyes followed me. They had gone from mad and moody to open, to maybe a little scared. And excited. Interesting.

"Dakota is unavailable for a few days. She asked me to convey her regret that she is unable to meet with you in the near future. She would like you to audition for Garrett. If that goes well, she'll take you on for a three-month trial period."

Hope sat up straight, letting her breath out with a whoosh. She smiled and laughed and clapped her hands like a little child. Then my face tipped her off and the smile faded.

"What's the matter?"

"Dakota is very trusting," I said. "I am not. Nor is Garrett. The audition is just the beginning. We will need to know more about you, not just whether you can play but background information."

"All right." It took her two tries to get it out.

There was a somberly grimacing Jesus over the front door, hand clutched to His heart, face drawn in torment. Jeez. Whatever happened to a good-luck horseshoe?

"Your cousin must be religious."

She was momentarily disconcerted but recovered quickly and nodded in agreement. "He's a real good ol' boy. He used to be a hell-raiser—drinking, gambling, running around. That was before I knew him. One night, coming home drunk, he wrapped his truck around a tree and almost got killed. When he got out of the hospital he was saved, or born again, whatever you call it. He saw the light.''

I looked around the dark, dreary room.

She laughed. ''Some light, huh?''

I was starting to like her. Except for the Link connection, of course. That was a tough one to like.

''He works a lot of out-of-town construction. These days you take work wherever you can find it. He has a newer truck with a camper shell and bunks in it on out-of-town jobs. Sometimes he comes home weekends, sometimes not.''

''May I see your driver's license?''

''Why?'' She stared at me in a puzzled-slow-learner routine.

''I have only your word that you're Hope Delaney.''

''Oh.'' Puzzled disappeared. She got up to fetch her purse. Jesus and I watched somberly. ''Here.'' She thrust a cheap wallet, the leather old and cracking, at me.

The name was right. The face was right. I copied down an address in Rio Linda, California, birth date, driver's-license number. Hope stood over me, watching, hovering. Opposite the license was a snapshot of a good-looking guy wearing a baseball shirt and a grin, his cap pushed back off his forehead. Dark hair and eyes. Great smile.

''Your husband? Or boyfriend?'' I asked, smiling as if it were an innocent question.

She looked at me for a long moment. ''Yes.''

Something flickered in her eyes. Sadness, maybe?

''Husband or boyfriend?''

Hesitation. ''Boyfriend.''

''May I?'' A token question. I was already flipping through the rest of her photos. Without permission.

Hope made a funny noise low in her throat like a kitten growling. I ignored it.

''Is this your mother?'' It was a picture of a woman in her forties, her hair softly waved and graying at the temples in striking contrast to the masses of red hair on her shoulders. A smile played on her lips almost flirtatiously. She looked like someone who loved life and excitement. She wore a pale sweater with a carnival-colored scarf draped over her shoulders and tied loosely at the neck. Pity Delaney was a very beautiful woman.

"Yes. It's the last picture I have of her before she died. We didn't have the money to get her medical care. It wasn't right, wasn't fair." Her voice lashed out, venom and hatred there, ugly and poisonous.

"I'm sorry."

She looked at me, eyes hard. "Sure you are."

I met the hatred in her yellow eyes, held her gaze. Her eyes dropped first. "I didn't mean that the way it sounded." It was lame but it was an apology. "It was just so unfair! She was so young, not even fifty."

"And you loved her very much." I was gentle.

"Yes. Yes, I did." She reached her hand out for the wallet.

I flipped over to the next snapshot, a younger Hope sitting cross-legged on a lawn, holding a brown and white puppy standing on its hind legs, front paws on her chest and pink tongue out to lick her cheek. Hope was smiling and happy.

"Your dog?" I asked the obvious.

"Chloe. She's dead too. A car hit her. The guy never even stopped." Her face was hard and ugly, nothing like the face of the girl in the photograph. "Everything I love has been taken away from me—has been *killed*," she corrected fiercely. "Anything you want in this life you have to fight for. You have to hang on to it no matter what because someone's always waiting to take it away from you, to take what you love and leave you alone and unhappy. You have to grab first, before they do."

Her right hand was balled into a fist and pounded her knee. A sudden flash of sunlight snuck in through the dust-streaked window and turned her red hair into a flaming coppery mass. Like her mother's. There was a smudge of dirt on her T-shirt just over her left breast. Her fingernails were bitten to the quick. She looked very young in that moment.

"You have to go after what you want, get it no matter how." Her voice came out in a snarl. A young woman with an old look in her eyes. And an old hatred.

"Is that why you slept with Link?"

Her eyes widened, her jaw dropped. She looked like a child caught in something forbidden.

Jesus gazed down on us from the cross, His eyes grave and filled with pain, not love.

Outside chickens cackled and a rooster crowed.

I almost did too.

twenty-eight

KAMIKAZE CHICKENS AND COPS

Y OU CAN'T KNOW THAT. I MEAN, I DIDN'T—NOT WHAT
you're saying.'' She stammered the words out. ''I
have no idea what you're talking about.'' She tipped her
chin up at an assertive angle and stated the last with more
firmness. ''None!'' She tacked that on and then the next:
''*Absolutely* no idea!'' Her voice was steady now and her
eyes met mine. Briefly.

''I hope you play the fiddle better than you lie.''

She glanced at me, then away.

I continued. ''The Merchant Restaurant and Grill. Five-
fifteen for drinks and flirtation. What happened to your red
lace top?''

She flushed deeply, a bright hot pink next to her red hair.
''Okay, I met him for a drink. Big deal.''

She shrugged in a decidedly poor attempt at studied casual. I know because I'm an expert on that one.

''He was really nice to me that night at the Bluebird. He
made me feel welcome.'' *And you and Dakota didn't*, were
her unspoken words.

I thought with a pang that maybe she was right. Maybe
we hadn't. Not out of malice or neglect but in preoccupa-
tion. Dakota was preoccupied with the benefit concert, I
was preoccupied with murder. And that's a full dance card.

"It was politeness, kindness. You needn't be making something sleazy out of it."

She delivered this with passionate and believable conviction. Up to now I'd considered her a poor to average liar. Obviously I would have to revise that opinion.

"He just offered to tell me about Nashville, to show me around a little. He's Dakota's friend. I'm her cousin. It was kindness, *neighborliness*, that's all." She stuck her chin out again. "I reckon you ought to be *ashamed* of yourself for thinking such thoughts."

I wasn't, though I was a little chagrined at assuming so quickly that she couldn't lie worth a damn.

Hope took a deep breath and sat up straight. "Now, may I have my wallet please." She held out her hand. "And it's time for you to go."

I handed over the wallet. "That was something." The approval in my voice caught her off guard.

"What?" Her voice was light, curious, relaxed now.

"I would have believed you too."

Hope wrinkled her forehead in a frown.

"Except for one thing."

"What *are* you talking about?" she snapped out in exasperation.

"Your lies. I saw you and Link come out of his house together this morning at eight-twenty. I saw you kissing in the parking lot of the Wild Boar."

"Oh." She glanced at me quickly, then away, then back again. Unsure. "Oh. Well. That."

She tried to make it sound like nothing but it didn't. Not to either of us. She started to chew on a fingernail, then caught herself and held her hands tightly in her lap.

"I don't have to tell you *anything*. I don't owe you the time of day." She'd settled on defiance. Her look said *Fuck you!* "Now get out. I *mean* it." She stood, fists white-knuckle-clenched at her side, and glared at me. "Out!" Shouted at me as if I were a misbehaving dog. Bitch, actually.

"Sure," I said, in the calm and agreeable manner of one

who holds all the aces. And I stood. "Forget about working for Dakota."

"Oh." Fists disappeared. Anger melted away.

I started for the door.

"*Hey*, wait a minute. Hey, I'm *sorry*. I spoke without thinking. Let's talk some more, okay?"

I kept on walking, reached out for the doorknob.

"Please." There was a desperate pleading note in her voice.

I stopped.

"*Please* sit down again. *Please* let's talk."

I retraced my steps and sat, avoiding Jesus' eyes. And then I waited.

"I don't know what to say." Hope twisted her hands in her lap, then wrung them as though she were squeezing water out of a dirty washrag. "I don't know how to explain."

Her eyes flickered and for just a moment I was reminded of the fruit—cherries, apples and grapes—on a slot machine as it flips past and you hope against hope that it lines up and pays off. And then her eyes settled and something lined up but I wasn't sure what.

"You sounded like my mama. She would have disapproved—no, she would have died if she found out I just up and slept with a man I'd only just met. She would have been so *so* ashamed of me." Hope hung her head.

But I hadn't disapproved. I hadn't sounded like her mama. I'd asked why she slept with Link. I looked at the bowed head of coppery curls and mentally revised my opinion of Hope again.

Her head came up. "Don't you think for even a *minute* that I was raised like that. My mama taught me better, taught me what was right and what wasn't. I was wrong, I know that. I know it *full* well." She placed her hand dramatically on her heart.

"I'm not your mama, Hope, and I don't care who you sleep with."

She frowned, looking like she didn't get it. Her hand dropped to her lap again.

"With one exception," I added.

"What? Link?"

"Yes. Only because he and Dakota have been dating for several months now. Seriously." I threw that in for effect, not accuracy.

"Link and *Dakota*." Her hands flew to her mouth covering it. Her eyes were wide and horrified. "They're *dating*? Oh *no! Oh my God*." The last was on a moan. "Please tell me that you're making that up. No, of course you're not. Oh my God! Dating? I didn't know. Honestly I didn't. I didn't have any idea. Link said that they were friends. He said that sometimes Dakota needed an escort or something and that he enjoyed her company and all, but that was it.

"He *never* said they were dating. I would *never* have gone out with him if I'd known that. *Never*. I wouldn't do that to anyone, especially not to my own cousin. You've got to believe me. You do, don't you? Say you do. *Please!*"

Oddly enough I did believe her. Not because of her professed moral standards in not sleeping with her cousin's boyfriend—I didn't know her well enough to judge that—but because I thought her music and her career were far more important than a one-night stand. Unless of course it wasn't a one-night stand but a relationship that had begun earlier. And maybe a relationship based not just on mutual attraction but on . . . I shook myself mentally. Interesting but way too many ifs. At least so far. Back to earth.

"Where did you first meet Link, Hope?"

"The other night at the Bluebird."

"You had never met him before that?"

"No."

Was there a slight hesitation before her denial?

"Or seen him in California?"

"No."

"The address on your driver's license—is that current?"

"Yes."

"How long have you lived in Rio Linda?"

"As long as I can remember. Since I was a little kid. Why?"

"What were you doing there?"

"Doing? What do you mean?"

"Working? Going to school?"

"Going to school and working in bands whenever I could."

"Where do you go to school?"

"American River College."

"What is your major?"

"I was going to be a nurse. Mostly because Ma wanted me to. She had wanted to be a nurse but never could so it was her dream for me. She wanted me to have a secure job, a future. But it really wasn't my dream, so I dropped out after she died. I was angry too. Medicine hadn't saved *her*. After that I got a job waitressing and then cocktailing. And I lived for *my* dream. Music."

"Will you play something for me?"

"Now?"

"Yes."

She walked over to the violin case standing against one end of the couch and picked it up, removing the instrument and holding it as though it was indescribably precious.

As she played I watched her face, her total absorption in the music, in the dream. The concentration. The love. And then I forgot and was lost in the music as it frolicked and meandered and played in my soul.

"That was the Mendelssohn violin concerto." Hope spoke softly into the silence that followed her playing. "I was trained in classical music."

"It was very beautiful."

"Yes." She spoke simply. "Music is God's gift to me. I can sing too." She smiled tentatively at me.

I smiled back. "May I take pictures of you?"

Her smile faded. "You're checking up on me, aren't you? All these questions, my driver's license, all of that?"

"Yes."

"All right. I understand." But she looked unhappy about it. I took half a dozen photos.

"Don't tell Link about our conversation. Or that I know the two of you spent the night together."

"Why?"

I raised an eyebrow to remind her who was calling the shots.

"Oh. Okay. Are you going to tell Dakota?"

"I'm not sure."

"You are, aren't you?"

"Probably."

"Please don't take my dream away. Please," she whispered.

Jesus' eyes followed me as I left.

The whisper did too.

I walked out the dirt path to my car. Hope was a gifted musician. And a gifted liar. I headed out to the main road barely missing a flock of kamikaze chickens who tried desperately to hurl themselves underneath my wheels. The radio was tuned to WSM, the Grand Ole Opry station, and Ernest Tubb was singing that he could waltz across Texas with his sweetheart in his arms. And that made me think about Hank.

I left with more questions than I had come with.

I made careful notes, not only of Hope's Nashville address but of how to get back there. Just in case. Better safe than sorry. Then it was back to downtown. I got off I-40 at Broadway and headed for lower Broadway past the Union Station Hotel, a beautiful old church—churches large and small, old and new, are everywhere in Nashville—past the Convention Center, the Federal Courthouse, the Customs Building—old and imposing in stone and gravity—past the Merchant and then, in a change of pace, past the Hard Rock Café, where today's concepts conflicted with yesterday's. There, where Broadway ends at First, I turned left and drove briefly along the Cumberland River and then twisted around to the James Robertson Parkway.

I found a metered spot (twenty minutes for a quarter, for crying out loud!) right in front of the Criminal Justice Center, fed the greedy meter three quarters and ran up the gracious steps, past planters bursting with pansies and snapdragons and into the modern glass-and-concrete building.

The inside was quite lovely, a large open area in the middle with doors around the perimeter. You could look up, to a balcony on the second floor bordered by an open railing. Above people walked, talked and disappeared into offices. All the doors that I could see had coded keypads. The floor was warm in red and yellow brick. I walked across it to a circular enclosed glass-and-metal cubicle that held two unsmiling uniformed men. Not so warm.

A reminder.

I gave my name and asked for Deeter, fervently hoping he was in. He was. I looked at trophies and photos of Officers of the Month until one of the locked doors swung open.

"Hey, Kat."

He gave me a big smile, which was nice. After chatting with Hope I could use all the smiles I could get.

"Hey, Jimmy."

"C'mon in." He held the door open for me. "How ya doing?"

"Busy. How about you?"

"Same." Another grin. He led the way down a long dull-beige corridor, turned the corner and entered an office. I followed. "Sit down," he invited. I sat. See? I can follow orders. "What can I do for you?"

"I'm just following up on Joni's murder. Dakota's out of town now but she'll be back soon. Maybe I can keep her out of town for a week or so. Maybe not. I thought I'd check in with you, see if you'd come up with anything promising."

He shook his head. "No. I've put a lot of manpower on it too. Door-to-door interviews didn't turn up a thing. We stopped cars going by a couple of nights running. Stopped them around the time of the shooting. Nothing. We'll try that again on Tuesday, maybe find someone who travels that route on a weekly, not a daily schedule. Lot of phone tips but nothing that panned out—just the usual bunch of fame or thrill seekers, wannabes and crazies."

"Joni's family and friends?"

"Far as we can tell everyone liked her a lot. Her family

all loved her, even her ex-husband got along with her real well. They shared custody of the child but had no hard feelings and no problems over it. No boyfriend in particular and none of her friends could think of a reason why anyone would want to hurt, never mind kill her. We didn't find any holes in anyone's story. Didn't find anything in her apartment or personal effects either.''

The phone rang. Deeter held up a hand in apology and answered it, spoke briefly. As he hung up he cocked an eyebrow in inquiry at me.

''Jimmy, do you know a society reporter or gossip columnist or whatever they call them these days who knows what's going on socially and would be willing to—'' I tried to think of something that sounded better than ''dish dirt.''

''Talk trash?'' Jimmy finished it for me with a grin.

''Exactly.''

''Sure. Lana. Lana Lansome.''

''Lana Lansome?''

''She thought it sounded classy. And it *is* better than Glory Butts.'' He flipped through his Rolodex and picked up the phone.

''Almost *any*thing's better than Glory Butts.''

He winked at me. ''Lana? Jimmy Deeter. . . . Doing fine. How you doing? . . . Well, good. . . . Yeah, they're all fine too. Look, I'm here talking with a friend, Kat Colorado, and she sure would appreciate your take on a couple of things. You going to be in your office—'' Jimmy broke off and looked at me.

''After lunch.''

''—after lunch? . . . One-thirty? Okay, that's great. . . . I'll sure do that. Y'all take care.'' He hung up and scribbled an address on a pad in front of him, handed it to me.

''Thanks, Jimmy.''

''You're welcome. Anything I should know about?''

I shook my head. ''Not yet. So far just another dash down what's probably a dead end. If it gets interesting, you'll be the first to know.''

He nodded. ''Just for the record. In our investigation into

Joni Ames's death we asked around about Dakota Jones too."

No surprise there. "And?"

"Didn't come up with a damn thing there either. Or at least nothing that wasn't yesterday's news. Her ex-husband, Cal Jenkins, didn't have anything nice to say about her, but then that's been true for years. Old news," he said wryly.

"Are you taking the note at face value then—assuming that the killer meant to kill Dakota, thought that he had killed her and not Joni?"

"I never assume anything, Kat. That's a possibility but I don't have anything to back it up at this point. Just the note itself."

The note: NOW WE'RE EVEN, DAKOTA.

"And it could have been written to throw you off, to make you think that Dakota was the intended victim?"

"Could have." He didn't sound enthusiastic.

"How did it happen that Joni got the studio time that had been Dakota's?"

"Apparently cancellations are pretty frequent so the studios will schedule one or two backups. Joni Ames was first on their list, so they called her and she took the time slot."

"So it was just a coincidence?" I didn't let myself start thinking about that, about how life is filled with apparent coincidences and near misses.

"Looks that way."

"How did Joni fall? On her back, the way we saw her that night?"

"Yes."

"Shot from close up or at a distance?"

"Fifteen to twenty feet."

"But someone had to get in close to leave the note?"

"Yes."

"And wouldn't they have seen that it wasn't Dakota?"

"They could have. Would they have?" He shrugged. "I guess it just depends on how cold-blooded the killer was. Remember he's just shot someone so he wants to get out of there as fast as possible. Maybe he drops the note and gets the hell out, doesn't even look at the face of the woman he shot and maybe killed. There would have been a lot of blood too. Not pretty.''

"Was she dead then, Jimmy?"

"No. Probably not."

I swallowed hard. "Do you hate them?"

Deeter referenced my vague pronoun. "I try not to. I try not to get emotionally involved with a case. That interferes with your thinking, clouds your judgment. You try to see everything at the crime scene, including the victim, as evidence that will point you in the right direction, that ultimately will help you solve the case. You feel for the victim and their families, of course, but emotion doesn't get you anywhere. The satisfaction, for you and the family, is in finding out who did it and putting him away for a long time."

Down the hall somewhere a phone rang and a woman's soft voice answered it, speaking in an unintelligible murmur. Talking about murder, maybe, or where to meet for lunch. *Barbecue? Meat 'n' three? Salad?*

"Can you always do that?"

He picked up a fountain pen and snapped the cap off, then on again. "Once I showed up at a scene. Middle of the night. The victim was a child, a boy about the same age as my son was then. He'd been burned with cigarettes, beaten, brutalized. I could see the tread of a man's shoe outlined in dirt on his naked, skinny, broken chest. I had to leave. Took me a while to get it together. Nobody can always do anything, Kat."

I drove away from the Criminal Justice Center with murder on my mind, and emotion interfering with my thinking and clouding my judgment.

twenty-nine

TABLOIDS AND PEACH PIE

TALKING WITH DEETER PUT ME IN THE RIGHT MOOD—mean—for what I wanted to do next. I stopped at a mini-mart, got a cold drink, then dropped change into a pay phone.

Hunter was abrupt, almost annoyed-sounding. "What can I do for you?" He snapped this out.

"I need to know Clyde Jones's local phone number and address. I need to know about your conversation, or conversations, with him."

"Hang on." He punched me onto hold. I turned my face into the spring sunshine and breeze and listened to a couple of college kids argue about Ibsen and Hardy and fatalism in literature. Ibsen? Hardy? I didn't know anyone still cared. I was a block away from the Vanderbilt University campus where, apparently, literature was alive and well. Fatalism? I hoped it was dead and gone.

"Kat, you there?" Hunter asked, then went on without my answer. "Here's the address. You know your way around? It's off the far end of Music Row. Not a great part of town; I don't recommend going there at night. Here's the phone number."

I jotted it all down. "Your conversations with Jones?"

"Nothing much. When he first called I didn't believe him. I get communications all the time from people who call themselves Dakota's relatives—aunts, long-lost fourth cousins twice removed, shirttail relatives, you name it. Not to mention college roommates, friends from high school, and the boys she dated in tenth grade. Most of them are bogus. So I gave Jones the brush-off. He called back three or four times, each time sounding as sincere as Santa on Christmas Eve. Finally I called Dakota's grandmother and verified the information he had given me. Then I called Dakota and asked her what she wanted to do about it.''

"What was her reaction?''

"Stunned. I don't think she expected to see or hear from him ever again. I think in her mind he was dead already. She thought it over for a while, not long, and decided she wanted to see him.''

"Why?" I considered Ibsen and Hardy and fatalism.

"Beats me. I was against it. Didn't see that any good could come of it and saw plenty of possibilities for—''

An eighteen-wheeler rumbled by spewing black exhaust. "What?" I hollered. "What did you say?''

"Thought it was a bad idea all around. Dakota's got plenty of people trying to ride her coattails; she doesn't need another one.''

Plenty of people, I thought, but not plenty of family. She was real short in the family department.

"Jones say anything else?''

"I didn't ask. That was up to Dakota, not me. That it? I got two calls waiting.''

So I hung up. Hung up curious. For all the money Garrett Hunter was making off Dakota you'd think he'd be knocking himself out for me. Sweet as pie, something like that. But he wasn't. Why? Every time I'd seen him with Dakota he'd been attentive, protective, good-humored. So what was with short-tempered and surly? Jekyll and Hyde? Bad day at the office?

"Ma'am, you through with the phone?" A twenty-year-old kid in baggy shorts, dirty sneakers and a tie-dye T-shirt smiled at me in polite inquiry.

"Yes. Sorry.'' I grabbed my cold drink and daydream

and moved away from the phone booth. Tie-dye? *Yuck!* When had that come back into fashion?

I climbed into the Pathfinder and lowered the windows. Garrett Hunter as bad guy? I thought it had a certain appeal but Dakota had scoffed at me.

"No way, Kat. You've been reading too many out-of-date novels. Or the tabloids." She had giggled.

The tabloids were an old joke between us. We used to make up story lines: "Woman with twelve toes marries hairless man with arms to his knees. What *will* their baby look like?" Or: "Elvis spotted in hamburger joint eating cheeseburgers with Richard Nixon and Marilyn Monroe!"

But these days we'd pretty much stopped that. Reading tabloid lies about Dakota and the people she knew had taken the fun out of it. Almost. I played with it now. "Dakota Jones's manager steals singer blind and leaves country after threatening her life." Hmmmm. "Was he a manager or was he a crook? Dakota is asking herself that now."

Dakota had scoffed at that, too. "Katy, for starters I've got a business manager, a road manager, a merchandise manager, a booking agent, two accountants, a lawyer and a bookkeeper. Everybody's checking up on everyone else. How is a scam going to get by? Country music's full of stories about managers robbing their clients. I should know—I put myself in that position with Cal. But that's when you put one person in charge of everything and neither you nor anyone else follows what's going on and holds him accountable. For obvious reasons nobody does that anymore. Anyway, I trust Garrett."

I dropped it. For then. I still wasn't convinced, still thought it was worth looking into. Because of Hunter's attitude alone. Although, why would a bad guy be surly, almost rude? If I were a bad guy, I'd act like a good guy. Camouflage. Of course, as a rule bad guys aren't all that smart. Or polite. I thought of Ivan Boesky and Michael Milken and tossed out that generalization. White-collar bad guys were plenty smart.

I sighed and started the Pathfinder. Off to Music Row.

Music Row is 16th Avenue spilling over onto 17th and

is country music. Sony is there and the United Artists Tower, and Mercury. The new buildings are huge, modern concrete-and-glass. Sony had a banner the size of a store-front stretched across the front of the building announcing an artist who had gone platinum. Mixed in with modern corporate edifices are modest homes converted now to of-fices or recording studios. The Country Music Hall of Fame is there, and Recording Studio B, where it all started. At the Broadway end are gift shops—Randy Travis, and Bar-bara Mandrell Country—filled with theme junk for the gul-lible and starstruck.

I was on 16th heading away from theme junk past brick and stone homes-turned-offices. Legend has it that many a deal was cut here on the porches under the trees. The deals are still made, but not on porches. After dark Music Row is not a great place to be. Burglaries, robberies and rapes are common. I passed residences with bars on the windows. Clyde was staying here, on past this end of Music Row.

I was taking a chance—dropping by, not calling—for the element of surprise, which I like, and also because I was hoping to get an unrehearsed version of his story. The house was two-story brick, once lovely, now dilapidated. The roof was shot; the wooden trim desperately needed painting; the sidewalk from the street to the porch was cracked and broken with weeds flourishing in the cracks. Weeds flourished in the lawn too. The bushes around the house were overgrown and three vast trees draped over the house in a menacing canopy. Parking was no problem.

I walked up the path noting a couple of beer cans tossed under a bush and a broken shutter. The porch light was a bare bulb. A faded note thumbtacked to the door said: *DOORBELL DOESN'T WORK. PLEASE KNOCK LOUDLY.* Homey was not a term that sprang to mind. I knocked loudly. And waited.

The door finally opened onto a gray-haired woman wear-ing a faded, rumpled housedress and a dour expression.

"I'm looking for Clyde Jones," I said pleasantly enough to Mrs. Dour.

"He has an upstairs room. Ain't no female company allowed up there.'' She said "company" as though she meant "whore" but was too proper to say that.

"Perhaps you could tell him he has a visitor then." I was still pleasant but it was taking more of an effort now. Much more.

She glared at me before turning and starting up the stairs in the dark hallway behind her. Everything was dark here, dark wood, dark wallpaper and paint, curtained windows. Dour clomped and dragged herself up the stairs, feet slapping down heavily, hands hauling on the banister as she dragged her shapeless body up to the second floor. The inside was far less homey, far more depressing than the outside—which was saying something.

"Who is it?" a man's voice asked upstairs. A shaft of light fell across the stairway now, breaking the darkness up into dust and must and different shades of gloom and brown.

The landlady mumbled something I couldn't quite catch.

"Tell her I'll be *right* down." Jones sounded excited. Footsteps followed hard on his words as he came down the stairs, easily beating the landlady. His face was open, excited, and it fell when he saw me, crumpled up like that of a disappointed kid whose ice cream was melting on a hot sidewalk.

"Oh. I thought it was Dakota. I—"

"Hi." I ignored the comment and the disappointment both. "Kat Colorado. We met the other day." I stuck out my hand.

He stepped forward to take it, almost tripping on the threadbare and treacherous ancient hall runner. His handshake was firm, his hand cool and dry. His eyes were still disappointed.

"I'd like to talk to you."

He nodded, gestured toward the parlor to my left. We both looked in on a roomful of hideous overstuffed furniture, china figurines and a variety of ghastly knickknacks, all shrouded in the now familiar darkness and gloom. I looked at the dusty grandfather clock in the hall. Eleven-thirty. And at Mrs. Dour, now standing at the bottom stair and watching us with an evil and predatory eye.

"How about lunch?" I queried, my spirits rising at the thought of getting out of there.

"Sure." Jones looked relieved.

"Mr. Jones, you plan on staying another month, I need my money by tomorrow and that's final."

"Yeah, okay." He flushed, embarrassed that this woman was scolding him in front of me.

So I left. I was out the door and down the sidewalk in a heartbeat, Jones hard on my heels.

"Anything in particular?" I asked as I snapped my seat belt into place.

"No. I'm not here for the food, but to talk about Dakota."

I headed back to Broadway, made a left, then cruised until I saw a little hole-in-the-wall place that said it had the best chicken-fried steak in the South. Ordinarily such an extravagant claim would put me off; today I didn't care. This place, unlike Dour's, was much nicer on the inside than out, clean and bright with perky red-and-white-checked tablecloths. The waitress was smiling and friendly, at our table in a moment with a "Hi, y'all."

I ordered an iced tea; Jones ordered a beer. And got right down to some serious menu reading.

"Y'all ready to order?" Patsy, her name tag said, stood with pad and pencil.

I ordered a chicken salad on toast with coleslaw. Jones had the chicken-fried steak, mashed potatoes and red-eye gravy, stewed tomatoes and okra, and biscuits. Doing okay, I thought, for someone who was more interested in the conversation than the food.

"And a piece of peach pie. À la mode," he added before Patsy left.

"I sure do fancy a man who can eat." Patsy winked at Jones. "Don't you?" she asked me.

I smiled politely, evasively. There are a lot of things I fancy in a man before I get to his appetite. I looked at Patsy looking at Jones. There were, I thought, a couple of things she fancied about him other than his appetite.

Jones looked at me, not her. Now that food was taken care of he was all business.

"We're here to talk about Dakota, aren't we?"

"We are." I lied. I was here to talk about him.

"Good." He sounded relieved.

"But first, Clyde, tell me about you. After all these years your showing up was a surprise." *To say the least.* Not that I said that. Or that it was an unpleasant surprise.

"Sure, I can understand that." He took a sip of beer, set the glass down carefully on the table. "Some might say I was no kind of father, not being around for Cody—" He shrugged a little. "Dakota, I meant. It's hard for me to think of her as Dakota and not as my little girl, as Cody."

I gazed at him noncommittally. I found it difficult to believe that he thought of her at all, never mind what he called her.

"Anyway, I know I wasn't around much for Cody when she was little—"

I couldn't let that one pass. "Much?" I raised my eyebrows. "Not at all. Not when she was a child. Or a teenager. Dakota's thirty-three now and you left when? When she was two or three?"

He flushed. The arrival of the waitress with his chicken-fried steak and multiple side dishes was obviously a welcome break. He took it gladly, picking up his utensils and diving right in. No, forget diving; try attacking. He slashed at the chicken-fried with a ferocity that wasn't just hunger.

"Sometimes things aren't always what they seem, you know." He put a slab of steak in his mouth and chewed. "A man can care deeply about his child and yet be torn apart from her, unable to participate in the everyday things of her life."

Torn apart? According to Jo, Dakota's mother, what "tore" him away was a tarty little bit of blond fluff with big hooters and no brains. Her words, not mine.

"Cody's mother and I didn't get along very well, you know. The last thing I wanted was for that anger and bitterness to affect Cody. I thought it would be best if I stepped out of her life entirely. I didn't want to bring any more pain to an innocent child. Of course I would have preferred to be a part of her life! It was a huge sacrifice on my part.''

I nodded in appreciation. I love it when people not only excuse and justify the wrong thing they did but make it commendable and then turn around and pat themselves on the back for it. Okay, I was being a little sarcastic.

''I never thought of *that*,'' I said and nibbled on my sandwich.

''No?'' His eyes were sorrowful as he forked in a bite of steak piled high with stewed tomatoes and okra. ''Most people don't. They think only of the child and forget the suffering of the absent father.'' He mopped up gravy with a wedge of biscuit and popped it in his mouth. ''They forget that the father would be there if only he could.'' He shoved his plate aside and looked around for Patsy. ''Miss, can I git my pie? Coffee, too.''

I finished half of my sandwich and took a bite of my coleslaw. ''When did you last see Dakota?''

He looked at me sorrowfully. ''When she was two.''

''But you stayed in touch?''

He shook his head. ''No. I explained that to you. I didn't want to interfere with my child's life. I didn't want to cause a problem. I really believed that that was best. I really did.''

''Here you go. Peach pie à la mode.'' Patsy gave us a big smile. ''Anything more for you, ma'am?'' She refilled my iced tea as I declined more food.

''Mighty fine pie,'' Clyde commented.

''It sure is. We make it here. We serve only the best here.'' She dimpled at him.

Jones nodded and turned back to me.

''Can you understand that, a man doing what he thinks best even though the rest of the world might say he was a no-account deadbeat?'' He said the last with scorn and as though anyone who would think that was not only no-account but brain-dead to boot.

''Yes.'' And I could even think of examples, though this wasn't one of them. I pushed my half-full plate away and took a sip of iced tea.

"But you sent money?"

He nodded. "Whenever I could, sure."

"And that was how often?"

He flushed slightly. "Not as often as I would of liked but as often and as much as I could. But enough of this. I didn't come here to get caught up in the past. In what was, and what wasn't, and what might have been. That's over and done with. I . . . came . . . to . . . talk . . . about . . . Dakota." He pounded his fist on the table in rhythmic cadence with the words. "And why the hell can't we get to that?"

The best defense is a good offense.

"Okay. Talk about Dakota."

"She's not a child anymore and now we can get to know each other as adults. I'm real proud of her. I want to help and support her and, by God, I think she needs that help and support now. A lot of things aren't going so well. The papers write about someone who's stalking her. That other girl—that singer, I don't recall her name—who was killed? We sure as hell don't want that." He pounded the table again. "Do we now?"

I let the question go; it was rhetorical, anyway. And I had one of my own. "Dakota was an adult at eighteen. Why didn't you get in touch with her then?"

"I was hoping she would understand. That she would reach out to me."

I stared at him in amazement. A child neglected her whole life was supposed, as a young adult, to see this neglect as heroic and then reach out to the neglecter? Could he *really* believe this scenario?

"I wanted nothing more than to be reunited with my daughter. I know that I told you that I thought what I was doing was all for the best." He leaned across the table and over the remnants of his peach pie à la mode toward me. "And that's God's truth. But there are some days, bad days, when I think what I did was wrong, that I never should have let go of my dear child and to hell with the cost. I think that on those bad days, and then I think that maybe Cody thinks that too, that maybe she wants nothing to do with me, that maybe she despises me. I guess maybe that fear kept me from coming to her. That way I could love her in my mind and I could hope to God that in some small way maybe she could understand and maybe even love me back.''

He looked down at his hands. "Kat, I've been weak sometimes when I should have been strong. I've told myself what maybe was wrong was right, just so I could sleep better at night. I haven't always lived up to my idea of what a man should be. And I'm not proud of it. But I'm not a bad man. And I do love my daughter.''

He met my gaze evenly. "I reckon what gave me the courage to show up now was reading that she was in trouble not of her own making. I reckon I hoped that maybe I could offer her something now, my help, that she didn't need before. And that in her need maybe she might take it.

"And maybe we could start over again,'' he continued softly. "That was my hope. It's still my hope.'' He opened his hands in an almost pleading gesture.

And I believed him. I believed him when he said he wanted to be in Dakota's life. I believed him when he said that he was a weak man but not a bad one. I even believed that there was good in him, perhaps quite a lot.

Patsy dropped our check off with a "Thanks y'all'' and another round of smiles and dimples. Jones made no move for his wallet.

I believed that Cal had good in him too, although in his case it was so often overpowered by greed. Weakness, to use Clyde Jones's word. Cal had a weakness for money; Clyde had a weakness for women and his own way.

And Dakota was sick of men with these weaknesses.

"It's not as easy for Dakota to dismiss the past as it is for you.''

"It is not easy for me, but I know what you mean,'' he remarked gravely. "Will you please speak to Dakota on my behalf?''

"I'll speak to her.'' Although not necessarily on his behalf. "May I take pictures of you?''

He grinned. "Suspicious?''

I grinned right back. "Cautious.''

"Sure."

And he smiled as I clicked away. I stowed the camera in my purse, took out fifteen dollars to cover the check. When I stood Jones made no move to follow.

"Give you a ride back?" I inquired.

"Thanks. I think I'll have another cup of coffee."

And another look at Patsy.

Weakness.

I left without a backward glance.

thirty
MISSILE MOTHS AND STARLIGHT

L ANA WAS SIXTY, EASY, HER HAIR WHITE AND POUFFY
and shellacked into an impressive helmet, her trim figure neatly tucked into a blue pantsuit trimmed with gold.
Her complexion was as flawless as her figure, although I
suspected an assist there. Not just makeup but plastic surgery. She tucked a pencil behind her ear and greeted me
warmly.

The walls of her office were covered with framed and
signed photographs: Reba, Paul Newman, Barbara Walters,
Peter Jennings, George Strait. Lana Lansome smiled sas-
sily, almost wickedly at me. At a quick glance she looked
like a sweet little old lady; a closer scrutiny belied that.

She waved at the photos. "Pretty damn good company,
wouldn't you say?" She didn't sound like a sweet little old
lady either.

"I'm impressed, Ms. Lansome."

She shrugged the "Ms." away. "You call me Lana and
I'll call you Kat. That Jimmy Deeter, he's something. I've
helped him out on a couple of things."

I tried to imagine Jimmy and Lana working together; it
was a stretch.

"I hear things he wouldn't, not in a coon's age and not
for love nor money. A good cop doesn't turn his back on
that, on talk and gossip and history."

"A cop turning his back on that? Shoot, I can't imagine *anyone* turning his back on that." I thought it over. "Well, maybe Mother Teresa—she's probably above gossip."

"Exactly." Lana twinkled at me like an elderly, over-coiffed Tinkerbell. "Sit down. What can I do for y'all?"

"The Davidsons."

"Ah." She tapped her chin thoughtfully. "An old, very highly regarded Nashville family. The Davidsons go back to well before the War Between the States. Harter Davidson was a captain for the Confederacy. After the War he married Amelia Hodges. They had a number of children and grandchildren, the most renowned of whom was a grandson, Harter Hodges Davidson. He died ten years ago at the age of ninety-two. He was active all his life in various endeavors, notably banking and farming, but is best known for founding Charitable Insurance. He married late in life—am I going over this in too much detail?"

I shook my head. "Not at all."

"Lucinda Allen Graves came from another prominent Nashville family. It was, by all accounts, a happy union, and one that produced three sons. Under Lucinda's influence the Davidsons engaged in charitable endeavors. Charitable Insurance endowed a number of charities for orphans, unwed mothers, the blind and the disabled, those whom yesterday's society had cast aside and forgotten. They were great patrons of the arts as well.

"Their children, as so often happens, while likable enough, lacked their parents' talent, compassion and dedication. And were averse to hard work in their youth."

"The grandchildren?"

She twinkled again, one step ahead of me. "You perhaps have someone in particular in mind?"

"Link."

"Yes." There was no surprise in her face. "He was named after his father, who was named after Abraham Lincoln. Harter Hodges named all three sons after presidents whom he admired. The qualities he most revered in the presidents did not, alas, show up in his sons or grandsons.

"Link's father was a hardworking man with no imagination who married a pretty fool. Alice didn't age well, fools rarely do. Link is the product of an authoritarian father and a foolish, doting overindulgent mother. It was not a happy combination.

"As a child he was a spoiled brat, as a youth he was constantly in trouble. Had he been the son of a less prominent family several of his escapades would undoubtedly have landed him in jail."

"And as an adult?"

"Ah. Well, my dear, we have two views on that. The tolerant and fair-minded view holds that he is quite a credit to his family now. He holds down a responsible position at Charitable Insurance. Still a bachelor, he is frequently seen escorting Nashville's loveliest, most charming and eligible young women to art openings, the symphony or charitable events. Rumor even has it that currently he is somewhat taken with Dakota Jones, a country music star. And that, I can tell you, will send quite a shudder through the family if it lasts."

"Really? Why?"

Lana leaned forward and pitched her voice low. "Oh my dear, old Nashville has *nothing* to do with country music. It is considered garish and tasteless in the extreme. The Grand Ole Opry and Opryland, the money and the ostentation, the lifestyle, are all considered a great embarrassment. Old Nashville has no truck with the likes of *that*. Should Link take up seriously with someone in the music business he would be considered to be going quite beneath him. And more to the point, quite beneath his family. Times are changing of course, and with that inevitably the old ways and traditions. Still it would be looked upon with considerable disfavor in the Davidsons' circle."

"Dakota Jones is a big star, talented, hardworking—"

Lana shrugged. "I did not say that the old ways were right, merely that they are. I myself find it refreshing that the youth of today pick and choose between the old and the new. Although," she added tartly, "I often wish they would use their brains to think with and not the seat of their pants."

"And the other view of Link Davidson, the one that is not tolerant and fair-minded?"

She looked at me sharply. "Ah, well, that one is not widely held."

"But you believe it?"

"Perhaps." She pushed her wire-rim glasses up the bridge of her nose. "It is sad, I think, to see the worst qualities of parents combined in the child. Where the father is hardworking and determined to have and enjoy the best, the son is merely eager to live luxuriously, unwilling to see the part that hard work plays. Add to that the absurdly fond indulgence of a foolish mother and—" She lifted her shoulders slightly as if to say: *Well, and what, really, can one expect?*

"What kind of trouble did Link get into when he was younger?"

Lana raised an eyebrow and ugly things danced in my mind.

"Did he pull the wings off bugs or set puppies on fire? Knock off Seven-Elevens or rape his prom date?"

"Oh my no, I never heard anything like that. He was just wild. He raced around in the fast cars his mother gave him, wrecking more than a few, and collecting speeding tickets like there was no tomorrow. On a dare he snuck into a stable and let out a champion racehorse, rode him bareback helter-skelter and pell-mell from hell to breakfast. A horse, mind you, that was worth hundreds of thousands of dollars. At seventeen he stole his father's credit card and made it all the way to Mexico and a Tijuana whore before they caught up with him."

"And now?"

"Now he works for his grandfather's company and I hear that he is doing well. Also that the very decent salary he makes doesn't even begin to cover his expensive tastes. I do trust that he is doing his job. The old days are gone now and I do not think that the Davidson name alone is enough to secure his position."

"Lana, is he a nice person, a good person?"

"I don't know." She smiled. "Gossip doesn't tell you

that. Gossip thrives on vice, not virtue, and so it quite over-looks the latter.''

''Your guess?''

''I report, I don't guess. At least not aloud.''

I could see that there was something in the back of her mind. I just couldn't read it.

I left Lana Lansome's office and headed for Music Row. Where was I?

Not one damn bit closer to finding out who was threatening Dakota, that's where. I'd turned over a lot of rocks and seen a lot of slimy things, but threats? No. Just the opposite. Not everyone liked Dakota. And some liked her, but for the wrong reasons. But most needed her and wanted her safe.

Dead cows don't give milk.

The list of people involved with Dakota was a pretty long one. Hope was on it. And Link. Cal. And maybe someone who was standing in the shadows still? Dakota had talked about that long ago.

''THE RULES HAVE CHANGED, KATY. NICE, GOOD, KIND: THEY don't seem to matter anymore. None of the things we were brought up to value do. What matters is not who you really are but whether you have a name, whether you went platinum. Your bank account matters and whether you know the right people and are invited to the best parties.'' Her voice was sad.

''People say they're happy for you and then tear you down behind your back. Some of my oldest friends don't want anything to do with me anymore. One even said she hated me for having what she wanted. She said she wanted what I had and hoped my luck wouldn't last.''

''Cody, she's not good enough to be third base, never mind your friend!''

''Katy!'' she had gasped, but then she giggled.

''Men, too.'' The giggle was gone. *''I see now why rich and famous people marry other rich and famous people. Then you know that they're marrying you, not what you*

*are. Shoot, this is the kind of thing that makes Cal look
straightforward.''*

*"Cal is straightforward,'' I said. ''Pretty women, good
music, illegal drugs, and money.'' We laughed. ''He's honest about who he is and what he wants, which is good. But
he's an unprincipled jerk, which is bad. Everyone's not like
that, Cody. Or like the swarms of missile moths who launch
themselves at your starlight.''*

And I hoped that was true.

"I'm not a person to the fans either, Katy.''

*"No. You're a star. They don't want you to be a person
just like them.'' I stopped, at a loss for words. I'd seen it
in their faces, heard it in their voices, but it was hard for
me to understand. ''You're larger than life; you're what
they can't be, their hope and escape both. They need you
to keep their dream alive because if the dream dies some
part of them does too.''*

And that's unbearable, I thought, living without a dream.

*"A dream seems so simple and beautiful when it's far
away, Katy. All the years I was a lonely, left-out kid and
now I feel like the homecoming queen, the class president
and the head cheerleader all rolled up into one. The love
is wonderful. I just didn't realize there would be hate too.''*

WHAT DOES IT TAKE TO CROSS THE LINE FROM HATRED TO
murder? And why was Dakota a target—because of something about her as a person, or because she was a star? I
didn't have the answer to those questions. Maybe Hunter
would.

The receptionist in the Music Row office was friendly
but aloof and cool. And she raised her eyebrows at my
name.

"Is Mr. Hunter expecting you?'' she queried, and
frowned when I shook my head, as though Hunter's busy
schedule had no time for unstructured visits from off-the-
street riffraff. ''Please be seated.'' She instructed me like a
schoolchild that had strayed. ''And I will check with Mr.
Hunter.'' She disappeared into the corridor partially hidden
by the partition behind her desk.

I sat. And promptly abandoned one of my half-baked plans. This was no Barbie and there was no way I could sweet-talk Ms. Marble Face into spilling secrets about her boss. On to Plan B.

"It will be a moment," she informed me after she had reseated herself at her desk and recomposed her face into marble.

"Thank you," I said and then I smiled—just for the practice. Smiling at friendly people is hardly a challenge. She didn't smile back. I picked up a magazine with a picture of Dwight Yoakam in skintight pants on the front cover. Yuck. Remember the story about Marilyn Monroe and how, for one of her movies, she'd put her jeans on wet and let them dry on her like a second skin? I wondered if that was how Dwight did it. On the other hand, who cared? I flung Dwight down on the table.

"May I use your bathroom?" I whipped out another smile and tossed it on my face, like a cherry tomato on a salad.

"Down the hall and to your left." She pointed behind her.

Off I went. I remembered the layout from our meeting here with Clyde. Behind the receptionist's desk was the bathroom and a storeroom. Hallways were set out in a rectangle around these center rooms. A series of offices and conference rooms opened off the hallway on the other side. Garrett's office was next to the conference room and both were around the corner from the bathroom.

I could hear Hunter as I passed the bathroom door. He was on the phone, his office door open and his voice loud. Such a deal. Just past the bathroom I stooped to tie my shoe. Only I was wearing boots, which kind of spoiled the effect. Hey, you work with what you have.

"Yeah, I know. We don't want to cancel either. Sure there's a lot at stake here. Don't worry about that. No. Dakota will do whatever I tell her to. Right. I'll get back to you." A phone slammed down and I heard the squeal of wheels, the sound of boots hitting the floor. I nipped over to the bathroom, opened the door and stood there as though I were exiting, one hand on the light switch, one foot slightly in front of the other. A tableau: Innocent with Washed Hands.

Hunter rounded the corner with a frown and a brisk pace. He looked surprised to see me but recovered quickly. "Hey, Kat." And peeled the frown right off. "C'mon back. Glad you stopped by." He held out his hand and grasped mine in a bear hug kind of handshake. "Want a cup of coffee or a cold drink?" he asked as we seated ourselves.

"A cold drink sounds good, thanks."

"Mina." He barked into the intercom and Mina came running. This time she smiled at me, a loyal office minion mirroring her boss. "Coffee for me, cold drink for Kat."

"Diet Dr Pepper?" I asked.

She nodded and dashed off. I surveyed the office and the smiling Hunter.

"Talked to Dakota this morning. She sounds great. That was a real good idea of yours, Kat, sending her home to her grandmother for a break."

I nodded, content to let him lead, interested to see where we were going.

And I wondered if his smile was a little too hearty.

Maybe even phony.

thirty-one

MY CRAZY LIFE

BUT—"

I was surprised. He got to the but faster than I thought he would. I tossed an eager-listener, can't-wait-to-hear-this smile on my face.

"We've got a lot of things to consider here."

"In addition to Dakota's safety."

"Yes." There was a slight hesitation and I knew that right now that wasn't one of the top-priority things he was considering.

"Dakota would not want to disappoint her fans. We've canceled the concerts this weekend out of necessity."

"Canceled or rescheduled?"

"They'll be rescheduled. We don't want to cancel any more."

"What have you done about security?"

"We'll put on extra people."

"A flash bomb could still get through. Or a real bomb. Or a gun."

"I don't think that's likely."

"So far it's one out of three."

"Dakota's made commitments. It costs us money if she doesn't meet them. Big money. And it's not just the money, it's her reputation. We can't afford to lose that any more than we can afford to lose the money. We've issued a statement that she will stick with her schedule as announced after this weekend."

I thought about the note on Joni's body. *Now we're even, Dakota.* If someone had meant to kill Dakota and killed Joni instead, nothing was even. The job wasn't done. Yet. Hunter knew about the note. Hunter and his money and scheduling.

"What does Dakota say?"

"She's with me on this." But there was a slight hesitation again. So maybe she was; maybe she wasn't.

"Remember the note on Joni's body?"

"That's not going to happen. Nothing's going to happen."

"Joni's not sticking to her schedule," I pointed out.

I DIDN'T BOTHER TO PACK. I WAS GOING HOME. I'D TURNED over all the rocks I could find in Nashville, it was time to start turning them over in California. There was a slimeball under one of these rocks. *And the clock was ticking.* So many rocks, so little time.

Rafe met me at the airport. Six foot three inches of gorgeous blond hunk in faded blue jeans, a tight T-shirt and dark glasses. It was ten forty-five. Evening, not morning. Good choice on the dark glasses.

"What do you know, hotshot?" He put an arm around my shoulders and hugged me into him.

Two women turned and stared at us, the envy raw on their faces. The short intense one licked her lips. Rafe always has this effect on women.

"Not enough," I answered. Look at that. Just home and already I was talking gloomy. Phooey.

"Impatient as usual." He winked at me. I think. It was hard to tell behind the dark glasses.

"Why are you wearing those stupid glasses?" I asked crossly. It's so much easier to be cross at someone else than at yourself.

He grinned. "So I can see. I lost my other ones."

"Oh. Good. I thought you were trying to look cool."

He shrugged, meaning: *Why bother? This is Sacramento.* "You check your bag?"

I shook my head and swung my purse. "I'm traveling light."

"Good girl."

It took us about two minutes, tops, to walk through Sacramento Metropolitan Airport. Out on the sidewalk a spring breeze ruffled through my hair and pouffed in my face. My heart lifted. It's always good to come home; I love Sacramento and California's Central Valley. Rafe took me by the elbow and steered me across the street where his Corvette was parked right in front of the terminal. Legally for a change. I glanced at the twenty-four-hour meter. Red flag. Forget legally. He always does that and never gets tickets. It makes me nuts.

Rafe tossed me the keys. "You drive, you can see better."

It was a moonless night. I couldn't see the rice fields, solid green now, a spring carpet of tender shoots. Or the old farmhouses and barns. Most of them you couldn't see in the daytime either—they were disappearing fast, slipping away in the wake of "progress."

We could see the Arco Arena lit up out there in the middle of parking lots and the nowhere that used to be some of the best agricultural land in the world. Our basketball team, the Sacramento Kings, plays there. Well, loses there. Dakota has played there. And the Rolling Stones and George Strait and Tom Petty. Nobody but me seemed to mind that our arena was named after a gas station. Rafe turned on the radio. Pam Tillis was singing "Mi Vida Loca (My Crazy Life)." It sounded like the same old same old to me. Bad sign, huh?

"Is everyone in bed, Rafe?"

He snorted. "Yeah. Right. They're over at Alma's 'whoopin' it up.' "

That was my grandmother Alma's expression and it usually meant trouble.

"It started out with homemade ice cream and brownies."

It always starts out innocently enough with Alma, I thought.

"By the time I left to pick you up Alma and Granny were making Manhattans and arguing about how many cherries the perfect Manhattan should have. Dakota was tossing down Chardonnay and Lindy was making popcorn. Dakota and Lindy were talking about clothes and getting ready to call Charity."

"*Lindy* was talking about *clothes*."

"Yeah. How's that for a switch?"

"Really interested, or faking it to be polite?"

"Sounded interested to me but I could've missed some of the fine points. She and Dakota pretty much took to each other once Lindy got over her shyness."

"*Clothes?*" Pigs could fly and I wouldn't be as surprised.

"You and Alma did a good job, Katy."

I nodded, a lump in my throat. Lindy had come a long way. We all loved her to pieces, as Granny would say.

We crossed over I-80 on I-5 south, cruised past Old Sacramento and the downtown exits, scooted onto Highway 99 Business 80 (don't bother trying to follow this one, even the locals get confused), off on H Street, and headed into Midtown and toward Alma's.

Alma's front door was closed but not locked.

"Rafe!" I snapped at him.

He shrugged. "It was locked when I left, Katy. You try to whip Alma into line."

I glared at him. Right. He wasn't fooling me for a minute. It was Rafe who took Alma out barhopping and pool playing. Pool sharks, both of them. Rafe hustles unsuspecting macho nitwits into playing Alma, who throws a few quarter games before moving in for the kill. They make a lot of money that way since—let's face it—macho nitwit is a bad combination for guys. They don't know how to lose with grace, they refuse to admit that a little old lady can beat the socks off them, and they're clueless about cutting their losses. You know the kind of grandmother that does charity work, crochets and reads large-print *Reader's*

Digest? Alma's nothing like that. Alma doesn't even *know* people like that.

I could hear the noise through the closed door. Voices, laughter, music. Whoopin' it up was right. We opened the door and pushed our way into the revelry.

"Katy, dear!" Alma gave me a big hug. She smelled like spaghetti sauce, Manhattans and popcorn. "It's good to see you. Sophy left Leonard. Can you *believe* it?"

"Really? Why?" I looked at my grandmother fondly. She was five two and shrinking, with her gray hair in a French braid down her back. Lately she'd taken to dressing like Lindy so she was wearing jeans, an oversize sweater and granny boots. Go figure.

"He invested a lot of the money from her trust fund in risky stocks—that chowderhead!—and of course they went belly-up and if *that* wasn't bad enough—"

Lindy hugged me from behind. Thank goodness she'd gotten over the stage where punching and socking people was the only way she could show affection. At five foot eight inches she was an inch taller than I and slim and beautiful.

"Holy shit!" I gasped.

Lindy laughed. "Do you like it? Dakota thought I should have a western outfit." *This* from a person who had scorned the western look for years. Now it was Rocky Mountain jeans, boots, a belt with a silver buckle the size of a salad plate and a shirt that was western in cut but ended just above the waist. Not a working shirt, a sexy shirt. "We had to go to three stores before we found—"

"You two went shopping?" I was horrified. No one in my family comprehends the term "low profile." Or even tries to.

"Yes, but don't worry. Dakota was disguised and Rafe was with us."

They don't understand the term "disguise" either, I reflected glumly. Dakota had probably worn sunglasses and a scarf over her head, looking about as disguised as Jackie Onassis had when she tried the same thing.

"Charity went with us too. It was a blast."

I shuddered. Charity is a life-of-the-party, center-of-attention kind of person. And a nationally syndicated advice columnist with a very recognizable face.

"Why didn't you hire a brass band and jugglers to go with you?"

Lindy giggled. "Charity said you'd overreact."

"Overreact! Give me a break."

Instead I got Granny Mae, Charity and Dakota and it was hugs and laughter all around. Granny wanted me to eat a plate of spaghetti—she and Alma are of the generation that insists on feeding people on every possible occasion. Dakota thrust a glass of wine in my hand and Lindy tried to tell me about Robbie, her new boyfriend.

"Just don't get involved with someone like Leonard," Dakota said. "Or Cal. Or— Oh, never mind, I'm going for more wine."

"Who's Leonard?" Lindy asked.

"Someone Alma knows." Dakota tossed the comment over her shoulder on the way to the kitchen and the wine.

Alma heard that, unfortunately, and jumped back into the conversation. "Not only did he spend all of Sophy's money, he slept with her little sister, Bernadette, who is a bitch, so of course she immediately told Sophy who went into shock before you could say howdy-do and almost miscarried her baby. Well, it turned out that she wasn't actually pregnant but—"

"Jeez!" said Lindy, who had drifted away and only heard a small part of this—not that a small part wasn't enough. "Where do you *meet* people like this, Alma?" She frowned. "You and Rafe have *got* to stop going to low-life bars."

"It's not low-life bars," I said. "It's low-life soap operas."

"Oh yeah! Duh." Lindy smacked herself on the forehead and walked off in disgust.

Dakota returned with a full glass of wine. It was rare that I saw her drink this much. An occasional celebration. Or stress. I hoped it was the former.

"Is everything going okay?"

She nodded. "I've been writing a lot. The ideas are coming so fast I don't know what to do with them. And walking. Or biking. Rafe and I go down by the river. He'll go for hours without saying anything if I'm working on something in my head. *God*, he's a hunk! Should I fall in love with him, Katy?"

I shook my head. "He's one of those men who makes a really great friend but a lousy boyfriend. He's kind of rotten to the women he dates, takes them for granted, is cavalier and cold. You know."

"Yeah," Dakota said. "I do."

"Have you been going out much? Lindy said you guys went shopping." I tried to keep the accusatory note out of my voice.

"Katy, she is such a *great* kid. I swear I'm adopting her as my sister."

"You didn't answer the question."

"Not too much." She smiled the bright, open, honest smile that always means she's lying.

"Liar."

Dakota blushed. "I had to get out a little, Katy. We always took Rafe and nobody really recognizes me out here, honest. One woman came up to me and said she thought I looked like Dakota Jones. I told her yeah, I got that all the time. Lindy"—she giggled—"said she thought Dakota was a *lot* prettier than me. Then she told her my name was Bette. With an *e*." She giggled again.

But I didn't. Sacramento was better than Nashville, true, but it was all relative. The doorbell rang. It was almost midnight.

"Who else is coming, Alma?" I asked.

"I don't know, dear." She said this with the wide-eyed, open look that means she's lying like a rug, all the while sidling, crablike, away from me. I sighed and watched Rafe head for the door.

"Hey, look who's here!"

Lindy sounded pleased and excited. Her boyfriend? He came around the corner and into the living room.

Not her boyfriend. Mine.

Hot damn!

thirty-two

CUCUMBERS AND DESSERT

WE WERE REALLY REALLY COOL. EVERYONE KNEW we'd just been through a hard time—okay, an unbelievably horrible time—and they were watching us like hawks out of the corners of their eyes, all the while pretending they were doing something else and could care less what we were up to. So we hugged and kissed and said all the usual stuff. Cool as cucumbers, you bet.

"What a surprise," I said conversationally, coolly.

He looked puzzled. "You didn't know."

Alma, who was hovering nonchalantly at our elbows, heard that and moved in like a sheepdog after a stray. Two seconds and she was herding Hank into the kitchen for a plate of spaghetti. I looked around for someone who would meet my eye. Guess what? Then headed for the kitchen for another glass of wine. Might as well, I wasn't driving.

Alma had parked Hank in a kitchen chair and was fluttering around piling spaghetti and meatballs, garlic bread, green beans and salad on his plate. He smiled at me when I came in, the smile that lights up his eyes. I found the wine and a bottle of Carta Blanca which I opened and handed to Hank.

He reached out, not for the beer but for me, pulling me down on his lap. The stubble on his cheek was rough on my skin, his arm tight around my waist. "Hey, sugar."

Alma plopped a huge plate of food on the table and beamed on us. "I changed the spices. See if you can guess."

I sniffed the spaghetti aroma appreciatively. "Hmmm. Easy on the oregano, just a tad of rosemary and a dash of—" I sniffed again. "Bay leaf," I announced triumphantly.

Alma ignored me. She and Hank are the cooks, not me. Charity drifted into the kitchen followed by Dakota and Granny Mae. Alma passed the freshly grated Parmesan. The doorbell rang again. Please—don't even bother to ask why my family doesn't have regular parties that start at reasonable times. It's an interesting but unanswerable question.

"Al!" Charity trilled and dashed off for the front door. Al is Charity's boyfriend, a really nice, stable guy whose patience is frequently stretched to the limit by Charity.

Hank hugged me again and offered me a bite of meatball and then a green bean and a bite of garlic bread. I hadn't eaten for hours. Alma had herded Al into the kitchen and was urging him to eat. Everyone was talking and laughing.

I looked up and met Dakota's eyes. There were tears in them. Only Dakota and Granny Mae were related by blood and yet we were a family, the kind of family that did everything with energy and passion, with tears and laughter, the kind of family that would do anything for each other.

Hank felt solid and muscular under me, our bodies warm wherever they touched. *It doesn't matter*, I thought, *how bad things got between us. What matters is that they're not that way anymore, that we love each other and are working on it.*

"You didn't bring Mars," I said, since I couldn't talk about love. Mars is Hank's black Lab. More family. He and Ranger, my dog, adore each other although Kitten, who is my grown-up cat without a real name, is pretty snotty to Mars still. Cat with Attitude—he has it down.

"No. Not when I'm working." He smiled at me and forked in a bite of spaghetti. "That's the part nobody told you."

I smiled back. Hank would tell me. And I could wait; there were no secrets between us now. He stood, picking me up too, kissing me as he set me down, and headed for the refrigerator and another beer.

"Man, are you ever in trouble now," Lindy walked in the room and announced.

"Oh yeah?" Hank didn't look worried.

"I've learned a *whole* bunch of new stuff. I mean move over, Bobby Fischer. Now I can really whup you. Want to play for money?"

"Sure."

I groaned. Rafe and Alma were a bad influence on Lindy, who was a good kid and not, thank God, a natural-born hustler like Alma and Rafe. Well, except at chess with Hank. Hank put his arm around me and I leaned into him, comfortable and happy.

And ready to go home.

"Hank, there's chocolate cake for dessert. Do you want ice cream with it?" Alma asked.

"No thanks, I'll wait. Katy's got dessert at home."

Yeah, I thought. *Me*.

Hank's arm tightened around my shoulders.

thirty-three
WAFFLES AND REDNECKS

THE WINDOW WAS OPEN, THE CURTAINS FLUTTERED IN the spring breeze. The air was cool and pleasant on our sweaty tangled bodies. I lay on Hank, totally relaxed, his hand stroking my bare back. Our heads were on the pillow pile and my nose was buried in his cheek. I wasn't breathing right.

Outside a bird was singing. It was three a.m.

"Why do birds sing in the middle of the night?"

"I don't know." His hand lingered in the small of my back. "Maybe they get confused too."

"Are we confused?"

"Not now."

"Mmmm." I reached down for the sheet and pulled it over us, cool now. "Hank?"

"Yes, Katy."

"That was pretty good."

He laughed. "*Pretty* good?"

"Yes." I kept my voice level and serious. "Of course, practice makes perfect. It never hurts to practice, do you think?"

"No." He rolled over, cradling me underneath him, covering my eyes and face and neck with kisses. "No, it doesn't."

The sheet got tossed again.

It was almost noon by the time we rolled out of bed. Nothing like a night of love and sleep to perk you right up. Better than vitamins. The birds were going nuts but it made sense now, it was daylight. Hank was in the shower. I had just gotten out. Damp and in my underwear, I made the bed. Ranger was prowling around, still hoping Mars would show up, and Kitten was pouting. His food bowl was full so I assumed it was just on general principle.

Hank walked out of the bathroom toweling his hair dry. I had just finished making the bed, true, but still . . . I put my arms around him. He was warm and damp, the muscles in his broad back hard under my hands.

He kissed me on the top of my head. ''Tell me there's food in the house.''

I wrinkled my nose. ''There's food, yeah, but nothing great. If I'd *known* you were coming there would be. Naturally.''

I looked around for my jeans. Where had I tossed them last night? Hank pulled on his Levi's, then sat on the bed and pulled on socks and Nikes. Hank looks just as good without clothes on as with them so I always kind of hate to see him cover up.

''I'm sure there's stuff for an omelet. Or waffles. Do they deliver pizza this early?''

''Waffles,'' he said, contentment in his voice. Hank's a sucker for my waffles, which are really good, I admit it. Breakfast and dessert are my kitchen specialties.

''Blueberry or plain?''

''Blueberry. I love you, Katy.''

The way to a man's heart is definitely not through his stomach. But it's not a bad detour.

''What should I wear to look like an important business associate of Dakota's?'' This wasn't clothes talk—which Hank, like most men, is bored with but dutiful about; it was undercover investigator talk—which he is interested in.

''Look Nashville. The jeans are good.'' He shook his head at the sneakers at my feet. ''Boots and a kind of flashy top. A little bit of makeup.''

''Okay.'' I pulled out a silk shirt in teal and turquoise

and silver earrings and bracelet. I put on the boots and jewelry and a T-shirt. The silk shirt would look a whole lot better without waffle batter than with it. I know this from experience.

Hank made coffee and juice and I made waffles. From scratch with fresh eggs from Charity's ranch. Also real maple syrup. From Maine, I guess. If you're going to detour, make it a good one.

Hank ate three waffles but refused a fourth.

"Really? You need to keep your strength up."

"Strength." He snorted. "Any more and I'll be lucky to waddle out of here."

"What are you doing?" We never did get around to talking about work last night. Odd, huh?

He pushed his chair back from the table and held his arms out for me. I sat on his lap facing him, my arms around his neck. It was a little difficult to concentrate on work.

"I'm babysitting Dakota. Rafe asked me to cover, said an emergency situation had come up. They're pressuring me to take time off work since I've got so much overtime built up so it worked out fine. Mostly I wanted to be with you, Katy." His hands were underneath my shirt on my bare back. I snuggled in closer.

"Emergency?"

We both laughed. It could be a real emergency or it could be a stock car race or a poker game. With Rafe it all depends. I've heard him define running out of beer or breaking his custom-made pool cue as an emergency.

"I'm glad you're here." Waffles don't make me contented but Hank does. "That's why you drove."

"Yes."

It was a non sequitur but he knew what I meant. Hank drove so he'd have a gun.

"What are your plans?" Hank ran his fingers through my hair and kissed my ear.

"Rio Linda. I want to talk to people who knew Hope and Pity."

"Hope and Pity?" He sounded puzzled. "Are those nouns or names?"

"Names."

He shook his head. It takes a fair amount to surprise a cop but it can be done.

"Ask Dakota and I'll fill in the blanks tonight." I gave him a last hug and got up to rummage through the kitchen drawer that is largely filled with miscellaneous unusable junk that I think I might need someday. "Here's a house key."

I've had a key to Hank's house for over a year but he has never, permanently, had one to mine. It's not that I'm less committed, it's that I'm more afraid. He put it on his key ring.

"Do you have Granny Mae's address?" I headed for the bathroom to brush my teeth and throw makeup inexpertly around.

"Yes. Dakota gave it to me last night."

"I think Rafe's been letting them run a little wild. Lindy and Dakota have been doing a lot of shopping. At Arden Fair Mall, for godssake!"

"We're going out to Charity's ranch. They're going to ride. And there's a new foal that Charity wants to show off."

"Is Al working this weekend?"

"No."

I laughed. "So you guys are going to sit on the front porch and drink beer and tell lies while they ride."

He looked a little sheepish. I was right, or close to it. I was glad, too. Glad that he'd be out in the country sitting in the sun and fresh air with friends, riding horses, telling stories, maybe losing at chess to Lindy. And I was glad he was away from homicide and Sin City, which is how I think of Las Vegas.

RIO LINDA MEANS "BEAUTIFUL RIVER" IN SPANISH. IT'S A community of less than ten thousand people about ten miles north of Sacramento. It's mostly white folks, blue-collar jobs and a heritage that is as much small Southern town as rural northern California.

There is no beautiful river here. There is no river at all. There is Dry Creek which is poorly named and rarely dry. Rio Linda and the surrounding area is in the floodplain and is semiregularly inundated with floodwaters. The East Levee (on the west side of town) protects the rice fields on one side but not Rio Linda on the other. Things are like that in Rio Linda.

It used to be agricultural. Once there were chickens and it was a major egg-producing center but then the chickens moved south to Petaluma. Rio Linda is mostly a dream that never happened but that people haven't quite given up on. Homes and land are cheap although there are a few million-dollar places—all built on high ground—and big ranches. There are horses and livestock, pigs and chickens. Lots of pickups, almost all with gun racks, most of them with guns. Redneck country.

The driveways of the sprawling, sometimes shacky homes are filled with cars. Some run, some are rusted out and on blocks. There are sagging sofas on front porches and washing machines on back ones.

There is no bowling alley or shopping mall. Demolition derbies are big here, as is the Little League Parade. There are wrecking yards and Bowinkle's drive-in (where President Clinton had a chili dog), flies and dogs and plenty of bars. They say there are more horses than people, more pickups than cars. It is not a cultural mecca.

But there are codes. People in Rio Linda take care of their own problems. Differences of opinion are settled with fists, and if that doesn't work, with guns. It's usually the neighbors who call the cops and only when the noise lasts too long or there's a lot of blood. The cops roll frequently on domestic violence complaints.

Rio Linda is Hope's hometown.

It took me about thirty-five minutes to get there and no time at all to find the house at 6th and O. The address on Hope's license belonged to a neat two-bedroom ranch-style house built low to the ground. The yard was nondescript but trim, the lawns recently mowed. Everything was green and lush, the way it is here for about ten minutes in the spring.

The driveway was dirt and gravel. Two vehicles, a battered white Toyota sedan and a newer red Ford Ranger. The Toyota was streaked and dusty, the Ranger had been recently washed. A shot-up, rusted-out mailbox with no name was perched on a wooden post next to the ditch that paralleled the street. No sidewalks.

I pulled into the driveway and parked next to the palm tree. Just for the record: I don't ever want to live in a place that doesn't have palm trees. Rio Linda has a lot of them. I parked, reached for my purse and started to get out.

The dog was huge—a cross, say, between a Rottweiler and a rhinoceros, and very vicious and unscrupulous-looking. I changed my mind about getting out. Just like that. And rolled my window up. Real fast. The dog had its front paws on the door of my Bronco and was eye level with me, barking and drooling with enthusiasm.

I chickened out and looked away before the dog did.

The guy I recognized immediately, though he wasn't wearing a baseball cap. He whistled at the dog, who stopped rocking the Bronco and went to stand next to his owner, who waved at me to join him. I took a deep breath and climbed out of the car.

"Hello," the guy said to me. He was a lot friendlier—plus he wasn't drooling—than the dog who lolled his tongue at me and drooled some more.

"Hi. I'm Kat Colorado. I'm a business associate of Dakota Jones's. I just got back from Nashville where I met Hope Delaney."

I had the right house and the right guy. Yup. His face lit up like a traffic light at the mention of Hope's name. I closed the distance between us cautiously, one eye on the dog, and held out my hand.

"Nice to meet you. I'm Rick. You want to come on in?"

I did, especially if the dog stayed out. I followed Rick across the lawn and up to the front porch where an old metal swing, big enough for a cozy twosome, sat. The screen door had seen many better days but had been sanded down and repainted, the wire screening carefully patched. He held it open for me. The inside was a surprise. There were a lot of nice pieces, slightly old-fashioned and elegant, that I was betting were Pity's choices, not Hope's. There was a Van Gogh still life and a Monet landscape on the wall—decent reproductions in ornate frames.

"Sit down. Can I get you an iced tea?"

"Oh, no, thank you."

"No trouble." He seemed eager to offer me his hospitality. "How is Hope?" he asked when I declined again.

I sat on the couch and he was in an easy chair across from me, leaning forward, elbows on his knees. "We only talk once or twice a week, trying to keep expenses down, so you've probably spoken to her more recently than I have."

I thought of Hope: cocky and sexy in the bar, smiling and satisfied as she climbed out of Link's car, with smeared makeup and angry demeanor as she sat under a bleeding Jesus at her cousin Tommy's house.

"She's fine," I lied. The truth was not only too complicated, it wasn't mine to tell.

"Good." He smiled at me. "What can I do for you?"

I had tried to figure out a way of saying this that didn't sound like the FBI. Not that I looked FBI. "Background check" was the term that came to mind, the term that sounded like the FBI. I wondered how much Rick knew, how much Hope had told him.

I walked away from FBI and toward the personal. "Rick, Dakota has been threatened a number of times in the last few months. An attempt was made on her life. It has made us not only very jumpy, but very careful."

He thought that one over. "And you want to know that Hope is who she says she is?"

Good. He was making it easy for me. "Exactly."

"Sure. I can understand that. What can I tell you?"

"Do you have any pictures of Hope? And of her mother? She and Dakota are related through their mothers."

He stood. "C'mon."

I followed him into the bedroom. It was more sunshiny and feminine than the living room, with a floral comforter, pillows edged in lace and curtains with pale stripes picking up the comforter colors. Rick was headed for a tall old-fashioned mahogany bureau and I was right behind him. A lace runner covered the top of the bureau and on it were crowded at least twenty framed photos in all sizes.

Rick handed me one, Hope in a simple short white dress, the veil pulled back from her face as she smiled up at her groom.

Is he your husband or boyfriend? I had asked Hope, looking at the picture in her wallet. Boyfriend, she'd answered, but she hesitated before she spoke. Hesitated and lied.

"This was at our wedding."

"Recently?"

"Last year." His face clouded over briefly. Was the honeymoon already over? He took the photo from me, handed me another one.

"This is Patricia."

I looked at the woman whom Hope had identified as her mother.

"Patricia?"

"Hope's mother."

"Did she go by any other name?"

"There were a few people who called her Pity but it was a nickname she disliked."

Pity had changed her name to Patricia. Good for her. "When did she die?"

"A year and a half ago."

I put that photo down and looked at the others, the ones of Hope and Patricia and Rick and people I didn't recognize.

"Did Hope know her grandparents or her family on her mother's side?"

"No. And Patricia never spoke of them except to say that they would have nothing to do with her. She was brought up by her father's family. I guess she was passed around a lot, not exactly unwelcome but not quite with a home either.''

''And Hope's father?''

''He left, or Patricia divorced him when Hope was very young. After that he never came back. The men in that family don't seem to stay around for long.'' He frowned. ''Myself, I don't understand that. When I married Hope it was for better, for worse, and forever. These pictures here are her father's family.''

They looked like a dour and unsmiling lot, I thought, as though life had been hard, grim and unrewarding. I studied a photo of a happy smiling couple in their mid-fifties.

''Your parents?''

''Yes,'' Rick agreed. ''Hope has an album too. It's in the front room.'' Dutifully I followed him as we retraced our steps. ''Patricia said that Hope looked at this album a lot as a child, that she would point at people and say 'I hate you,' and 'I will never never never be like you.' '' I flipped through the pages of the snapshots and sympathized. It was the same dour unsmiling group of people in more informal, but apparently not happier, situations. I would not have wanted to be like them either.

''Do they live around here?''

''Some of them. Hope won't have anything to do with them though. She says they're bad news and bad news is catching. I'm gonna get me an iced tea. You want to change your mind?''

''Okay,'' I said, mostly to be polite. I drifted along behind Rick as he headed for the kitchen. ''Has music always been important to Hope?''

''Always.'' He got out a jug of tea and a tray of ice cubes. ''There's a lot about it I don't understand, Kat. It's almost like a fever, a sickness deep inside her. It makes her life something better, she thinks. But sometimes I just see it eating away at her, chewing her up and spitting her out into something smaller.''

Rick took glasses down from a cupboard and filled them with ice, carefully poured the tea. When he put the jug

away I could see a clean refrigerator neatly stocked with
food—Styrofoam trays with meat and poultry, fresh fruits
and vegetables, milk and juice. It was the opposite of Cal's
refrigerator. Or mine. Though mine at least was clean. I
hoped Hank would remember to make a grocery run, wine
and beer too.

"Does that seem strange to you?" Rick asked.

Ooops. I should have been thinking about Hope, not re-
frigerators and refreshments.

"No. Music does that to people. Maybe not just music
but anything you feel really strongly about."

The phone rang. Rick put his tea down and walked over
to the inexpensive wall-mounted extension.

"Hey, honey!"

Rick turned and smiled at me. I smiled back, pointing at
myself and shaking my head. I preferred that Hope and
Rick not put their heads together on me. He shrugged and
nodded. I picked up my tea and walked into the front room
to give him the illusion of privacy.

But I could still hear.

Easily.

thirty-four

BAD SEEDS, SWEET BITTERNESS

Is EVERYTHING OKAY? YOU WEREN'T SUPPOSED TO CALL until tomorrow. . . . Good. . . . Okay. How much? . . . *How* much? . . . Hope, you know we talked about that, what we could reasonably afford and all. We're already pushing it, you know, what with you out there three weeks. . . . I *know* a lot is riding on this but we still don't have the money and I don't get paid until next week. Hope. Hope! Aw, *shit!*"

He hung up. I pretended to flip through the photo album. *Hope had been in Nashville for three weeks?* I quit pretending the minute Rick walked back in.

"Everything okay?"

"Yeah. I guess." He ran his hand through his hair, which didn't take long—it was very short. "Aw shit, Kat, I'll be honest. I don't know what the hell is going on here. I'm not even sure I can figure it out.

"Hope's a complicated person. I'm not. I'm a simple guy, a fireman like my dad. I love my job and I work hard. I like to play softball. I'd like to start a family sometime soon. And I love my wife, I really do, but I'm not sure I understand her. Sometimes I'm even afraid that I'm not what she wants.

"Honest to God, I don't know what she wants. Some-times I think it's me. Sometimes I think it's getting even with the past. I don't think you can do that, but *she* does, and she's got a whole list of wrongs that need to be put right. But most of the time I think it's her career.''

"Music?''

"I don't know. That's part of it, yeah, but it's not that simple. It's not just the music, it's fame and fortune and wanting to hit the top and show people. We were fighting about money, you probably heard. She'll go into debt, she'll do anything to get what she wants. That scares me. I'm not like that.''

I thought of Link and thought he was right to be scared.

"I want her to be happy, I want her to get what she wants but that scares me too. I'm afraid that will take her away from me.'' He got up and walked over to the window, stood with his back to me. "I risk my life on the job. Not every day but often enough. That doesn't scare me, but this does.''

He turned and faced me. "Do you ever think about names? Hope. Is that a name or something she's stuck with? Always to be looking, wanting, hoping for something different and better, maybe even for something that chances are you'll never have. I don't do that, do you?''

I shook my head. "I don't think so. I have dreams and goals, and I work for them, plan for them, but hope? Not really. Your wife works to make things happen, though.''

"Yeah.'' He rubbed his temple. "Yeah, she does. She gonna get the job with Dakota?''

"Dakota's willing to take her on for a trial period. I don't know what will happen after that.''

"Is Dakota a nice person, Kat?''

"Yes.''

"And she runs a good operation?''

"Yes.''

"So Hope would be safe, wouldn't get into any trouble or anything?''

I thought of Link, of all the willing guys that every city everywhere spits up and out, of the trouble that finds you, and of the trouble that you have to go looking for. And I thought that I could see Hope, no problem, in all of those situations and more. And I could see her here, sitting next to Rick, smiling up at him, loving him like tomorrow was a long ways away. I couldn't call it. Rick couldn't call it. Maybe even Hope couldn't call it.

"You can get into trouble anywhere, Rick." I said it gently.

"Yeah," he said. "You can." He sounded defeated.

"Where is Hope staying in Nashville?" I asked.

"Outside of town with her cousin Tommy and his wife. She said she could borrow Joanne's car and keep expenses down that way."

"Who's Joanne?"

"Tommy's wife."

So she had lied about that, too.

"Did Patricia remarry?"

"No. She had a boyfriend, though, a nice guy. Things had just started going real good for her when she was diagnosed with cancer. It was a goddamn shame. She was a good person who'd had a hard life, a real hard life, and there it was over just when things turned around for her."

"What was her boyfriend's name?"

"Harding. Tom Harding."

"Is he in Rio Linda?"

"Yeah. On West Fourth. I don't remember the number."

Rick got up, headed for the kitchen, came back with a phone book. There were three Hardings, a Terry, a Thomas and a T. Only one on West Fourth.

"What was it about the past that had a hold on Hope? Who or what did she want to get even with?"

"I don't know. I didn't like to encourage her to talk that way and neither did Patricia. Patricia was always one to look on into the future and to look for the good side of things. You know what a crazy quilt is?"

I nodded.

"Hope said that life was like a crazy quilt, that it was made of random bits and pieces that didn't make sense but got stuck together. But then she'd try to make sense out of it. She'd drive herself and everyone else crazy trying to make sense of something that didn't or couldn't make sense. Hell of a deal." He shook his head. "Look, Kat, I gotta go. I coach a Little League team and it's almost time for practice. You gonna see Hope again?"

"Yes."

"Watch out for her, okay? Please."

"I'll do my best."

He nodded as though he really appreciated it.

I took a deep breath and then a risk. "You love Hope very much." I stated the obvious. "I'm sure she loves you too. Love takes faith but sometimes you have to fight for it."

He started to speak, then thought better of it, nodded and picked up his keys.

"Thanks for your help, Rick. If my house ever catches on fire I hope your truck responds."

He laughed.

The Rottweiler rhinoceros walked me to my car.

I made it fine. I didn't make any wrong moves.

RIO LINDA'S NOT THAT BIG AND TOM HARDING WASN'T difficult to find. I didn't call ahead and I was a little over-dressed for the occasion, but what the hell?

Harding's house was a three-bedroom ranch much like Rick and Hope's place only a lot nicer and probably worth twice what theirs was. No dog but a big garden with bunches of early spring flowers. No patched screen door either. I rang the doorbell and gazed at the etched glass in the door panels. Couldn't see a thing through it. Rats.

A good looking man of about forty-five answered the door. He was five foot eight or nine and stocky, with dark hair graying at the temples. He wore worn jeans and a plain shirt. His smile was warm and open.

Mine, too. And innocent and charming. "Hi, I'm—"

"Collecting for the Cancer Society?"

I shook my head.

"The Heart Foundation?"

"Nope."

"Your kid's a Girl Scout and if I buy ten boxes you'll

throw in a free one and she gets a shot at the trip to Disneyland?''

"Not that either." I laughed.

He folded his arms across his chest, leaned back against the doorjamb and grinned at me, a slow, friendly could-have-been-sexy-with-any-encouragement grin. "I'm outta guesses."

"Hope Delaney."

Harding folded that grin and stashed it away like a camper with a camp stool. He still leaned against the door but his posture was rigid, his face ugly.

"What kind of trouble is she in now?"

"What kind of trouble is she usually in?" It was an outside chance but he didn't fall for it.

"Who are you? What do you want?"

"Hope is applying for a job. I'm doing a background investigation. I understand you were a good friend of Patricia Delaney and that you knew Hope as well. I was hoping"—I paused. It's confusing having someone's name be the same as a common verb—"that you would help me."

"I reckon not."

"May I explain?"

"Go ahead."

"Hope's cousin on her mother's side is Dakota Jones."

His eyes flickered in recognition.

"The country star."

"I know of her."

"I work for Dakota."

He nodded.

"Hope approached Dakota's grandmother, Mae Parneter. Mrs. Parneter is also Patricia Delaney's aunt. She wanted to adopt Patricia—Pity—as a baby but Pity's mother, Louella, refused and gave the child to her father's people instead. It just about broke Mae's heart. She tried to keep in touch with the child but the father's family refused to allow that. When Hope came to Mae and asked for help Mae agreed gladly. Hope wanted to meet her cousin, Dakota, and she wanted Dakota's help in getting a start in the music business."

He shrugged. Everything about him said he didn't care about Hope or this conversation. Or maybe that was too polite, it was more that he didn't give a shit. "This doesn't have a thing to do with me."

"Someone's threatening Dakota's life."

"Threatening?"

"Tried to kill her."

He unfolded himself. "Come in."

I followed him back to the kitchen, an unadorned room in yellow and white and appliances. At his invitation I seated myself at the kitchen table.

"Coffee?"

"No. Thanks, anyway."

He pulled a mug out of the cupboard and filled it from a pot on the stove, then sat across from me. "You work for Dakota?" He was buying time, thinking things through.

I took a card out of my purse and handed it to him. "We've been friends from childhood. I'm helping her because she needed someone from the outside." *Someone she could trust.*

"It's that serious."

"Attempted murder is serious," I agreed.

He spoke slowly, thoughtfully. "I thought the world of Patricia Delaney. Things pretty much fell apart for me for a while when she died almost two years ago. I didn't feel that way about her daughter though. I never have had any use for Hope and I sure as hell don't now. Out of respect for her mother I'd prefer not to go into it."

He looked at his coffee, which had an oily slick on the top of it and looked cold and uninviting. "Is Hope involved in the murder attempt?"

"If that weren't a possibility I wouldn't be here wasting my time and yours."

He sipped his coffee, made a face and put the mug down. "You ever see the movie *The Bad Seed*?"

"No."

"It's on late-night TV once in a while. It's about a little girl and her mother. The girl is angelic-looking but she's no angel. Anyone crosses her, she gets 'em. Like she pushed a playmate of hers who did something to her into a lake. Kid couldn't swim and drowned while she stood there and watched. Stuff like that. The mother, who is a really decent person, finally figures it out. She decides to kill herself and her daughter. Only she dies and they save the kid.''

There was silence in the kitchen except for the sound of a bee. It buzzed around the yellow and white room looking for sunshine and flowers, finding only stainless steel and chrome and bad coffee. Harding got up and opened the back door. Sunshine and the sweet-smelling scent of spring fell in on us.

''Mr. Harding—''

''Tom.''

''Tom. What are you telling me?''

''I'm telling you what I'm telling you.'' The bee flew outside. I waited. Shivered.

''I've never met a person I distrusted more than Hope. She was obsessed with the past, thought the world had done her and her mother wrong, thought it was up to her to make it right. No, not just make it right but get even. Get ugly,'' he added. ''She is a mean, vicious person and she likes to get ugly.''

I thought about the beautiful, sometimes shy, sometimes vivacious woman I had just met. It was difficult to reconcile the two images.

''We're not talking playing by the rules here, Kat. We're talking winning. Doing whatever it takes. She cheated in school, sabotaged a kid on the basketball team so she could play, stole her friends' boyfriends, got a kid fired so she could take her place at work in a drive-in.'' He ran his hand through his curly hair. ''That was at school. She didn't get any better outside of school, I just didn't hear about it as much. Patricia knew it made me angry and tried not to tell me things.''

''Do you know any of Hope's friends?''

''No.''

''Did you ever meet or hear about a man named Link Davidson?''

"No."

"How did Patricia react to all this?"

"She was a smart woman but she was a fool over her daughter. She knew what was happening but she wouldn't really look at it. She made light of things, made excuses for Hope. She made it worse is what she did.

"I think it killed her, the fear of what was, the disappointment, the anger she couldn't admit to—all that ate away at her as surely as the cancer. Hope talks it up that her mother died because there wasn't enough money and she couldn't get decent medical care. That's bullshit. Patricia put off the surgery and chemotherapy that could have saved her life. Hope sucked up money like a five-hundred-dollar Hoover. She was buying guitars and amps, drugs and good times with money that could have saved her mother's life."

I didn't know what to say so I didn't say anything.

"I didn't find out about it until it was too late or I would have done something. By the time I knew, the cancer was too far gone. So I lost the woman I loved more than life itself. I don't know what you're asking me specifically but I'd be real careful. Hope wants something from Dakota Jones and she'll do anything to get what she wants. She's capable and intelligent. If Hope wants to, and if she can, she'll pull Dakota down out of greed or meanness or out of this obsession with the past that's all twisted up in her mind." He shoved his coffee cup away.

"Murder? Depends how you define it, doesn't it? There's probably not a person in the world that would call Patricia's death murder. Except me. And I'm real clear on it."

He looked at me. His face was calm, his eyes clear. He'd cried his tears a long time ago. But he was bitter, and he remembered.

"Sometimes I wish that I had Patricia's faith in God, her faith that things work out for the best even though we don't always understand how. But I don't believe any of that. I sure as hell don't believe that Patricia's death was for the best."

The bee flew back into the kitchen, a slow learner in the garden of life. As Patricia had been?

"I once walked in on Hope going through her mother's purse, taking cash out of her wallet. She stuck what looked like a couple hundred dollars down her blouse and then she walked over to me bold as brass. 'This can be our little secret, huh Tom?' she said to me and put her hand on my crotch."

Revulsion set in on his face like quick-dry cement. "She'd sell her body, like she tried to offer it to me for my silence, if it got her somewhere. She doesn't really count the consequences the way you and I would. Murder? Why not? She'd figure that she was smart enough not to get caught and it would be worth it to get what she wanted."

"How would killing Dakota get her what she wanted?"

"I dunno. I can't think like she does and I don't want to. But if she's the one threatening Dakota I'll bet you dollars to doughnuts that's how she's got it worked out." He pushed back his chair. "I don't believe in God but I believe in bad seeds. You tell your friend Dakota to be careful.

"*Real* careful."

thirty-five
THE DIP OF ANGEL WINGS

THEY BUZZED ME IN THROUGH THE ELECTRONICALLY controlled metal gates. I drove up to the house, then sat in the car and waited. Jack was loose, that's why. Jack, who is named after Jack the Ripper, made Rick's dog look like a pussycat. It's not as though I haven't been to Charity's ranch a million and two times; I have.

But it doesn't matter with Jack. He has bonded to Charity and she is the only one who can control him. He would just as soon rip your throat out as blink. Actually, I think he'd prefer to rip your throat out. He stood silently staring at me—locked up in the Bronco—with evil in his heart. It was more frightening than the barking and slobbering of the rhinoceros dog. Once he caught my eye and licked his lips. *Jeez*.

Charity opened the car door and gave me a hug as I climbed out. Jack sighed in disappointment—dog language for *another wasted day,* I guess. Dakota was right behind Charity. They were dusty, smelly—horses, not sweat—and Dakota had a smudge on her cheek. She was smiling. I hadn't seen that in a while.

"We had a wonderful day, Kat. You should have been here." The pressure of the anonymous letters and the scares, even the pain of Joni's death seemed to have slid off her. She looked like a young and carefree Cody, not the frightened and troubled country star Dakota. "We rode forever—it was great. Charity's naming the foal after me!"

I laughed. She sounded like the kid with the most Easter eggs.

"How was your day?" Dakota asked me.

"Interesting."

I hoped that was as unthreatening as it was noncommittal. A troubled look flitted across Dakota's face. Charity, who is the world's most sensitive and discerning person (not counting her love life), jumped right in.

"Little Dakota stood up almost immediately. She cocks her head to one side and has the stage presence of a star, just like her namesake. She has a white splash on her face and white markings on three legs."

"Katy, she's a darling!"

"I can't wait to see her." I looked around. "Where's Hank?"

"Inside. He went through the kitchen and is making cioppino."

"Yum!" I've had Hank's cioppino many times before.

We reached the front porch and trooped on through the house and into the kitchen—a fragrant and delectable paradise. Hank smiled at me, his hands full of . . . whatever . . . I couldn't really tell.

Al stood and grinned, saluting us with his beer bottle. "Hey."

"Hey," I said in return and put my arms around Hank, my cheek against his warm back. New lovely smells drifted up from the pot where Hank was tossing things.

"Wow!" Charity exclaimed, standing in front of the open fridge. "There's an hors d'oeuvre tray in here."

Hank chuckled. I filled up a plate for us; Charity grabbed a chilled bottle of wine and wineglasses; then we headed back to the front porch, leaving the boys in the kitchen.

I love role reversal.

I sat in a rocker on the porch—rockers and porches are another thing I love—and watched the sun start its quick slide toward the horizon. The need to talk to Granny Mae, and maybe Alma, was gnawing at me. I wished I'd been able to do that this afternoon. Tomorrow. I spit an olive pit between two porch rails and smiled in satisfaction. I was reaching for a chunk of cheese when Charity spoke.

"Dakota, I've been too polite to ask but I think you should start talking. Now." She spoke kindly and she patted Dakota's knee and filled up her wineglass.

Dakota was crying, tears drifting down her cheeks like sad little fallen stars.

Well *shit*, wasn't I just the hotshot investigator—covering all the bases but home? "Dakota?" I asked, better late than never.

"I wish I had a guy who loved me, like Hank and Al love you two."

"You will," I said. "It's only a matter of time."

Charity ignored me *and* my comment. "That's not it, Dakota." She spoke as an advice columnist, not a friend drinking wonderful Napa Valley wine on a front porch watching the sun go down.

"No," Dakota agreed. "I guess it's not."

What was going on here? What had I missed? I had the sense to keep quiet, I had the sense not to brush away Dakota's tears. I had the sense not to do anything but listen.

Dakota spoke. "A lot of my life I felt like nothing. My father deserted my mother and me when I was two. I don't remember him and Jo destroyed all the photos and memories that would have made him a part of my life. She told me that he left because of me, because I was a bad child. I believed that for years."

I made a sound that had more to do with anger than understanding. Part of me couldn't believe that a parent would say that. The other part knew Jo and understood perfectly. She never blamed herself, always someone else, preferably someone helpless and unable to fight back.

"Jo didn't love me—"

"Was incapable of loving you or anyone else," I interrupted, trying to get away from hatred and bitterness and back to understanding.

"Yes, all right. But I didn't understand that then. I didn't figure that out for years. For years I was just a kid whose daddy had run off and whose mommy blamed her. Do you know, I don't ever remember Jo doing anything with me. Mostly I remember watching her get dressed and made up to seduce whatever man she longed for then, the man she thought would make her life complete. She would clip on her earrings and smile at me. I took those smiles, treasured them as though they were for me and not for a stranger. Maybe I learned it from her.'' Dakota sipped her wine and stared at the sun sliding down the sky and falling into a puddle of rainbow sherbet on the horizon.

Huh? Learned what? Smiling? Clipping on earrings? Makeup?

"What?" Charity asked finally.

"The idea that something else could make you complete. Later I thought that music would do that for me. Sometimes I still think that."

Dakota picked up a piece of cheese and tossed it to Jack who caught it in midair. I could hear his teeth snap.

"When I was a kid I would wake up in the middle of the night crying, feeling lost and alone. I had nightmares all the time. If Jo heard me she would storm into my room to scold me. More than once she slapped me. I remember how beautiful she looked in her filmy, floating nightgowns. Sometimes I would be lucky and Granny would hear and be the one to come.

"She tried to protect me from Jo. Every night when I was small she would read to me or tell me a story. Then she would kiss me good night and say that I was God's precious little angel. I didn't believe that. Once I said that I wasn't an angel, that angels were good and I was bad— Jo had told me so—and so God couldn't possibly love me. I didn't even cry. If God didn't love you things were so bad that there wasn't any point in crying over it.

"But Granny was tougher than that. She told me that God loved everyone and that you could be an angel if you always tried to be good and said your prayers. And she kissed me and told me I was her little angel. Sometimes I wonder who I would be without her. Not just a lost soul but worse, someone consumed with hatred and anger and

revenge—a Bonnie looking for her Clyde and guns and
ammo and pointless destruction.''

Like Hope? I wondered.

Birds were singing, calling out to each other and to the
world, bidding the sun good night. Charity and I were silent. Jack snapped at a fly. Close by a dove cooed its cloudy
mournful entreaty.

''Sometimes I think that maybe I wanted to be a star so
that people would see me, would recognize me and value
me as my parents never had. Maybe I even wanted to make
them see. To see the dip of angel wings, not the child they
resented and abandoned.''

I wondered if those early hurts, hungers and needs, once
denied, are ever filled. It takes a lot. More than bright lights
and a stage. I thought of Cal. More than drugs and alcohol
and endless lovers. More than hate and anger, bitterness
and resentment.

More than murder.

''The first time I sang on my own an old man came up
to me and said, 'Honey, you just knocked everyone's hat
in the creek. You keep it up and don't lose heart now.' I
have never forgotten him. Those are the people I'm singing
to, good-hearted, down-home people. Music is a gift to
them and they love you for it. They come there for your
music but it goes both ways—you come there for their love.
The roar of the crowd fills you up.''

There was a loud noise inside and then a shout of male
laughter. Momentarily it drowned out the birds and the
crickets. But not the loneliness.

''There's an ache in me all the time. It's like a hole that
can't be filled up. I am not a person who can lay her heart-
aches down. I carry them along with me. Only when I put
them in a song it sometimes gets better.''

Temporarily. Stopgap.

''I didn't really get into music to be famous or rich. I do
it because it's in me, heart and soul. It's wonderful that the
recognition and money came. But it's confusing, too. I have
never had a real good notion of who I am. Now, standing
in the spotlight, it's real hard to tell.''

A dove cooed and another one—its mate?—answered

and there was a soft flutter of wings. The rainbow sherbet puddle on the horizon had turned to a pool of pinks and grays. Charity picked up the wine bottle, saw it was empty, put it down. The rocking chair creaked as I tipped it back. The crickets chirped and the frogs from the pond out back started tuning up for the evening.

"It's easy to forget who you are. People have their own image of you and they want you to be that. They're angry at you if you're not. Sometimes I think I'm forgetting what's real and what I made up in my dreams and songs along the way. I became a star and I got lost," she said softly. "And if I don't know who I am, how can anyone else? If you don't know someone, you can't love them."

"Yes you can. People do it all the time." Charity, the voice of common sense and reason.

"Not really *love*."

"Dakota, love is not something, like a CMA award, that someone hands you and is yours forever."

"I know that."

There was more spunk, less sadness and defeat in Dakota's voice. Charity's good at this, much better than I am.

"Love grows and you build on it and often it has wildly improbable beginnings," she said in a firm voice.

I thought about how I met Hank and how Charity met Al and thought that that was true. A dove warbled and cooed and a loud squawking dusty black bird flew by and drowned it out. Jack was snoring as well as drooling, his sleeping head on the grass, his ears pointed in Charity's direction. It was his concept of love. Inside I could hear kitchen sounds and male laughter. Love. Charity picked up the empty wine bottle and headed indoors.

All I could think of were fortune cookie platitudes: *Love is just around the corner. Do not give up hope. True love will soon be yours.* One of my greatest fears is that someday we will all sound like fortune cookies. Jack yawned. I sighed. And then I had it.

"If you beat the odds to become a country star you can do anything."

Dakota looked at me for a long time and then laughed. "You know, I think you're right."

We left dusk and Jack on the front porch and headed into the house. Light and laughter, food and wine.

But I remembered a line Dakota had told me long ago: *Sorrow flew into my heart and stayed.* I have seen Sorrow do that, move in with her cold smile, damp linens. She is a difficult tenant to oust, feeding on herself and others as she does.

Tomorrow I would talk to Granny, then see if I could track Clyde down, peek into the missing years of his past. I couldn't concentrate on sorrow yet, not until Dakota was safe.

Sorrow could wait.

We had to beat the odds on murder still.

thirty-six

BAD APPLES AND STRANGE JOY

"WHAT HAS DAKOTA TOLD YOU, GRANNY?"
The house was quiet. Dakota had gone off somewhere with Hank and Lindy. We sat in the front parlor—Granny is probably one of the three people in the world who still uses the word "parlor"—and drank tea.

"That she came home to rest and write. She stays up late at night, Katy, working on her songs. Sometimes I hear her walking around in that restless way of hers at three or four in the morning. Singing." She smiled. "It's so nice to have her home again."

"There's more to it."

The smile slipped off her face and faded into yesterday. "It's not good, is it?"

"No."

"I wondered about that. Her visit seemed so sudden. I thought she was on tour. The child didn't want to worry me."

"No. And I don't want to worry you now but I do need your help."

Her hand trembled as she put the delicate china cup in its saucer. "All right."

"And I need the truth."

She nodded.

"Don't leave anything out."

"All right."

"Tell me about Clyde."

A half smile played across her face. "He was a very handsome man. Even as a young man there was something about him. It wasn't just women who noticed. Men, too. Everyone liked him. And charm? Oh my yes. Why, he could charm the stripes off a zebra.

"I was there when he and Josephine met at a church social. I saw them look at each other and I knew in the blink of an eye that we were in for trouble." Her voice shook a little. "Would you pour more tea, dear, I can't quite reach it." She waited for me to pour, then stirred sugar and lemon into her cup. "I knew from the moment I laid eyes on my Billy that he was the one for me. He courted me for a year before we were married but I knew it in my heart all along.

"That wasn't the way it went for Josephine and Clyde. I don't even know if it was love, ever, between the two of them. They had a hunger for each other that neither of them could ever say no to. Not," she added tartly, "that either of them ever tried. The first time I turned around that evening they had slipped out somewhere.

"It wasn't until the end of the social that I saw Josephine, her eyes all bright, her cheeks flushed, her clothes mussed about. Theirs was the kind of trouble that started right off and kept right on until it exploded and there was nothing left but pieces to be picked up."

Granny sipped at her tea and looked at me thoughtfully. "I think you ought to marry that young man of yours, Katy. He's not the trouble kind at all."

The expression on my face gave me away. It was not so long ago that Hank had gotten involved with someone else and the memory was still clear and painful.

"Well," Granny qualified, "no more'n any man. Even Billy was a mite of trouble."

I heard the rush and then the clatter of skateboards, the shouts of children outside.

"What's this all about, Katy?"

"It exploded, didn't it—the trouble between Josephine and Clyde?"

"Yes."

"I think we're still picking up the pieces. I'm trying to understand what pieces belong and what don't."

"So many things go back so far," Granny said sadly.

"Some of that's good. Dakota loves you very much, Granny."

"Yes. I love her too." Her voice was soft.

"Without you and Billy, but especially you, she wouldn't, she says, be the person she is today. Jo would have destroyed her."

"Love is a blessing," Granny said. "And she was the blessing to us that we were to her, that is God's truth. Josephine was our only child. We loved her dearly and yet could never reach her. Nothing reached her but pretty things, money and—"

"Men."

"Yes."

Which brought us back to Clyde. Granny's rarely a reluctant storyteller but she was today. "Won't you finish your story, please."

"They could not stay away from each other. Like animals in season, they were. Billy caught Clyde in Josephine's bed one night. *Imagine!* And only just down the hall from us! It was a craziness that blinded them to everything else. They were utterly shameless. He made Clyde marry her. They weren't talking marriage, you know."

"It doesn't sound like they were talking at all."

Granny giggled, sounding suddenly as young as Lindy. "Isn't that God's own truth. Now I wonder if perhaps the marriage wasn't a mistake. At least it made the child, made Cody, legitimate. Do you think it was a mistake?"

"I don't know. You did the best you could. And things were so different then. Today having a child out of wedlock is a walk on the beach. Thirty-some years ago—"

Granny nodded. "Yes. That's very true. Not that it lasted long. He was gone before the child's second birthday. Gone for good, I mean, he was gone most of the time anyway.

And not working much either. Even then they lived with us. They both liked money and the good things it could buy but neither one of them was overfond of hard work. Like two peas in a pod, they were.''

"Money, or lack of it, is that what broke up the marriage?"

"Josephine never spoke of it to me but my guess is no. Their physical need for each other had no love to pin it down and make it last. The fire burned hot and then the coals died out. Clyde came home later and later in the evening and once or twice not until the next day. One day he just stopped coming home at all. We heard he'd left town.

"We didn't see hide nor hair of him for a year or more. Then he came back with sweet talk and tall tales galore. And Josephine took him in."

"*No.*"

"The fire was burning again."

"Just as hot?"

"Just as hot but not nearly as long. When he left he took all the cash we had in the house, which was a goodly sum. Josephine said then she would never speak to him again. To the best of my knowledge she kept to her word. Of course he never came back either."

"What about his daughter? What about Cody?"

"He never had anything to do with the child. Not when he was there. Not after he left."

"Did he send support money, letters, presents?"

"No, and it hurt Cody terribly. Sometimes I wish that he had died. It would have been simpler for all of us."

"Dakota said she thought that he had written, maybe come back—to you, not Billy—for money. And she thought that you helped him out."

Granny sighed. "How did the child know? I kept it from Billy and Josephine. I thought that I had kept it from her, too. It's true, though it was never much. I did not like him nor think well of him but he was the father of my beloved grandchild. I could not ignore that."

"Do you think he ever cared about Cody?"

"No."

"He came to you to find Dakota. He told us he cared and wanted to make up for the past. Do you believe him, Granny?"

The expression on her face said no but it was the good Christian in her that spoke. "I don't know, dear, I hope so. The Bible tells us not to judge. Perhaps he has changed."

Perhaps.

"Is there anyone around here who knows Clyde, who is still in touch with him?"

"Years ago there was a brother. His name was Charles Wilkins Jones but everyone called him C.W. I don't know where, exactly, he lived."

Outside the skateboards clattered and crashed. One kid hollered and another laughed.

"Granny, tell me about the crazy quilt."

"Oh Lord." She put her face in her hands. "Oh Lord, oh Lord, oh Lord."

It took her a moment to calm down and continue. "It was a wonderful thing. It was pieced out of scraps but it had a beauty that was impossible not to see or feel. I have seen beautiful things come from great love and joy. This came from sorrow and pain.

"It was my sister, Louella, who made it. She was very different as a young woman, very beautiful and alive. You cannot imagine."

I thought of the dried-up, bitter prune of a woman I knew and agreed that I could not imagine it.

"Louella and Josephine were very much alike. I thought of that often and how very odd it was that Josephine, a child so unlike me, should be my daughter. Well," Granny said briskly, "that of course is neither here nor there except to remind us that God works in mysterious ways."

God and murderers both.

"Did Cody tell you what I told her of Hope's family history?" Granny asked.

"Yes. But please tell me again. All of it. Just in case she missed something."

"Louella and Josephine had more than hot blood, and tempers to match, in common. Men. Put either one of them in a room full of nice hardworking, churchgoing young men and they'd leave with the one bad apple in the bunch. Every time. They had an eye for them, a taste for them. Worse, a strange joy in them.

"I don't know, dear. Maybe that kind of thing is not so bad today. Such a disaster, I mean, to choose a young man like that. You women today are so strong and self-sufficient with jobs and lives of your own. And thank goodness for it. But back then, sixty years ago, it was very different. If a woman picked a man who couldn't take care of her and the children there was trouble indeed. What was she to do? There weren't the jobs and opportunities there are today.

"Now Clyde was irresponsible, there's no getting around that. He was a real good-time man, as Billy used to say, but not a bad man, not really. Louella's Homer was a different story. Homer was bad through and through. His mama and God could find something to love about Homer but there wasn't no one else that could.

"I didn't tell all of this to Dakota, but you asked me not to leave one thing out, so I won't. Now, you use your common sense on this, Katy, and don't be telling everyone who turns the corner."

I shook my head.

"No, of course you won't. Well, Homer got Louella— we called her Lou back in those days. I can remember when Daddy would bounce her on his knee and sing 'Skip to My Lou' to her. I was jealous then—she was always Daddy's favorite. My, isn't it something what we remember?"

She smiled at me, a little sadly I thought, and I reached over to pat her hand, small and white with blue veins standing out in stark relief. Vulnerable. I felt a sudden stab of pain at the thought of losing Granny or Alma.

"You're *my* favorite," I said, meaning every word.

"Thank you, dear. I guess it's a blessing that everyone is someone's favorite. Even Homer. Though I do wish someone besides Lou had chosen that particular blessing."

After all the years that had passed I was surprised to hear the depth of the sorrow in her voice. I couldn't see it on her face or in her eyes but I could hear it.

"Anyways, Homer got Lou in the family way. Well, and we weren't one bit happy about it. The family way part we could have lived with. Plenty of girls had a hurry-up wedding, after all. But *Homer*, why that was something else again.

"I reckon you know, Katy, that Billy was a railroad man all his life. And mighty proud to be. Well, he got Homer a job at the railroad. He didn't like that man no more'n anyone else but Billy was crazy for me and I wanted the best for my little sister, so he did it."

I could hear the slow, measured beat of Granny and Billy's ancient grandfather clock.

"Homer stole from the railroad, stole every goldang thing he could lay his hands on and git away with."

I didn't need a map, I saw it coming. "And Billy found out and turned him in."

"Yes. It was an insult to God, the railroad and my honest Billy who had gotten that no-good Homer the job. And then, by golly, the fat was in the fire. Or . . . what is it you young people say?"

"The shit hit the fan."

"Yes. That's it. Exactly. Well, Homer lost his job of course. It was only out of respect for Billy that they didn't put Homer in jail and take him to court. Lou and Homer's whole family had conniption fits. You'd a thought, listening to them, that Homer was innocent and Billy was to blame. That's what they thought, you know. They talked themselves right around to believing that."

"I'm sure no one else did."

"Oh no. It was just Lou and Homer's family, all of them acting like they didn't have the sense God gave dirt." Her tone was weary, as if the old sorrows pulled her down.

"Homer started hanging out with a bad crowd then and it wasn't no time at all before he was in really big trouble. Him and the boys in that crowd tried to hold up a payroll office and a man was killed. They all went to jail for it and the charge was murder. And Lou and his family—they blamed it on Billy." There were tears in her eyes. After all these years. She tried to talk but couldn't.

So I did. "They said that it never would have happened but for Billy, that he had pushed Homer into a life of crime."

Granny wiped her eyes and nodded. "Yes. That's it, exactly. You like to wrote the book. But I don't suppose it's the first time you've heard such a story."

"No."

"They weren't married then—Lou and Homer—and I begged her not to marry him. She said she wasn't bringing a child into the world without a daddy. Well, and it got worse. She cursed that poor little unborn child like it was the guilty one and she the innocent. It like to make me sick but I kept it to myself for the sake of the child.

"I told her that we could go away toward the end of her time, that she could have the baby and I would raise it for my own. No one need ever know save her and me and Billy and she could start all over again.

"Billy and me wanted another child to love and it wasn't no nevermind to us whether it was our blood child or not. I begged Lou and she wouldn't listen. She married Homer. Had to go out and buy her own ring and go to the jailhouse to do it, but she did. Later she tried to get rid of the baby before it was born. I thought I'd never be able to forgive her for that.

"By the time that poor little child was born her daddy was dead in a prison fight and her mama couldn't wait to get rid of her. Again I begged Lou for that baby but she wouldn't listen to me. She named her Pity and gave the child to Homer's family. And I never have nor will forgive her for that." Granny rubbed her hands on her temples. "Will you put on water for more tea, dear?"

I put water on. We would get to the crazy quilt, but it would be in Granny's time, not mine.

thirty-seven

CRAZY QUILT MAP OF LIES

WE LOST THAT LITTLE CHILD, KATY. I KNEW SHE WAS gone from us forever. The minds of Homer's family were poisoned against us and for sure they would do the same to the child. They called her Pity, just like Lou had. Can you imagine? What a burden to lay on small shoulders.''

"She changed her name to Patricia as an adult."

"Well, good for her. I didn't give up entirely though I might just as well for all the dang good it did me. I called Homer's family every now and then. Once or twice I went over. They treated me like dirt—froze me out and slammed the damn door in my face."

Granny blushed. From "dang" to "damn" in a single paragraph. I thought her point was well taken. "You're a good woman, Granny, and you did the right thing."

"The it-ain't-gonna-work thing," she snorted. "But I had to try. I couldn't get the image of that sweet innocent little girl out of my mind. I don't even think they wanted her. She was a burden but they kept her out of stubbornness or meanness or maybe just so I couldn't have her. Well, after they slammed the door in my face a few times I gave up." She sighed. "You know what, Katy?"

"What?" I asked affectionately.

"For a long time I sent birthday cards and Christmas

cards and presents of clothing and things I thought she could use. I just wanted to reach out to the child."

"To send her your love."

"Yes. That was it, really. They kept the things so I hope she got them. Little Pity. Then, after a while, they started coming back to me so I stopped that too. I just really gave up then. I figured that later on when she was grown she could come to me if she wanted, but she never did."

"I don't imagine she ever heard anything more than their version of the story. Hope's husband told me Patricia thought her mother's family wanted nothing to do with her."

Granny shook her head sadly. "I saved every one of those cards and presents. Every one. All these years. Isn't that something? Shucks. Maybe I don't have the sense God gave dirt either."

"I think you do." I held her small hand in mine. "Patricia didn't come to you but her daughter did."

"*Well*, and she wanted something, didn't she?" Granny asked tartly. She snatched her hand away from mine and patted her hair fiercely. "It wasn't like she came to call."

"Hardly anyone ever comes out and asks for love even when it's the one thing on their mind. Asking for help is hard but it's easier than asking for love."

"Huh!" she snorted, still fierce.

"What was the quilt about, Granny?"

"Hate. That was it pure and simple." Granny stood up and smoothed her dress down over her slim hips and fragile bones. "Once I saw a picture of the Taj Mahal in the light of a full moon, that beautiful beautiful building that a man built as a testimonial to his love for a woman. The crazy quilt, beautiful as it was, was a testimonial to Lou's hate. You sit there. I'm going to go get it."

A testimonial to hate? I couldn't think of any examples. To love, yes. Poems, palaces and churches. Love builds. Maybe hatred only destroys. Gossip, envy, backbiting; wars, rapes, murders. A beautiful testimonial to hatred? I didn't get it.

Granny came in clutching a bundle to her chest. "I kept

it locked up all those years because I didn't want to share the hatred. I was afraid of it." Granny looked at me, a quiet, frail, elderly lady. "I still am."

Yes. The fear showed on her face. She unfolded the quilt.

The beauty came through first. It was made of silks and velvets, taffetas and brocades and materials I didn't recognize or have names for. The piece I held measured roughly three feet by four. Three edges were cleanly bound with a kind of satiny fabric; the fourth had been cut by pinking shears and was unfinished. I looked at Granny.

"Lou cut it in half. She wrapped the child in the other half when she sent her off."

She wrapped her child in hate.

The quilt was made of many small irregularly shaped pieces carefully stitched together. There was intricate top-stitching and embroidery and the embroidered designs were simple and clear: cracked and broken hearts, tears, weeping willows, forget-me-nots, fading and wilting roses, funeral lilies, an empty cradle, a sad-looking pair of baby booties, a path that led nowhere.

I looked at Granny's stern, unforgiving face. "You said it was a quilt of hatred but I don't see that. Loss and sorrow, love and pain, but not hatred."

"That's because you haven't read the story—'The Story of the Quilt' is what Lou called it."

"Oh? Where is the story?"

Granny continued at her own pace. I swallowed my impatience. "When Lou married Elmer, her second husband, she left some things behind. I guess she wanted to start afresh. She had never mentioned the story to me, I found it years later when I was going through the old things. When I shook out the half of the quilt she had left with me, this fell out."

Granny reached into her pocket and drew out a letter. "The quilt was made of hatred and stitched with tears. The letter is made of lies." She handed me the envelope and walked from the room, her back stiff and unyielding.

The envelope was yellowed now and with a water stain

on one outside edge. The sheet was closely written in an old-fashioned spidery hand, the black ink now faded.

TO MY DAUGHTER

I write you this in the hope that someday you will read it and questions in your hart may be answered. I keep a copy of this letter for myself as I do half the quilt which I made in the time that I awaited your birth into this cold world of ours. The other half was wrapped around you when you were taken from me. It is rite and proper that you should know the truth of this matter. I am a poor penniless woman unable to care for herself or her child. Your father died an innocent man in jail where he was wickedly and wrongly sent by the betrayal of those nearest to him. It is for these reasons that I am compelled to give you up in the hope that your father's family will offer you more than I can.

Your father was a good man falsely blamed for others misdeeds and put into the jail house. These false accusers were none other than my own sister and her husband. By these lies they profited. Money and land and property that rightfully was your fathers and mine and one day yours was all taken from us. But that is as nothing. Your fathers life was taken from him as was mine. He was dead. I was dead inside. And then they took you, forcing an innocent child to suffer the sins of others.

I am powerless to do anything but this. I give you a mothers blessing.

It was unsigned. I looked through the lacy curtains floating like unspoken thoughts in the spring breeze and at the new green leaves on the trees, the red and pink flowers of the azaleas and the white of the puffy, dreamy clouds, and I wondered where such hatred came from. I jumped, startled, when Granny spoke. I hadn't heard her come in.

"I have searched my heart and mind over and over, Katy, but still I do not understand what can make a person do such a thing. I believe it was God's judgment on Louella that she never bore another child, not even in her marriage to Elmer when she wished and prayed for that. And, though I know it is neither right nor Christian of me to say this, I am glad.''

In the silence the grandfather clock ticked, the minutes marching on inexorably from the unheard future to the present and then into the past.

''Why, Katy?''

''Some people cannot face the truth and they will do anything, make up any lie so they do not have to.''

''Even if it means ruining the lives of others?''

''Yes.'' I looked at Granny's tears and reached out for her hand.

Even if it means murder.

thirty-eight

EUPHEMISM, WHITE TRASH, DARK STALKERS

T HERE WAS ONE C. W. JONES IN THE PHONE BOOK AND it was a wrecking yard and not a person. Close enough.

I left Granny in Roseville—once a thriving railroad town notorious for its bars and bordellos, now a quiet suburban community—and headed west on I-80 for Elverta. Elverta is a next-door neighbor of Rio Linda. Same rural atmosphere, maybe a little bit more down at the heel.

Hardly anyone, in our current age of euphemism, says "wrecking yard" anymore. Usually it's something cleaned up and dignified, like "auto dismantler." Not C.W. Looking at him I realized he was not a man of many things, including euphemism.

"How ya doin'," he said from behind an old wooden desk piled with greasy papers, auto parts and leftover fast-food containers. The dim light filtering in through the dirt on the one window didn't illuminate much but it wasn't hard to see C.W. Gray stubble on a filthy face and a huge beer belly mostly covered by what had once been a white T-shirt was what jumped out. He was eating (okay, devouring) powdered-sugar doughnuts out of a box with a

day-old red mark on it and drinking a Classic Coke. The
mousse craze had pretty much passed him by; he was still
styling his hair with WD-40.

"Whaddya need?" He belched. Such a charmer.

"Are you Clyde Jones's brother?"

"Not if the bastard is in trouble, in jail or in debt." He
belched again and lit a cigarette. "Who wants to know?
You a cop?"

"No."

"Girlfriend?"

"No."

"Shit. What's left?" He grinned at me. Ooops. He didn't
brush his teeth much. Or floss. I could tell.

"You got an address for him?"

"Naw. Clyde don't let the grass grow under his feet.
He's always moving around, changing jobs, changing
places. I don't try no more to keep up with him. He comes
by coupla times a year, we go out, drink beer and get
fucked. That's about it."

"Does he have any other family?"

"I asked you once, I'm gonna ask you again. What's this
about?"

"Credit check. Mr. Jones is applying for a loan to buy
a piece of property."

"You from the bank?"

"No, a credit agency. Apparently his credit history and
references were a little, uh, unusual, so they sent me out to
check."

"Unusual?" C.W. snorted. "Fucked is more like it."

"Does he have any other family?" I asked again in a
firm and businesslike tone.

"Naw."

"Wife?"

"Naw. Clyde there, well, he likes the ladies and that's
the truth but he don't ever marry 'em. He fucks with them.
Nobody fucks with him. You fuck with him, he turns into
one mean son of a bitch."

"I understand he was married once."

"Long time ago. He was young and dumb. He ain't

young no more and he ain't dumb. He likes the ladies, like I said. And they like him. He's a nice guy and he shows 'em a good time while he's around. It's just that he ain't usually around all that long. He don't want no responsibility.''

C.W. was wheezing by the time he finished that thought, or maybe it was ''responsibility.'' Those six-syllable words can get to you. He stubbed out one cigarette and lit another, a poster thug for How Not to Live Your Life.

''He has one child, I understand.''

C.W. dragged on his cigarette, then blew the smoke out of the corners of his mouth.

''Yeah. Technically. He don't have nothing to do with it. Never has. It's grown now, anyhow.''

''Did he ever contribute regularly to her support?''

''Right.'' He snorted. ''Look, I tol' you, Clyde's a decent guy, he just ain't big on responsibility.''

This is how it works, I guess: One person's ''decent'' is another's ''deadbeat.''

''I hear the daughter's rich.''

''Yeah. Right. I ain't never heard that.'' C.W. slugged down the rest of his Coke and belched again. ''What's your name? I didn't catch it.''

''Crystal.'' I read the brand name of a milk container sitting next to what looked like a filthy coffeepot.

''Yeah. Say, Crystal, you wanna go out for a coupla beers one of these days? Maybe shoot a little pool?''

''Wish I could,'' I lied, ''but it's against company policy to date someone you meet on work time.''

''That's fucked.''

''That's life.''

''I won't never tell.'' He leered at me.

''Thanks for your help.'' I made a dash for sunlight and fresh air and a place where people brushed their teeth and didn't say fuck all the time.

WE WERE AT FLORENTINE'S, AN ITALIAN RESTAURANT IN Old Folsom down by the river. At least they say it's by the river, and technically, it's true. The American River isn't far away but you can't see it, although you can see a bunch of asphalt and one of the ugliest Radissons in the world.

Old Folsom is a historic town, early-California and gold mining. There are still the old names of places—Negro Bar, Humbug Creek and Prairie City Road. Also Folsom Prison, which Johnny Cash made famous and numerous others called home. (And I bet you anything those were guys who didn't brush their teeth regularly and said fuck way too often.) Now there are supermarkets and outlet stores and, most recently, a Wal-Mart, but all of that (except the prison) is in the new part of town. Old Town is still quaint and charming with raised sidewalks, cobblestone streets, old hotels and bars and an occasional hitching post.

I hadn't wanted to go out to dinner—too high-profile— but it was a compromise. Dakota's first choice was Lake Tahoe. Speaking of high-profile. Her second choice was clubs and dancing and wild nightlife, not that we have a whole lot of any of that in Sacramento on a Sunday evening. So dinner it was. We were five: Dakota, Charity and Al, Hank and me. And two of us were off-duty cops (Al is California Highway Patrol) who—I'd put money on this, no problem—were carrying guns. They also brushed their teeth and hardly ever said fuck in a social conversation.

"It's great to get out," Dakota announced.

We were having drinks in the downstairs bar at a window table with a nice view of the Radisson parking lot. Dakota was like a tightly coiled spring. She didn't quite meet my look so I knew there was something going on.

"You look different tonight, Dakota, but I can't quite put my finger on it." Al looked puzzled.

"I'm disguised," Dakota said. She almost always wears her hair loose. Tonight it was pulled back completely off her face into a French braid.

Al shook his head. "That's not it."

"I'm trashy."

"*That's* it."

We all laughed. I thought what an easy and effective disguise it was. A little too much, too bright makeup, slightly garish costume jewelry, a T-shirt that was too small and . . . goodbye Dakota Jones, hello Miss White Trash.

"Garrett called today." Dakota's voice was elaborately casual.

So that was it, or a part of it. The cocktail waitress drifted by and Hank ordered another round.

"I'm flying home Wednesday. I'm playing Thursday through Saturday. We're picking up our regular concert schedule from here on out. The benefit for Joni is two weeks from next Sunday." She whipped through that like it was one long run-on sentence.

"I'm not sure that's such a great idea." I kept my voice level and even.

"Katy, what choice do I have? Really? I can't cancel concerts indefinitely. It's not fair to the fans and it's a *disaster* for my career. It's not the loss of income, though God knows that's bad enough—I have a lot of people depending on me. It's the lack of exposure and the damage to my reputation. You have to be out there all the time. Country music fans used to be really loyal but that's not true anymore. If you're not out there, they forget about you. I worked too hard for everything to watch it slip through my hands now."

"I don't want that to happen either, Dakota. I just want you to be cautious for a while yet."

"How can I? It's all or nothing. Either I perform or I don't. Garrett's put a lot of extra security on. It'll be all right."

"Extra security?" Hank and Al spoke at the same time.

"A lot more security people at the venues, a bodyguard for me. There's an alarm system at my home and he's got someone patrolling the area."

"That's all good but—" I looked my question at Hank and he nodded in response. I started to speak, then stopped. "You explain," I said to Hank. Maybe it would have more of an impact coming from a cop than from a friend.

"You can't stop someone who's willing to trade their life for yours."

That was it. Stark. Simple.

Dakota's face went white. "What do you mean?"

"If they're willing to get caught or killed, they can get you. Lee Harvey Oswald, Jack Ruby, Sirhan Sirhan, Mark David Chapman—our history is full of examples."

The blue eye shadow and red lipstick stood out in severe, ugly contrast to her white face. Her lips were parted slightly and her eyes were scared.

"But you'd have to be crazy to do that," she whispered.

We all nodded. We were thinking of the anonymous letters, the coffin pictures, the dead flowers, the magazine subscriptions and Joni's murder. We were thinking this, and we were thinking that the perpetrator did not sound like a sane person to us, not one who passed his Rorschach blot test on the first try and with flying colors. Not even close.

Dakota was thinking this too.

Finally.

"Oh God, what am I going to do?" She was whispering still.

I didn't answer. I didn't have the answers; I just had the questions.

"Are we any closer to finding out, Katy?" she asked.

"No. I know a lot more about a lot of things and a lot of people, most of whom technically qualify—that is, they were around and have, or could have, a bad attitude. There is nothing to connect up any of these people with what has happened. That's been the problem from the beginning."

"And Joni's death?"

"Same thing."

"The police investigation?"

"Same thing."

"Do you think it will just stop?"

Dakota asked me but Hank answered. "No. People engaged in this kind of behavior—"

"What kind of behavior?" Dakota asked.

"Harassment, stalking," Hank answered.

Or thrill killing, I thought but didn't say.

"Stalkers don't give up. It's obsessive behavior that almost always gets worse over time. If the behavior is interrupted it rarely means that the stalker has lost interest; rather that something out of his control has intervened. A military transfer, for instance. Or maybe he's in jail on another charge. Or dead.''

''He?'' Dakota asked weakly.

''It's usually a man. Violence in a stalking case almost always indicates a male perpetrator.''

Who is crazy as a bedbug. This is what we were all thinking. Crazy is frightening not just because we don't understand it but because it is so unpredictable. And because a lot of the crazies in this country have guns. Crazy as a bedbug, unpredictable and armed is a really bad combination. We were all thinking this too.

''If I were to drop out of sight completely what would happen?''

''Would it stop, do you mean?'' I asked.

''Yes.'' Dakota looked at me and then at Hank. I let him take it.

''I doubt it, not as long as he knows where you live and can find you. It's possible that eventually he might refocus onto someone else.''

''Eventually? Is that weeks, months, years?''

''Not weeks.''

There was despair on Dakota's face. ''If this is going to continue no matter what I do, except totally disappear, what's the point of changing my schedule? I can't stop living my life.'' Her voice rose on a note of hysteria.

''Sooner or later he'll make a mistake. We'll identify him. We'll get him. Until then the point is to keep you safe.'' I made my voice as calm and soothing as I could.

''Sooner or later? That could take days, weeks.''

''Yes.'' *Or even months, but why bring that up?*

Dakota slugged down the rest of her wine. ''I'm going back Wednesday as planned. Will you come with me, Katy?''

''Yes.''

She relaxed in relief and smiled. ''I was so afraid you'd quit.''

I shook my head. Not a chance.

I could quit this job, but not our friendship.

thirty-nine
FOR SALE: SABOTAGE

I SAT IN THE FOURTH ROW FROM THE STAGE. DAKOTA'S voice soared out through the arena, filling it, floating up to the domed ceiling and sifting down onto me.

> "And He walks with me,
>   and He talks with me,
>   and He tells me I am His own..."

There was a plea, almost a prayer in her voice. Her voice broke and then it climbed and soared again. I had been to sound check more times than I could count but I had never heard her sing a hymn. The last notes trailed away in the darkness and emptiness of the arena.

I got up and walked the arena floor again, the map in my hand, different expectations in my mind. Except for parts of the stage, the arena was in darkness, the outer reaches dim and unclear. But the X's on the map stood out, as did the routes marked in highlighter pens of different colors. Dakota's voice filled the arena.

> "No more saying I'm sorry,
>   no more asking you to stay..."

The security plan. I could find no fault with it. Nothing had been overlooked or skimped on. Hunter and the people he was working with had done an excellent job. This was the setup at all the venues now. The buses came in early, long before the crowds, and were parked in locked, gated, guarded, often underground areas. From there Dakota was escorted to the stage. She was never alone. If we could get them, off-duty cops—with guns and uniforms and attitudes—were Dakota's personal escorts. And me. I had an attitude a lot of the time now too.

Thirty rows back I stopped and looked at the stage. Dakota seemed both small and far away—the effect of the stage—and larger than life—also the effect of the stage. She stopped singing, played with a phrase, stopped, played with it again.

> "No more looking back,
>   no more hoping for yesterday . . ."

She stopped again, walked around the stage. Silence and then the drummer started a solo, occasional beats that built slowly to a wild crescendo ending in the slam and crash of cymbals. And then Dakota.

" '*No* more looking back . . . No more looking *back* . . .' James, what do you think? I can't get it just right. 'No more *looking* back . . .' "

She sang it again, then tossed up her hand and walked into the pool of darkness at the center of the circular stage.

At first it was just a blur, a dark movement on the edge of my peripheral vision.

It happened so fast. That's what the innocent bystanders always say.

And then it coalesced into a huge shape, a stage light that was falling.

There was no time for a warning. None. They say that too.

It hit the stage at the spot where, seconds before, Dakota had been standing.

We were all in shock. Nobody could believe it. We were frozen in place.

And exploded in a flash of colored glass and lights and electrical energy.

There was silence and then I heard, as I ran, Dakota's voice rising a cappella into the darkness and above the shouting:

" 'And He walked with me, and He talked with me . . . ' "

As I reached the stage she broke off abruptly. The mike squealed, screamed and then resounded as though it had been dropped. I put my hands on the stage and vaulted up, still running. Dakota was surrounded, by the guys in the band, the bodyguard, you name it.

"I want the lights up in here," I yelled. "Someone hit the lights now!" Lights flicked off and on and then finally on, the glare almost blinding. I stepped back out of the pool of light on the stage until I could see clearly. He was rigid, motionless, easy to miss—dark clothing blending in with the heavy steel beams and huge cables.

"Hey you, up in the lights. Come down here."

I stood, one hand shielding my eyes from the stage lights, the other held out, index finger pointing, like a sailor hollering "Land ahoy!" What was this: Killer ahoy?

It seemed like a long time to those of us who waited in silence as the dark figure scrambled overhead and then clambered down the ladder. It wasn't, of course; it was remarkably fast. He was remarkably agile.

And white-faced and shaking. "Miss Jones, are you all right? That's never happened on a job that I've worked. Never. It was an accident but it could have— Oh my God. Are you all right? Please tell me you're all right. I'm so sorry about it. It wasn't my work but that doesn't matter. I'm sorry. Are you all right? Please tell me."

Dakota nodded weakly and that, mercifully, put an end to his babbling. That and Rolli's sharp nudge in his ribs. Killer ahoy? He didn't look it. He didn't look like a bad guy. Or a good guy. Just an average joe, unremarkable in every way. Except for the remorse and contrition, and that seemed genuine.

"What's your name?" I asked.

"Chuck Blaine." He stammered it out.

"It wasn't your work?"

Chuck's eyes swung around wildly, not as though he was

guilty but as though he wanted to account fully for everyone and everything.

"No. I was doing the final safety check and any last-minute safety adjustments, if necessary, on work done earlier. Miss Jones is the main act and all of this is usually done when the opening act is rehearsing. That's what we aim for, anyways. Look I gotta call. This kind of thing happens, we got to get someone else up there to check it out. It's rules."

"Garth was almost hit like that a while back," Steve said. "Same thing. Huge spot just missed him."

"Garth Brooks?" I asked him.

"Yeah."

"Does it happen often?" I asked anyone.

"No. But it happens." Tommy answered me.

I turned back to Chuck. "Had you checked out the light that fell?"

"No. I was heading in that direction but I hadn't got there. I gotta call, okay?"

I nodded, then looked around until I located Dakota's bodyguard. "I'm taking off for a while," I said. "Don't let Miss Jones out of your sight, I don't care if she's going to the bathroom." He nodded by rapidly jerking his chin down a very short distance two or three times. Maybe it's hard to nod if you have almost no neck?

And then I followed the lighting guy. Chuck went into a glass-enclosed office and picked up the phone. It looked as though he made two phone calls, quick ones—I couldn't hear, of course—and then he was out of there.

Me, too.

Our cars were parked in different areas—I was in the high-security lot—and I was afraid I might lose him. I almost did. I saw one car at the far end of the parking lot cruising through the lot diagonally and heading for an exit. That was my only choice so I took it.

We were in Atlanta. I don't know Atlanta. It's a name on the map to me, nothing more. If I lost Chuck, that was it. End of chapter. I was driving a rental. Dakota, Hunter and I had flown in on a private plane; the band and equipment had come by bus.

Chuck—I had gotten close enough to be reasonably sure it was him—was driving a battered Ford Escort in an unappetizing color that was somewhere between a disgusting beige and a yucky mustard. He drove carefully, stolidly, keeping to the speed limit and signaling every lane change and turn. A model citizen, at least in the driving department. I was grateful for it. Model citizens are a breeze to tail.

He could have lost me at several light changes but I never even saw him glance over his shoulder or look back to see if he was being followed. Model citizens never think they're being followed. They aren't. Usually.

The Escort's left-turn light started flashing and the car slowed for the turn, stopped to wait for an opening in traffic. I yawned. I never get to have wild car chases, not like Clint Eastwood and Bruce Willis. Blaine turned left; I went to the end of the block and did the same, circled back and parked not far from the Escort.

The parking lot of the home-style restaurant was reasonably crowded but not full. Inside Blaine was sitting at the counter with a cup of coffee and an agitated expression. There was a short line of people waiting to be seated at a table so I stood in line as though I, too, were waiting.

Blaine got up and headed for the rest rooms. Me, too. Isn't the power of suggestion amazing? The phone bank was right before the rest rooms. He stopped there. Me, too, suggestible as I am. He dropped a coin. I flipped the coin release and jiggled the receiver. Then we both punched numbers, Blaine for real, me faking it. I had my back to him two phones away but I could hear him just fine.

"Yeah," he said. "This is Chuck. I need to talk to—"

"Missing a side of sausage, hash browns and a buttered wheat toast!"

The kitchen doors flew open. The bathrooms and phone bank were right next to the kitchen entrance. Did I mention that? I ground my teeth in exasperation. A side of sausage, hash browns and buttered toast? *Nobody* needs that much grease, never mind cholesterol. And for that I missed an important conversation? Shoot!

"Yeah," said Blaine. "I just come from there."

I leaned—okay, teetered—in his direction.

"Someone fill up the cream pitchers. Is there any syrup around here? Who opened this morning? Nothing, I mean nothing, is done around here!"

"No, it's a done deal. Light came down just like I said it would. Scared the shit out of everyone, especially her. Course it missed her. I said it would, didn't I? Look, I did what I agreed to—now you pay up the rest of my money."

"Hey, Lulu, you got a clean apron? This one's trashed."

"That's the deal, man. I want the rest of the money by tomorrow or I'm making trouble. You tell him that." He slammed the phone down and started to walk away, paused as he passed me.

I hunched over my phone. "Hey, no way!" I said in an exasperated tone of voice—a frantic high-pitched tone of voice. "Don't put me on hold *again*. I've been on hold *all* morning and I— Aw, phooey!" I muttered a string of damns and darns and other annoyed sounds as Blaine walked on past me to the dining area.

I considered how to play this one. Took me two seconds to decide to go for it. The counter was almost empty so sitting right next to Blaine was noticeable. Very.

"Hey, Chuck."

He looked at me and frowned in concentration. I was familiar but he couldn't place me. Of course I wasn't where I should have been, doing what he expected me to be doing. That's always puzzling.

"Say, do I know you?" He asked only after his frown and concentration failed to come up with the answer.

"I'm with Dakota Jones. We spoke right after the lighting accident." I smiled at him in a friendly fashion.

He tried to smile back but he was too nervous to really pull it off. "Oh," he choked out finally.

And the ball was back in my court. "And then," I continued, still ever so friendly, "I couldn't help overhearing your phone conversation a minute ago."

"Couldn't help hearing?" he stammered.

"No. I wasn't really on hold; I was eavesdropping." I smiled again.

Blaine stared at me, lost. He couldn't reconcile my friendly expression with what I was saying. To be frank, I didn't get the impression that he was rocket scientist material.

"Who hired you?" I asked.

"I don't know what you're talking about."

"You want to order?" a waitress asked me. She must have been the one who wanted to borrow Lulu's apron. Hers was trashed, just like she said.

"No, thanks."

She frowned, disapproving of sitting at the counter and not ordering, Blaine took out a dollar and tossed it on the counter, then started to rise.

I didn't move. "You don't want to answer? No problem. I'll just talk to the cops. They're real interested in attempted murder, especially when it involves a superstar."

He sat down again. "It wasn't attempted murder, it was just a joke."

"A joke?" My voice was hard; I was tired of pleasant.

"Yeah. Sorta." He stared at his coffee cup. "Well, maybe not a joke—it was to scare her. That's all. Honest to God. There was no chance she coulda been hurt. I was real careful. It was just supposed to look like an accident and scare her, that's all. It was no big deal, honest."

"Who hired you?"

"I don't know."

"This conversation is beginning to bore me. When I get bored enough, I'm calling the cops."

"I don't know. This guy in Nashville called me. I don't know his name either but he does the same kind of work that I do, and he said there was five hundred dollars in it for me if I did the job no questions asked. I got the idea it was someone in the music business, someone who was jealous of her success."

"Give me the number." I held out my hand.

"I can't. I won't get the rest of my money. They only paid me half."

"You go to jail, you won't get your money either—only for a much longer time."

"Look, I know it wasn't right. I only did it 'cause I got a kid that's sick and I really need the money. You're not going to go hard on me, are you?" There was a whine in his voice.

"Give me the number."

He took a piece of paper out of his pocket and shoved it across the counter toward me. I glanced at it—a Tennessee area code and a Nashville prefix—and put it in my purse.

"You're not gonna go hard on me, are you?" The whine again. "Hey, I got a sick kid."

"No harder than you were on Dakota." I stood as his jaw dropped and hung there slackly.

Chuck wasn't entirely satisfied with my answer.

Who could blame him?

forty
BROKEN ANGEL

I CALLED HUNTER'S OFFICE AND BLEW THE WHISTLE ON Chuck first thing. We had a hole in security and it had to be plugged. Or, if that hole was at management level—Hunter, say—then I wanted him to know that I was on it.

Chuck? Maybe he had a sick child, maybe he didn't. Ask me if I cared. People who try to solve their problems by dropping a two- or three-hundred-pound weight from a forty-foot height to "just miss" someone don't get any kind of a sympathy vote from me.

The concert that night was okay. Dakota was either stiff and nervous or awkward and jumpy. I could hear the tension in her voice too. The lights had been checked and double-checked but it was obviously very difficult for her to stand under them. She wandered around the stage a lot, as if to stay out of range. Out of range of anything: falling lights, guns, flash bombs, hatred.

We got through it and nothing ugly happened. Some days that's the best you can say and that's not bad at all. It was almost two before we got home to Nashville and much later before we got to bed. Dakota insisted on making breakfast. This is a very old tradition of ours going back to the days when I was a bartender.

She'd lost weight and looked thin and pale. I was worried

about her. *Understatement*. I was worried about a lot of things. *Major understatement*.

"Dakota, you need to get some sleep."

We had eaten and Dakota was now playing with her food, building little forts out of potatoes and scrambled eggs.

"I know." She carefully piled a potato on a corner mound, where it teetered slightly before it settled. "I'm afraid to relax, to even close my eyes for a minute, Katy. I know that's dumb but . . ."

"It's certainly understandable. We're okay, though. Checking the lighting has been added to the security list at every venue." I hadn't told her that the sabotage was deliberate. I was afraid it was more than she could handle right now.

"Okay, that's good. But there's something we've overlooked, there always is."

"Hunter's got top security people on it. I'm on it too. It's a good tight operation."

"But someone *could* get through. *Somehow*."

"Yes, but it's very unlikely."

Dakota knocked her potatoes over with her fork and started rebuilding her fort.

"Would you like to reconsider, maybe cancel some concerts and reschedule for later?"

"No." She cemented a few potatoes together with ketchup. "But I'm an emotional wreck getting worse, not better. I want it to be over, Katy."

I did too. One person didn't, though. And so it wasn't.

It was after three. We went to bed.

I woke up to the sound of breaking glass. It wasn't all that loud. *Nothing* like the sound of the alarm system. *That* was loud. I hit the ground running, gun in my hand, and headed for Dakota's room—the sirens raw and wild and fearful in the night. Dakota had leapt out of bed and stood in the center of the room, apparently rooted to the floor. I yanked a quilt off the bed, grabbed her and hauled her off to the small half-bath, the only room in the house that didn't have windows. There I dumped her at the dressing table, wrapped her in the quilt and snapped on the night-light. "Stay here," I shouted over the alarm. "I'm leaving the alarm on until the cops get here. Don't turn on any lights." She nodded dumbly.

I moved through the house quickly. A rock had come in through the plate-glass window in the front and set off the alarm. I saw no one out front now, no vehicles, no move-ment, though I stood there and watched for several ear-splitting minutes. I saw no one from any other vantage point and I checked them all. Someone threw the rock and was long gone, that was my bet. Three patrol cars rolled up. I turned off the alarm, turned on some lights and went to the door. I'd pulled a pair of jeans and a sweatshirt on in my trip around the house.

After I let the cops in I went to retrieve Dakota, huddled and shaking in the quilt in the windowless bathroom.

"It was a rock." A short, beefy cop stated the obvious. "Came through the window here." More obvious. "No signs of entry or attempted entry. Could've been a prank. We'll look around the neighborhood. Why don't y'all just forget about it and go on back to bed." That was their parting recommendation.

I looked at Dakota as the front door shut. Her face was white and drawn, her eyes the size of dinner plates. She looked like someone who would never be able to sleep again. An emotional wreck before, she'd slipped off the edge now, way past the comforts of things like words or tea.

"Katy, I feel like this is never going to end."

I'd finished sweeping up the glass, reset the alarm and called Hunter. "It will," I said grimly.

"Why would someone do this? It's not as though I did anything, is it?"

"No. You didn't do anything and it doesn't make sense. We can't get into the mind of a deranged person and have it make sense. It's not about sense, it's about power and control. A stalker wants you to be threatened and afraid, to feel as though he has the power in your life, as though he is the one making the decisions, not you."

"I am beginning to feel that." There was despair in her voice. "That I have no control and it will never end."

"If you give up, he wins." *Or she*.

"Yes. I haven't given up yet." She tried to smile.

We didn't go to bed until Hunter's guard had arrived—no more patrolling, he was stationed right out front with orders not to move.

Later that same morning we flew to Mobile, on way too little sleep, for the Friday evening concert. Dakota was, without question, a serious wreck but she was trying to smile and chat and act normal. It was pretty awful to watch. I wasn't in much better shape. The strain was starting to tell on everyone now. I'd asked for Deeter's help on the phone number I'd taken from Chuck Blaine. Nothing. The guy was a mostly unemployed musician. No record. No apparent connection to Dakota. Nothing that led anywhere, at least not without my leaning on him—which I hadn't had the time to do.

It was a waiting game.

And the stalker had the high cards.

Jokers were still wild.

Dakota! Dakota! Dakota!

My footsteps echoed loudly off the concrete in the corridor. I wasn't thinking, just running. Adrenaline racing, I flung the door to Dakota's dressing room open.

The red was splashed like fresh blood on the white tile.

Dakota! Dakota! Dakota!

In the arena the audience clamored for her. Guys were whistling and waving their hats. Women held up flowers.

Dakota! Dakota! Dakota!

White bathroom tile. Red satin. Makeup streaked and smeared on her face. Dakota sat on the floor, her arms around her knees, shaking and crying.

"He's won, Katy."

"No he hasn't."

"Look at me. I'm a mess. I can't go on."

I reached down a hand and pulled her up.

"I want to go on but I can't. I'm too afraid. He's won."

I picked up a towel and splashed warm water onto it. "Wash your face." And when she did nothing, I started scrubbing the makeup off. "People have come to see you. Some of them have come hundreds of miles. They love you. Their love is your protection." I took a step back, towel in hand. I couldn't see any more makeup. Good enough.

"What do you mean?"

"Tell them the truth. Ask for their help. Listen." I tossed the towel on the floor. The arena was some distance from the dressing room but it didn't matter. There were fifteen thousand people out there and we could hear them clearly.

Dakota! Dakota! Dakota!

"They want to give to you the way you've given to them. Let them. Let them be your eyes and ears. Every cowboy out there is ready to be your honky tonk hero."

Dakota!

I hauled Dakota back into her dressing room and pushed her onto the stool in front of the makeup mirror. The light was harsh, pitiless and unforgiving. Dakota looked young and beautiful even without makeup.

Dakota!

"Hurry. They're waiting."

She looked at me quietly and then reached for her makeup.

Jokers were still wild but we were about to deal a new hand.

A SPOTLIGHT FOLLOWED DAKOTA AS SHE RAN DOWN THE cordoned-off aisle to the stage. The audience exploded. She opened with "Broken Angel" and then she held her arms out to the crowd.

"Tonight I opened with 'Broken Angel.' I don't usually do that. Let me tell you why." And she told them, asked them "each and every one to please be my security tonight." They roared with their love and acquiescence. And the cowboys hitched up their belts, straightened their hats, rolled their shoulders and looked around. The Christians had better odds against the lions than a troublemaker had there that night.

> "Broken angel, broken wings,
> reaching for the rainbow . . ."

Dakota sang her heart out. Spunk, red satin and heart.

> "Stumbling over yesterday's dreams . . ."

And they loved her.

> "Broken angel, broken dreams . . ."

At the end she thanked them for their love and asked them for their prayers and brought the house down. After her last encore she sang and then the audience sang with her:

> "And He walks with me,
> and He talks with me,
> and He tells me I am His own . . ."

They threw roses on stage and in the aisle as we left. Roses and wildflowers and cards and letters.

"Dakota!"

The spotlight caught the pretty young woman who leaned down over the railing to the bleachers. Dakota hesitated. In the woman's hand was a plate of cookies wrapped in clear plastic and tied with a red satin ribbon.

"I love you and your music and I thought you might fancy some homemade cookies. I made them *just* for you!" She held them out to Dakota with a smile.

The bodyguard moved in to shoulder Dakota along but she held him back and reached for the gift. "Thank you. What's your name?"

"Patsy."

"Thank you, Patsy."

And Patsy smiled as though a dream had come true. "*Oh no*, thank *you*!"

The spotlights and the bodyguard swept us along. In the security area the car that was to take us back to the plane was parked beside the band bus. Dakota ignored it, flying up the steps to the bus.

The guys hugged her, jostled her, shoved her around. It was a homecoming, a reunion. They would have hoisted her on their shoulders if there had been room. Dakota was back; the pale, frightened shadow gone. The cooler in the bus was open and bottle caps were flying.

"Where's the champagne?" Dakota asked.

"Wrong bus, darlin'." Rolli handed over an opened beer.

Dakota tipped that beer back and drank half of it, sucked it down sweet and easy at first but came up sputtering slightly.

"A lightweight," Steve announced in mock scorn.

"A girl," James agreed with a grin.

Someone opened a bottle of Jack Daniel's and started passing it around. I took the cold beer that was shoved in my hand.

"She's got promise, I don't care what they say about her," Rolli said and winked at Dakota, then reached for the cookies. "You been slavin' over a hot kitchen stove, dar-lin'?" He pulled the ribbon off the cookies. "All *right*. Chocolate chip, my favorite."

"Cookies and beer?" someone asked.

"Whatever." Rolli grinned, already on his second cookie.

I was suddenly starving. There was chili on the stove and it smelled wonderful. Chili and barbecue-style potato chips. Life was sweet again.

We were on our second beer, second bowl of chili, and Rolli had almost finished the cookies by the time Hunter showed up. He leaned over and kissed Dakota on the cheek. "Good work, sweetheart. Real good."

Dakota smiled and nodded. Someone handed Hunter a beer.

"T-shirts and poster sales are off the chart. We're going to run out. It's been one hell of a night. Any more of that chili?"

Someone handed him a bowl.

"How many empty bunks on the bus?" Dakota asked no one in particular.

"Three," James answered.

"I'm riding back with you guys. I'll sleep better here than at home. I'll feel safe—no one knows I'm here. *And* we get to party."

Hunter looked at me and I nodded.

Sleeping, partying and safety. Three good ideas. Dakota had been a little short of all of them lately.

Then Rolli started throwing up.

"The chili?" Steve asked. "How the *fuck* long has that *goddamned* chili been sitting on the stove?"

It wasn't the chili, of course; it was the cookies.

I thought you might fancy some homemade cookies. I made them just for you.

She was pretty in her youth and fresh complexion and western shirt. There are a thousand girls like her at every concert. Almost like her.

What's your name?

Patsy.

Now I remembered.

forty-one

GOLD RUSH AND
RATTLESNAKE HATRED

IT TOOK ME A LONG TIME TO FALL ASLEEP IN THE BUS that night though, like Dakota, I found the movement and the noise soothing.

Rolli was okay. According to the hospital the cookies had been laced with syrup of ipecac, an easily available medication that causes vomiting in case of accidental poisoning. I am here to tell you that Rolli, who is an overcautious parent with small children, will never stock it. It had been a bad night.

I closed my eyes to the sound of the diesel engine, the whine of the tires as endless miles slipped away under us. The rhythm of the road and of memories. It was arenas now, Dakota a star. Before that, almost a star, opening for Alan Jackson and George Strait.

And before that? Paying dues in dives and honky tonks: the smoke, the drunks, the men, anything to get her music out there, to get heard and known and recognized.

The bus hit a pothole. I rolled over in my bunk and pulled the comforter up under my chin, glad that the dives and honky tonks were a thing of the past. Like a two-by-four right between the eyes, the memory hit me then.

WE WERE LATE THAT DAY AND DAKOTA WAS NERVOUS. Late was unusual, nervous wasn't. She was real new then and didn't realize that in a dive bar late doesn't matter. Nobody gives a damn if the band starts on time. I was along for moral support; I was along a lot in those days.

"Do I look okay?"

I looked at Dakota, her hair short, almost white, bleached out in the California summer sun, no makeup except for a splash of pink lipstick. She had on tight, worn jeans, a white blouse and a black vest. Funky western.

"You look great."

"My jeans are too tight."

"They're fine. When you're a size seven, nothing is too tight."

We were five miles from the Broken Spoke in Rio Linda. Or was it the Broken Wheel? Odd that I should forget after all those gigs. Five more miles of this stuff. I gritted my teeth a little.

"Are these earrings okay?"

"Cody—"

"Dakota—don't forget."

"All right." She had started singing under her name, Cody Jones, but had decided—with this new gig—to change her name to Dakota. "Dakota, Dakota, Dakota," I muttered.

Cody cleared her throat. "I won't be able to sing." Her voice was choked up. "Oh God, what am I going to do?"

"You'll be fine. There's gum in my purse. Chew up."

"Suppose they don't like me, Katy?"

"They will."

"But suppose they don't?"

"They will."

"Oh God." She put her head in her hands.

"They'll love you, they always do. Cody, it's Rio Linda, where country music is breakfast, lunch and dinner to ninety-four point eight percent of the population."

"You really think so? Really?"

"Yes." The neon of the Broken Spoke flashed at us. "The parking lot is full. A lot of people came out to see

you." I parked on the far edge of the dirt-and-gravel lot close to the street. I like a clear exit route.

"Oh my God."

Cody didn't know whether to be happy and excited because so many people had come to see her, or horrified because if she failed there would be so many witnesses. She sat in the passenger seat, hands clenched and white-knuckled.

I turned off the ignition, pulled on the brake and spoke sternly. "Out here you're Cody Jones and you're scared silly and that's okay. But the minute we walk in you're Dakota Jones. You're a star with nothing to be scared about. Got it?"

"Got it," she said in a shaky voice.

"Okay. Let's go."

I'd exaggerated about the star part just like I'd exaggerated about the "a lot of people came out to see you" part. It was Friday night in Rio Linda and people were here to get drunk and happy, drunk and stupid, or drunk and laid, depending.

Dakota threaded her way through tables and people and approached the stage. The drummer was the only one there, smoking and talking to a guy lounging off to one side, and when he saw Dakota he hit a cymbal and played a short drum riff. The rest of the band started drifting over from the bar and taking their places. Dakota just stood there looking about as lifelike and relaxed as a mannequin in a department store window. She'd be all right once she started singing. I crossed my fingers.

The keyboard player began picking out a melody, the bass picked it up first and then Dakota. She wasn't all right, she was something else. The audience knew it too—she had them from the first note. At the end of the song she said, "Hey, I'm Dakota Jones and this is Gold Rush. We'd like to welcome y'all tonight. Hope you have as much fun as we plan to."

It was funny but standing there, watching her, I knew with absolute certainty that she would make it. The worn jeans, the cheap blouse and vest faded into the background *and I saw Dakota on stage and a star. I shivered. I remember that too.*

Now I don't remember when I first noticed him. Early, I think. He was tall, maybe six foot, with wide shoulders and narrow hips, dark hair and dark eyes, the kind that women fall for. He had regular features and a strong full mouth. Guys talked to him, women asked him to dance but all he really looked at or paid attention to was Dakota. He asked her silent questions: What are you into besides music? What are you doing later? Sleep with me tonight? *And then his eyes drifted over her, caressed her. His hands caressed a beer bottle.*

He didn't make a move in the first two breaks, although one of the biker guys did. Up close I could see that he had metal teeth, too. A bonus, huh?

"Hey, you sing just as goddamn good as you look. How about I buy you a drink?"

"No thanks," Cody said and turned away, walking toward the door. "Katy, c'mon." That was before she got good at handling guys in bars. She scooted out the door, me right behind her.

The night air was cool and fresh with a slight breeze. I could smell honeysuckle and roses. A dog barked and a confused rooster crowed. We walked away from the front of the building, leaned against it around the corner. Cody sucked in fresh air.

"Don't do it that way."

"What?"

"Turn guys down."

She shrugged. "Give me a break, Katy. Who cares?"

"You do. You work here."

She snorted.

"Well, it's true. I learned this the hard way as a bartender. You should be grateful."

"Okay, okay. How?"

"First of all, the truth is out."

"You mean like: 'No thanks, I don't date lowlifes or slimeballs'?" She giggled.

"Exactly. Or: 'No guys with IQs lower than their age.' "

"Or metal teeth."

"Or rap sheets." We both laughed.

"Here's what you say: 'Thanks, but I've got a boy-friend.'"

"But I don't."

"So what? The truth is out, remember. If you say you have a boyfriend, they'll leave you alone—that's all you care about. If you say you're busy, or you're not dating anyone right now, or that the two of you have nothing in common—all of which are true—they'll just keep asking. They'll figure they can wear you down."

"Okay. Does it get easier?"

"Guys?" I thought it over. *"I don't think so, although I hope it does."*

"Not guys. Singing."

"Oh. Yes." I was sure of that. *"There will come a day when you are standing backstage listening to the crowds cheer for you and you can't wait to get out there."*

She sighed. *"I wish it was here now. C'mon, break is over. I have to go back."*

There was fear in her voice, not longing. The day when she couldn't wait to get on stage was a long way off. We walked back into the noise and smoke and jukebox scream of the Broken Spoke.

Dakota ended the next set with "Honky Tonk Angel." Now, sometimes, I wonder how many times I've heard her sing that song.

The biker beauty with metal teeth was waiting, hadn't given up. He was convinced he was irresistible. *"C'mon, sweetcakes."* He grabbed for her elbow. *"Let's go for a drink."*

"Oh no, thank you, but I've got a boyfriend." Dakota smiled at him, bravely not recoiling from the stench of beer breath blasting in her direction.

"Just a drink, tootsie."

"I can't." She smiled again.

"Well, shit," he said. *"Hey, you change your mind about your old man, you let me know."* And he ambled

drunkenly off in search of the willing, the desperate or the buyable.

Dakota kept her brave little smile pasted on until his back was turned.

"You don't really, do you?"

"What?" Dakota asked the man who couldn't take his eyes off her.

"Have a boyfriend."

"Ummmm," she said. Cody never was real good in the lie department. She looked at him and tried to smile nonchalantly.

"It's just easier to get rid of guys that way, huh?"

"Ummm," she said, winging it again with the same lack of success.

"You're new at this, aren't you? You're going to be a hit, I can tell." He had a nice voice and sounded intelligent. Add to that good-looking, personable and a sense of humor. Not to mention that he wasn't drunk. All these were pluses.

I looked at Dakota and could read the truth in her eyes: You're nice but you're too old for me. I'm twenty-two with my whole life ahead of me. You're not. I looked at him looking at her. He didn't see it, couldn't read it. Was blinded by his desire, was probably more like it. He was, I thought, as hot and hard as the biker thug but smart enough not to be so obvious.

"Thank you," Dakota said finally. Smiling, she started to turn away to something that interested her more.

"I could help you."

She turned back. "How?" There was naïveté and curiosity and even disbelief written on her face.

A drunk who'd had about six bourbon-and-Cokes too many smashed into Cody, spilling half his drink and almost toppling her. Mr. Older but Suave caught Cody, held her, steadied her and released her—all in a moment. Had I imagined it? I looked at Dakota and saw the same question on her face. So no, I hadn't. His hand had just touched her breast and slid down her hip, the inside of his thigh stretched along her leg. Quickly. Over and done. But there.

"Are you all right?" he asked at a respectful distance.

"Yes, thank you," she answered, the question leaving her face.

"Anyway, I know people in the music business."

"Who?" Curiosity pulled ahead.

He named names we didn't recognize. Not difficult. Assured us they were big names. Hmmmm. *"And I'd like to get to know you,"* he added. *"I'd really like that."*

Curiosity and naïveté slid into a tie for last place as suspicion and cynicism pulled into first and second. Cody hadn't been around long but ten minutes was long enough to recognize that line. I stayed curious a little longer. I believed the sentiment and the sincerity underneath the line. I believed he wanted to help her. I looked at the naked emotion on his face. I believed how much he wanted her; I had seen it.

"I have a boyfriend." Cody had her lines down even though the delivery left a lot to be desired. *"I need some fresh air. C'mon, Katy."* She put her hand on my arm even as he reached out to her. Cody recoiled as though he were a rattler about to strike.

"Hey, Cody! We made it. Better late than never, right?"

Cody forgot the snake and laughed with Annie and Joe, friends of ours who had just arrived.

"Cody?" the man whom she had treated like a snake the moment before asked.

"Yes?" She smiled at him, safe now, that moment forgotten.

"I thought your name was Dakota."

"My stage name—my real name is Cody."

"Jones? Is that your real name?"

"Yes." She looked at Annie and Joe. *"Thanks for coming, you guys."*

"And how old are you, Cody Jones?"

"Old enough to know better." She said it without a smile and then laughed and tossed her head. *"Twenty-two."* And walked off.

He stared at her. I stared at him. Then he walked too. I didn't see him for the rest of the evening, not until the last *song of the last set, "Tennessee Waltz." All the couples were on the dance floor wrapped around each other. There was no longing on his face then, no love. Just hatred.*

Putting a positive spin on rejection clearly wasn't his strong suit. I watched him for the rest of the evening and his expression never changed, never lightened or varied. It worried me, almost frightened me.

But I never saw him again and so I forgot about it. About him. About the hatred.

HOW LONG CAN HATRED LAST?

Was it Cody or Dakota?

Briefly I wondered about both those things before I fell asleep.

forty-two

KILLER ON THE LOOSE

I'VE BEEN KICKED OUT, TOSSED OUT AND LAUGHED OUT of cops' offices for a lot of things but only once for saying: "I know it, I just can't prove it." Live and learn. Hunches might get you a winning lottery ticket but they won't get you a warrant or an arrest.

So I didn't bother calling the cops.

I'd called Granny Mae from the bus that morning. Early. It felt like night to me still but it was dawn in Sacramento. Granny is a big believer in the it's-the-early-bird-that-gets-the-worm theory. I am usually not a believer in anything where worms figure that prominently.

Yes, Granny told me, that was true. How did I know that? And yes, she had all that and of course I could borrow it whenever I wanted. Oh yes, it would be ready whenever I sent someone by to pick it up. And was everything okay? I told her it was just peachy.

I lied.

The last two incidents—the rock through the window and the tampered cookies—had been annoyances rather than serious or life-threatening situations. (This was not a viewpoint I shared with either Dakota or Rolli, who would have smacked me silly on the spot.) But something was happening almost every day now; the pace was picking up. So was the seriousness.

That wasn't a hunch, it was a no-brainer.

Tonight's concert. That was the hunch.

You can't stop someone who's willing to trade their life for yours.

Dakota flatly refused to cancel or postpone the concert. So it was Plan B.

"HEY, Y'ALL. HOW YA DOING? IT'S GREAT TO BE IN FORT Worth." Dakota stood center stage, the spotlight on her. She shimmered in the short, sparkly emerald-green dress with long sleeves, a scooped neck and a plunging back. Her hair was twisted into a knot on top of her head. Gold sparkled in her earrings and necklace.

The crowd roared its approval as she opened with "Cadillac Cowboy" and paced around the stage in flashes of quicksilver, green and gold, her smile, her hands reaching out to embrace her fans as they embraced her. I could see signs in the crowd: *WE LOVE YOU, DAKOTA. YOU'RE SAFE WITH US. WELCOME TO FT. WORTH.*

One hit followed another: "Leftover Love," "Back Door Man," "See Ya!" "String of Yesterdays," "Broken Angel," "Lost and Found," "Solid Gone."

In the middle of "String of Yesterdays" Dakota's hair started tumbling down.

> "Honey, since you left me,
>   Monday, Tuesday, Wednesday, Thursday,
>   Friday, Saturday, Sunday,"

She reached up, pulled the clip out and tossed her hair back, not missing a beat.

> "They're all the same.
>   There's no today or tomorrow . . ."

A broken barrette? Was that all the hunch was about?

Security circled the stage—no one without a special ID badge could come within thirty feet—and patrolled the aisles. Dakota's bodyguard was on stage in an unlit and inconspicuous place. I was there in the aisle just below the stage.

"Nothing but a string of yester—"

"Ladies and gentlemen, may I have your attention, please." The band stopped playing. Dakota stood there, hands at her side, mike dangling loosely. The arena was silent.

It wasn't the barrette.

The PA system crackled again. Our collective mood shifted from music to fear. Fear on the edge of panic.

"Do not be alarmed. I repeat: Do *not* be alarmed." His voice broke in alarm and we believed his fear and not his words. People started to shift in their seats and stand. "We will be evacuating the building as a safety precaution. Please file quickly and quietly out of the building. Once outside continue to move away from the building. Do not be alarmed. I repeat—"

His voice broke completely. The PA system snarled and whined. People began moving, mostly in a quiet and orderly fashion. And then another voice on the PA. "It's a bomb big enough to blow us all to hell and gone. A bomb. Get out of here. A bomb . . . a bomb . . . a bomb . . . Get out."

In a heartbeat fear shifted to panic.

People shifted to animal instinct.

It began. The panic. The stampede. The pandemonium. I looked in people's eyes and saw everything blacked out but survival. Love, caring, humanity—those were to be the first casualties. A row of the collapsible wooden chairs was kicked over and I saw a man go down, twisted, struggling, maybe as broken as the chairs. People clawed at me, trying to pull me back in an effort to propel themselves forward. Survival of the fit and strong. The security force had stopped being security and had joined the panic; I guess they figured they weren't being paid enough to be blown up. I was almost to the stage when the first notes filled the stadium.

"Oh, say, can you see
by the dawn's early light,
what so proudly we hailed
at the twilight's last gleaming?"

Dakota's voice, a cappella, beautiful, pushed through the panic, scrambled and climbed over the fear and then soared above us. People stopped in mid mad flight all over the stadium. A moment only, but it broke the panic and the stampede and the fear.

"And the rocket's red glare,
the bombs bursting in air,
gave proof through the night
that our flag was still there."

She dared us to remember that we were Americans, not an ugly, mindless mob. That we are people who care and help each other. She stood there on stage, singing not running, and she dared us to live up to that.

I saw a man put his arm around a youth and hold him, help him, a woman disentangle another from a maze of collapsed chairs, people holding hands and linking arms, working together not fighting. The last words, "O'er the land of the free and the home of the brave," had barely died out when Dakota's voice rose again.

"Silent night! holy night!
All is calm, all is bright . . ."

I stood beside her on the empty stage as she sang. The bodyguard, Butch—who would soon be looking for a new career if I had anything to say about it, which I would—was gone.

"Sleep in heavenly peace . . ."

Christmas in April. I signaled to Dakota that after this song, we were leaving. I didn't think there was a bomb but I wanted Dakota out of here. The back way, the way we had come in, was almost clear now. It was time.

The last words died out. Dakota let the mike fall to her side, shook her head at me and spoke. "I can't, Katy. Not yet. There are too many people here still. It's too dangerous for them still. I'm staying here and singing them out." I nodded. I know that tone of Dakota's.

It would have to be Plan B. Again.

> "My country, 'tis of thee,
> sweet land of . . ."

I pulled Dakota farther away from the spotlight and into a dark patch on the stage. The .380 dug into my waist. I was wearing an inside holster clipped onto my belt and covered by my blazer. It was some comfort, but not enough. And there was always the chance that I was wrong about the bomb. I looked again for security and couldn't see anyone.

If they're willing to trade their life for yours . . .

We were back to Christmas with "O Little Town of Bethlehem." And then "Home on the Range" and "Battle Hymn of the Republic" and "Red River Valley." And then the arena was close to empty and Dakota was jumpy. She was no longer afraid for others.

Now it was us.

She ran her fingers through her hair, pushing it back off her face. "Which way?" Her voice was scared.

I pointed to the way we had come in. It was the fastest way out for us. And I didn't want Dakota in the middle of a crowd as we emerged from the building. Crowds were dangerous for her now. We moved quickly across the stage.

"The band?" I asked.

"I told them to go on, that I would meet them out back."

"Ted?" Her road manager should have been here, I thought, no matter what she said.

"Him, too. I told them I'd be okay with you and Butch. Where *is* Butch?"

"Getting his nails done."

She tried to smile but it proved to be too difficult. "I can always count on you though, Katy. *Always.*"

We were moving right along, just entering the short tunnel that led from the arena to the underground maze of corridors, offices, function rooms, dressing rooms and God knows what else when the music started.

Music?

Rap lyrics. Loud. Pounding. They filled the arena. They pounded on us.

> *Killer on the loose,*
> *killer on the run,*
> *killer with a bomb,*
> *killer with a gun.*
> *Say, whatcha gonna do,*
> *where you gonna run,*
> *when there's a killer on the loose,*
> *killer with a gun?*

Dakota froze in place. "Katy."

"Let's go. Fly!" I grabbed her hand. We ran but we didn't fly. Dakota was in high heels.

> *Where you gonna go,*
> *where you gonna run . . .*

I could hear the footsteps behind us now. Heavy. A man's. They were running too. And faster than we were.

> *Killer on the loose,*
> *killer with a gun . . .*

I didn't look back. I didn't have to. Dakota hadn't heard them yet. She stumbled and I pulled her up and along. The footsteps were gaining on us.

"Katy!" Dakota looked at me, her eyes wide with fear. She had heard them.

"I know. Keep running. Turn left up here."

We skittered around a corner, Dakota flying wide on the turn, me holding on to her, pulling her in, keeping her up.

> Killer on the road,
> killer with a gun.
> Whatcha gonna do,
> where you gonna run . . .

The blood had oozed out, puddled and trickled into an unreadable Rorschach blot. Butch sat on the floor, slumped over and half propped against the wall. One hand lay on the floor, palm up and smeared with blood.

Butch was on the job but he was dead.

Dakota skidded and tried to stop, or at least step over the blood, then stumbled, twisted and crumpled to the floor.

Where you gonna run?

He was right behind us. I could hear him breathing now. I turned around.

"Hello, Clyde."

"You knew. I was afraid you might." He smiled. "Not that it matters now."

Dakota was struggling to get to her feet.

"Clyde? What are you doing here? Look, we've got to get out. There's the bomb. And that music. And Butch." She sucked in a breath. "There's a killer . . . *C'mon*, let's go!" She was trembling and trying not to look at Butch, reaching out for me.

Clyde's right hand hung loosely against his leg. There was a .45 in it. "We're not going anywhere yet."

"Are you *crazy*?" Dakota stared at him. "You said you wanted to help. Well, *help*." Dakota took a step, winced, then took her heels off. Another step. "Katy, let's go!"

"I surely do wish you ladies would join me for a bit," Clyde drawled out.

Like a Southern gentleman instead of a killer on the loose.

"Are you *nuts*?" Dakota took another wobbly step away from the body. *She twisted her ankle*, I thought.

Clyde brought up the hand with the gun in it.

Dakota looked at it, at Butch, at me. "Oh *my* God."

He ignored her. "How did you figure it, Kat?"

I figured I'd talk up a storm right now, buy as much time as possible, that's what I figured.

"I knew you were here for a reason. Everything in your past said you weren't the kind of man who stuck around out of duty or sentimentality—so that made all your talk about family, fatherhood and love bullshit.

"I found out you'd been in Nashville for some time, considerably longer than you let on. You arrived about the same time the harassment started. You said you wanted to help Dakota but it was just the opposite: you wanted something from her."

Dakota made a sound that was a cross between a sigh and a moan.

"I didn't have time to connect you up with the recent small stuff but I could; I will if I need to."

"Small stuff?" Dakota asked.

"He hired someone to drop the spotlight on stage."

Dakota gasped. "Did you?"

Jones stared at me, acquiescing in his silence, waiting.

"And Patsy. I recognized her, though I didn't put it together until afterwards."

"Patsy?" Dakota asked.

"The one who gave you the cookies that made Rolli sick. She was the waitress at a restaurant where Clyde and I had lunch."

He smiled. "You're good."

"I knew you liked to get your own way and that you didn't take rejection well." I thought of his face years ago when Dakota turned him down. "You like to get your own way, and if you don't, you're a mean bastard. That's what C.W. told me."

"Yeah." He grinned. "C.W.'s right; I am."

"He's nuts." Dakota whispered it.

It wasn't that simple. And it was more dangerous than nuts. A lot more.

Clyde had dealt this hand.

Jokers were still wild.

Good thing I had an ace up my sleeve.

forty-three

JOKERS ARE WILD

Is THERE A BOMB?" I ASKED.

"No."

"You phoned in the bomb threat?"

"Yes."

"Why?" Dakota sounded amazed. "Why would you do that?"

"You tell her," Clyde ordered me.

A fly buzzed Butch and then settled down for lunch at one of the blood pools. We were underground, probably a quarter of a mile from fresh air. How had a fly gotten in? I stepped away from Dakota. I wanted her to keep talking. I wanted to put distance between the two of us so that he couldn't watch us both.

"Don't do that. Get back there." He waved me over with the gun. "Let's go to your dressing room," he said to Dakota. "Show me how a star lives."

Another fly had arrived and was in the middle of a territorial squabble with the first one, even though there was plenty of blood to go around.

Clyde pointed the gun at us. "Move it!"

And there would be more blood real soon.

"You think you're slicker than snot on a doorknob, don't you? Too damn fucking good for the likes of me."

I heard the anger in his voice. Dakota heard it too. The

flies echoed Clyde's anger in a shrill and combative buzz. Otherwise there was silence. The rap music had stopped. Clyde waved us along, our footsteps loud in the silent corridor, in the silence everywhere in this underground pit. I wondered where the bomb squad was. They were bound to be here somewhere, sometime.

> "Killer on the loose,
>   killer on the run.
> Whatcha gonna do,
>   where you gonna run?"

Clyde chanted the lyrics and mocked us as he kicked open the door to Dakota's dressing room. "You like it? I wrote it."

"Yeah?" I asked.

"Yeah." He sounded pleased. "Like it?"

"Don't quit your day job."

I thought of Butch—blood-smeared with flies fighting over him—and realized that Jones had already quit his day job. Murder is inevitably a turning point in a career.

"Killer on the loose? Slicker than snot? Guns? I don't get it." Dakota looked scared and tired and small. "You're my *father*. Even if you were never around we're still related. How can you *do* this?"

"Tell her, Kat."

"No." I sat on the edge of the dressing table that was in front of the mirror squared off in light bulbs. Dakota sank onto the stool at the other end where her makeup was. I could see them both from my vantage point, directly and in the mirror.

Clyde looked around the room. Off to one side was a wardrobe rack with three backup dresses in red, silver and white. Shoes and accessories were scattered around. The white dress was pulled out slightly and facing us. Clyde held his arm out, point-shooting not aiming, and pulled the trigger. The bullet went through the dress at chest level, ricocheted off the cement wall and blasted out a light bulb in the vanity mirror.

"Tell her, Kat."

I took a deep breath. Nothing like a loaded gun and a trigger-happy asshole to change your mind and turn you into the talkative type.

"When you hit the big time, Dakota, Clyde wanted in, wanted a piece of the action—money, power, fame, the spotlight. He wanted a piece of you. Again."

"Again?"

"He wanted a piece of you before but it was a different kind of piece."

"What are you talking about?"

"Clyde put the make on you, wanted to sleep with you."

"Sleep with me?" Dakota said this with utter revulsion. "Sleep with me? No, *oh God*, no!" She looked sick to her stomach.

"A long time ago. You were singing in Rio Linda with Gold Rush then," I said, remembering the night she had looked at him as if he were a snake.

"You turned me down. You were too good for me. Thought you were slicker'n snot on a doorknob even then," Clyde snarled.

"Turned you down? Turned you down . . . You were my *father*."

"I didn't know that. You didn't either. You wouldn't have anything to do with me and I didn't forget that, Cody. I only wanted to help you. Back then. Now."

Dakota swallowed with difficulty, looked at him, then away. "I think I'm going to be sick."

"Help?" I asked. "How is trying to get sex and money out of someone a help?"

Clyde shrugged me off.

"How was killing Joni a help?" I asked, no quitter in the question department.

"*You* killed Joni?" Dakota shrieked. Not sick now, enraged. "You *son* of a bitch. You *goddamned* motherfucking son of a bitch!"

Jones stalked over to the wardrobe rack and savagely ripped the red dress off its hanger, ripped it down the middle, tossed it on the floor. And the silver dress, only he spit on that one too. The white he flung at Dakota.

"Hold it up." He used the gun as an exclamation point in a gesture that said *Do it!* and *Fuck you!* both.

Dakota held it, gripped it in her hands almost at arm's length as though she were holding a snake.

"Hold it up. *Up!*"

She pulled it up to her. Her hands were shaking. "You son of a bitch," she whispered.

"The dress has a bullet hole in it. The star doesn't. Yet." He yanked it out of her hands and used it to swipe the counter clear of makeup, jewelry and accessories. His back was to me. I started to make my move.

"Stay where you are, Colorado—I'd shoot you as quick and easy as I'd spit." He was looking in the mirror, staring me down. I shrugged and sat again on the counter.

"Why?" Dakota asked.

"Why what?" Jones snarled again.

"Why did you kill Joni?"

"I followed you to the studio that night. I'd planned to throw a scare into you. Only you left early and I wasn't prepared. When I saw Joni—of course I didn't know her name—I saw my chance and I took it. I figured it would scare you."

"You killed someone to *scare* me?"

"Yeah."

"You didn't even know her name, she was nothing to you, and you *killed* her—just as a way to scare me?"

"You got it."

"The letters, dead flowers, coffin pictures, magazines . . ."

"Yeah. All of it."

"This is *not* because I turned you down. After all these years? It doesn't make sense."

And she was right. It didn't and it wasn't. Or no more than the icing on this cake whipped up out of greed and bitterness and hatred.

Jones didn't answer her question. "I figured you'd turn

to me, Cody. I figured you'd see I was family and I could help you. I figured you'd see you could trust me, turn to me.''

"You did *all* this, you created a problem so I would turn to you for help? So that I would, in effect, trust the person who was the *problem*?"

"Yeah."

"*My God.* You're crazy. *Crazy!* That would never have worked. Not . . . in . . . a . . . million . . . years.''

"He had a backup plan." I spoke.

Dakota looked from Jones to me.

"Yeah," Jones said. "I figured it might not work, though I hoped it would. I would've liked it a lot better that way, Cody honey." His voice was heavy, sweet.

"A backup plan?" Dakota spoke carefully.

"Tell her, Kat, you're so fucking smart."

"He knew that you had no will. He got it out of Granny not so long ago. If you died, he inherited. Or that's what he figured.''

"That's what I figured," Jones agreed, "and I figured right. I wanted it to go the other way, Cody baby. I really did. I was hoping it'd be you and me, but I guess it's just gonna be me. Kat, you git over there with Cody. Take your hand out of your pocket. Slow. Real slow.''

And, slowly, I took my hand out of my jacket pocket. Real slowly. My right hand. My gun hand.

"Get up. Slow. Real slow. Keep that hand where I can see it.''

We'd argued about it, Hank and I. I said it was stupid. Why would anyone ever bother with a left-handed back cross-draw if they were right-handed? But cops do. They train for that in case their right arm is disabled. I'd said it was stupid but I was wrong. I'd like to go on record with that.

I got him twice in the chest. He didn't see it coming until it was too late.

He spun, slipped, fell on the white dress. Blood everywhere. Red blood. White dress. Blue carpet. The .45 slid across the floor. I picked it up, then walked over to look down at Jones.

"Goddamn." He forced the word out in a whisper, looking at me. There were bubbles of blood on his lower lip. "Goddamn."

"I guess it's just going to be Dakota," I said.

forty-four

TOUGH GUYS AND
WINNING TICKETS

W E WERE ALL THERE. GRANNY, ALMA, LINDY, CHAR-
ity and Al, Hank and me. Even Hope. Dakota had
sent us a fistful of plane tickets.

And front-row seats at the concert. "There are a *million*
stars here," Lindy said, awe in her voice.

I nodded. She was right; there were.

The Ryman Auditorium was originally a gospel hall built
in 1891 by Tom Ryman—a riverboat captain, a drinker,
gambler and sinner—after he heard the Reverend Sam
Jones preach and was saved. In 1943 the Grand Ole Opry
moved there. Later, after the Opry moved to Opryland, it
had been beautifully restored.

The stiff-backed pews and pulpit were long gone but that
night, at the benefit concert in Joni's memory, the echoes
of prayers and hope could still be heard. At the end all the
artists joined hands and sang "Will the Circle Be Unbroken." We sang too.

It was something.

Lindy hummed all the way back to Dakota's party. "Do
you believe that, Kat?" She stopped humming.

"What, Lindy?"

"That there's a better world awaiting us?" Lindy para-
phrased a line from the song. She didn't look at me, just
stared out the window at darkness and then at lights.

"I don't believe in that kind of heaven. I think it's important that we do the very best we can in life."

"For ourselves?"

"Yes. And for others." I squeezed her hand.

Dakota's place was a carnival of lights. People filled the
house and spilled outside. There was food and champagne,
smiles and laughter.

The darkness and trouble were gone from Dakota's eyes.
She handed me a glass of champagne as we walked in.

"Katy, it's all over, isn't it?"

"Yes."

We clinked our glasses together in a toast.

"And it's just beginning." Dakota laughed.

The unbroken circle.

Hank took a picture of "us girls," as Granny put it—
Alma and Granny, Dakota, Lindy and me. Lindy and I were
glittery and beautiful, red and gold, in two of Dakota's
swellest dresses. Dakota wore a white dress like the one
Clyde had shot up and then bled on. We were dazzling and
gorgeous.

The Supremes in vanilla.

"If you can't run with the big dogs, stay on the porch,"
Alma announced as she and Granny waltzed off in search
of good times and more champagne. They were whoopin'
it up.

"You did a good job, Kat."

It was Jimmy Deeter; I had invited him. "Thanks." I
smiled but first my heart stopped, then tried to skip a little.
"How's Jones?"

"He's gonna live."

My heart eased.

"Worse luck."

I understood. It would have been cheaper, easier and
more satisfying, I know, if he had died. For everyone but
me—I had enough on my conscience already.

"We found materials that matched the ones used in the

anonymous communications to Miss Jones and we tied him to Blaine, the guy who sabotaged the spotlight.''

"Patsy?''

He grinned. "Can't get her to shut up. Jones made a shitload of promises and didn't deliver.''

"Ballistics?''

"Just came in. Jones's gun killed the bodyguard and Joni Ames. We got this one nailed down tight. He's looking at free room and board for a long time.''

Lindy scooted by, her back to me.

"Hey!'' I hollered.

She tossed a smile over her shoulder and kept scooting.

"Are you drinking champagne?''

"Just one glass. Alma said I could, *honest*.'' She smiled brightly and was gone.

Deeter winked at me. "Gonna go find me a beer,'' he announced.

Across the room Link was trying to look comfortable and relaxed, even though he hadn't been invited and Dakota was as warm as a glacier on a January day. I was no help in the welcoming department.

Hope came too. I shouldn't have been surprised, I guess, but I was. She was talking with Dakota when I saw her. I barged right in on the conversation. Hope wasn't all that pleased about it, which was understandable considering what I had on her.

"Hey,'' I said.

"Hey.'' Her eyes were wary.

"Dakota is a lot more polite about this kind of stuff than I am.''

"Katy—'' Dakota politely tried to stop me.

But there was no way. Actually, I am not polite at all about this kind of stuff. "Dakota is giving you a chance because you're family. I wouldn't. Not after learning how you treat your family and friends.''

Hope stared at me, white-faced and silent.

"Bitterness, hatred and revenge. It seems sweet but it's not. You need to talk to Granny.''

"All right.'' She nodded like a puppet on a string.

"Life isn't a crazy quilt, it's a chance. You blow this and I'll toss you. Dakota doesn't have the heart for it but I do."

"I won't blow it."

I nodded, a Sam Spade/Philip Marlowe/Lew Archer tough-guy expression on my face. And then I walked; I can't sustain that expression for more than a minute.

"How come you're looking so tough?" Hank asked. I smiled up at him as he leaned down to kiss me.

Sam Spade, Philip Marlowe and Lew Archer?
They didn't know everything.

If you enjoyed *Honky Tonk Kat*, you won't want to miss Karen Kijewski's newest mystery featuring Kat Colorado...

KAT SCRATCH FEVER

Here is an excerpt from this provocative new novel—available in hardcover from G. P. Putnam's Sons...

IN DEATH THERE WAS NO LOVE IN HIS FACE. OR KINDNESS. Or peace. There had been little of any of these in life either but I had not known him then and would not learn that until later.

What they say about the dead—that they look peaceful— is a lie. Or perhaps the undertaker's magic. When I saw him, he was flung out across the floor—bloody and destroyed—as though carelessly tossed there by a lackadaisical giant.

He did not die immediately. There was time to think and feel and, perhaps, regret. I could not imagine that someone would choose a death like this. I could not imagine it, but James Thomas Randolph had. I could not imagine what Randolph had thought, felt, regretted in those agonizing minutes as he lay alone and dying. But I needed to. That was the job.

"What the hell you doing in here, Kat?"

I looked at homicide detective Bill Henley. The sickness in my heart and mind was, I knew, written on my face.

His voice softened. "They shouldn't have let you through."

"Suicide." It wasn't a question; that wasn't one of the questions in my mind then.

"Yeah. That's my guess. But it's early yet. Catch up with me later."

I left before he threw me off the crime scene. Timing is a funny thing, is everything, they say. I wondered if it was the same "they" who said the dead look peaceful. If so, what did they know? I threaded my way through plain-clothes and uniformed police officers and Crime Scene Unit equipment and out into an early-winter night, the darkness split by revolving police lights.

"Hey, ducky-lucky."

Lean, compact, and wiry with blond—almost white—hair, he was slanted, hands in pockets, against a black-and-white. He wore a shit-eating grin and was casually, disingenuously gorgeous and charming à la a dissipated Robert Redford.

"Hey news-slime," I replied halfheartedly. Blood and death had taken the starch out of me. A uniform lifted the yellow POLICE LINE DO NOT CROSS tape and I scooted under with a quick nod of thanks.

"Buy you a drink."

"Lost my taste for hemlock." I shoved my hands into my pockets and started for my car.

"Was it murder? Did you see a body?" A shapeless woman in a black silk designer warm-up suit and an avid look plucked at my elbow.

"Was there blood? Huh? Huh? Did they blow his head off like on TV?" The child was *Sesame Street* age. His words echoed his mother's, as did his empty, avid eyes.

I could taste the bile in the back of my throat. I pulled up the collar on my jacket.

"C'mon tootsie-pop." J. O. tucked his arm through mine. "You look like you need a drink."

I sucked in a breath, walking fast now. It was cold and damp. And dark. At six it was still clear. By ten the fog would clamp down on the city. I hate winter in Sacramento.

The Bronco was parked at the corner of American River Drive and Thornley. I shook off J. O.'s hand and unlocked the car. "Okay," I said to him. I didn't want to be alone with my thoughts. Not yet.

"Atta girl." He started around to the passenger side.

"You take your car."

"You got it, baby-cakes."

"Kat. Not ducky-lucky, or tootsie-pop, or baby-cakes."

"Sure, babe." He winked at me.

I didn't say anything, just got into the car. So now you know how bad it was. J. O. was nothing to what I had witnessed: the blood, the pieces of red and white and gray things falling out of the body and blasted around the room. The empty staring eyes that mutely testified of horror. *If the eyes are the windows of the soul, what had his been open on?* "Where?" I asked, trying to turn away from the eyes.

"The Sacramento Bar and Grill?"

"No."

"Great atmosphere."

"Cheap drinks," I corrected. And probably full of newspaper people.

He shrugged. "Paragary's? Zelda's?"

I nodded at Zelda's and got in the Bronco. *Why would someone choose to die slowly and painfully? To make others suffer? To do penance?* And it was a choice, not an accident. Randolph had been in Vietnam; he knew about guns, he knew about death. It was a long time before I turned the key in the ignition.

J. O. beat me to Zelda's. A full beer and an empty shot glass sat on the bar in front of him.

I pulled out a stool and ordered a chardonnay. "Get out a credit card, weasel."

"Kat," he reproached me. "Like I'm not good for it."

"Exactly," I replied. "Like I'm going to fall for that one again." I stared at him until he got out a credit card and then, after a short tussle, I handed it over to the bartender. "See if this is good for fifty."

The bartender nodded, her eyes blank and uninterested. *But not dead.*

"Hey!" J. O. protested the amount.

"All set." The bartender gave me a thumbs-up sign so

I ordered stuffed mushrooms and garlic bread. Grease as comfort food. And all on J. O.

"Dammit, Kat." He said it glumly.

I smiled. "Remember the two extra-large pizzas with everything and the three pitchers of beer you stuck me with?" *Payback is a bitch.*

"Tell me what you saw." He ignored my question and signaled for another shot of Gold.

My smile disappeared. "Not until I have a couple of drinks. What do you know about Randolph?" *The dead man. The suicide.*

It is important, with J. O., to get information before you give it. And J. O. has information. J. O. Edwards has been in the newspaper business for over twenty years. He says J. O. stands for John Osborne; rumor says it stands for Jerk Off. So far rumor has gotten more votes for truth than J. O.

He worked in Texas before he came to California to write for the *Sacramento Bee*. J. O.'s a very good reporter, his stories cutting-edge and solid, but he doesn't give a good goddamn how he gets his information. Doesn't give a damn how he lives his life, either. His loose brawling ways are more suited to Texas than California, and nobody who knows him can understand why he's never been fired or killed. But he knows everything: hears things, sees things, and remembers both the trivial and the profound.

The bartender plunked the shot down. There were limes and a saltshaker on the bar already. J. O. drank the shot, sucked a lime, and stared at me for a long moment. On general principles—which are the only kind he has—J. O. hates to part with information. Especially for free. And never—these are his words—when he's buying. The food had arrived, reminding him of this. I ate four stuffed mushrooms before they started looking like empty eyes; then I stuck to the garlic bread and waited for J. O. to get over his snit and start talking. Which he did.

"Randolph was a decent enough guy. Well liked and respected, known for the right reasons. Had his own business, been in insurance forever, I guess. Good family man, loved his kids, belonged to Rotary and went to church, did charity shit, and coached kids' basketball.''

"Fuck you, J. O.'' I stood, reaching for my purse and jacket.

"Katy, c'mon, what's the matter? Sit down. You haven't even finished your wine."

"Fuck you, J. O.,'' I said again, too exhausted to fight.

"Okay, okay. I'll tell the truth. I promise." He held up his hand like a Boy Scout.

I happen to know that he was kicked out of the Boy Scouts three times. I started putting on my jacket. It was slow work, as if the sleeves were full of Jell-O. God, what a day.

"I swear on my mother's grave," he said, the sadness and sincerity clear in his voice.

"Godmother's, you lying sack of shit," I said, the fatigue clear in mine. He had hated his mother, his godmother was the one he had loved—as much as he was capable of loving anyone.

"Godmother's," he corrected.

I sat down and let him pull off my jacket.

"What was it?"

"It?"

"That tipped you off?"

"You always lie."

"There must have been something?"

"He wasn't in insurance, he didn't have kids, and he wasn't that good a family man." I tossed in a lie myself.

"Yeah? What did you hear?"

I shook my head. "Your turn first, remember."

J. O. ate a mushroom. "He was the last guy I would have pegged for it, Kat."

"It?"

"Suicide."

"Why?"

"I dunno. He wasn't a sensitive guy. I can't imagine something getting to him enough to make him want to kill himself. He struck me as the kind of guy who'd shrug and ride out the bad times. He'd seen his share of shit, too.

Vietnam. A failed marriage, maybe two of 'em, come to think of it. He's in a successful partnership now but he had earlier ups and downs."

"Is he really in Rotary and involved in charity stuff?"

"Yeah, though I didn't get the feeling it was because he cared. More that Rotary was a place to make business contacts and charity work a way to look like a good guy."

"Which he was, or wasn't?"

J. O. shrugged. "Depends on your definition. He never committed a felony, filed for bankruptcy, or screwed a client in a way that wasn't strictly legal. So, yeah, I guess he was an okay guy."

"What charity?"

"Some sob-sister shit about dying or fucked-up kids." He signaled the bartender for another shot and a second glass of wine for me.

"Did he ever lose a child?"

"Dunno." Mr. Warmth and Compassion shrugged. "Anyway, you wouldn't figure a guy like that to commit suicide, would you?"

"I don't know." I watched the faces in the mirror behind the bar smile and laugh and talk. "I never thought about it. Maybe anyone will commit suicide if they get pushed too far."

"No." He was emphatic. "There are some people who would never consider the possibility."

"Like you?"

"Yeah—as long as we're not counting suicide by alcohol. And I would have said Randolph, too."

"His marriage happy?"

"Never heard anything else."

"He get along with his business partners?" Randolph had been a partner in Bradshaw, Bellows & Emerson, a prestigious law firm. As I well knew—Carter had put me on the payroll to check out Randolph.

"Yeah, so far as I know. Maybe a disgruntled client got to him."

I laughed. "In probate work?"

J. O. smiled. "That what it was?"

"Wills, living trusts, probate matters."

"And the dead don't cause trouble."

I thought of Randolph's eyes and wasn't sure. And I thought that death, and the dead, cause plenty of trouble.

J. O. eyed my wineglass and the empty plates. "Time to sing for your supper, Kat. Spill your guts."

Pictures of Randolph again. *Guts literally, not figuratively, spilled. Ugly. Horrible.*

"Thanks for the drinks." I stood, pulling on my jacket. "And the snack."

J. O. half stood, his mouth open. "Well, I'll be a son of a bitch."

I smiled. "Night, J. O." *Payback is sweet.*

Driving home, I listened to a medley of Christmas carols: "Joy to the World," "Hark the Herald Angels Sing" and "Silent Night." But with suicide there is neither joy, nor singing, nor silence.